FATES PROMISED

CALL OF THE NORNS
BOOK 2

AIMEE VANCE

REVEL BOOKS

For my daughters

*Shine bright, my girls.
Blind those who can't stand the light,
but don't dull yourself for anyone.*

This book is a work of fiction. Names, characters, places, and incidents are products of the author's imagination or are used fictitiously. Any resemblance to actual events or locales or persons, living or dead, is entirely coincidental.

Text Copyright © 2022 Aimee Vance
All rights reserved. No part of this book may be reproduced or transmitted in any form or by any means, electronic or mechanical, including photocopying, recording, or by any information storage and retrieval system, without written permission from the publisher.

Revel Books
Paperback ISBN: 979-8-9863649-4-0

Cover Art and Illustrations
Copyright © 2023 Aimee Vance

Editing and Proofreading by
Brittany Corley and B. Perkins

aimeevancebooks.com

AUTHOR'S NOTE

The book you are about to read contains subjects that may be difficult or unappealing to some readers. This includes violence, graphic language, on-page sex, and mental health struggles. In addition, there are references to rape, attempted suicide and child abuse, but not depicted on-page.

PLAYLIST

If you'd like to get the full experience as I intended, I've created a chapter-by-chapter playlist on Spotify and Apple Music that you can find by searching for AimeeVanceBooks, Fates Promised playlist.

- P: *Edge of Seventeen,* Stevie Nicks
- 1: *Vor í Vaglaskógi,* KALEO
- 2: *Bruises,* Lewis Capaldi
- 3: *Stuck Here Without You,* yaeow
- 4: *Three Little Birds,* Bob Marley & The Wailers
- 5: *At Last,* Etta James
- 6: *Nervous,* Maren Morris
- 7: *Maybe It's Time,* Troy Ramey
- 8: *Way Down We Go,* Kaleo
- 9: *Heaven (Acoustic),* Calum Scott
- 10: *Days Like This,* Dermot Kennedy
- 11: *I Want More,* KALEO

- 12: *Dragon (feat. Skybourne)*, Built By Titan, Skybourne
- 13: *Fallin' For You*, Colbie Caillat
- 14: *White Christmas (with Shania Twain)*, Michael Bublé, Shania Twain
- 15: *Break My Baby*, KALEO
- 16: *The World I Know*, Collective Soul
- 17: *Cowboy Take Me Away*, The Chicks
- 18: *Hold My Girl (Acoustic Version)*, George Ezra
- 19: *I Get to Love You*, Ruelle
- 20: *Broken*, Seether, Amy Lee
- 21: *Numb*, Linkin Park
- 22L *Hallelujah*, Theory of a Deadman
- 23: *One Step Closer*, Linkin Park
- 24: *Going Under*, Evanescence
- 25: *Before You Go - Piano Version*, Lewis Capaldi
- 26: *The Reason*, Hoobastank
- 27: *How Did You Love - Acoustic*, Shinedown
- 28: *Clarity*, Vance Joy
- 29: *Issues*, Julia Michaels
- 30: *Clubbed to Death - Kurayamino Variation*, Rob Dougan
- 31: *I Am His Vengeance*, Robin Carolan, Sebastian Gainsborough
- 32: *Gimme Gimme Gimme (a man after midnight)*, Syzz
- 33: *Raven's Omen*, Robin Carolan, Sebastian Gainsborough
- 34: *Storm at Sea / Yggdrasil*, Robin Carolan, Sebastian Gainsborough

- 35: *Draugr*, Robin Carolan, Sebastian Gainsborough
- 36: *Bring Me To Life*, Evanescence
- 37: *Eye of the Storm*, Pop Evil
- 38: *Pretty Handsome Awkward*, The Used
- 39: *Survivor*, 2WEI, Edda Hayes
- 40: *In the End*, 2WEI, Edda Hayes
- 41: *Insomnia*, 2WEI
- 42: *Supermassive Black Hole*, Muse
- 43: *Heavy*, Collective Soul
- 44: *Let the Chaos Reign*, Pop Evil
- 45: *Mama's Got a Brand New Hammer*, Michael Giacchino
- 46: *Valkyrie*, Robin Carolan, Sebastian Gainsborough
- E: *The King*, Robin Carolan, Sebastian Gainsborough

PROLOGUE
DOMARI

Flames danced in the evening air, warm against the chill of a summer night long ago. Four friends — old enough to have experienced life but young enough not to be bogged down by the burdens of adulthood — hovered around the fire as they did every night, away from the village and under the watchful eyes of so many others. Laughter floated high above them, casting its glow over the scene just as much as the light from the fire.

The youngest, a blonde youth growing in the beginnings of a beard, smiled broadly as he flipped a dagger in his hand, tossing it end over end into the air, catching it repeatedly.

"Eventually, you'll stab yourself," the oldest said, but his tone held more amusement than scorn. "Of all the ways to prove your prowess, Gunnar, this doesn't seem the best idea you've ever had."

"See, Domari," young Gunnar grinned at his cousin, a darker, larger version of himself, with golden-brown hair and deep chocolate eyes. Domari's beard was much fuller than the younger Gunnar's and accented Domari's chiseled cheekbones, shadows playing across his features in the evening light. "I have to practice. Winter Nights will be here before you know it, and I plan to win every event this year. You and Raud don't stand a chance."

"But I do," a girl's voice rang over their chattering, and the words had both young men turning to her. A laugh broke free from her lips as the last in the clearing, another young man with short-trimmed hair as black as night, pulled her to her feet into an embrace, swinging her around in a circle. The skirt of her dark dress flowed freely around her as she danced to the song of the surrounding night, her movements as mesmerizing as the flickering flames. His hands settled on her hips possessively as he pulled her to a stop, trailing kisses up her neck.

"Little brother," she smirked at Gunnar under a half-lidded gaze, "I intend to embarrass you as I've done every year so far."

The cocky grin on Gunnar's face fell as he squinted at his older sister. She was the female version of him — lithe muscles filled her feminine frame, and long golden hair braided tightly against her scalp accentuated the sharpness of her features.

"It's true," the young man, Raud, behind her paused, where he still kissed her neck. "My future wife is a force all her own. There has never been anyone like her. If Valkyries were still among us, I swear my Tove would be one."

The girl threw her head back, resting her head on Raud's chest as a broad smile spread across her face.

"That's only because you don't listen to her snore at night," Gunnar shot back, and Tove's happy smile turned to a scowl. Gunnar grinned, knowing he'd landed the comment as intended.

"Soon enough," Raud said, kissing her neck again as he pulled her back tighter into his front. "Although, who knows how much *sleeping* will happen when I finally get you to myself every night, Tove?"

Domari only shook his head, having heard these conversations so many times before, so he changed the subject, tired of the lovesick fools and sibling squabbles. "Thorsten has agreed to meet us here tomorrow to finish our tattoos."

As expected, his statement was shocking enough that all three figures around the fire snapped their gazes to him. Domari reclined back on a hand where he sat on the ground and adjusted his shirt, intentionally showing the ink along his hip — a giant shield covering his side. He was the only one with tattoos yet, and a contented grin spread across his face.

Thorsten, another one of their villagers and a fellow hunter with Domari, had refused to tattoo the others for years, insisting they wait until they'd grown out of their *"childish ways."* The summer before, Domari had mentioned to Thorsten in a private moment what he'd wanted to be tattooed on his skin, and the man — only ten years his senior — had readily agreed. Strong and silent, Domari sat for days while Thorsten worked his wood ash ink into his skin, never showing a hint of the pain that seared his skin with every poke. The tedious work was worth it when

Domari saw the final product, in awe of the detail Thorsten had worked into his father's shield along Domari's hip. Njal — a warrior through and through and Domari's idol — would always be with him, as would the reminder of what it means to sacrifice for those you love.

Fourteen years had passed since Njal died, headed for Valhalla, along with many others from their clan. Like Domari, Thorsten remembered Njal from before that final battle that had left Domari, Raud, Thorsten, and so many others, orphans.

"Truly?" Gunnar asked, excitement glittering in his eyes. It had taken days for Domari to convince Thorsten that Gunnar, Tove, and Raud were ready for their own ink, but finally, the quiet man acquiesced to this new request.

"Have we agreed on the knot, then?" Gunnar insisted, sheathing his dagger on his belt as he stepped closer to his friends. Domari shrugged in response, and Gunnar rolled his eyes at his older cousin's indifference. "Tove? Raud?"

Raud focused on the girl in front of him, his hands roaming her body, and only mumbled an assent.

"Whatever you want, brother," Tove said in a breathy voice, spinning in Raud's arms as she grabbed her lover's chin, holding his gaze. "I'm already tied to you by blood, Gunnar, but I like the idea of a knot tying all four of us together in spirit."

Raud and Domari exchanged a glance — the outsiders here. While Domari was Gunnar and Tove's cousin, it wasn't quite the same as the siblings' bond. Raud and Domari's was a bond built on shared grief, far deeper than a simple friendship. Neither Gunnar nor Tove remembered the days before their peaceful life under their father's rule here in the village, but Raud and Domari did.

Raud's focus shifted back to the girl in his arms, but Domari continued to appraise his oldest friend. So much had changed between them in recent years, and darkness clung to Raud that shrouded his actions and words in bitterness, always painting himself as the victim. But none of their lives had been easy since that day their fate turned; Raud wasn't alone in his pain.

With a silent plea to the gods, Domari wished his friend could find peace and contentment in their new lives here under Erik's wise rule, but wishes wouldn't solve the haunted look Raud wore these days. No matter, Domari's heart belonged to the three friends standing around the fire. As his father Njal had done for his brother, Erik, Domari would die for them in an instant.

Breaking his eyes away from his friend, Domari turned his focus back on the fire as Gunnar dropped to his side on the ground. "If Raud can let go of Tove long enough to let Thorsten tattoo her, I'll consider it an act of the gods," Domari muttered quietly, and Gunnar's answering laugh boomed over the crackling fire.

But Tove and Raud didn't respond, now pressed into a tree further back from the fire, kissing passionately. While Domari was happy to see that Raud and Tove's tumultuous relationship seemed in one of its easier, albeit obnoxious, phases, he missed his friend; no one knew Domari better than Raud.

Sometime later, the fire died down, and the four friends walked back towards the longhouses in the distance. A small boy with gleaming white blonde hair bounced on his heels, waiting and watching for their return.

"Mama! They're back!" the younger boy called out, and Gunnar pulled him into a headlock. The boy fought back, swinging at Gunnar's torso, but missing.

"Someday, I'll be twice your size, and I'll take you down easily in a fight," the boy growled.

Gunnar's chest shook as he chuckled, shoving his little brother away. "I await that day, Knut."

"Magnus. Why are you not in bed?" an older woman called from the door, and the boy's shoulders slumped as he walked back towards his mother.

"I want to go with them," he mumbled. "I'm almost ten. Other boys are off fighting battles, and I'm stuck here at home picking berries for you."

Tove slapped the back of Magnus's head before pulling him into her side, kissing where she'd walloped him. "Someday, you'll be grown and can have your adventures," Tove said into her little brother's hair. "And I'll be right by your side."

The boy grinned up at Tove, wrapping his arms around her waist. Already he was nearly her height — he would be a giant among men.

"Björn is expecting you, Raud," Frida called from the door with a pointed look.

Raud met her stare, reading between the lines, and Domari couldn't help but watch how his friend would react. Raud's shoulders were thrown back, and a defiant look lit his eyes, even though he knew Erik's strict rules regarding his daughter. Tove glanced in Raud's direction, and the heated gaze between Domari's two friends told him everything he needed to know. Raud would have stayed, breaking the rules yet again, if not for Frida's watchful eye.

"I'm leaving," Raud finally said, turning to leave as his shoulders sagged. The look of defeat on his friend hurt Domari's heart, and he extended his hand, stopping Raud's steps.

"Sneaking behind Erik's back with Tove isn't likely to win you any additional favor," Domari said in a hushed tone. Raud's furious gaze swung to Domari, and Domari raised his hands in defeat. "I'm not saying I agree with Erik's judgment, but walking away instead of rising to challenge Frida is showing Erik your control. You're doing the right thing."

"I would *die* for Tove, Domari. What more could Erik want in a partner for his daughter?" Raud answered as he shoved Domari's hands away from him. "Just because I have no family, no wealth, no legacy, I'm unworthy." Raud spat on the ground, anger clouding his vision.

Domari sighed, unsure why he'd even started this discussion. It always circled back to the same thing, anyway.

Raud was wrong.

Erik didn't care that Raud was an orphan like so many in this village, with nothing to his name. Erik, their clan leader and Domari's uncle, was the most generous and kind man Domari had ever met, but it was easier for Raud to blame him than work on his own actions.

If Domari was being honest, he wasn't sure he

disagreed with Erik's answer when Raud asked to marry Tove two years ago.

"Learn to control your temper, Raud," Erik had said. *"You only fan my daughter's flames, and a fire that burns hot and bright also burns out quickly. Show me you can control yourself first."*

The older they'd gotten, the more Raud demonstrated a need to prove himself. Better. Faster. Stronger. *More.* Seeking attention and love. Maybe this was the life of an orphan — needing constant affirmation of love when so many things in life felt lonely.

While Domari could understand that, he'd always been more reserved, focused on perfecting his skills, not for notoriety, but to remake his father's tarnished legacy. Domari was a protector; someday, it would be his job to watch over Gunnar when he became chieftain, as Njal had done for Erik, even with his dying breath.

Domari watched as Raud turned from the house and headed down the worn path between Erik's longhouse and onto Björn's, where Raud had lived off and on for almost his entire life. He stayed in the clearing, waiting until Raud's shadow blended in with the trees around their land, a wolf howling in the distance. No other answered, as lonely as the man turned away from the warm home at Domari's back.

Rubbing along his neck, Domari turned to enter his uncle's longhouse. Maybe the tattoo tomorrow would take some of the weight off of Raud's shoulders — make him feel a part of something bigger. Give him a sense of belonging. Gunnar's idea of having them swear to protect each other until their dying breath seemed unnecessary to Domari, but if it helped ease this growing rift, he'd do it.

"Hold still," Thorsten's voice rumbled the command the next night. His short-trimmed hair nearly matched the flames, light glinting off the strands of copper amongst the red in his beard. Back hunched, his thin, muscular frame leaned over the girl sitting below him on the ground. Tove's golden braid draped over one shoulder as she tilted her head to the side, face screwed into a grimace of pain.

"Can't you go any faster?" she snapped the words at Thorsten, and he swatted her across the top of her head.

"Don't touch her again," Raud growled from nearby, his black beard standing out against his pale skin.

"Raud," Gunnar laughed with a shake of his head. "Thorsten is tattooing her. He *has* to touch her. What a stupid thing to say."

"It's fine," Tove answered, reaching out to touch Raud, who now squatted near her, his hands draped casually across his knees.

"I hate seeing you in pain," Raud hissed the words, and Tove rolled her eyes. "I won't let anything happen to you, Tove."

"If we have to have this conversation again — have to remind you I refuse to be controlled, coddled, like a *woman*," the word was laced with venom as it left her mouth, "then I will end this relationship right now. Besides, you know more than anyone that I can take care of myself."

"Never say that." Raud reached forward, lightly gripping her by the neck on the opposite side where Thorsten worked the ink into her skin. She grinned up into Raud's face, one brow raised in a challenge. "You are *mine*. Forever."

"Move your damn hand," Thorsten grumbled, shoving Raud's grip aside. "You four are impossible. Why did I ever agree to this?"

"Because the solemn, lonely man you portray is an act," Gunnar smiled easily, "and you like us."

The redhead shook his head with a scowl and kept working on Tove's tattoo, but he didn't deny it.

Domari said nothing, watching everything from a distance, casually sipping his ale from a drinking horn.

"Show me yours, Domari." Gunnar strode to his side, and Domari tilted his head to the side, showing off the fresh black ink beneath his golden brown hair. The skin was hot and red where Thorsten had poked him repeatedly, sinking the burned ash deep under the skin, leaving behind the same design Thorsten was finishing on Tove's neck — a knot of four strands. Inseparable. One.

"The same as yours, Gunnar." Domari raised his brows with amusement. "And on Raud's. All the same, just as you wanted it."

Gunnar beamed, rubbing his hands together in excitement. "This seals our bond."

Thorsten leaned back, wiping Tove's neck with a wet cloth, and rose to his feet. Raud reached out, pulling Tove up as well, and gripped her face, pulling her into a savage, possessive kiss as if he could erase the other man's touch from her skin. Her arms flew around his neck as she kissed him back with wild abandon, ignoring everyone else in the area. Domari cleared his throat, and the two broke apart, breathing heavily.

"I'm done here." Thorsten gathered his things and walked into the trees, back towards their village without another word.

Raud draped his arms around Tove's waist in a possessive hold, pulling her back into his front as he leaned his chin over her shoulder. Her smile was mischievous as she stared at the two other men in front of her.

"Together," Gunnar said, hands outstretched, and the four of them stepped around the fire, clasping hands to forearms, creating a circle around the flames. "From this day until our last. We'll forge new paths and defend each other with our lives until we enter the gates of Valhalla."

"Until Valhalla," the other three repeated.

The flames seemed to lick higher, dancing in the wind, hearing their promise and sealing it into the fresh ink on their skin.

"Together." Gunnar smiled. His eyes shifted to Domari, his cousin, and brother in spirit. Then to Tove, his sister in blood. Then to Raud, his friend and someday brother by marriage. "Unbreakable."

"Until Valhalla," Tove repeated, and her gaze danced with joy.

1

DOMARI

Thunder rolled in the distance, matching the mood of the weighted hush that filled Frida's longhouse. No one had bothered to light the sconces on the wall tonight, the fire in the hearth the only light in the ample space, and the darkness pressed in on Domari just as much as the sound of screaming in the distance. An echo of a battle cry rang in his ears, and each one sent a shiver of fear down his spine.

He brushed a hand through his golden-brown hair, feeling where he'd shaved it along the sides the day before, as he glanced down at the two sleeping children curled into the furs behind him. One dark-haired, one fair. One fearsome, one kind. One green-eyed, one grey. Opposites in every way, like their parents.

In the three seasons since Domari had returned home from his service in the Varangian Guard, Revna and Ulf had wormed their way into his heart, seizing it more than he'd ever expected. Each time he looked upon the twins was a reminder that Gunnar, their father, had changed so much — grown, with a family, and now the chieftain of the Eriksson clan after his father's passing. Everything in his village had changed in the ten years Domari had been gone, and everyone had moved on without him.

Another scream.

Domari glanced to the door as his aunt Frida rushed from the space, her greying hair swaying behind her hurried steps. Lightning pierced the sky, revealing for an instant the sheets of snow coming down before the door clanged shut behind her.

Each moment that ticked by, each *pop* of the fire seemed an eternity.

Restless energy seized him as he rose to his feet, pushing off the low platform beds built into the walls of the immense one-room house, and he padded across the dirt-packed floors, headed for the fire. The flames cast a shadow over his dark features, so different than the other Vikings of his village, as Domari dropped to the ground, pulling free his knife and a block of wood.

"Can't sleep?"

Domari glanced up, taking in the giant man in front of him, pale blonde hair skimming his shoulders. From Domari's seat on the ground, it was more evident than ever how large Magnus was, filling the space in both body and spirit. Tattoos painted the young man's muscled chest, bare even with the cold air leaking between the cracks in the wooden walls, and Domari couldn't help but roll his eyes at his younger cousin. His question didn't need an answer, so Domari only looked back at the carving taking form.

"What are you making?"

A heavy sigh escaped Domari; again, he didn't bother answering.

"Can I see it?"

Domari's hands dropped to his lap, and his dark gaze settled on Magnus. "How is it that everything in this village has changed, yet you are still as much of an irksome child as when I left?"

Magnus's laugh rumbled through him, his chest shaking as he poured a horn of ale, passing it to Domari before pouring another for himself. "It's been a long time since I was a child, Domari. Last I checked, I stood taller than even you, and my wife was madly in love with me, carrying my child in her womb."

"A startling thought; a child with a child," Domari answered, settling the wooden block on his lap and taking a sip of the ale.

"Were you *ever* a child, Domari?" Magnus tilted his head, inspecting Domari on the ground through squinted eyes. "Or were you born this much of a Grinch?"

Numbness spread through Domari's body at the word, remembering the first time he'd been called that.

Her word.

His hands stilled, ale in hand hovering midway between his lap and his mouth, but any interest in the drink or the conversation was long gone.

"I shouldn't have said that, Domari," Magnus said, his voice taking on a more somber tone, no doubt seeing how Domari's face shuttered of all emotion.

Needing space, Domari pocketed the carving and his

knife, shoved the ale back into Magnus's hands, and crossed the space to the door. Grabbing the furs draped across a table, he shrugged them over his shoulders, pulling them tight over his woolen shirt to guard against the cold that awaited him outside. But anything was better than this stifling space.

Before he could push open the door, it swung open violently, snow blowing through the space as Gunnar stood in the doorway, beaming with happiness.

"A boy!" he cried, slapping Domari on the chest before pushing into his mother's longhouse. "Oh, Domari, you should see him. He's perfect. And Signe," he paused, spinning towards Domari as his grin spread wide, rivaling his younger brother's. "You should have seen her. I've never seen anyone as strong as my woman."

Relief washed through Domari, fearing the worst after listening to Signe's screams through the night. But Gunnar's words also sent a lance through Domari's heart, bringing up other memories of another woman, one strong enough to face down a dragon.

Snow whipped around him as Domari pushed through the door and headed out into the night, the sound of the two brothers' celebrations for the new baby not enough to warm his frozen heart. The storm raged on in the distance, heavy clouds with snow blocking out the magenta and green lights that whirled overhead on clear winter nights.

With no true destination in mind, Domari found himself standing in front of the barn, pushing the door aside as he stepped into the warm space, smelling the many animals hunkered inside. A dun-colored head leaned over the beam across his stall in the back, and Mjölnir nickered when he spotted Domari approaching. Several other horses, their coats varying from tan to gold, but each with the matching black-and-white-striped mane, leaned out as well.

Domari stopped in front of his horse, running his hands over the stallion's shaggy mane, taking the simple comfort his steady companion offered. The horse's large head worked along Domari's side, lips moving as he searched the layers of Domari's furs and shirt for a treat.

"I brought nothing but my friendship," Domari said as he pushed the horse's face away. "Hopefully, that's enough for you."

With a huff, the horse lifted his head, resting it on Domari's outstretched arm.

"I know you hate being cooped up in here," he went on, scratching along the thick fur on Mjölnir's neck. Domari's eyes scanned the surrounding barn, full of animals since he had helped construct it several months ago. Goats and sheep huddled in the back, munching their feed while several chickens pecked at the ground at his feet. Between Magnus's earlier words and Gunnar's elation over his new baby, Domari's heart ached for all he'd lost and never had. Even here in the barn, everything reminded him of her, of their last night in the village before they began her journey home. "So do I."

With the baby's birth, the next nine days would be a flurry of activity, getting ready for the celebration to welcome the new child into their clan. Gunnar had already visited the blacksmiths multiple times lately, waiting for the baby's arrival, planning in case he had another son. Now that he was here, his son's first sword would be all Gunnar could talk about, and Domari had already had enough.

Mjölnir stamped his hoof on the ground, drawing Domari back from his thoughts, and he scratched along the horse's side once more. The horse's striped mane waved as it tossed his head, stamping again, knocking the board that kept him in the stall.

"Easy, boy," Domari said, laying his hand flat across the horse's neck. "We can't go anywhere tonight. It's still storming outside. Maybe it'll pass, and we can go for a ride in the morning."

The thought of celebrating, of drinking and listening to the merriment around him, of watching Magnus croon over his unborn child growing in Astrid's belly, of Signe and Gunnar's shared excitement over the new baby's arrival, made this idea sound even better.

Without further thought, Domari grabbed the saddle hanging over a rack in the center of the barn and began to pack. He needed space, time to think, time to heal. Decision made, Domari settled his things near the front of Mjölnir's stall and returned to the longhouse for the night.

He'd leave in the morning.

Darkness clung to the chill air as Domari waded through the fresh snow the next morning, determination settled into his bones. Donning his warmest furs and cloak, he'd left the longhouse before the others were awake, making for the barn with his travel bags in tow. Long trips in the middle of winter were treacherous, the storms brutal, and shelter scarce, but Domari had been a warrior for ten years in the elite Varangian Guard and a hunter for his entire life before that. He knew these lands, and he knew how to survive. Physical battles, he knew how to win. Battles of the heart were much less familiar to him.

"You're leaving, aren't you?" Magnus said from the barn's door, surprising Domari. But he didn't stop working, cinching the saddle on tight to Mjölnir's back, never casting a look over his shoulder.

"Are you coming back?" Magnus asked, and, this time, Domari turned, glancing over at his younger cousin where he leaned against the door frame. "Or is this like last time, and I'll have to tell them I watched you ride off in the night, not to be seen or heard from for ten more years?"

Domari opened his mouth to answer, but paused. He thought he'd be back, but he also couldn't explain the pull he felt to be back on the shoreline of the lake where he'd spent his last moments with her. After he'd left the barn last night, his dreams circled around the Tree, calling to him, demanding he go. He *had* to.

Reading Domari's hesitation, Magnus scoffed, pushed off the wall, and turned to leave. "Find her, Domari," he said, and Domari's head snapped up at his words, eyes wide with disbelief. "Find her, or find yourself. But come back to us either way."

Domari watched silently as Magnus left, the door closing behind his cousin, offering wisdom far beyond his years. Maybe Magnus had grown up, after all.

2
DOMARI

Storms plagued Domari's journey to the lake, and the trip that should have taken three days was stretched into nine, dreams of the Tree becoming more vivid with each passing night. Each morning he rose, determination pushing him forward, even if only to travel to the next cave. But on the ninth day, as the moon rose bright in the sky, Domari paused at the shore's edge. Clouds hovered overhead, blocking most of the stars, but magenta and green wisps still danced in the sky, oblivious to the man below.

Everything was how he'd left it all those months ago. A boat lay shattered and broken on the snow-covered beach, another intact, now frozen into the ice along the water's edge. Wood was gathered there as if someone had returned to build a new boat and then abandoned the effort. But who had done that, or why — it didn't matter.

Nothing did.

Mjölnir's breath filled the night air with fog as the horse

panted from their winter ride. The furs covering Domari's body were caked in snow that had fallen on the last leg of his journey, dusting everything with white, but he hadn't even bothered to brush it off. With each step they took, Domari's mind drifted to those last days with her.

The clearing where she'd faced down a dragon.

The cave they'd shared.

Even here at the lake — the way she'd done what she needed to, returning to her time with the Norn's warning of danger to come, breaking her own heart and his in the process. Memories of his last moments here had haunted him, drowning him in thoughts of what could have been. But that wasn't his reality, and he needed to move on.

The snow glittered in the moonlight, and Domari kicked at it absently as he hesitated, staring out at the ash tree rising from the island in front of him. He had hoped that being here — being closer to her — might bring him some semblance of peace, of closure. But the only thing here for him was a tree on an island, barren and broken, like him. His heart was dark, as empty as the limbs rising high into the sky.

Domari sank to the snowy ground as he stared at the island. Hands draped across his knees, he sighed as he rested his chin on his forearm and watched.

Waited.

For what, he didn't know.

The night was silent around Domari, the wind rustling the trees around the lake his only companion other than his horse standing nearby. It was peaceful out here, with no one's eyes following his every movement. He was tired of the sad stares shot in his direction and the loneliness that clung to him as it had for years. Coming here had been the right decision, if only to have the space to feel these emotions away from the watchful eyes of his clan. Thoughts became distant as his mind wandered, curling into himself on the shore.

Suddenly, a gust of wind flew off the water, whipping snow in every direction as it blurred his vision. One arm came up to block his face while the other hand gripped the axe at his side when he heard it.

CRACK.

The sound filled the air as the ice covering the lake took a hard hit. Mjölnir nickered loudly. Domari jumped to his feet, grabbing the reins while the horse did his best to break free and run. He reached up, running his hands over the horse's neck, whispering to calm him as he glanced back at the frozen water.

Finally, the snow settled, and the moonlight glittered off black and gold scales.

"Hadriel," Domari's rich timbre said with a laugh. At his words, he dropped to one knee, bowing before the enormous dragon posed on the ice.

A shriek was Domari's only warning before fire filled the air, ice crackling everywhere at the sudden wash of heat. Domari's hood blew off in the gust as warmth filled him to his core. A smile spread across his face at the memories this dragon brought to the surface. Blonde curls, wild and free, blowing in the wind as a beautiful face didn't cower, didn't back down from the terrifying creature in front of her. Domari's head was still down, his brown hair now filled with snow, as he shook his head at the memory.

"Unbelievable."

Even though he felt the heat of Hadriel's fire, it was still hard for him to believe this was real. A dragon. The Norns. Time travel. These existed in legends for his people, but never had he experienced anything of the sort.

When Domari returned to his village after escorting Shelbie to the Tree, he hadn't had the heart to discuss their journey, so overcome with bittersweet memories. He'd forgotten to even mention to Gunnar that he'd met the dragon of legend.

Hadriel panted, steam rising from his nostrils — reminding Domari how very *real* he was — but didn't unleash a column of flame again. After a moment, Domari finally raised his head, eyeing the dragon. His green, slitted eyes glowed in the evening light, brimming with questions.

"She's not here," Domari whispered, barely loud enough for his own ears.

A whine crawled out of the dragon's throat, a strange sound for a creature so large.

"I know," the man said, hanging his head again. "Me too."

Thwack.

Something hard hit Domari's shoulder, bruising instantly. His head shot up, looking for the cause of the sudden pain, and he saw only the dragon in front of him. Hadriel's eyes seemed different, warmer, as his mouth hung open.

"Is that what you'd call a smile?" he asked the dragon

aloud as if he could answer, and a smile rose to Domari's face as he remembered her doing the same.

The dragon huffed, then whipped his tail in an arch towards Domari, who rose at the last minute to avoid the crushing blow. Instead, Hadriel's tail shifted the surrounding snow, plowing an area clean. There, in the middle of the clearing, was a necklace.

Domari stooped to retrieve it, brushing off the snow gathered on the surface. His brows came together as he flipped it in his gloved hands and peered up at the dragon. Without another sound, the giant creature spun and flew towards the Tree in the distance.

Unsure of what to do, Domari stood idly on the beach, flipping the pendant in his hand. If he wasn't mistaken, this was the same necklace she had bribed the dragon with months ago.

"Why are you giving it back?" he called. His eyes came up, watching the dragon's flight across the frozen lake as he landed hard on the island, stalking towards the Tree.

Without another thought, Domari eased his way onto the ice, testing it to ensure it held after the large cracks the dragon caused. He worked his way across slowly, but each step seemed a little surer as the Tree from his dreams stood tall overhead.

Domari's feet touched down in the snow on the shore, sinking in the untouched mounds piling along the island. The dragon repeatedly circled the Tree, smoke rising from his nostrils.

"I've lost my mind," Domari muttered to himself, shaking his head as he made to follow the dragon.

As he neared the trunk, Domari noticed the large cavern under the roots where she'd dropped her bracelet. His heart broke at the sight, emotions spiraling through him as movement suddenly became impossible.

After a moment, a heavy nudge landed on his back, throwing Domari off-balance enough to bring him out of his fog. His chin tipped up to find the dragon, too close for comfort, staring into his eyes.

Hadriel's green, glowing eyes shifted to the right and down to where the roots were exposed closer to the shore. Curious, Domari followed the dragon's gaze, brushing the snow away with his boot.

Carved on the root was another rune, different from the one she'd knelt in front of. He stooped to inspect it while the chain dangled from his hand into the snow.

$$N$$

Hope. Before he even had time to consider why Hadriel would usher him here, something heavy smacked him in the center of the back. Domari's grip on the chain slipped as it flew into the air. He grappled for the necklace, but it was too late. It fell, bouncing off the exposed root before sliding underneath.

Everything went black.

3

DOMARI

As Domari's vision returned, faint sunlight crept through the trees, but he recognized nothing. Gone was the frozen lake in front of him. Gone was the rainbow of lights in the night sky. Gone was the giant black and gold dragon. Gone was the Tree.

His eyes scanned the snowy landscape around him, but the snow was the only thing familiar to him. Thin white trees rose high into the sky, clustered tightly together in a large grove. Light sparkled off the fresh snow in spots, and Domari glanced into the sky. This time of the year, he was used to the never-ending darkness that clung to his homeland. It wasn't until he'd moved to Constantinople following the Varangian Guard he learned the rest of the world wasn't like his home in this.

Wherever the Tree had transported him, Domari knew he was far from home.

He turned, glancing behind him for any sign of how he'd arrived here, but nothing stood out to him. There were no roots exposed or runes carved into the bark. Nothing like the Tree in the middle of the island he'd left behind.

Just as Domari moved to step away, his eye caught on something black in the snow. He knelt, gloved hand brushing over the onyx stone suspended in a gold pendant. Warmth radiated from the stone the longer he held it, inspecting the intricate dragon circling the stone. He didn't remember feeling any heat from it when Hadriel threw it at him, nor when he carried it across the ice.

Unsure what to do with it, Domari removed his gloves, lifted his furs, and moved the axe hanging at his side, exposing the pocket in his trousers beneath. With one last glance at the stone, he slid the pendant into his pocket, the golden chain slipping through his fingers as it dropped.

Gloves in hand, he turned to the sky, searching for the sun. Light radiated from his left, soft pink in the early morning light. Dark clouds hovered to his right, looming over the trees, evident of a storm to come. He turned back to the trees once more, hesitating briefly. Domari had no idea where he was, but somewhere here was his way home. Trusting his instincts, he removed his knife from its sheath at his side and stepped up to the closest tree, marking it with a rune before he wandered further from his starting position.

N

Hope. His heart beat rapidly as he gave in to the driving force, telling him this was right. This was why he was here. Why he'd come to the Tree in the first place. Pushing hard on the knife, he carved. Wood scraped away with each forceful move, easing the tension and heartache Domari had carried with him for months.

Hope. This wasn't the end for him, and he'd find his place, whether here, wherever the Tree had transported him, or back at home again with his clan.

Hope. Like the sun rising to the east, a new day was upon him, even with storms looming nearby.

Each pass of the knife had the rune standing out clearer, tan against the bright white bark. As he finished, he stepped back to admire his work, feeling the deep grooves with his fingers.

Domari sheathed his knife, sliding it into its place on his belt, then dropped his furs back over his weapons. His chin tipped up to the sky as he studied it once more. The storm was moving in from the west, so he spun on his heel, moving to the east, headed towards the sunrise, hoping to find shelter before the snowfall began.

His boots crunched through the snow as he moved, working his way towards a clearing ahead. Before he reached it, a low growl rent the air, forcing Domari to stop. Hand slipping to the dagger on his belt, he scanned the area, searching for the animal. It sounded like a wolf, but he couldn't be sure, since he was unfamiliar with the land. However, he *did* know that wolves were hardly ever alone.

Eyes sweeping the surrounding trees, he searched for movement or footprints, something that would give away their location. Pulling his knife free, he took another tentative step, eyes peeled for the predator nearby.

The growl came again, this time from up ahead in the clearing, followed by footsteps, and Domari paused.

"What is it, bud?" a voice floated through the air, and Domari sucked in a gasp. Heart racing in his chest, he whipped his head to the side, searching for her. The growl sounded again, and Domari increased his pace as he chased the sound, hoping beyond hope that this wasn't his imagination playing a horrible trick on him.

He knew whose voice that was.

Her voice.

As he neared the clearing, he spotted movement. A large black dog stood there, a woman in a blue coat, blonde curls peeking out in two knots at the nape of her neck, leaning down as she rubbed her mittened hand over its head.

"Shelbie."

Just saying her name after the last two months was enough to have his emotions crashing down on him, his breath becoming uneven.

The dog growled again, and Shelbie followed his line of sight, finally spotting Domari in the trees. Shelbie's hand slammed over her mouth as she sucked in a breath. Her eyes blew wide in shock as she stepped back, tripped to the ground, and knelt in the snow.

Domari dropped his gloves and rushed to her side, closing the distance between them in several long strides, and dropped to the snow in front of her, hands drifting up to cup her jaw.

"Are you real?" Shelbie whispered, tears brimming in her eyes as she stared up at Domari. A tear escaped, running down her cheek, flushed from the cold, and Domari swiped at it with his thumb. Words were lost to him as he stared into her ice-blue eyes, only nodding in response.

"How is this possible?" Shelbie sniffled, then shifted her focus away from Domari, darting to the dog as he growled again.

Domari dropped his hands from her face, moving back a fraction to access the knives at his waist. He didn't want to hurt the dog, but no way in Hel would he let anything happen to Shelbie now that he'd found her once more.

Shelbie's eyes flicked down to Domari's hand hovering over his belt, then grew wide as she threw her hands out between Domari and the dog. "WAIT. He's mine. This is Thor, my dog I told you about. He won't hurt you," she paused, glancing at the dog nervously again, "Probably. At least, I don't think he will. You never know with Thor. He hates everyo—"

Before finishing her sentence, Thor brushed aside Shelbie's arm, inching closer to Domari's face.

"Thor," she drew out his name, tugging on his collar as she jumped to her feet, attempting to pull the giant dog away from Domari. But the dog charged, and Shelbie's arm jerked forward as Thor pulled loose from her grip, closing the distance between himself and Domari. He jumped up, paws coming down hard on Domari's shoulders. Shoved back into the snow, Shelbie screamed as Domari turned his face to the side, feeling the cold snow under his cheek.

"THOR!" Shelbie yelled, yanking uselessly on the dog's collar to pull him off Domari, but the dog didn't budge. His

wet nose slid across Domari's cheek, sniffing furiously as Thor inspected his beard, neck, and furs. Tentatively, Domari brought his hands up, letting his fingers slide through the thick coat along the dog's side, hoping he would see the gesture as friendly rather than threatening. A low rumble escaped Thor's throat right before a warm tongue slid across Domari's cheek. Domari pulled back as giddy laughter rumbled through his chest.

Thor continued to lick him until Domari brought his hands up to his face, pushing the imposing beast off and back into the snow. Domari sat up, wearing a wide grin as he stared at Shelbie.

Her jaw hung open as her eyes moved between her dog and Domari, brows knit together in confusion.

"You were saying?" Domari said as he brushed the snow from his trousers, rising to his feet.

"What the hell, Thor?" Shelbie looked down at the dog padding back to her side, tail wagging. Her eyes came up to settle on Domari's again, and her jaw snapped shut. "Well. I guess I take it back. He hates *almost* everyone. Apparently, that does not include you."

Domari's chest felt instantly lighter as he moved to stand in front of her once more. "Where are we?"

"In the woods." Shelbie smiled, holding her hands out to the side. Domari fought not to roll his eyes, glancing back in the direction he'd come, but Shelbie's mittened hand snagged on his furs, pulling him back towards her.

"Sorry," she said, a nervous laugh escaping her. "I get weird when I'm flustered, and this *definitely* has me flustered." She closed her eyes, mitten still pressed against his chest as she drew a steadying breath. Domari couldn't help but notice her long eyelashes draped across her freckled cheeks, rosy pink from the cold. She exhaled, opening her eyes once more, gaze settling on Domari's.

"Hi."

A smile spread across Domari's face as he quirked a brow. "That's it? After all of this, I get one word. I expected more from you."

Shelbie stuttered a laugh and a smile as bright as the sun settled on her face. "Sorry to disappoint. This is all shocking, and then I thought Thor was going to murder you, which would have been unfortunate. I wasn't even sure you were *real* after I returned. I would've been furious if he killed you right after I found you again. Thankfully, that didn't happen, though. And he likes you?" She twisted her head back and to the side, nose scrunching in confusion. "*That's* a total mystery. I'm not sure I've ever seen him take to anyone like that. It took Sabrina *a year* for Thor to let her into my apartment, let alone pet him, and here he is, licking you like you're his best friend. I'm honestly a little jealous; he only likes me like that. It's bizarre. But here you are," she paused, seeming to realize her hand was still on Domari's chest as she dropped it to the side, "in the woods I used to hike in as a kid near my parents' house, standing in front of me like it's no big deal. But this *is* a big deal because you're now in *my* time, Domari."

"There she is," Domari chuckled, eyes sparkling as he slid one hand across her waist, pulling her into his chest. "I missed you so much."

Tears brimmed in Shelbie's eyes, cheeks turning even redder as she nodded in return.

Waiting no longer, he placed a knuckle under her chin, tipping it up. Her lips parted, eyes closing, and Domari savored the sight for only a moment before he gently touched his lips down on hers. The kiss was full of longing and hope, lips brushing as they melted into each other. Her mittened hands curled into his furs as much as they could, holding on as a tidal wave of emotions threatened to pull them both out to sea.

At last, they broke apart, and he rested his forehead on hers.

"That felt pretty real to me," she whispered, and Domari pulled her into him. She laid her cheek across his chest, and he turned, resting his chin on her head, rubbing his hands down her back.

After a moment spent soaking in each other's presence, she sighed, breath escaping her in a fog. "How did you get here? How the hell are you in *my* time now, Domari?"

Domari chuckled as he thought through the morning he'd had. He didn't understand any of it, but there wasn't a doubt in his mind that this was where he was meant to be.

"You won't believe me when I tell you," he answered. "Hadriel pushed me into the Tree."

4
SHELBIE

My head was spinning, and the only thing that seemed to keep me in place was Domari's hands on my back.

Domari.

My throat tightened, and I couldn't tell if it was because I wanted to sob or shout for joy. Two months had passed since I'd left Sweden behind and returned to a life I could hardly stand. Two months of torture, questioning everything I thought I'd experienced on my trip, but it shouldn't have been possible. Two months of missing a man gone for a millennium, if he wasn't a figment of my imagination.

None of that mattered anymore, though. Domari was holding me, chin resting on my head as my lips tingled with the memories of our kiss. I could hear his heartbeat, feel his chest expand with each breath, and smell his pine and fresh air scent. He was *real*.

A snowflake landed on my eyelash, drawing my attention away for a moment. I swiped my hand across it, clearing my eye, and looked around. The dark clouds that had been in the distance when something called to me, insisting I stop here in the woods, weren't so distant anymore. Thor rose to his feet, shaking the snow from his black coat, and stretched. With a quick look in my direction, he turned back towards the path.

"Crap," I muttered to myself before glancing at my watch. It had been an hour since I'd parked at the trailhead, and the snowstorm was moving quickly. I looked up to find Domari's gaze on mine and smiled.

I'd missed this man so much.

"So, as much as I'd love to stand here making sure you are, in fact, real," I grinned, letting my eyes drift to the dark clouds behind him, "We need to go. Now."

Without waiting for us, Thor began walking down the path, and Domari inclined his head towards the storm. "Snow is coming."

"Yeah," I nodded, patting his chest. In all the many times I'd daydreamed of Domari, I'd still forgotten how huge he was, which was saying something since I stood just under six feet, and the top of my head was below his chin. "And we have a bit of driving to get out of it. We kind of need to hurry."

Domari dropped his arms from around me, and the sudden loss of his body heat sent a chill through me. "Lead the way."

"You're... coming, right?"

He glanced behind him towards where he had arrived and then back at me, nodding.

We made quick work of the trail heading back to my

Jeep, which fortunately wasn't too covered in snow yet. Domari suddenly came to a stop behind me. I turned around and found him studying my Jeep, eyebrows raised and mouth slightly open.

"What *is* this?"

My eyes scanned him, then my surroundings, before internally smacking my forehead. Everything would be new for him here. *Everything.*

"This is a car," I said, trying my best not to sound condescending, talking while I worked. I turned on the engine to defrost it and dusted the snow off Thor's coat before loading him into the back. The Eagles played through my speakers, picking up where I'd left off after leaving my parents' house that morning. Grabbing the brush off the floorboards, I cleared the snow accumulated in the hour I'd been gone — much more than I'd realized.

"It's like…" I waved my hands in the air, urging my brain to think of some way to explain this to him, "a sled. Or a wagon without horses. There's an engine — a machine — under here," I patted the hood, "that powers it." I glanced at the sky, trying my best not to hurry the conversation, but we had to get going. "I live about two hours by car from here, so why don't I explain more on the way?"

Domari stood to the side, eyes scanning everything I'd just done. I dropped the brush to my side as I opened the driver's side door. "Are you coming?"

He stepped towards the Jeep hesitantly, but ultimately grabbed the passenger door as I reached across the console and pushed it open for him. Before climbing in, he unbuckled his belt, dropping the sword and axe sheathed onto the floorboards with a loud *thunk*.

Hope I don't get pulled over, I momentarily thought to myself. Shivering, I pulled my mittens off and shoved my fingers towards the vents.

His gaze swung over the car after he settled, taking in all the buttons, screens, and gauges filling the dashboard. Hands grazed over the fabric seats and leather console, exploring. Mirroring what I'd done, he leaned forward, inspecting the air vents.

"It's hot."

"Yes, a heater," I nodded. *Yeesh, this was going to be complicated.*

I turned off the music before showing him his seatbelt and how to buckle it, briefly explaining its purpose as well. With a deep breath, I checked my mirrors. "Ready?"

Domari said nothing.

Unable to contain myself, I leaned across the console and planted another chaste kiss on his mouth. "Making sure you're still real."

Domari's eyes crinkled in amusement at my words, and I was delighted to see the joy I felt at this moment reflected on his face.

I talked as I drove, doing my best to explain the fascinating details of automobiles, which was more like a brief overview because that wasn't my area of expertise. Domari seemed too overwhelmed to ask many questions, and I could hardly blame him. Sure, traveling back in time had been shocking for me, but I'd already been on a horseback-riding trip, camping, and riding with him for two days before I fully realized what had happened. That made it seem much more reasonable than traveling forward in time by a thousand years.

Cars whizzed past us on the highway, but I watched the road for any signs of danger as the snow came down hard around us. My windshield wipers drummed a steady beat as I downshifted, talking less as I concentrated on the twisting, icy mountain roads.

"You doing okay over there?" I asked after several minutes of silence had gone by.

A weird, mumbled affirmation drew my attention for a moment. Domari was looking green, sweat beading on his brow.

"Oh geez," I sighed. "You're carsick, aren't you?"

He said nothing, lips sealed to keep whatever was brewing in his stomach locked down tight, but the sheer concentration on his face told me everything I needed to know.

"Think of it as a boat," I explained. "Watch the horizon. Keep your eyes open and up. Breathe as deeply as you can, and let me know if I need to stop and pull over."

With that explanation, Domari seemed to settle. He sank back in the chair, staring out the window at the snow falling hard.

Switching the radio to Bob Marley and the Wailers' *Three Little Birds*, I sang along with the radio, my stress easing as my windshield wipers worked furiously to keep the snow from blurring my vision. We weren't in a hurry, though — my only goal was to make it home safely.

The drive out of the mountains and back to Denver took far longer than usual, but eventually, the highway opened up on our final descent into the city. We left the worst of the snow behind us, but flurries still floated through the air, making the view in front of us almost magical.

The sun had risen hours ago, high in the sky, even though it was muted behind the looming clouds. Just enough light passed through to make the city shimmer, glowing off the buildings rising in the distance.

I glanced at Domari to gauge his reaction and noticed he'd shut his eyes, dozing lightly as his head rested on the window. The color was back in his cheeks, and relief rushed through my veins. I was glad he'd relaxed and had one less thing to explain. While he slept, I quickly stopped by my apartment to grab the last of my belongings and turn in my keys.

The key slipped into the lock, and I pushed open the door, flicked on the lights, and took in the last view of my apartment. It was empty now; I'd moved all my furniture a few days ago using one of Charlene's horse trailers. All that remained was a box of kitchen utensils, cookware on the counter, and a suitcase containing toiletries. Stacking my last box on top of the suitcase, I turned off the light, closed the door, and locked it.

My grin spread wider as I rushed back to my car through the snow, thinking of all that life was presenting to me now. I'd chosen to change, to move forward, and look where it had taken me. The man of my dreams sat waiting for me in my car's passenger seat. I didn't have to go to my job tomorrow; my life now revolved around horses, reading, or maybe even writing books at my leisure, and whatever I decided made me happy.

"This is it," I said with a giddy smile, flipping the keys through the air before dropping them in the landlord's mail slot. "Good riddance, old life."

5

SHELBIE

Domari was awake by the time I got back to the car, and Thor was standing with two paws on the center console, practically smothering the man.

"Back!" I scolded Thor as I opened the door, shooting my best glare at my misbehaving dog. "You know you're not allowed in the front."

Domari rubbed his hand over Thor's head one last time before my dog let out a huff of frustration, returning to his bench seat in the back. He circled, then dropped to the seat, dark eyes heavy on me.

I jumped back in the car, studying Domari once more. He leaned towards the windshield, taking in the large apartment building four stories tall. My eyes drifted over his dark hair, enormous beard, furs draped over his shoulders and thick woolen trousers. Here, in my world, Domari looked very *Viking*.

"This is my apartment, where I used to live," I explained. "But it's not all one house like you're used to.

The whole building is split into 24 smaller homes, and I lived in one."

He looked away from the apartments and back, studying my face. "Alone?"

Thor released a low moan, stretching languidly as his paws crept back onto the center console. I pushed them back, but chuckled. "I don't think Thor appreciates that you don't count him as part of my family. But yes, it was only Thor and me here."

Domari glanced back at the building again as I reversed the car and headed out to the street. "Where are we going now?"

Nervousness buzzed under my skin, causing me to tighten my grip on the steering wheel. "Home, Domari."

I felt his eyes linger as I drove, trying to focus on the snowy roads around us instead of the distracting Viking in the passenger seat. It had been years since I'd last lived with a roommate, and never a man. The house on Charlene's ranch wasn't large, but what other options did we have? We were right back to the same one-bed trope all over again.

Snow fell steadily and piled up quickly by the time we pulled up to Charlene's ranch on the outskirts of Denver. With a push of a button, the red electric gate creaked open slowly, taking its sweet time accepting me into this new chapter of my life. Domari had said little the entire car ride, and I'd done my best to let him sit in silence — a difficult task for me. He had a lot to absorb, and I was sure his mind was reeling. Hell, *my* mind was spinning, and I wasn't the one surrounded by everything new. I snuck a peek over at Domari in the passenger seat while I waited, but he was preoccupied with studying the ranch. It still didn't feel real that he was *here*, but that could be said about so much of my life lately.

I'd spent the last two months spiraling into a dark hole, tossing and turning over whether any of my trip's memories had even happened. That I had told no one in my life what I *thought* happened had isolated me in a way I'd never prepared for. Charlene was the only one I'd mentioned anything to, and even then, it was only Domari's name. But how *could* I explain time travel without sounding like I needed to head straight for the looney bin?

Maybe Domari had more answers than I did about how this was possible, but we hadn't discussed it yet. With each passing second of silence, tension pulled my shoulders tighter to my ears, all the lingering stress from the day piling heavily on me. I wanted answers, to understand what to expect, to know if the emotions building between us last fall were real.

Everything had happened so fast in Sweden, a whirlwind romance in the best sense. But real life didn't work like that. It was messy, complicated, and full of turbulent changes you had to learn to weather together. We'd had passion in our brief fling before, but was that all there was to it? A desperate desire driven by the fact our time was cut short?

I chewed on my lip as the car lurched forward through the rising snow and scanned the ranch. Three mismatched barns sat scattered on the property, along with all the equipment Charlene used for training horses, framed by a forest behind the property, trees dusted with snow. The mountains rose high in the distance but were blocked from view by the low cloud cover of the storm.

Smoke rose from the chimney on Charlene's house, curling into the clouds above. Lights were on inside, and her truck was parked out front. From what I could tell, all the horses had been brought in from the pastures, barn doors closed, waiting out the storm. Since Charlene wasn't expecting me until tomorrow, she must have done all the chores today without me, and I sighed in relief. It wasn't that I didn't want to help her — in fact, I was excited about my new job here on the ranch, helping with the horses a welcome change from my lackluster office job before. But before I faced Charlene, I needed to gather my thoughts and figure out how to explain the man I was positive I couldn't hide for long.

I drove behind the smallest barn and headed for my new house, tucked between the barn and the forest behind. Nausea rolled through me as my nerves ramped up, feeling the intensity of our situation; a mixture of anxiety over all the changes that had happened rapidly over the last few weeks and excitement about everything to come. My life was suddenly full of possibilities if only I were brave enough to take the chance. With a deep breath, I shifted into park. Thor pawed at the door restlessly, and I turned off the car.

"Hang on, big guy," I said, gathering my keys and phone as I slid from the Jeep. I quickly reminded Domari how the handle worked once more as I let Thor out, watching the hulking dog drop into the snow on the ground. He padded around the side of the house, and I pulled my bags from the trunk. Snow fell faster, clinging to my eyelashes and hair as I hurried to remove my belongings from the car, shivering in the brisk winter air. Domari's arms circled me momentarily, and I stiffened at his closeness out of instinct, but he only lifted the suitcase from my arms as he followed me onto the porch.

The little house was dark, lights off inside, two rocking chairs on the porch piled high with snow, but the coral door with its crystal knob was inviting, promising happiness and warmth beyond. Excitement bubbled in my chest as it sank in that this was *my* house. I didn't have to return to the cold, boring apartment and my dull life again. I couldn't help but smile as I reached for the note taped to the door.

Welcome home! Glad you're here. It's colder than a witch's titty, so I'm not coming over. Knock if you need anything.
XO, C

I giggled as I peeled the paper off, shuffling my grip on the box in my hand to pull out my key ring. The ostentatious and so very Charlene leopard-print key stood out against the other boring silver ones, and I slid it into the lock. The smell of clove and nutmeg reached me as the door opened, and immediately, I was happy I'd left a reed diffuser here the last time I'd brought over a load. It smelled like home.

Reaching in, I flicked on the light overhead and stepped inside. Domari was right behind me, standing on the threshold, staring into the house, and I glanced between him and the house's interior.

Straight ahead was my small living room — I'd moved my couch and TV over from my apartment, but still needed to get some more furniture. This house had once belonged to Marlene, Charlene's equally flamboyant twin sister, and old floral wallpaper still covered three of the walls, giving the space a feminine feel. The other wall was painted a bold blue that overwhelmed the small space. I hadn't purchased a dining table yet, but my two bar stools from my apartment sat useless along the wall between the couch and the kitchen. Until I had a table, I'd either be eating on the couch or standing over the sink — both perfectly acceptable options according to my lifestyle.

The kitchen looked the same as the first time I'd seen it, with pots hanging from the ceiling over the island and white cabinets. I'd piled my boxes in the kitchen corner when I'd moved them over last week and dropped the last one in my hands on the stack. Tomorrow I'd work on unpacking and settling in. Right now, though, I turned back to the doorway where Domari stood on the threshold, silhouetted by the snow falling behind him.

His eyes were wide, moving around the space as he took it all in, and I couldn't help but think how different my home was from the Viking longhouse I'd stayed in with him. The massive, one-room wooden structure with platforms built into the walls, dirt-packed floors, and an outhouse all centered around the hearth in the middle was an entirely different sort of *home*. I'd also be standing in shock in the doorway if I were him.

Thor suddenly pushed Domari out of the way to enter the house, making straight for his bed under the front window. He shook, sending snow flying everywhere, much to my annoyance, and then curled up on his bed. A strong gust of wind sent flurries floating on the porch, blowing in through the open door and jarring Domari's attention.

As he stepped inside, the low ceilings of the house made Domari seem even taller; his golden-brown hair, still longer on the top and shaved close on the sides, nearly brushed the doorway when he closed the door behind him. Framed against the bright coral door, his brown furs draped over his shoulders emphasized his rugged appearance, and my mind stuttered over the fact that a Viking warrior was standing in my living room.

"So," I lifted my hands, waving them around the house, "This is my home." Any further explanation was lost to me as I let my hands drop, nervousness eating up every drop of energy in my body. I could feel all the nonsensical words ready to spew out of my mouth to fill the awkward silence between us, but I bounced on my heels instead.

Chill the fuck out, Shelbie, I couldn't help thinking as Domari continued to stare at the interior of my house. Seconds ticked by, and the silence stretched until I couldn't take it any longer. Turning my back to him, I pulled open the coat closet door, shrugged out of my coat, and hung it inside. I unlaced my boots, placing them underneath, then paused for a second, searching for even an ounce of calm.

"It's weird, right?" I said, scrunching my nose as I followed his gaze around the space. "Too much floral. I need to paint it and get rid of these colors, maybe something more neutral. But I'm not sure I'm a neutral-type person. Could do yellow, or maybe a paler blue, I suppose. Anything would be better than this kaleidoscope of color. Charlene's sister Marlene used to live here, and they have some old beef they need to work through, but that's none of my business. Also, I've never painted a wall before, so this will be an adventure. All comes with the whole *first home* gig, I suppose."

Nope.

That wasn't calm.

That was word vomit.

Even worse, as I thought back over my words, Domari probably didn't understand half of them.

His deep brown eyes settled on me, sparkling with merriment as he set the suitcase still in his hands down, shrugged out of his furs, and opened the closet door as I had moments before. Domari attempted to drape his furs over a hanger as I had, struggling to keep it on the flimsy plastic until I took it from him, choosing the hook on the back of the door instead. He kicked out of his boots, setting them next to mine, then glanced at the weapons belt in his hand. With a raised brow in my direction, he lifted it in question, then motioned to the closet.

"Sure, you can put them in there, too. That works," I shrugged because where else would one casually place an axe, a sword, and about a dozen knives? As the door clicked shut, I spun on my heel, moving through the living room, searching for anything to do other than stare awkwardly at the man in my home.

Good God, I'm weird.

Domari followed close behind me as I moved into the kitchen. "It's warm in here," he said, and I nodded, still avoiding eye contact.

"Yep. There are heaters in here, like in the car. But it comes from down there." I pointed to the radiator at the far end of the kitchen. Domari looked towards it, eyes squinted as he studied the metal contraption, and I prayed he didn't ask how it worked because I had no idea.

"You hungry?" I said, hoping to change the conversation before making even more of a fool of myself.

"Yes," he replied, standing in front of the radiator, touching the metal bars. "Food would be good."

6

SHELBIE

DING! The timer on the ancient but functional oven startled me, scattering my thoughts to the wind. I hadn't had time to grocery shop for the house yet, so our options were limited to what I had left in my fridge and the freezer from my apartment. I'd settled on a frozen pizza, hardly the way I'd have chosen to introduce Domari to the culinary delights of our time had I known about this beforehand.

Please don't burn it, I chanted in my head.

Domari knew from our previous conversations that I considered myself a cook in no way, shape, or form. A baker, yes. I could do that. But cooking? Couldn't do it. Only omelettes, and that was it. Nevertheless, I was terrified something catastrophic would happen, imagining flames licking out of the oven I had yet to use.

After closer inspection of the radiator, Domari seemed to loosen up, chatting more easily, and the uncomfortable tension between us dissipated. While we waited for the oven to heat and the pizza to cook, he asked question after question about all the different kitchen appliances. The sink especially impressed him; running water was a novel concept. I watched as he turned the faucet on, then off, on, then off, running his hand underneath in awe. Immediately, my mind wandered to how he'd react when he discovered the shower.

The wind shrieked outside, moving past howling and into full blizzard mode. It was a white-out outside the windows, but my new little house was warm, and we had *some* food, so we'd survive.

I slipped on my oven mitts and opened the door, steam rising and carrying the delicious scent of melted cheese into the room. The sight of the browned but unburnt pizza had me almost giddy, glad I hadn't embarrassed myself any further, incoherent rambling aside. I slid it onto a cutting board to cool while I leaned in and grabbed two hard ciders from the fridge, popping the tops off the glass bottles and handing one over to Domari. He looked at it for several minutes before finally raising it to his lips, tentatively taking a sip after watching me do the same.

Even though I'd drank the ale they'd handed me in his village, I wasn't much of a drinker. Cider was as close as I got, and the only reason I had any in my fridge right now was that I'd bought it to take to a Christmas party last week at Sabrina's house that I'd later bailed on. I'd been avoiding my best friend recently — she asked too many questions and knew me too well for me to dodge them without raising more suspicions than my actions already had. Plus, the party would be most of her other married, parent friends, and I wasn't in the mood to be the lone single friend.

"It's not exactly ale." I took another sip, my gaze still locked on his face.

"No," he responded, pulling the bottle away from his lips to scrutinize it, "but it's not bad. They had bottles like this in Constantinople full of wine, but I've never seen one this small before." Domari tipped the bottle and chugged the rest of the cider as I shamelessly watched his throat work.

Another sip for me, because *whoa*. In my memories, I remembered how ungodly attractive he was, but seeing him again in real life was jarring. His dark beard was full, but not scruffy in the least, neatly trimmed and kept to just below his chin. Paired with his broad chest, towering frame, strong cheekbones, and beyond-sexy undercut hairstyle, I fought the urge to fan myself, bite my knuckles, shove my face into the freezer… anything that would make me look completely ridiculous. Domari put the bottle down and looked over at the pizza.

"And this is *pizza*, you said?" His brow scrunched, trying to process all of this new information.

"Yes." I cleared my throat, drawing my attention back to the food. I did a terrible job explaining it, trying to put into words the deliciousness he was about to experience as I sliced it, cheese stretching as I laid it on a plate for him. He took it from my outstretched hand, hip leaning on the counter, and stared down at it. I plated my slice and walked to a cleared part of the counter before hitching my hip up and onto it, taking a seat.

"Grab it like this." I showed him, pinching the crust, picking up the slice, and then taking a bite. He observed as I chewed and then did the same.

Suddenly, I was glad I'd splurged on the *expensive* pizza on my last trip to the store. It wasn't fantastic, but it was pretty good as far as frozen pizzas go. I took another bite and then glanced up at Domari. His jaw worked as he chewed, taking in everything new.

"What do you think?" I asked after he swallowed.

"Different," he said, and then took another bite.

I finished my slice, grabbed another, plating one for him while I was at it, and handed him a new cider.

He drank it like water, which I shouldn't have been surprised by, considering how I'd seen him drink in his village, but it was something else to see here in my kitchen.

"So," I said, hopping back onto the counter once more, feet dangling in front of the cabinets. "Hadriel, huh? How'd you end up at the Tree again? Isn't it the middle of winter? That journey was hard enough without mounds of snow on the ground."

My eyes couldn't seem to focus on any one thing, bouncing between the cabinets, the pots hanging from the ceiling, anywhere but Domari's face.

"Am I making you nervous, Shelbie?" Domari asked, amusement lacing his deep voice.

"Yes," I nodded enthusiastically and shoved the slice of pizza in my mouth, taking a too-large bite as I peered back his way. "You absolutely are."

His eyes stayed on mine as he set his plate and cider on the counter, stepping between my legs. God, he smelled so good, like pine, and fresh air, and so very Viking. I struggled to swallow the pizza in my mouth as my eyes darted between his, unable to focus. Was he going to kiss me again? It was all I could think about on our drive down to Denver, and then real life came crashing down around me when we entered the house. I barely knew this man in front of me, yet I was drawn to him in a way I'd never felt with anyone before.

The insides of my knees touched along his hips as my breaths came quicker, waiting for him to move. To say something. *Anything.*

"What about now?" he asked, his lips turning up on one end as he lightly trailed a finger over my thigh. The touch seared my skin even through the denim fabric, and I fought not to move. "We need to talk, but you're tense. So, tell me, is having me closer making it better or worse?"

My hands trembled as I touched his chest, feeling the wool fabric under my spread fingers. His hands tightened on my thighs, and I closed my eyes, pulling in a deep breath. Before I opened them again, Domari's lips were on mine, and without thinking, I melted into the kiss.

It was sensual and sweet, demanding nothing further than this moment, and I couldn't help myself as I laced my fingers behind his neck, pulling him closer. His chest settled on mine as his mouth moved, parting slightly, and I opened for him. I sank into the feeling, enjoying his warmth, attention, and the depth of emotion pouring off him.

This wasn't just a kiss.

This was coming home.

I sighed deeply as he pulled away, my forehead dropping to his chest, and my nerves soothed for the moment. "Better."

"Good," he said, his finger resting under my chin, lifting until my gaze met his. "Then let's go sit, and I'll try to answer your questions."

We finished our meal, and I let Domari try out the sink as he washed off our plates and laid them to dry on the rack Charlene gave me. Before leaving the kitchen, I quickly fed Thor, flipped off the light, and headed towards the couch, plopping down on it. Domari followed me, sitting on the other end, and I pulled my feet up on the cushions, hugging my knees as I turned to look at him.

"I can't answer your question about Hadriel without explaining the rest first," Domari started, his fingers circling my ankles and tugging my feet into his lap. Calloused thumbs worked against the arches of my feet through my socks, circling slowly as he rubbed, and any lingering tension evaporated as I leaned back in the pillows.

He began his tale, and my heart ached as he talked of Signe and Gunnar, Magnus and Astrid, Frida and the children. In an attempt to numb myself to the loss I felt over the people I'd come to love in such a short time, I'd buried my emotions, and now they were bubbling to the surface. A tear slipped from my eye, and I quickly swiped it away as Domari told me of riding to the Tree, driven by an instinct he couldn't explain. I had felt the same when I'd stopped at the trailhead to walk Thor on my way home, pulled by some invisible force to the clearing where he'd spotted me.

"Why is this happening to us?" I asked, sniffling to pull back any further tears that wanted to fall.

"Not everything is so easily explained, Shelbie." His hands stilled on my calf, and his gaze settled on my face. "I don't know why this is happening, but I'm grateful that my fate is tied to yours, even a millennium apart."

My lip trembled as I fought back the tidal wave of emotion crashing down on me, and Domari tugged me across the couch, pulling me into his arms. "I missed you so much. I couldn't explain how any of our story happened to anyone, and I've been so alone."

His beard tickled my forehead as he kissed me there, pulling his arms tighter around me. "You aren't alone anymore."

The weight of his words sank in, and I nodded in understanding. The feel of him wrapped around me was enough to banish the darkness that had clung to me since October, to loosen the last of my control over my emotions. After the last two months of ignoring my pain, I felt my shoulders sag in relief.

Domari's hand moved slowly over my back, comforting me in a way I hadn't even known I needed. The silence between us was no longer uncomfortable when his every action, every touch, reassured me he was right where he wanted to be, and I closed my eyes, reveling in the moment.

My body is falling, arms and legs flailing in the air as I descend into my dream. Magenta streaks blend with the greens I know as the Northern Lights, pulsing to the beat of my racing heart. I scream, but no sound breaks through.

I fall faster now.

After what feels like an eternity, the lights begin to fade, and my motion slows, dropping me into a dark void.

You're dreaming, *I tell myself, and yet, it doesn't feel like a dream.*

Wherever I have landed is foreign to me. Darkness envelops the world here. In the way only the pure absence of light can do, every other sense seems to come alive.

Drip.

Drip.

Drip.

The sound echoes off walls that can't be seen, bouncing back to me. Somehow, even without a corporeal body in this world, I can smell a sulfuric scent filling the air. A tremor runs through me, both from the chill in the air and a lingering sense of dread.

Panic.

Death.

Something here is dying.

I reach my hands forward, feeling my way through the inky black, but the darkness is so complete I can't even see if I have *hands. I feel nothing, though.*

Emptiness.

Sorrow.

This is a dream, *I tell myself again. This same dread has followed me for months, but never before has it been so vivid, even in the darkness.*

If only I could see…

7

SIGNE

A chill wind whipped through the air, seeping through the slats in the wood of Gunnar's longhouse, but even that did nothing to cool his temper. He fumed, pacing the length of the floor and putting everyone on edge. Signe rocked back and forth near the hearth in the center of their home, the skirts of her simple blue dress swaying with her long strawberry-blonde hair as she moved with her tiny baby in her arms. Sensing the tension in the room, the baby let out a long wail.

"You need to calm down," Signe sighed heavily, and Gunnar stopped to stare at his wife.

"He hasn't returned," Gunnar seethed, shaking his head as he clenched his teeth in frustration. "Why does Domari do this? Every time something gets difficult, his response is to run. To leave us all. Last time, it took him ten years to return."

"I know you're upset," Signe attempted to appease him, and Gunnar scoffed, "and rightfully so. This day is important to you, and Domari isn't here to share in the celebration. But think for a moment. Put yourself in his position. Today is a celebration for our newborn son, our growing family. We've gained a new love, while he is still mourning a lost one."

Gunnar paused near the raised platform that was their bed, covered in furs and blankets, built into the wall of their one-room longhouse. His hands dropped from where he'd had them placed on his hips, down to his sides, and the bright, golden man Signe loved so much shone through. Without meaning to, she smirked. There was something so satisfying about knowing this fearsome man was so well and truly *good* down to his core. And he was all hers.

Crossing the space between them, Signe handed him their baby. Gunnar's anger from only moments before curbed even more as he stared down at his newborn son.

"We have so much in our lives to be grateful for." Her hand stroked along Gunnar's chest, feeling his hard muscles beneath the pale blue fabric of his thick woolen shirt. The color matched his eyes beautifully, and Signe admired how it fit him. "So much that Domari doesn't have. Maybe never even wanted. Until her."

Gunnar seemed to deflate as his eyes found Signe's. "He hasn't been the same."

"But he will be." Signe rubbed her hand over his powerful arm. A strong physique was essential for all Vikings, dependent on their physical strength to survive the harsh climates and the harsher way of life. Her husband was undeniably Viking with his short-cropped golden hair, pale blue eyes, strong jaw, and close-trimmed beard.

"Domari is loyal, like you. He's been gone for nine days, and no one knows these woods as well as he does. He needs time, but he'll be back."

Gunnar's gaze turned alert, searching her face. "Is that what your intuition says?"

She shook her head lightly, her long hair swishing with the movement, and dismissed what he asked. Signe's intuition had always been exceptional, particularly around those she loved, but no matter how much she thought of Domari, she didn't have a sense of him the way she did the rest of her family. Perhaps it was because she hadn't known Domari as long — he had only returned from the Varangian Guard the summer before. But only the faintest glimmer of a feeling burned deep in her soul, reassuring her he was safe, wherever he was — that was all she knew.

"He loves you, too, you know." She leaned in close, letting her palm drift down Gunnar's arm to slide her hand into his much larger one. "But not as much as I do."

Gunnar leaned down to kiss her, their baby still between them in his arms. The kiss lingered for a moment as two little bodies darted between their legs, sprinting for the door.

"Mama, is the feast now?" Revna asked excitedly, light brown braids swinging wildly as her bright green eyes lit with excitement. Her twin, Ulf — her opposite in every way with his almost white hair, narrow frame, and quiet demeanor — bounced on his feet at her side.

"Soon, babies," she smiled at them as she sat on the bed. "Soon."

Revna's bright eyes fell at her words, transforming quickly into a glare. "I'm *not* a baby, Mama."

Gunnar and Signe both chuckled at her response. At four years old, the twins were still young but had earned a sudden dose of independence with the arrival of their new brother, and little Revna was delighted to no longer be the youngest.

"You're right," Gunnar said, laying the infant down on their bed. He scooped up the twin children as their giggles wafted through the high ceilings, dangling them upside down over his shoulders. "I can hardly lift you anymore."

Ulf grinned like his uncle Magnus, but Revna snarled, smacking Gunnar's side. "Put me down, Da." Each word was punctuated with a hard slap, and Gunnar cried out in feigned distress. "Fight me like you mean it!"

Gunnar flipped them back down to their feet, and Revna immediately laid a hard slap on Gunnar's leg while Ulf giggled at her side. Gunnar winced, yelping as he hopped around, pretending she'd hurt him. Revna's hair pulled free from her braids in a halo of frizz around her head from the tussle, but the little girl smirked, eyes alight with mischief. A small chuckle rose through Signe's body as she shook her head, watching as Gunnar ran from their daughter wearing a look of terror. Revna chased him out the door and into the snow with a battle cry, and Ulf giggled as he followed behind her.

Tonight, nine days after his birth, as per tradition, they would accept the new baby into their clan. As the chieftain after his father Erik's passing last fall, Gunnar held a dual purpose at the feast — he was the clan leader *and* this boy's father.

The baby whimpered where Gunnar had left him on their bed earlier, drawing Signe's eyes to the sleeping child. Exhaustion pulled on her as she breathed deeply, searching for a sense of calm. Her eyes lingered on the weapons hanging from the wall, light dancing off the spear she'd hung up years ago when she'd joined the Erikssons. With a sigh, Signe scooped the baby up, nuzzling him into the fabric wrap on her torso. His little head worked its way across her chest, mouth open, seeking what he wanted. Adjusting the cut of her low-cut dress, Signe helped him settle alongside her breast, and the baby latched immediately. Waiting for a moment, Signe rubbed a finger across his dark hair, downy soft and far longer than the twins' hair was when they were born. Signe's heart beat outside her chest, residing in this tiny form and those of her twins, so fragile and needy, so unlike her own heart encased in steel.

The empty longhouse was quiet now, only the sounds of the hearth crackling and the suckling this tiny creature emitted. Everyone would wait on Signe in Frida's house across the clearing of their small village, but she paused, relishing this moment just for herself as a sleepy smile spread, recognizing how much her life had changed in the last eight years with the Erikssons.

Signe's life was broken into two — before and after Gunnar, and the former was never to be spoken of again. Even the thought of her life before the Eriksson clan instantly melted the smile from her face, steel sliding back in place over her heart, hardening her against the memories that would never fade.

Eight years ago, Signe had arrived here in this village to compete in Winter Nights against the chieftain's cocksure son. She had been looking for a new beginning, where she would welcome being ignored as she hid from a past she preferred never to revisit. Before the prophetic words of the Norns had changed everything in her life to send her fleeing from her village, Signe had only pictured one future for herself. She would have left with her father's people on raids, destination unknown. It didn't matter to her — she was born to fight battles. To breathe fire.

And yet, here she sat, gently rubbing the pad of her finger over the baby at her chest instead. The ties to a peaceful village and motherhood should have chafed, but here, Signe found an inner peace she'd never known. Just as she was meant for battle, she was meant for these people. Signe could feel it in her soul.

Her eyes burned with unshed tears as the baby dozed off. She patted his back, and he settled against her chest, heart to heart. A small burp escaped him, and a tear welled in the corner of her eye.

"Are you ready?" Astrid's high, musical voice drifted into the house as she stood on the threshold. As always, Signe's young sister-in-law looked ethereal in her pale green gown showing her growing belly, nearly white hair braided into a halo. Magnus loved to wax poetic about how his wife was as beautiful as the moon, and normally, Signe was the first one to roll her eyes at the man. But tonight, with the light flickering off her pale skin, Signe couldn't help but agree.

With a sniff, Signe fought the misty emotions swirling inside her and rose from the bed. Bouncing and swaying as she walked to lull the baby on her chest to sleep, Signe followed Astrid from the house.

Boisterous voices reached Signe before she opened the door to Frida's longhouse. The baby stirred in the wrappings along her chest at the noise, and Signe soothed him by bouncing some more.

The door creaked as she entered, and the sound was enough to draw the eyes of many. Of course, Gunnar was the first to find her gaze — he always was. His eyes sparkled with joy as she approached him.

"Feeling okay?" he asked her in a whisper, wrapping his arms around both Signe and the baby on her chest.

She nodded, peeling back the wrap. The baby whimpered as she pried him from the cocoon, but Gunnar wrapped his large, warm hands over the infant as he rested him on his shoulder. For such a big man, Gunnar was exceedingly gentle with the baby, and it sent Signe's emotions into overdrive as she watched her husband move through his mother's longhouse.

Like Signe's home across the clearing, Frida's house was set up in a long rectangle with platforms covered in furs built into the wooden walls, all centered on the immense hearth.

For the last 25 years, this home had served as both a town hall and home for the Eriksson clan. As such, it held more beds than the others in the village for visitors. Tables pushed up against the many platforms now, serving as seating instead of beds, and Signe gazed at them longingly, wishing for sleep.

"Thank you for joining us tonight," Gunnar's voice rang loud and clear from where he stood near the hearth. At least one villager from each of the ten families from their clan was present, but the howling storm outside had kept many at home. Signe nodded to Yrsa and Björn, huddled close together on a bench nearby, then to Thorsten, Kare, and his grown twins, Arne and Bodil, back from their latest hunt, standing to the side beneath one of the flickering torches on the walls. It warmed Signe's heart to see their show of support for the baby and Gunnar as their new leader.

"A new life is always a blessing, one to be honored and celebrated," Gunnar went on, his blue eyes twinkling in the hearth's firelight to his left. Several cheers followed his words, drinking horns raised in agreement, and he smiled. "Today, the honor is mine as Signe has blessed me with another son." Loud hoots rang through the room again, led by Magnus, grinning where he stood with his large arm wrapped around both his mother, Frida, and his wife, Astrid. Gunnar raised his hand in a gesture Signe had seen his father, Erik, and former chieftain, make several times. Silence flowed through the room, and Gunnar dropped to a knee on the packed dirt floor of his mother's longhouse, lowering the baby to his bent leg. The infant's small face screwed up at the loss of the warmth of Gunnar's chest, but he didn't cry.

"My son," Gunnar whispered, emotion riding hard in his voice. "Erik."

It shouldn't have surprised Signe that Gunnar chose his late father's name to give their son, but he hadn't mentioned it, and her heart squeezed at hearing the name he chose. Erik, Gunnar's father, was a wise and loyal leader for their people, and Gunnar perpetuated his legacy with this gift.

Magnus approached then, the gigantic man towering over his brother and leader, hands outstretched. A sword, glistening in the firelight, lay in his palms, the hilt molded into a wolf's head, and runes engraved in the cool steel blade. Signe's lips tipped up when she saw it, so large next to her tiny son, but pride radiated from her as she watched the scene before her.

Gunnar met his brother's eyes momentarily before he seized the handle with his free hand, raised the sword high into the air for all to see, and then drove the blade into the ground next to his knee. The baby flinched at the sudden movement but didn't wail. His little clenched fists rose, drifting through the air as the room stilled around them, everyone observing. Magnus sniffed, sentimental as always, wiping at his face with his tattooed hand as he bent down to place a bowl of water at Gunnar's feet.

Signe watched with rapt attention as Gunnar reached down, dipped his hand in the water, and drizzled it over Erik's dark hair. "I honor you, Erik Gunnarson, and accept you into the Eriksson clan. All that's mine will someday be yours, my son. May the gods watch over you. May glory find you. And may wisdom and honor lead your decisions until you enter Hel."

The room erupted in applause, and Signe beamed with delight.

Gunnar rose, eyes glistening with emotions not so different from his younger brother, and Signe stepped forward. Gunnar's thick arms encircled her waist, pulling her to him as he kissed her hard in front of their people, and whistles filled the room. Signe couldn't help but laugh as he broke the kiss, then took their baby back from his hold.

As soon as she tucked little Erik back into the wrap on her chest, he wiggled, seeking her warmth. Heart nearly bursting with happiness, Signe patted him until he settled, savoring his sweet coos as she joined the party.

Laughter and singing filled the room long after the ceremony, drifting as easily through the air as the smoke from the hearth and torches in the ample space. The revelry was contagious and much needed in their village since Gunnar's father passed last fall. Despite how tired she was, Signe had missed this.

Sitting in a dark corner on a raised pallet, Signe rested her feet as the twins played on the floor below her with wooden toy animals Domari had carved for them. Astrid sidled in next to her, dropping onto the soft furs with a sigh as she rubbed her hands over her pale green gown and growing belly beneath.

"The baby is kicking from this noise," she grumbled as she fiddled with the wisps of hair escaping from its neat halo. Astrid seemed much more annoyed than her usual pleasant demeanor, and Signe patted her hand in comfort. The woman still had months to go before the baby's arrival, and soon, she'd find out that *this* discomfort was nothing.

Some women claimed to love being pregnant, even saying they loved labor, but Signe couldn't agree. She adored her children and was happy to sacrifice her body to bring them into the world, but that was precisely what it was — a sacrifice. For months, it forced her to sit out of battles, games, hard work, and everything she'd known for the first nineteen years of her life. If only her father could see her now...

Before her mind could drift down that path, the wind whipped through the house, dousing several of the torches. Voices cried out in the sudden darkness as they all turned towards the open door. Gunnar withdrew the sword he always wore at his side, approaching the entryway, lit only by the dimly glowing hearth.

"Show yourself," his voice boomed as the crowd gazed into the dark, snowy night outside.

Signe rose, her hand drifting into her pocket and through the hole she cut in each gown, withdrawing the dagger she never removed from her body, always sheathed along her thigh. Magnus stood on Gunnar's left, an axe held loosely in his grip, and Signe approached his right.

Tilting her body, the baby at her chest behind Gunnar's back, she peered into the night.

Four figures trudged through the snow towards them, almost to the house. They stopped, and the tallest tilted its face to the sky. Caught in the moonlight for a moment, Signe gasped as she took in the face of a young girl covered in blood.

"They're children."

8

SIGNE

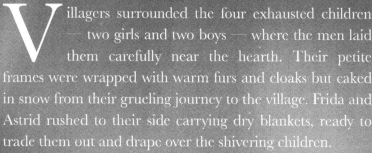

Villagers surrounded the four exhausted children — two girls and two boys — where the men laid them carefully near the hearth. Their petite frames were wrapped with warm furs and cloaks but caked in snow from their grueling journey to the village. Frida and Astrid rushed to their side carrying dry blankets, ready to trade them out and drape over the shivering children.

Yrsa stooped, kneeling in front of the children on the packed dirt with a wet cloth, wiping at their dirty, soot-covered faces. Her eyes scanned them as she cleaned, searching for injuries.

"They're safe," Yrsa whispered almost to herself after her work was done. Her gaze shifted up, finding Gunnar in the crowd. "Not a scratch. Not even a sign of frostbite."

Gunnar stepped forward, crouching low to speak to the children as Signe watched. "How did you find us?" he asked, directing his words to the oldest girl. She wore thick pants and furs, and her dirty brown hair was braided back, but her cerulean eyes squinted, appraising the man in front of her. "How did you make it here? Are you alone?"

The girl hardly blinked, her hand wrapped tightly around the hilt of the sword at her side. Watching a child staring down her large husband in defiance had Signe fighting back a smirk.

"Are you sure you didn't misplace a child ten years ago?" Magnus whispered at Signe's side. "That girl is as fierce as you."

Signe shook her head, swatting at Magnus for his words. Her large brother-in-law stepped back, but the words stung in a way he could never have known. She shoved aside the sudden pain in her chest as she returned her attention to the children in front of her.

The girl still said nothing, fingers flexing on the sword as she took a warm blanket from Yrsa's outstretched hand. As the girl dropped the snow-caked furs from her shoulders, Signe briefly glimpsed the blade, long and polished, nearly the length of her legs. Yet, the way her hand rested on the pommel easily, Signe was sure the girl knew how to use it. If only her eyes had been green, it would have been as if Signe was staring into her past.

"We were guided here," she spoke at last, her eyes scanning the adults around her before continuing. "He protected us."

Gunnar's brow scrunched in confusion at her words, waiting for her to clarify who *he* was. Although exhausted, the children were unharmed, making Signe believe *someone* had watched over their journey. Whoever *he* was, though, either hid from the village or was already gone.

Was that where Domari had gone?

But if so, why hadn't he returned with the children?

The girl's gaze was hard and unrelenting, so Gunnar changed tactics. "And where are you from? Are your parents not with you?"

At those words, her eyes turned downcast, and she seemed to retreat in on herself.

"Our parents were killed," a small voice squeaked from under a pile of blankets at the girl's right. Gunnar's weight shifted as he leaned towards the tiny child bundled there, barely older than Signe's twins. Her hair shimmered in the firelight, the same copper tone as the flames. "Our whole village is dead."

"What happened to them?" Gunnar asked, and Frida scolded him.

"That's enough for today, Gunnar," Frida scowled, her eyes sharp on her son even though he was now her chieftain. "Let them rest. We can talk more tomorrow."

"You're right." He frowned but nodded his head. "I'm sorry. We have food, water, and beds you can share. I'm glad you're safe."

"Thank you," the oldest girl answered, pulling the three smaller children into her side protectively.

Astrid and Frida shuffled the newcomers from the hearth, headed for a nearby bed set into the wall, and Signe and the baby at her chest stepped forward to follow. Copper curls bounced before her until the younger girl stopped, turning to Signe.

"It was a man," she whispered, her eyes on Signe's baby, inherently understanding that a mother could be trusted. "A bad man. He was covered in black ink, even on his head. And his eyes were red."

Signe paused, staring down at the small child. As the blankets slipped, she noticed the girl clutched a dagger so like the one Signe had at that age. "The man who killed your parents?"

"Yes," she said, her dark eyes drifting up to meet Signe's gaze. "Mama told us to hide, so Kára took us to the barns. We climbed in with the sheep, letting them move around us, but the men came even for the animals." The girl's lip quivered as she looked up at the oldest girl — Kára — before continuing. "When they found us, they dragged us before the bad man. He ordered the other men to leave, and they lit the hay on fire on their way out. Bo cried at the sound of the horses, and the bad man stopped. He started slapping his head, yelling curses that Mama tells Yvar not to say." She glanced at the older boy, who averted his eyes. "And then the man told us to run."

Signe's lips turned down, taking in his words as a chill spread through her body, tingling under her skin. "He spared you?"

"That's enough, Birgitta," Kára stopped, returning to pull the red-headed child into her side as she carried the littlest boy on her hip. "Let's rest." Birgitta stepped into Kára's arms but turned her face back to Signe for a moment. Eyes finding each other, the girl dipped her chin in a nod.

Signe said nothing after the children settled, and the party diffused. The celebratory air that had filled the longhouse only an hour ago was replaced with a somber foreboding. Men huddled in silent conversation while the women shuffled around the house, tidying the space, fetching water, and helping however they could.

The twins hovered at Signe's feet while she sat, nursing her baby in the corner. Gunnar would still be here for a while, overseeing the new guests, and she was torn on whether she should leave the house and return to her own.

No matter she had been a mother for four years, nurturing young children wasn't Signe's expertise. She watched the other women fawn over the new additions, but instead of feeling a motherly urge to soothe, Signe's mind wandered. Her impulses were not to comfort but to protect.

A bad man, covered in black, even on his head, the girl had said.

Tattoos weren't uncommon among Vikings, as was evident from the number she could see openly around the village. But tattoos on his head? Those were less common. Men painted themselves with symbols when preparing for battle, adorning the sides of their heads and faces with the dark stain in a plea for the gods to protect them and lead them to victory. But tattooing symbols onto your scalp was another matter, painful and permanent, and Signe's mind immediately drifted to Raud.

Just speaking his name was enough to upset Gunnar most days. She knew his story was intertwined with Tove, Gunnar's deceased sister, but no one spoke of why Raud had been banished. Whenever she'd breached the topic,

Gunnar quickly changed the subject. With most things, Signe was relentless, but the pain that filled Gunnar's expression at the mention of Raud's name was enough to stay her words.

She *hated* to see Gunnar in pain.

The thought of someone hurting him made her blood boil in a way she couldn't describe, but she knew the violent urge had been there since birth. It was a gift from her father, one of the few ones Draugr the Demon had ever given her, and one she'd gladly have him take back. It had taken years to learn to control her temper, thinking first through her actions instead of surviving on pure instinct.

Almost a decade had passed since she'd last killed a man, but the thought of someone causing harm to her family — Gunnar and these three children of hers — was enough to pull those instincts, those urges, to the forefront of her mind. Instead of wanting to dote on the children here, Signe wanted to hunt down the man who had hurt them.

"Come, children." She stood, working to control her breathing. The twins sleepily followed in her footsteps, out the door and into the cold, stormy night.

Once the twins settled in bed, Signe unwrapped baby Erik, laying him on the furs of her own pallet while she changed his cloth. He shivered in the cool air, releasing a soft wail of distress.

"Hush," Signe scolded the tiny baby. "I'll pick you back up in a moment. I'm not going to leave you in the cold."

The words brought a bitter laugh out of Signe, shaking her head at her own commentary. She scooped up the infant and settled herself down into the furs. By the time she'd nestled back against the wall, he'd wiggled his way across his chest, fists clenched in frustration.

"Calm down," she said, smoothing her hand over his head, talking to both herself and the babe at her chest. "Don't have a temper like me."

She pulled down the edge of her dress, and the tiny infant latched immediately, sighing contentedly as he ate. Signe's head tipped back, leaning against the rough wood of the walls as her eyes drifted shut. Gunnar would be back soon, and then she'd lay down once they had time to talk.

The moon was still high while Signe stared at the sky from the roof of her father's longhouse. Although the building was immense, it had only ever been home to the two of them. As with everything, it wasn't about the functionality of a home; it was a show of status. Of wealth. Of power. That's what everyone expected of Draugr the Demon, after all.

Signe's favorite place in their village was lying flat on her back against the thatched roof. Here, she chose to be alone rather than watch the way the rest of the village avoided her. Here, she heard the tales no one dared speak in front of her.

On a night not so different from this one, she'd learned her own story, one her father never dared to speak of. No one had ever shared the story with Signe outright, and it was forbidden to speak Hilda's name in their village, at least in her father's presence. But Signe's fondness for climbing roofs and eavesdropping on adult conversations had told her everything she needed to know.

A storm blew in on a cold day eight years ago, bringing the first snow of the season. That day, Signe's mother, Hilda, gave birth to a girl and fled from their village, never to be seen or heard from again. Hilda knew full well what would happen to the infant she left behind in their village. An unwanted child would be left in the cold to die, a waste of life, a pointless mouth to feed. Still, knowing the fate of her child wasn't enough to keep Hilda there. The number of times Signe had wondered why Hilda hadn't taken her with her when she fled... well. Those were wasted thoughts.

But Signe's fate was bigger than her father knew, even from birth. Draugr had left his daughter to die, a sacrifice to the wilderness, but she had persevered, shouting her demands into the cold night as she waited for someone to find her. The story was told often, but never when Draugr was within earshot, eyes glancing her way as they watched her with a mixture of unease and awe.

"Signe," they said Draugr muttered the following day as he took the baby back from the villager who had retrieved her. Victory.

Even though Draugr allowed her to live that day, gaining his respect for her ability to persevere, it hadn't earned her his love. As she grew, Draugr allowed her to speak to no one save a few of his trusted men. His only hope for his daughter was to marry her off to secure a strategic alliance when the time came.

Raucous laughter sounded from below, following the men as they entered the hall where her father waited. The warriors had returned from the last raid for the season a few days ago, just in time for Winter Nights, and each night was a drunken celebration. More often than she could count, Signe had watched her father return home after long raids covered in the blood — sometimes literally, but always figuratively — of others. Each of the weapons hanging on the wall inside their longhouse had been pried from the cold hands of the dead as a trophy.

Tonight, the town meeting was to recap the raiding season and *discuss preparations for Winter Nights. Signe was supposed to stay home, but she did many things she wasn't supposed to.*

"The entry age for tomorrow's fight is eight," Signe heard Draugr mumble in his deep, scratchy voice. Several voices murmured in the audience, but no one ever spoke against Draugr unless they had a death wish. "Boys eight years and older may enter. It's time we raise them to understand victory must be seized by their own hands."

Victory, above all else, *her father always said. Failure was something Draugr didn't tolerate, not from anyone. Especially not from his daughter.*

"And what of the girls?" someone voiced from the back of the room, and silence descended on the room, shocked at the boldness of speaking out in Draugr's presence. Signe sucked in a breath from her place on the roof, panting in excitement as she waited for her father's answer.

"No."

The word was cold and harsh, a bucket of freezing water over Signe's hopes and dreams. But she should have known. Draugr only ever saw women and children as a weakness. If they couldn't fight, couldn't bring him more glory, they were useless to him. If only she could win an event, maybe her father would see that even though she was a girl, she was his.

Signe slipped from the roof, dropping to her feet lightly in a crouch as the torches from the room flickered in the evening light. A chuckle rose from behind her, and Signe spun at the sound, a small dagger in hand. The dim light glinted off the polished metal, sparkling for a moment as she stared at the large man in the shadows. His stance was relaxed, legs spread apart, as he raised his hands in mock surrender. Still, Signe's scowl never left her face.

She could overcome a size difference with an opponent — it was only a matter of leverage. She was small, yes, but she was also nimble. Signe ducked, stepping swiftly between the man's legs and letting the blade slide across his inner thigh. He gasped as the thick fabric of his black trousers split, following her swipe, revealing his pale skin and a trickle of blood. Faster than she could react, he reached down and grabbed her by the collar of her dress. Signe's legs kicked at the air as she fought, and the man chuckled again, a sound she instantly recognized. Vermund had been Draugr's right hand for Signe's entire life, with him through the worst of their raids. He was a constant presence in Signe's world and her favorite among her father's men.

"I should've seen that move coming," Vermund said. "After all, I taught you to go low."

"Put me down," Signe growled, and Vermund shook her lightly. Still, Signe fought back, snarling in his face.

"What have I told you about sneaking around after dark alone?" Vermund's chest rumbled as he lifted her higher in the air, now eye to eye.

"Don't get caught," Signe spat back at him, and he smirked.

"And what did you do?"

Signe sighed, the fight draining out of her as he set her back on her feet. "Got caught."

"You can do better than this. I know you can." He leaned down, face to face with the small girl in front of him. Her expression twisted into a sneer of determination, and he seemed to soften at the sight of it.

"Why won't he let the girls compete?" Signe whined, kicking her foot in frustration. A dust cloud followed the movement, and Vermund exhaled. "He thinks we can't fight, but we can. I can."

"Don't ask questions you already know the answer to," Vermund said.

"They are only wasted words," the two said in unison, and Signe

stuck her tongue out at him. Although his signature smirk wasn't present, Signe saw the sparkle in Vermund's eye for a moment.

He turned his head, listening intently to the meeting inside, and Signe studied him. His hair was pale blond, as many of their people were, but Vermund's features were unique. His nose was straight and sharp, but his deep emerald eyes, the color of the pines in the forest, made Vermund stand apart. No one else in the village had eyes like that — only he and his twin, Hilda. And now Signe, her only child.

"I want to compete," she pouted, and Vermund clipped her on the head. She swung back at him, but he deflected it easily. "You know I could take all of you down."

"That's why he can't let you compete." Vermund reached down, wrapping a large hand around her calf and swinging her quickly upside down, the dark, thick skirts of her dress pooling around her face.

Her red-gold hair hung down to the ground in waves as Signe bent and turned, trying to break free of the hold. A tiny fist connected with his crotch, and Vermund's hand slipped for only a moment as he groaned. Signe used the slight move to free her leg, back slamming into the ground.

"That was foolish," Vermund said after a moment as they both worked to recover. "Would've worked better if you hadn't knocked the wind out of yourself simultaneously."

"I see that now," Signe moaned, and Vermund laughed.

"Think first, Signe. Think first, and victory will be yours every time."

With a swat to the back, Vermund sent her home, and Signe stomped into the empty house. Her father's home differed from most — walls were built to separate Signe's small pallet from the rest of the house, as if the reminder of his daughter's existence didn't fit with Draugr's lifestyle.

Throwing herself onto her bed, Signe stared up at the rafters, frustration making her toss and turn as she fought sleep. The door to the house creaked open, and she stood, peering around the wall to watch as Draugr returned to the longhouse with a drunk, giggling woman thrown over his shoulder. Even with the walls to separate them, the sounds of her father and his woman carried through the house and into the rafters. Whether she wanted to or not, Signe was forced to listen to them long into the night.

Her uncle's words still rang in Signe's head hours later while she stared at the rafters, furious with the man snoring loudly only a room away. Finally, she rose, her feet dropping to the floor. Signe's eyes scanned the quiet home before she reached down under her bed and withdrew a pair of trousers and a loose tunic top. Slipping out of her dress and into the trousers, Signe straightened, feeling more herself already. She tiptoed through the house, glancing at where her father slept as she made for the door, pushing it open only enough to slip through and into the night. Remembering Vermund's words, she paused to take in the area, ensuring she wouldn't be caught this time, and made her way into the forest.

Signe stepped on light feet through the thick copse of pines, always conscious of her surroundings. Reaching a clearing along a small creek she knew well, she paused, sliding her back down the trunk of a nearby tree.

Runes were carved into the bark — blessings, wishes, hopes, and dreams. Signe withdrew her small knife, glittering in the moonlight that drifted through the trees overhead. She placed her knife along the edge of the bark, pushing deeply as she carved a symbol.

↑

"*I* am *a warrior. I'm not just a girl,*" she muttered as she deepened the cut, etching it with all her strength. "*If I were a boy, he wouldn't question me.*" Her words were a growl — fury and determination coursing through her veins.

"Change," *a deep, male voice said from the woods. Signe spun on her heels, rising swiftly with her blade in hand.*

"Show yourself," *Signe commanded into the dark, gazing between the trees, heart racing in her chest.*

But no one came forward.

Only the sound of the leaves rustling in the wind overhead drifted through the night. Quietly, Signe made her way in a circle, her back to the tree as Vermund had always taught her. No matter how hard she listened, watched, and waited, no one was there.

"Change?" *Signe whispered to herself later, splashing water over her face from the cold creek.* "*To what? A* boy? *If only it were that easy.*"

The water settled, shining in the moonlight, as Signe caught a hint of her reflection in the water. Dressed in the tunic and trousers, she looked like her uncle Vermund. Newcomers who hadn't known Hilda made passing comments about her being his, and Signe always wished that could be true...

But she knew the truth.

She carried far more than Draugr's red-blonde hair. It was the brutal Demon's blood that ran through her veins, and his rage boiled deep in her bones.

"Think first," *Signe whispered into the night. Glancing one last time at her reflection, she brought her blade to her scalp and sheared off her long tresses. The strands drifted into the water, swept away into the night as she hacked at her hair. Delight filled her as she concocted her plan, a smirk so like her uncle's sliding into place. Once the hair was gone, she slid the blade close to her scalp as she'd seen her father do so many times, cutting it as close as she could. It wasn't perfect, but no one truly paid attention to the young boys.*

Once her hair was gone, she slid her hands into the muddy soil along the creek's edge and began to rub it over her clothes. Boys were always dirty, and she needed to blend in. Holding her breath, she squeezed her eyes closed, grabbed a handful of loose dirt, and rubbed it into her skin.

"Ugh," she spat, removing the particles from her mouth. Leaning over the water again, Signe stared down at the reflection shining back up at her in the rippling water. Nothing she could do about the emerald eyes, but she'd have to keep her head down, which wasn't uncommon behavior for younger boys. She could do it.

Invisible armor as strong as that which her father's men wore into battle settled into her blood as Signe stood, transformed. Her smile grew as she crept back through the forest, slipped into Draugr's house as quietly as she'd crept out, and returned to bed. Glancing back at her father one more time, still snoring with a woman curled next to him, Signe removed the sword hiding below her furs. The blade was long, and the light flickered off the metal, illuminating it for only a moment.

She slipped the sword under her belt and headed back out of the house. Her father didn't speak to her often enough to notice her absence in the morning, so she only had to hide out until the games began.

Signe wouldn't be left behind — not ever again.

The soft touch of Gunnar's hands as he lifted the baby from her arms shook Signe awake. She sat upright and came to attention swiftly.

"Easy, *elskan min*," Gunnar whispered, "it's only me."

"How are the children?" she asked, shifting to lie on the bed. Gunnar sighed as he sank beside her, baby Erik in the middle.

"They're sleeping, but we still have much to learn from their story."

"Did you hear what the fiery one said to me?" Signe yawned, trying to remember the children's names, but lost to her memories.

A moment of silence passed as Gunnar's eyes screwed shut, his brow furrowing. "Birgitta. Yes, I heard."

"Do you think it was Raud?"

At the mention of his name, Erik let out a soft wail, and Gunnar placed his warm hand over the baby's torso, rocking him softly back and forth. It was always amazing to Signe how easily parenting came to Gunnar, but watching Erik and Frida with their grandchildren, she understood. They were strong and strict as parents, but love radiated from their every action — a far cry from her own brutal, lonely childhood.

"I do." The words came out in a hush. If the house hadn't been silent, Signe would have missed it. "But I don't understand."

"The child said it best, Gunnar. He's a bad man." Signe's gaze turned sympathetic as she watched the battle take place on Gunnar's countenance. "I know you want to believe that there's still some good in Raud, that the man you once knew is still there… but he has done terrible things. Leaving so many of our own people dead is only one example. You've heard the rumors that follow him."

Her mind drifted to the orphans sleeping next door with Frida and added the list of reasons to hate the man to her mental tally. Foremost, though, was the emotional damage he had done to so many in their village.

That fact alone fueled Signe's need to end the man.

9

DOMARI

Shelbie dozed as she rested her back against Domari's side on the couch, fighting sleep that pulled at her, and he could hardly blame her. When he'd arrived at the Tree that morning, he never thought it would bring him to her. The storm outside seemed to ebb, the wind whipping through the chimney quieting as the flames licked across the crackling logs in the small fireplace. The snow, the fire, the warm house, and the woman at his side were familiar to him. Everything else around him wasn't.

Avoiding the overwhelming thoughts about this time he'd found himself in, Domari's fingers moved through Shelbie's curls, loose after she'd unpinned them earlier, and listened to her soft, even breathing. Her long eyelashes accentuated her freckled face and pink cheeks, adding to the natural beauty Domari had pictured so many times in the last two months since she returned home. Sitting with her, his heart felt whole in a way it never had before.

What he'd said to Shelbie earlier was true — fate wasn't always easily explained. Vikings believed this wholeheartedly, but the popularity of seers in their world was enough to show how most of his people didn't easily accept it without question.

Of course he wanted answers.

Why *had* Hadriel given him the necklace back, then pushed him into the tree?

What *had* the Norns meant when they gave Shelbie her warning last fall, insisting she return to her time? *"Danger follows you, the last of your kind…"* they'd said, but what danger did they speak of?

"To be ready for what is to come, you must remember what you are to protect," the Norns had told him, which he felt needed less explanation. For as long as Domari could remember, he'd been the strongest of his clan, the quickest to pick up new fighting skills, and the swiftest to strike. But was it Shelbie he was to protect? Or his clan, who he'd left behind?

Guilt should have weighed on him at the thought of leaving his people, but it didn't. Winter in his world was harsh, and few traveled. The threat of attack was little, and there wasn't much he could do around the longhouse. Hand settling over Shelbie's back, he felt as her chest rose and fell, relaxed in sleep. Somehow, in a brief period, she'd changed him forever, and Domari didn't know if he'd ever be able to return to the cold, lonely life he'd led before. Nothing he'd ever felt compared to this feeling blooming in his chest.

Placing a gentle kiss on her head, he stood from the

couch, lifting her into his arms. He moved down the hall and towards the room beyond that Shelbie had pointed out earlier in the night. Her arms looped around his neck as he carried her, head resting on his chest, and he savored the feel of her against him.

"Sorry," she muttered sleepily as he stood beside the bed, her words slightly slurred. "You can put me down. I'm awake now."

Domari set her on her feet, and she pulled back the white blankets, yawning deeply, then unbuttoned her pants, shimmying slightly as they slid down her legs. As if suddenly remembering he stood only inches from her, Shelbie's eyes snapped up, finding his as her hands stilled.

"Sleep tonight." He kissed her lightly, and she eyed him warily, then dropped her pants to the ground. He watched as she slipped between the blankets and slid away from him to the far side of the bed. With a flick of her hand, she pulled the blankets down, patting next to her in invitation.

The house was warm, so Domari lifted the wool tunic over his head, muscles flexing as he removed it and let it fall to the floor next to her clothes. Black tattoos laced his forearms and torso, along with the many scars he'd earned in battle, each telling its own tale. He undid the simple ties at his waist, feeling the fabric slip down his legs, the necklace in his pocket clanking to the wood floors. But it was long forgotten as he felt the weight of Shelbie's eyes on him, raking over his bare chest, the thin pants he wore beneath his trousers the only clothing left on his body.

The room was dark around them, but he felt the heat of her gaze as he placed one knee on the bed, which sank beneath his weight. Instantly, he looked down at the soft material, placing a hand over it. He pushed once, feeling it compress beneath him, then spring back. Then again. Never had he felt a bed like this before. In his home, he'd had a wooden platform softened by layers of furs and wool blankets. In Constantinople, he'd had a cot. Whatever this was, he liked it.

"It's called a mattress," Shelbie said, fighting the smile that tugged on her lips, and clutched his hand to pull him onto the bed. He climbed on and felt it bounce beneath him, his eyes swinging to hers with playful heat.

"You're far too tired tonight," he leaned over her, his bare chest pressing into the soft cloth of her t-shirt, feeling her heart race beneath him, "but soon, I'm sure this will be fun."

A breathless giggle escaped Shelbie as he kissed her, then slid back to his side, pulling her back into his chest. "I hardly knew what to do sleeping without your ass grazing my body, endlessly wiggling."

"Oh, you've missed that, have you?" Shelbie laughed, glancing over her shoulder at him, but her eyes were already drifting shut again.

"Yes," he replied as he brushed her blonde curls over her shoulder, kissing her exposed neck. His arm settled back over her waist, fingers dug into her torso, needing to be sure that this was real, needing to hold her, no matter the many unknowns. "I've missed it all. Everything about you," he whispered, and she sighed, lacing her fingers through his. "Now go to sleep, *haski*."

❄

Light streamed through the windows the following day, almost blinding even in the early morning. The sun hadn't fully risen yet, but compared to the darkness of his world, it seemed scintillating. Domari closed his eyes again, soaking in the feeling of the woman still sleeping in his arms.

The quiet following a snowstorm was a different sort of calm; still, peaceful, untouched. The sound of Shelbie lying beside him, leg thrown over his, breathing peacefully in sleep drifted through the air. But the dog lying on the floor at the edge of the bed? He was snoring loudly.

Domari turned his head to the side, staring down at the large black dog. There was something familiar about Thor, something *more* in his eyes, but Domari couldn't quite place it. As if sensing Domari's lingering gaze, Thor stretched, head snapping to the side as he peered at Domari. No matter how domesticated this dog was, a predator shone through his black eyes. They stared off for a moment before the dog finally slumped back to his side, snoring again. Domari couldn't help but chuckle, wishing sleep would find him again as well, that he could sink back into the warmth from Shelbie's body and the house around him, but his mind was awake.

Carefully, Domari slid from beneath Shelbie's sleeping form, dropping his feet to the floor below. He stepped lightly down the hall and returned to the bathroom Shelbie had shown him yesterday. Everywhere he looked, Domari was overwhelmed by the changes he saw. There were lights overhead on the ceiling that stayed on, not a hint of a flicker from a flame. The walls were smooth to the touch and covered in bright-colored pink paint. Even the furniture, soft and pliant underneath him, had been strange yet comfortable. The world had changed drastically in the last 1,000 years, and Domari wasn't sure where he fit in. What good was a Viking warrior here in Shelbie's world? Hopefully, he was given some time with her to figure that out.

Brushing that thought aside, Domari stepped into the bathroom and turned on the light. The room was a far cry from the outhouses in his village, but he'd seen the brilliant baths and aqueducts in Rome. While it still wasn't the same, he understood the basic functions. Turning the faucet on, he splashed water on his face, watching it drip off his dark beard back into the sink below.

It wasn't often he saw his reflection, and never this clearly. The black knot tattooed on his neck so many years ago was beginning to fade, but still stood out prominently against his pale skin. The shield on his side he had darkened again this summer after returning home to his village, spending hours with Thorsten as they planned their hunt. But never in his wildest dreams had Domari thought his life would change as it had on that same hunt, finding Shelbie on the shore.

In the mirror, he noticed the handle on the wall behind him. He turned to face it, studying the faucet high on the wall. Leaning over, he cranked the handle as he'd done on the sink, watching as a heavy flow of water poured out above his head. He stepped back, shocked as he watched steam rise moments later, and tentatively stuck his hand into the warm water. Without further thought, he dropped his trousers and stepped under the stream.

Water sluiced the last of the dirt from his body, running down the tiled walls and into holes in the floor. He closed his eyes, turning his face into the spray, letting it wash his former life down the drain. The soap, a fresh, floral scent that instantly reminded him of Shelbie, sat perched on a small indent in the wall, and he grabbed it, scrubbing his hair and body. Hair dripping, he turned back into the water as he rubbed a hand over his neck, feeling the tension in his muscles ease.

"Oh!" Shelbie cried, and his eyes snapped open, glancing to where she stood in the bathroom doorway with a hand over her eyes. "I'm so sorry. You can, uh, close the, uh, curtain, fabric thing, hanging there."

Domari glanced at the turquoise fabric hanging from the ceiling at the edge of the tile with a confused stare, then glanced back to Shelbie. Her fingers were partially spread, peeking through the cracks as she walked forward, grabbed the fabric, and slid it shut.

"Have you forgotten that you've already seen all of me, Shelbie?" Domari asked, turning his face back into the spray as a mischievous grin spread across his face.

"Nope! No. Haven't forgotten that."

With a smile, Domari pulled the curtain back open, finding Shelbie wide-eyed in surprise on the other side. Before she could say more, he wrapped his hand around her wrist, pulling her into the water.

She gasped in surprise as he pushed her back against the tile wall, water drenching the shirt she'd slept in.

Without waiting another moment, his lips seized hers as steam rose around them. Between the warmth of the water and the heat of their embrace, she melted under him, her hands settling on his hips as he deepened their kiss. He couldn't help himself as one hand settled on her jaw, tilting her head up just right for him, and the other slid under the wet fabric, feeling her skin beneath. She pulled back, gasping as his fingers traced across her stomach, bunching the fabric higher on her torso, and Domari kissed along her neck.

A decadent moan escaped her as his fingers trailed under her breast, feeling the way her heart slammed against her ribs.

The sound of Thor barking snapped Shelbie's eyes open, glancing at the bathroom door and out into the hall. Domari turned, scowling at the intruding dog for ruining their moment.

"Shelbie!" A woman's voice called out from somewhere in the house, and Shelbie's hands pushed hard on Domari's chest, her blue eyes blown wide.

"Shit shit shit shit shit," she said as she hopped out of the water, grabbed a towel hanging on the wall, threw it around her chest, and ran from the room.

Confused, Domari reached for the handle and turned it again, waiting for the water to stop. He listened to Shelbie speak to someone but couldn't make out what they said as he grabbed another towel, dried off quickly, then slung it over his hips.

10

SHELBIE

Charlene calling my name snapped me out of the heat of the moment faster than anything I'd ever experienced. I slipped from the shower, not even bothering to remove my wet shirt, and threw a towel over the top.

"Rise and shine, Sleeping Beauty," Charlene's voice rang through the house. I hadn't even closed the bathroom door earlier, and my heart slammed in my chest as I hurried from the bathroom, snapping the door shut behind me.

"Time to get goin'. I need help with the —" Her eyes fell on me as I slid around the corner into the living room, leaving a water trail in my wake. "Honey. You're supposed to take your clothes *off* before you get in the shower."

A nervous laugh bubbled out of me, too high-pitched, and she squinted at me. "Why is the shower still running, hun?"

"Oh!" My eyes were too wide, but I couldn't seem to make them return to normal. Subterfuge wasn't my thing.

"Can't keep my head straight this morning. First, forgetting to take my shirt off, and now the water. Slept kind of weird last night. Bizarre dream."

"Uh huh," Charlene said, her chin tipping up as she appraised me. Right then, the shower turned off, and I swore under my breath. Her eyes darted to the hall behind me. "Funny, I never remembered Marlene telling me about a magic shower that turned itself off. I feel like that's something she would've mentioned before moving out."

I smiled sheepishly, staring at my friend as I thought about how to explain this. Her caramel brown hair was styled expertly in a curled ponytail, framed by a leopard-print headband covering her ears from the cold. Even her black coat was bedazzled, rhinestone buttons placed down the front. As always, the woman looked every bit of the Western woman she was. She waited for an explanation, tapping her boot with her eyebrows raised, craning her neck towards the hall, but I moved to block her view.

"So, here's the thing, Charlene," I began, reminding myself that I was a grown woman. Thirty-one-year-olds didn't need to explain if they had a man stay the night, especially since Charlene wasn't my mother. But before I could go on, two hands slid around my waist, and a loud whistle sounded.

"Well, who the hell are you, and what do I have to do to meet your brothers? Maybe your dad? I'm assuming you're taken already, considering the way you draped your hands all over my girl, but *hot damn*."

My heart pounded as I spun to the side, feeling

Domari's hand slide across the towel draped over my chest as I turned to look at him.

Shirtless.

Of course he was shirtless.

My cheeks flamed, heat searing me from the inside out as embarrassment sank in.

"Please tell me your name is Domari," Charlene added before I could come up with anything else to say, and Domari nodded in recognition. I, however, waited patiently for a sinkhole to open beneath my feet and swallow me whole.

Domari kissed my temple tenderly, then slid past me into the living room and through to the kitchen.

"What the hell, Shelbie?" Charlene whispered, her eyes wide with excitement as she glanced between Domari and me. "Suddenly, I get it. I'd also go on a two-month bender after a romp with that man right there. I don't blame you even one bit. I bet he's hung, too, isn't he?" She bit her lip, and I choked on nothing, spluttering a cough as I clung to my towel. Quickly, she held up a hand and shook her head. "Nevermind. Don't tell me. I'm picturing him hung, whether or not he is. Do I need to worry about tiny Shelbie's running around here soon? Because I sure as shit would hump like bunnies if I were you."

I fought to catch my breath, my face on fire as I looked anywhere but at Charlene or Domari. I shook my head lightly as I calmed down, exhaling slowly. Fortunately, I'd been on birth control for years, even though nothing had gone further than the shower kiss since he'd arrived. A *bender* wasn't even kind of what happened, but I hadn't thought through how I planned to explain our time travel story to her yet, either. I moved out into the living room, looking to my right where Domari stood in the kitchen, leaning against my counter.

And then I realized he was drinking a hard cider.

At nine in the morning.

I was positive Charlene noticed it, too, considering she couldn't take her eyes off his every move.

"We, uh," I stammered, "got in late last night as the storm was picking up."

Her eyebrows shot up as she peeked at me momentarily, then back to Domari. "And he came in from *Sweden?*"

I glanced over at Domari, who took another sip of his cider while he waited for me to explain. Charlene wasn't the type to judge, so I wasn't worried about what she had to say concerning that a man had stayed at my house last night. But I *was* terrified of everyone's reactions if I tried to explain how he had randomly appeared in the woods, traveling a thousand years into the future. I couldn't even explain it myself, for that matter.

"Yep. Just arrived yesterday morning."

"Sure." Charlene squinted at me, seeing straight through everything I was leaving unsaid. "Anyway. I need you to help with the horses, so quit leaving puddles all over your wood floors and get changed. Come find me in the barns when you're ready."

She turned to leave, winked pointedly at me, and walked out the door.

"Was that your mother?" Domari asked as the door snicked shut behind her.

An uncontrollable cackle burst out of me at his comment. "Oh god, no. And don't let her ever hear you say that." I couldn't even *imagine* what it would be like to be Charlene's daughter.

He tilted his head quizzically at my reaction, but waited for me to go on.

"Charlene's my friend. This is her property I'm living on; her house is the one up there." I pointed out the window, showing him. "She owns the horses in the barns, and I'm staying with her for a while to help her train them."

"I see. I can help with that, too, then." He rose, heading towards my bedroom to get his shirt, and my mind raced for reasons I could give him for why I needed him to wait.

"You'll be a huge help, yes," I said as I followed him down the hall. "Just… not today."

He turned, staring at me again with the same perplexed look as before.

"I need to talk to her about you. I need to find a way to explain our situation since you're staying here with me." I paused at that. "How long do you think you'll be able to stay? Do we know that?"

"However long fate will allow."

"Okay, well. One day at a time, then." I nodded, mostly to reassure myself because what the fuck was I supposed to do with that answer? Melt into a puddle of emotional goo? "Maybe we'll find some answers soon. But for now," I snagged my jeans off the floor and a clean shirt from the closet, "we'll make the most of it." I stood on my tiptoes and planted a kiss on his mouth. His arms circled my waist, holding me steady against him before I finally leaned back.

This was a luxury I never thought I'd have again with him; it was such an everyday moment. My heart beat wildly in my chest as I tried to picture what this could be like, having him in my life. Before I could be swept down that rabbit hole of emotions, I forced myself to move. Slipping into the bathroom, I quickly changed, brushing my hair up into a wet bun, then shoved a hat over the top.

"I'll be back in a bit," I called as I walked towards the door a few minutes later. "Eat whatever you can find, or take another shower. Take a nap. I don't know. I'll be back soon."

My hand hesitated as I turned the knob, peering back at where he sat on the couch. Part of me was afraid that if I left, he'd be gone again when I returned. Charlene was helping me by letting me stay here, though, so I needed to go live up to my side of this bargain and help.

I had about 50 yards between my house and the barn to figure out an explanation for how Domari came to be here, and my mind raced to come up with *something*. Boots planted in the snow, I paused outside the barn, listening to Charlene singing to the horses as she walked from stall to stall.

"Good morning, babies," she crooned. "Did everyone sleep well? Nice and cozy here inside? I bet you're ready to roam, aren't you?"

Her voice made me smile, easing some of the tension I felt at the coming conversation. My mind wavered back and forth on whether I should tell her the truth. Charlene, of all people, would probably be the least likely to cart me off to a psych ward at my time travel admission. I chewed my lip as I thought it through.

"Are you coming, or what?" I jumped at the sound of her voice ringing loud and clear. My feet finally stepped forward, and I turned into the barn.

Charlene led one of the horses, a jet-black gelding whose back rose to about eye level for her, out to a hitching post in the center of the barn. She loosened the blanket on his back and removed it, picking up a brush and throwing another to me.

"Speak," she commanded. I stared at the horse, hoping he'd answer her call first so I didn't have to. Unfortunately, this wasn't Mr. Ed, so the job fell to me.

"That was Domari, the man I met in Sweden."

"I figured that part out on my own, thanks." She rolled her eyes at me. "I'm more curious that he's now standing in your living room half-dressed."

"He surprised me yesterday morning. I didn't know he was coming, or else I would have said something about it to you."

"Listen." She dropped her hand to her side and stared at me. "It's not my job to have an opinion on what happens behind that little pink door. I didn't let you move out here to judge your decisions on who comes and goes. You could have a different man every night of the week, and I'd keep my thoughts to myself. But that man? In there?" She pointed her brush back towards the house. "That man had you reeling for *weeks* after you came home. That's not just a pretty face in there, honey. That man holds a piece of your heart, whether or not you realize that, so it has become my business."

I took a moment to think through what she'd said before I answered.

"You're right. And thank you," I smiled at her. "It's a little hard to explain."

"What? How you f—"

"No, no. Not that," I spat on a laugh. "I meant how I met him."

"I thought you met on your trip?"

"We did." I chewed on my lip, indecision racking me. "There's a lot about my trip I haven't told you. Haven't told anyone."

Her eyes turned serious, mouth straight as she studied me. "I'm listening."

I puffed my cheeks out, delaying the inevitable for a moment longer. "On our first day of riding, I had a panic attack at the sight of an English saddle." Charlene cackled at that, gripping her side as she doubled over laughing.

"*English?* Oh, girl." She wiped at tears gathering under her eyes, and I couldn't help but chuckle with her. "Oh my. That's too much. Did you ride?"

My eyes wandered around the barn, delaying a moment more as my heart raced in my chest. A dozen saddles hung on racks on the wall, and not a single one was the tiny bike-seat English saddle style — Charlene had taught me to ride Western, and that was all she rode. She understood my predicament. "No. I never actually got on the horse."

Charlene's laughter stopped, and her expression turned serious again as her eyes found mine.

"They warned me that Freya, the mare I was assigned, loved to wander. I let her lead me down a path through the woods as I walked her, trying to calm myself back down after a panic attack over the saddle. I wasn't paying attention, and we were on a rocky cliff face. Before I knew it, she'd nudged me, and I fell."

Now I had Charlene's rapt attention. She circled the horse, trailing a hand over the gelding's tail, then stopped in front of me. "Were you hurt?"

Without even realizing it, my hand migrated to the back of my head, feeling where the bump had been two months ago. "Yeah. I had a concussion, and when I came to…"

My heart beat erratically in my chest, lungs constricting, and I couldn't get the words out.

"When you came to…" she repeated, waiting.

Staring up at the ceiling, I took a deep breath. "When I came to, Domari was there. He was hunting in the woods with a group of men from his village, and they helped me. I was so confused, and I'd hurt my knee as well. Out of options, I agreed to let them take me to their village."

"Girl," she *tsk*ed, her expression grave. "That was a dumb move."

"*I know.*" My head fell forward, staring down at her. "Clearly, I wasn't thinking correctly. Can you imagine what my mother would say if she knew I really hitchhiked with strange European men?"

"Like I said. I ain't your mother. Hell, I've made plenty of dumb decisions when men were involved. I'm not judging. I'm just glad you're safe." Charlene's eyes were full of warmth at the moment, and I knew she meant it.

"They were wonderful men, and his whole village took good care of me. I was unbelievably lucky."

"Good, then. I'm glad to hear it," she nodded, but her eyes never left my face. "But why haven't you told me, or anyone, this yet? Falling for your hero who rescued you after you were injured sounds pretty romantic."

"Well," I paused, still deciding if I would go on, but, at that point, I didn't think I could stop myself. "This is the part I don't understand."

She said nothing, but I had her full attention.

"Domari..."

"Is he married?"

"No, no, nothing like that." The longer I waited, the worse this was going to be. "Domari is a Viking."

"Like, reenactments? I could see that. He has the figure, that's for sure. I'd pay to see that in a heartbeat. Are there more like him? Maybe I need to go with you next time."

"No, Charlene. *Not* like reenactments." I twisted the brush in my hands, and the bristles cut into my skin. This was so hard to admit. "Charlene... what I'm trying to say... what I'm trying to tell you... is that... I somehow... I time traveled."

Charlene was mute, her head cocking to the side as she appraised me, probably wondering if I was joking.

"Charlene, none of it makes sense." I fiddled with the red leather bracelet on my wrist, feeling the deep groove of the *perthos* rune there. "Like, how is this possible? I still don't get it. It took me a bit to realize it, but then these women — these Norns — showed up and said I had to go home before time was changed forever. So we went to this tree on an island," I intentionally skipped over the whole dragon portion of the story, not sure I was ready to explain that part, "and I noticed runes carved all over the tree. One of them matched this bracelet," I held up my wrist to show her, "that a weird lady, who ended up being one of the Norns, had given me in town before I left on the trip. Maybe that was how it all happened, I'm not sure, but I ended up back in our time and had to come home."

Charlene still said nothing, listening as the story spilled out of me. I'd needed to tell *someone* all this, and it was all unraveling from the knot I'd kept it in faster than I could stop it.

"I came back here and couldn't tell if it was all real. I mean, how could time travel be *real?* How could any of it have been real? Then, yesterday, I left my parents' house early to beat the storm but stopped at the hiking trail Thor and I had gone up this summer. I'm not sure why I did, just a feeling, really, but we were about halfway up the trail when Thor growled, and I stopped. There, standing in the trees, was Domari. We were both in shock, unsure how he'd suddenly ended up here, but had to move because of the storm. So, we drove down here, and now we've caught up to where we are."

Air whooshed out of me as I finished the abbreviated version of my story and dropped my hands to the side.

Silence descended quickly in the barn, even the horses seemingly stunned by my wild admission.

"I know it's all unbelievable," I said after a minute, the silence weighing heavily on me as anxiety took over.

"Well," Charlene said, turning back to the horse and running her brush over its coat. "It's a little much to absorb, but there are many things in this world we don't understand. My second husband believed vampires were real. So much so that he led a cult, the Church of the Silver Stake. They fully bought into a life dedicated to vampire slaying."

My jaw dropped at her admission, eyes bugging out of my head as I stuttered over her words. She said it so casually, so flippantly, the way Charlene tended to drop bombs on me, but this was something else.

"Did you…" I couldn't even find the words as my mind had gone completely blank. This conversation had gone from unbelievable to straight-up *paranormal* faster than my mind could handle. "Did you ever see any vampires?"

"No vampires." She dropped her brush in the bucket. "Took me almost a year to realize how insane he was, and then I ran as fast as possible. I stopped at a diner in a tiny town once I thought I'd gotten far enough, and Nash was sitting on the barstool next to me. He was the angel I never knew I needed and didn't deserve. I never looked back after that."

Grief filled her voice at the mention of her third and last husband, and I pulled her to me, wrapping her in my arms. "I'm so sorry."

Her tiny hands patted my back as she accepted my embrace. "Some days, it plain sucks being a widow," she sniffed. "But there's still so much in life to be happy about. And that beautiful man standing in your kitchen is certainly one of those things, no matter how wild your story is."

I hugged her tighter, so thankful for her easy acceptance of me. She didn't pick and choose which parts to accept, didn't shut me out when I was sullen, and didn't judge me when I didn't want to pull it together and smile.

Charlene was *there*, steady and present. "I love you. Do you know that?" I said as I kissed the top of her head. "I don't deserve *you.*"

She chuckled and eased out of my hug. "I love you, too, Shelbie Ann. Now, go get that crap out of my horse stalls."

I grinned and turned to grab the shovel as she went about her chores in easy silence.

11

SHELBIE

I finished my chores in the barn as fast as possible and rushed back to the house to check on Domari. As desperate as I'd been to have a moment alone with my thoughts and to explain all of this to Charlene, I hadn't thought through leaving Domari alone for an hour. Everything here was foreign to him, and while I had been prepared to rough it while camping in Sweden, nothing had prepared him for the future.

Midway across the yard, Charlene yelled my name, catching my attention as I stopped by the porch. I turned, gazing back her way as she walked towards me with a large pile of clothes in her hands.

"I figured Domari might need these," she said as she handed over the pile. I glanced down at men's jeans and t-shirts, plus a pair of large cowboy boots. "Nash was a big guy. Not as big as Domari, but I thought this was a good enough place to start."

My heart warmed at her words, knowing how much it must mean to her to part with these items from her deceased husband she'd been hanging on to. "I don't deserve you." I smiled down at her, repeating my earlier words.

She waved me off, shooing me into the house, and I grinned broadly as I stepped onto my porch. The moment I opened the door, Thor stood from where he'd been sitting on Domari's feet by the couch.

"So glad you two are such buddies," I laughed, shoving the door closed with my foot. Domari stood as I dropped the pile of clothes down onto the couch. "These are from Charlene. They were her husband's clothes; she thought you might need them."

He nodded before grabbing a pair of jeans and holding them up. "These are like yours," he glanced in my direction.

"Yep, denim." I handed him a soft, cotton black tee and ushered him towards the bathroom. "See if those fit, and then we'll talk."

I watched as he went into the bathroom, the door shutting behind him, and threw myself down on my couch. My conversation with Charlene this morning spun through my head as I stared at the ceiling fan. It had gone far better than I'd thought, but I guess it shouldn't have been unexpected from Charlene. I hadn't seen the vampire cult coming, however. That was a trip. And also… I needed to know way more about this.

The sound of the door opening had me lifting my head

off the couch, staring at the man walking down the hallway towards me. "It's all a bit tight," Domari said as he moved his arms and legs around.

My jaw hung slack as I sat up. Tight wasn't the right word. The black tee was painted across Domari's broad shoulders, stretched taut around his biceps, and hung loosely over his trim torso. He shrugged his shoulders as I stared at him, and the shirt rose away from his waistband, showing a peek of the black shield I knew was tattooed across his skin.

"Turn around for me." I motioned to him, spinning my finger in a circle. His look was questioning, but he did as I asked, and I bit my lip, holding in a moan.

He glanced over his shoulder at me, taking in the odd expression on my face, before reaching behind him to run his hands over the back pockets. I watched as his darkly tattooed forearms brushed over the tight denim and almost came undone at the sight.

"If I bend down, I'm afraid this fabric will rip," he mumbled as he squatted a little, his butt filling out every square inch of those jeans.

His words stuttered a laugh out of me, positive that was precisely what would happen. "We'll get you some new ones in town tomorrow." Until then, I'd admire the view. Charlene was going to flip when she saw him in this outfit.

He shrugged into a jacket she'd left for him and pulled on the cowboy boots. Holding out his arms to the side, he turned to me. "How do I look? Like I'm from 2022?"

The combination of his rugged Viking look, golden

brown hair long on top and shaved close on the sides, combined with his beard and then the cowboy gear, was one straight out of my dreams, I was sure.

"One sec," I said as I grabbed my phone, snapping a picture of him.

"What was that?" he pointed at my phone.

"This?" I turned it towards him, quickly explaining my phone and then pictures, shaking my head at how complicated this was. I showed him the picture I'd taken and then walked to his side, standing on my tiptoes as I reached high. "Smile!"

He looked down at me right as I took the picture, and I smiled at the camera. The look in his eyes, full of adoration for me, made this instantly my favorite picture I'd ever taken.

Domari leaned down, kissing my shoulder as he walked towards the door. "We've wasted enough of the day. Show me how I can help."

We left the house, aiming for Charlene's, where she was shoveling snow off her front porch. I glanced over at Domari, checking to make sure he was ready for this second introduction, but his face was severe, set on the task ahead of him. As he approached her, Domari reached out, gently resting his hand on the shovel. Charlene stilled her motion.

"I'll do this for you." He nodded, taking the shovel from her hands. "Let me help."

Charlene's eyes drifted from his face down his body, so very slowly. "Mm," she smiled, "Mmm mmm mmm. Yes. I don't know what you just said, but yes."

"Wait…" I turned, brow scrunched at her words. "You can't understand him?" I glanced at Domari already shoveling snow, not paying attention to our words.

"No, girl. I don't know Swedish or whatever language he's speaking."

But… that didn't make sense. If I had been gifted the ability to speak the Norse language fluently when I time-traveled, why had it not worked in reverse for him?

"Domari?" He glanced over at me, stilling his hands. "Can you understand me?"

"Of course, *hàski*."

"Whoa, hold up there." Charlene put a hand out in front of him. He stopped at her words, standing to his full height and glancing down at the small woman in front of him. "Nobody here is calling my girl husky. Sure, she's tall and broad, but that's offensive here in the States, and you seem like a nice guy. Nice guys don't call girls *husky*. She's *curvy*."

I giggled, hand over my mouth, as they both stared me down. "I'm sorry," I said after a moment, wiping at the tears on my face. "He didn't call me husky. You really can't understand him?"

I glanced back and forth between the two, who both wore exasperated expressions at my questioning.

"I don't understand you, *ástin mín*." Domari's hand grazed my shoulder, brushing down my sleeve.

"Can you understand me now?" I looked up at him.

"And here I thought you went to Sweden knowing not a lick of the language other than the few sentences I heard you practicing in the car. Color me surprised."

"I'm so lost." I turned back to Charlene. "I'm speaking a different language when talking to him?" My hand came up to my head, rubbing my temple as I tried to understand this dynamic.

"You're speaking Norse with me and something else with her." Domari rubbed my arm reassuringly. We were in *my* world now—why was I the confused one here?

"But I can't tell I'm switching back and forth between English and Norse; it's so natural to me. How can that be?"

"The Norns must have gifted you the knowledge of Norse, for some reason. But I wasn't given the same gift. Maybe it's because Hadriel sent me, not the Sisters."

I supposed that made sense, but it still left me with many unanswered questions. Before I could dwell on them, though, Charlene sent me off with a list of chores.

The day passed quickly as the three of us worked in harmony while I played translator between the two. I was exhausted when the sun dipped below the mountains, painting the sky a brilliant coral, the same shade as the door on my tiny house. The worst of the snow was cleared, though, and the horses were well cared for.

I fell into bed later, and Domari scooped me into his side, snuggling in close. His arm drifted over me as his whiskers brush along my shoulder. Warmth spread through my chest as I smoothed my hands over his arm, tracing the black tattoos.

Tomorrow, we'd head into town for groceries and some better-fitting clothes for Domari, but right then, I closed my eyes, praying that I would continue to be gifted more time with this man.

12

SIGNE

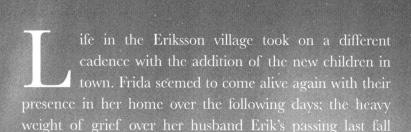

Life in the Eriksson village took on a different cadence with the addition of the new children in town. Frida seemed to come alive again with their presence in her home over the following days; the heavy weight of grief over her husband Erik's passing last fall momentarily lifted, replaced with this new sense of purpose.

As the children settled, they shared more about their lives, explaining they were from a town further west down the river, and from three different families. Little Birgitta with her copper curls was five, and talked incessantly to anyone who would listen. Her older brother, Ivar, wore his shoulder-length blond hair tied up, and was as silent as his sister was talkative. Kára, ten, was from the neighboring longhouse, the youngest child of her family, and little Bo was her nephew.

Astrid also rose to the occasion, taking on the role of mother to Birgitta and Bo. Each time Signe saw Astrid,

Birgitta hung from the pregnant woman's legs, and Astrid had little Bo propped on her hip. How Bo had survived the trek through the woods to their village, Signe couldn't comprehend. With his flaxen curls and doe eyes, Signe guessed he couldn't be over three.

Ivar seemed to adjust the quickest, choosing to return home with Yrsa and her grandchildren.

Kára was quiet, helping where Frida directed, but Signe could see in her posture that this wasn't a girl fit for housework. Unlike Birgitta and the other village women, Kára refused to wear dresses, wore her dark hair tightly braided back against her scalp, always carried her sword at her hip, and watched everyone with calculating eyes. More than once, Signe had been reminded of her past when appraising the girl.

Signe's days were spent with baby Erik strapped to her chest, working in her house and Frida's, strategizing with Gunnar on how to make their winter rations last to cover four more villagers than they had planned. They decided that the men would continue to hunt locally in their forest on fair weather days, making the most of the few hours of daylight whenever they could.

"Take her with you hunting," Signe whispered to Gunnar later that morning as she watched Kára from a distance, sitting stiffly as she played with the children, sword across her lap.

Gunnar paused as he strapped on his bow, an axe slung at his side, and turned to Signe with a severe gaze. "The snow is knee-deep."

"She made it through the forest in a storm with three

children to look after," Signe scoffed. "I doubt she'll slow you down. Unless," she smirked, one eyebrow climbing, "you're afraid of being outpaced by a girl?"

"I've no issues losing to a girl, as you know," Gunnar chuckled, leaning down to place a kiss on his wife's nose. "You beat me at nearly everything."

Signe couldn't contain the smile that crept over her face. How had she gotten so lucky to find this man? Even after eight years with him, it was shocking to compare the men of this village to the ones she grew up with. "I could have at her age as well. Have I ever told you about when I shaved my head to enter the Winter Nights fight as a boy?"

"That doesn't surprise me even the least," Magnus said, interrupting their conversation as he slapped a hand on Signe's back. "Kára! Want to hunt with me today?"

The young girl's eyes flew up at his words, and her back straightened. She said nothing, but the fire in her eyes told Signe everything she needed to know. Kára nodded brusquely, and Magnus grinned at her. She quickly glanced away, blushing, and Signe elbowed her brother-in-law in the ribs.

"Don't terrify the poor girl," she glanced up at him. "Just because she could probably cut you down with that sword at her side doesn't mean she's ready for your charm."

The men left with Kára in tow shortly after, snowshoes strapped to their feet.

❄

Later that afternoon, the men returned home from hunting, and set venison to smoke. Traps were set in the forest that they could reuse, and the mood was upbeat. Signe and Gunnar stayed for the evening meal at Frida's, the twins playing on the floor with Birgitta and Bo. Kára stood to watch nearby but didn't join in with the younger ones. Frida had taken the baby from Signe, and Signe reclined against her husband, enjoying the momentary reprieve.

Astrid drifted off to their bed to rest, and Magnus folded his large body onto the ground, grabbing the dragon carving the children were playing with.

"Is this Nidhoggr?" he asked, examining the intricate details along the small toy. The name sent a chill down Signe's spine as she watched him turn it over in his hands. Carved from the lightest wood, the toy was almost white, with large spikes protruding down its spine. Red dye was painted onto the eyes, giving the creature an eerie feel.

"Who's Nidhoggr?" Ulf asked, and Magnus clutched his chest in feigned despair.

"Who's *Nidhoggr?* Has your father taught you nothing?" Magnus bugged his eyes in Gunnar's direction, but his older brother didn't take the bait. "Nidhoggr is perhaps the most legendary dragon of all time. Would you like to hear the tale?"

The children all cried in delight, urging him on, and Magnus grinned broadly. "If you insist," he chuckled.

Signe's eyes drifted shut, but she listened intently to every word. Legends of dragons soaring over the lands had been passed down from generation to generation, but she had never seen one herself. Nidhoggr, though — she knew his story well.

"Long ago, in a dark cave far in the mountains, a stark white dragon egg lay forgotten," Magnus began. The children leaned in, eager to hear more. "Dragons filled the sky in those days, aiding the Vikings who worshipped them and hoarding for themselves. The rarest and strongest dragons hatched at the exact moment that their Promised was born. Working in tandem, the dragons and their Promised were charged with protecting our people. But more importantly, protecting the Sacred Tree.

"It was a cold winter day, far from what you'd expect for a dragon to hatch. And yet, the stark white dragon egg deep in the cave cracked down the center." He clapped his hands together loudly, and the children jumped where they sat on the floor.

"His mother had long since abandoned the egg, and the new dragon was alone. There, in the dark cave, surviving off the animals who mistakenly wandered in, Nidhoggr grew, and grew, and grew. So big he hardly fit into the cave!"

"Bigger than you?" Revna asked, head tilted to the side in question.

"Oh, yes. He could eat me in one bite." Magnus clashed his teeth together, and Birgitta whimpered, her eyes darting to where Kára stood near the wall. Signe couldn't help but chuckle at Magnus's antics, rolling her eyes at his elaborate story-telling.

"As the winter wore on, fading into spring, Nidhoggr made his way to the edge of the cave, squinting into the bright sunlight over the mountains below. As white as snow dusting the trees, his pale scales glistened everywhere but where he was caked in the dried blood of his prey."

"Why didn't he bathe?" Revna asked again, unfazed by the gory description. Bo burst into tears, hanging on Birgitta's sleeve.

"Hush, Revna." Gunnar patted her on the shoulder. "Listen to the story."

Magnus winked at Revna, not bothered by her interruptions the way her father was. "But dragons are not meant to grow up alone. Nidhoggr knew no others of his kind, and was never gifted a Promised. Every day, he gorged himself on any life he could find, both animals and Vikings. Small children were his favorite, like you."

At this, Astrid paced to where Bo was sobbing, scooped him up, and glared down at her husband. He shrugged innocently and went on.

"Nidhoggr's only goal was to stave off his never-ending appetite. While other dragons focused on hoards of treasure, Nidhoggr returned each night to his cave with his kills, making himself a nest of bones deep in the recesses of the mountain."

Signe shivered at the description, seeing the picture he painted all too clearly.

"He grew, and grew, and grew," Magnus stretched his arms wide in a demonstration, "until Nidhoggr was the largest of the dragons, even though he remained Unpromised. Stories were passed down of the fearsome white dragon, the Terror of the Skies, as they called him.

No one knew where his cave was, and not even the most fearless Vikings were brave enough to search for him."

"I would have," Revna mumbled under her breath, and Signe's lips tipped up in amusement.

"As time passed, many Vikings forgot the dragons were sacred creatures, chosen by the Norns to protect our people. Instead, it became a sport to hunt the winged beasts, a sign of true glory to defeat the fire-wielding demons. Men risked being charred beyond all recognition as hoards were seized, men were cursed, and the dragons were no more.

"As Nidhoggr watched the destruction of his world, he became anxious. It was only a matter of time until he was the last of his kind. Never aligned with the dragons' true purpose, he was filled with rage," Magnus roared, and the children jumped, "set on vengeance against the people he was supposed to protect."

Ulf drifted to Signe's lap, still watching his uncle intently but seeking the safety of his parents.

"Ragnarok, the brutal end of days was foretold, and the creatures of the darkness were determined to see it through in hopes it would revive the Viking culture of old. No beast was more invested in this than the dragon Nidhoggr." Despite the harrowing tale, Magnus's eyes glittered with excitement as he drank in the rapt attention of everyone in the room.

"For years, he attacked Yggdrasil, hoping to unleash all that was locked away in the Sacred Tree. If he could unleash the giants, chaos and destruction would rain down on the lands. The dead would rise again to defeat even the gods in Asgard, burning the world as we know it."

Birgitta burst into tears, and Astrid called for her, glaring at her husband again as the little girl climbed into bed with her.

"That's enough for tonight." Magnus leaned back on his hands, relaxing.

"Is Nidhoggr still alive?" Revna prodded, leaning forward, her eyes sparkling in the hearth's warmth. Signe noticed how Kára stood in the corner, listening intently as well.

"No one knows." Magnus shrugged.

Revna pulled on his arm, begging, "Please, tell me more, Uncle."

"I shouldn't." Magnus shook his head, but his smile betrayed him.

"Please," she dragged out the word, glancing up at him through her dark eyelashes.

Magnus looked at Gunnar, seeking his opinion, and Signe turned to eye her husband.

"You've scared them already. What's a little more?"

"Exactly." Magnus beamed, ignoring the sarcasm in his brother's voice as he pulled Revna into his lap. "All right, where was I?"

"Is Nidhoggr dead?"

"Oh, yes." Magnus dramatically slapped his forehead. "How could I forget? This is the best part." He waggled his eyebrows at her. "The *battle*."

Revna bounced on his lap, clapping her hands together, and Signe only shook her head. But Magnus was right — this *was* the best part of the story.

"Another dragon was born. Hadriel, *The Dark One*, they

called him. The last of the Promised dragons. He was as black as a moonless night, dusted with gold on the tips of his wings, and the opposite of Nidhoggr in every way."

Kára's foot dropped back to the floor, her posture straightening instantly at attention, and Signe couldn't help but watch the girl.

"Nidhoggr made several appearances to terrorize the Tree after Hadriel was born, but the sight of the black dragon growing larger slowed his attacks. Nidhoggr watched, becoming more jealous as he saw the way the Norns favored him, and he waited for Hadriel's power to expand upon meeting his Promised. But, for some reason, that day didn't come.

"Finally, Nidhoggr took his chance. As the fog slid over the water of the Well beneath the Tree, he flew in and attacked the roots of Yggdrasil with all he had, determined that this would be it: the beginning of Ragnarok."

Revna gasped, eyes wide as she listened, and Ulf turned his face into Gunnar's chest.

"Hadriel waited in the water below, watching as he liked to do. He'd found a cave under the water that was perfect for a dragon of his size, and it kept him close to the Norns in hopes they'd one day find the thread that belonged to his lost Promised.

"Nidhoggr flew overhead, flames erupting from his mouth as he clawed at the roots of the Tree. Hadriel shot to the sky, black and golden wings sending waves rippling across the Well. His screech shook the Tree's roots as he collided with the white dragon in the sky. Rage lit Nidhoggr's red eyes as he stared at his opponent. Turning from his task, he spun to meet Hadriel, the sound of wings flapping drowning out the call of the Sisters below."

Magnus stood, scooping Revna up in his arms as he lifted her into the air, pretending to make her fly about the room. She squealed in delight, taking on the act perfectly as she roared in anger. But Kára didn't laugh.

As Magnus set Revna down, he continued, "The Norns could only watch, unable to see the fates of the last two dragons battling overhead. Their long hair blew in every direction in the gusts, clutching each other as they waited.

"*Oh no!*" he cried in a high-pitched voice, pretending to fling his hair over his shoulder in an impression of a woman before returning to the story.

"Fire shot from Hadriel's mouth and Nidhoggr retreated for a moment. That was all Hadriel had needed, though, as he darted through his cloud of fire and raked his talons down Nidhoggr's wing."

"*Yes!*" Revna called out excitedly, bouncing where she stood at Magnus's feet.

"A roar shook the earth as the dragon wailed. His wing came in close, pulling it in to prevent further injury as he flapped harder, retreating. Draining the last of his power, Nidhoggr shot into the sky."

Kára gripped the hilt of her sword, and Revna was panting, eyes wide as she grinned. Gunnar cleared his throat, and Magnus glanced up at his brother. "Legend says that after the two battled under the Tree, Good versus Evil, Nidhoggr was never seen or heard of again, either dead or biding his time," Magnus finished the story quickly. "Time for bed, everyone!"

Revna pouted as she moved towards her parents. "I wish I could fight a dragon," she said as she crossed her arms. "Kára could teach me how to use her sword, and I could kill him for good."

Signe laughed, but Gunnar stooped to eye level with the little girl. "Nidhoggr is only a story, my girl. And fighting dragons for the sake of glory isn't a smart decision. But if a dragon ever comes for our people, I will make sure I stand back and let you take the killing blow." He winked at his small daughter, and she beamed up at him.

It took longer than usual for Revna and Ulf to settle after Signe returned home with them; the boy disturbed by his uncle's tale and Revna plotting the demise of a mythical creature fifty times her size. Signe stared down at her baby, sleeping easily in the bed between her and Gunnar, then glanced at her husband.

Tonight's story brought up so many memories of her past. Signe's mind was a whirlpool she didn't have the strength to paddle through.

"Do you think the stories of dragons are real?" she asked him, sounding foolish even in her mind.

He turned onto his back, arm drifting behind his head as he stared at the ceiling. "I don't know," he answered honestly. "I think they once roamed the skies. As far as I know, they're gone from our lands and have been for some time. Rumors still pass of them, but I've never seen one in my travels."

A mischievous look passed across his face as he turned to smile at Signe. "When Domari and I were younger, we were convinced that Hadriel and Nidhoggr still lived. We even tied Magnus to a tree one night, circling him with the bones of our recent kills while we watched from the trees. We were *sure* that if we could tempt a dragon with such an easy kill, one would show."

The laugh that bubbled out of Signe's chest was manic, shaking her to her core as she imagined the scene. A broad smile filled Gunnar's face as he reached across and rubbed a thumb across her cheek.

"And what did you find?" she asked him, tears leaking from her eyes in humor.

"My father, furious with us for such a foolish plan," Gunnar's chest shook at the memory. "And a bear prowling nearby."

"So, no more dragons?"

Gunnar shook his head. "No more dragons."

Signe nodded, accepting what she thought to be true, but the look on Kára's face as they'd listened to the story stuck with her. The girl wasn't telling them something, Signe was sure of it, but she was too tired to solve that riddle tonight. "I do love the stories of the Promised, though. To fight side by side with a dragon?" A long sigh escaped her as her eyes drifted shut. "That would be a dream."

Gunnar leaned across, planting a kiss on her forehead. "*You* would be a dream."

She smiled to herself as she drifted off to sleep.

13
SHELBIE

Over the next three days, Domari seemed to settle into life on the ranch and here in my world. Part of me was surprised by how quickly he could adjust, but he always seemed to carry that same sense of distanced calm in everything he did.

I, on the other hand, was struggling to find that same sense of peace. Every time I woke up to the sight of him lying in bed next to me, my heart leaped into my throat. No matter how many kisses and touches we shared, it all felt like a pinch-me moment. A Christmas miracle, maybe. My face hurt from how much I'd laughed and smiled since he arrived, and it was a welcome change from the last two months since I'd returned home.

We drove into town on Christmas Eve, and the streets were bustling with cars and pedestrians out grabbing last-minute gifts before everything closed for the holiday. Domari watched in silence, taking in the large brick buildings lining both sides of the road, eyeing everyone and their movements. I skipped the big-box stores, knowing both the crowds and contents would overwhelm him, and instead focused on clothing. Still, the sight of tables of clothes to choose from had been too much for him to take in.

In the end, Domari hadn't strayed too far from the original outfit Charlene had given him, favoring soft black tees that hugged his muscles paired with jeans. He continued to wear the hand-me-down boots and jacket from Charlene, and neither Charlene nor I were complaining.

"You doing okay over there?" I asked, peering at Domari in the passenger seat as I pulled into the grocery store parking lot before we headed back to the ranch. It was time we had some staples other than frozen foods in the house. He nodded, but said nothing.

We entered the store as the doors slid open automatically. Domari paused, eyes wide as he watched the movement, but was quiet as he followed me. I grabbed a cart and beelined for the produce section. A lot had been picked over between the winter storm preparations and Christmas week, but anything was better than the frozen food I had in my fridge.

While I browsed through the fruits and vegetables, I couldn't help but watch Domari. He brushed his hands over vegetables I was sure he'd never seen before, looking around with a mixture of wariness and awe. It didn't escape me I wasn't the only one who watched him. While he dressed the part of a modern man in jeans, a Carhartt jacket, and boots, fitting right into this little pocket of a Western town on the outskirts of Denver, not much else about Domari was typical. He towered over most of the other store patrons at six-and-a-half feet, and his tattoos showed along his neck, even when no one could see the rest that painted his arms and torso. While his beard was a little messier than it usually was for him, he was still neatly kept. Several other women seemed to be lingering in the produce section, eyes on him. I smiled at that, laughing silently as I observed him as well.

Domari's hair was a little longer on the top than I'd seen it this fall, tied in a knot at the back, but still, he'd shaved it close along the sides — an undercut *and* a manbun. Usually, that wouldn't have been my type, but on Domari?

Absolutely.

Yes.

No doubt about it.

My heart surged a little at the thought that he was *mine*. Gratitude swelled in my chest at how my life had changed in the last week. Gone were the lonely, melancholy thoughts that had filled my mind since I arrived home from Sweden last October. Not only had I taken control of my fate, changing my job, my home… everything, but this man had been dropped back into my life. I didn't understand how that was possible, but my heart was nearly bursting with happiness.

"Domari," I called, and the eyes of the women shot to me as he looked up to find me. He grinned, eyes crinkling as he studied me, and I was positive their panties all melted.

"I've seen nothing like this before," he said, awe filling his voice as he walked to me with a head of broccoli in his hand. Once he was within arm's reach, I grabbed the front of his jacket and stood on my tiptoes, planting a kiss on him right there in the middle of the produce aisle. His arms laced around me, and I felt drunk, woozy on his attention alone.

I leaned back, and he studied me. "What was that for?"

"Because I can."

"It had nothing to do with those strange women staring at me?" His eyes sparkled with mischief, and I bit my cheeks to stifle a laugh. Unsurprisingly, the women had all moved on, leaving us to our PDA moment by the cantaloupes.

We strolled through the rest of the store, picking up steaks, a few potatoes, asparagus, and anything that caught Domari's eye. We also bought nearly every bottle of cider the store carried. I snagged ingredients for some cookies and a cheesecake, and we made our way to the self-checkout. Before I could finish explaining how debit cards worked, I snagged my receipt, and we made for the exit. I slipped on my sunglasses as the doors slid open, and a chill went down my spine that had nothing to do with the cold air outside. I paused.

Domari's face was concerned as he asked, "What's wrong?"

Promised, a voice rasped in my head. The same word I'd heard so many times before.

The last variegated purples fade from the evening sky, giving way to the pinks and greens overhead as a young woman approaches the water's edge. Snow had fallen on the mountains in the distance, coating the

trees in bright white, but the ground is dry here. The water is as still as glass, as if the entire place is frozen in time. A small hut sits back from the water, smoke curling into the air from a small chimney, the only disturbance to the silent scene.

There, waiting for the girl, are three sisters in hooded cloaks. Pebbles crunch underfoot as she approaches the trio, head high, shoulders back as she moves with confidence. The fitted bodice of her dress, sapphire with gold embroidery, seems to blend into the night sky behind her, sparkling as the stars shone through the darkness. In contrast, her fiery red hair shines bright in the moonlight, flowing freely over her shoulders, braided only along the sides of her head, swaying gently with each step. A light gleams in her eyes, anticipation filling her every move as she glances up into the sky, searching.

But neither the stars, moon, nor the bright colors of the moving lights overhead can compare to the faint light that shines from what the sisters hold in their joined palms.

The young woman's chest rises and falls quickly as she floats over the ground. When her eyes meet those of the sisters in front of her, they smile at her approach, happiness radiating from within as one who watches a bride descending into a new life with a loving bridegroom.

In a sense, that's what's happening; what lies in the sisters' hands would change this young girl's life forever, and she'd waited her entire life for this moment.

Promised.

"My dear," the middle sister says with a faint smile, brown hair greying with age. Her pale skin softly glows in the night as her hand comes up to cup the girl's chin lovingly. "It's time."

The girl nods, ducking her head in respect, and lowers herself to her knees. She stays there, genuflecting, as her red hair falls around her face while the oldest sister steps forward.

In the woman's wrinkled palm is a glowing chain, golden and bright. A long white braid tumbles from beneath her hood, hanging down over her elbow as she lifts her hands over the young girl's head, holding the chain high, eyes drifting shut.

The woman begins to chant, the sound melodic and soothing, and soon, the lights above in the night sky dance to the same tune. As one, her sisters join in, legs spread wide as they reach their hands into the air, heads tilted back.

Waiting.

The chanting continues as the young woman stays bent over, ducking her head.

Waiting.

The chain gleams, the soft purple glow brighter in the night sky, almost glaring when a clap of thunder fills the sky. A bright light illuminates the evening sky for a moment. In an instant, the stars, the moon, and the lights above wink out, plunging the world around the women into darkness.

The women collectively draw in a startled gasp, the chanting ending suddenly.

"I don't understand," the oldest woman mutters. Her hands drop, and the chain in her palm is dull.

Lifeless.

Dark.

It's still gold with a large onyx pendant in the center, but now… it's but a trinket.

The magic is gone.

"Try it on her," the youngest sister adds nervously, taking the necklace into her hands.

The redheaded girl glances hesitantly into the sky, confused, but says nothing as the sister lifts the necklace over her head, clasping it around her neck.

Nothing.

No life.

No voice.

No power.

No dragon.

"She's gone." A single tear slips down the young girl's freckled cheek as her eyes drop from the sky back down to the beach below her. Her shoulders sag as grief takes over. "That's why she isn't here. Vyara's dead."

"No…," the sisters say in unison. The youngest clutched at her chest, falling to her knees.

"This can't be," she wails, her soft blonde curls fluttering in the air as she throws herself over the young girl, holding her close.

"Calm now, sister," the middle sister consoles. "It's not over. We still have one chance left."

"In an egg that has never hatched!" the youngest sister cries out as she rises, throwing her arms in the air in defeat. With a sudden gasp, her eyes flash white; the color leeched from them as she stares up into the sky, breathing heavily. Barely above a whisper, the words leave her lips. "I can't see a future that lies ahead, Verandi. Something is missing. Something is so very wrong."

A horn honked, and I jumped, brought back to attention. Domari stood in front of me, gripping my face in his hands as I fought to catch my breath.

"*Shelbie,*" his voice was laced with concern, his thumb moving over my jaw. "Are you okay?"

"Yes," I nodded, trying to shake off the strange, ominous feeling that dug its claws into my skin. Blinking rapidly behind my sunglasses, I tried to clear the momentary fog that had me pausing in the middle of the street and pushed the cart towards my Jeep. "I'm fine. Got lost in thought there for a second."

The way Domari's eyes wouldn't leave me as I loaded the groceries into the trunk told me he wasn't convinced, and honestly, neither was I. What the fuck *was* that?

We climbed in the car, and he entwined his fingers through mine on the gearshift, running his thumb over my hand.

"Do you have any winter traditions?" I asked, trying to change the subject away from my weird moment in the parking lot. "What would you be doing right now in your time?"

Several beats went by before he answered, but then the conversation seemed to flow once more, restoring the peaceful happiness of earlier. We chatted idly on the way back to the ranch, making plans for the week. Domari wasn't a Christian, so the holiday wouldn't particularly matter to him, but he told me of the Winter Solstice traditions they practiced. It was mostly similar to what I'd experienced at Winter Nights — lots of drinking and merriment that lasted for twelve days. Apparently, that was how they celebrated just about everything in Viking society.

I didn't know about twelve days' worth of drinking, but I was excited at the prospect of Christmas together.

Between Charlene, Domari, and me, surely we could figure out how to cook these steaks, and I could try my hardest to follow a mashed potato recipe. Couldn't burn those, right?

Lauren, my brother Jacob's wife, was the best cook in our family, and the thought of her legendary twice-baked potatoes had me missing my family. It would be strange to spend the holiday without them, but I'd already committed to helping Charlene this week while I settled in, even before Domari showed up. With so much uncertainty in our future, I couldn't deny that I wanted to spend as much time with him as possible. Plus, it was time to create my own traditions.

Parking outside my little house, I glanced back at the woods framing the picturesque mountains behind me, an idea sparking in my brain. A grin spread over my face as I turned in my seat, eyes wide with excitement, and the last of the uneasiness faded from my mind.

"Think you could cut down a tree for me?"

14

DOMARI

Shelbie chatted incessantly as they made their way to the barn, pulling on her hat and gloves. He'd grabbed his axe from the closet, sliding it into this belt, feeling more himself with the weapon at his side. Despite her evident excitement, Domari couldn't brush off the panic that had shot through his body when Shelbie had paused outside the store. She'd gone stiff, motionless, hands gripping the cart handle tightly as her breathing came in ragged breaths, reminding him of the way she'd lain lifeless in the root of the Tree last fall.

Now that they'd shared the last few days together, he couldn't bring himself to imagine his life without her again. As much as he missed his family — Gunnar, Magnus, Frida, and the twins — back in his time, Shelbie made him feel *home* in a way he'd never experienced. While they hadn't picked up where they'd left off, Shelbie seeming almost shy with this new dynamic, it was far more than her body he was interested in. The way she glowed, radiating joy and happiness, was something he had needed in his life, and he was desperate to stay in her bright light.

Together they quickly saddled two horses — a large black gelding for Domari and a smaller black-and-white mare for Shelbie. They proceeded out of the barn, through the pasture, past Shelbie's little house covered in snow, and into the forest behind. The surrounding trees were dusted with white, branches heavy from the recent snow. Everything sparkled in the sunlight, and the feeling in Domari's chest seemed to match with each passing moment.

Shelbie picked a small, sturdy-looking evergreen, and Domari hopped off his mount, axe in hand. A quiet moan passed her lips as he shed his jacket, black tee painted over his broad chest, and he adjusted the grip slightly more than necessary, giving her a show of his power. Domari couldn't help but smirk as he worked silently, hacking away at the tree for several minutes, the only sound the creaking wood. The tree groaned as it tilted to the right, away from Domari, and landed in the snow with a soft thump.

"Why are you so hot?" Shelbie said breathlessly, her eyes roving his body. Domari glanced down at his exposed arms in the frigid winter air, confused by her statement, but she laughed, drawing his eyes back to her. "Nevermind. It's an expression."

Shrugging the comment off, he tied a rope around the tree trunk, then around the saddle horn, before climbing back on. Shelbie returned his jacket, which he donned, then kicked the horse forward. The tree branches scraped across the ground as they returned home while Shelbie excitedly explained ornaments, garland, and other words he didn't understand, but it was easy to feel light in her presence.

Thor bounced off the front porch as they passed, following as the horses made their way to Charlene's little house at the front of the ranch. The door swung open as they approached, and the dog padded to Charlene's side on her porch.

Charlene smiled at them, saying something Domari couldn't understand, then pointed down to the tree behind the horse. Shelbie clapped excitedly, sliding off the horse and taking the reins from Domari's as well. He followed her, then untied the tree from the saddle, carrying it up to where Charlene held the door open for him, pointing inside.

"She's going to put the horses away for us," Shelbie said as she kicked off her boots, snow piling around them near the door. "Figured she was more useful there than trying to explain this to you in English, which you can't understand."

Domari nodded, one hand on the tree holding it upright. Shelbie stooped to the ground, pulling out a green circle with a hole in the center, instructing him to set the trunk inside. He followed her instructions, watching as she adjusted it to stand level in the little living room. Looking around the space, he took in the cozy room centered on the fireplace. The kitchen was off to the side, but still open to the living room, like in Shelbie's home. The walls were painted pale turquoise, and pictures of horses, wolves, and a man in a brown hat filled the walls. Many of them featured Charlene standing, smiling broadly as she held up prizes, barrels in the background behind her and her horses.

The door opened and closed again, and Domari looked at Charlene standing at the door with a hand on her heart. A small smile tugged on her lips, but her eyes brimmed with tears as she glanced between the tree and Shelbie.

"I think she likes it," Shelbie whispered as her arms circled Domari's waist from the side. He draped his own around her shoulders, squeezing her as he dropped a kiss on her head. Staring down at her bright smile, Domari quickly realized he'd do anything to capture every one she offered him, anything to be the one to put it there.

"Good," he answered, warmth spreading in his chest. "I'm glad."

Charlene disappeared down the hallway, and Domari couldn't seem to take his hands off Shelbie, needing to feel her close and soak in her merriment. Hands running over her back, he clung to her, savoring how her fingers tangled in his jacket.

"You good?" Shelbie asked, looking up through her lashes.

"Better than good." Kissing her nose, he watched as a blush crept across her freckled face.

Charlene's voice carried as she talked excitedly to Shelbie, who let go of him to take a large box from the petite woman. Gold and silver glittered within, mixed with small trinkets Domari didn't recognize.

Plopping a pair of fake antlers that blinked with lights

on her head, Shelbie turned to Domari, holding a sparkling star. "This goes on the top of the tree. Can you reach?"

He took it from her hands, turned back to the tree, and did as she asked. Charlene and Shelbie clapped behind him, and with his back turned to them, he felt the smile spread on his face.

The evening passed quickly as they decorated the tree. Charlene cooked while Shelbie hung ornaments, and Domari did his best to help. He asked many questions about the different trinkets depicted on each decoration, confused by the pickle, the hot air balloon, and the tiny lighthouse — all souvenirs from Charlene's many adventures. Thor had taken up a place in front of the warm fireplace, observing everything in the room.

Together, they settled at Charlene's table as she passed out spaghetti and meatballs with fresh bread. Domari leaned in, letting the smell waft over him. He studied Charlene, how she held her fork, swirling in the noodles, and then made to copy her. It was a mess, and Charlene's cackle filled the room. It was hard for Domari not to smile with her, joy spreading through his bones at this happy sight.

This life was a gift and one he would choose to cherish. He wasn't foolish enough to see that this couldn't last, and the likelihood that he and Shelbie would be ripped apart again sat heavily on his shoulders.

Charlene tapped Shelbie's hand across the table, speaking to her briefly as her eyes were heavy with a tinge of sadness. Shelbie smiled at her, then at me.

"She said Merry Christmas Eve," Shelbie grinned,

grabbing my hand in her free one and rubbing her thumb across it. "Thank you for this. It was lovely."

Charlene nodded, and Domari's eyes followed Shelbie as she pushed back from the table and began clearing the dishes. Domari followed her, working in silence. Shortly after, he held her hand as they walked across the yard back to their home.

15

SIGNE

A cloud of flour puffed into the air around the table as Signe smacked the dough down hard on the table by the hearth. With a day left to finish the preparations for Solstice, everyone worked in frenzied haste. Celebrations in the Viking village were a joyous occasion, set to the tune of heavy drinking, singing, bawdy behavior, and a plethora of food. But with the newcomers in the village, Domari's continued absence, and the sudden unease over the possibility of a threat even in mid-winter, the mood was more somber than years past.

Gunnar had announced the night before that he planned to cut the Solstice celebration short this year. While they would still honor the day, it would be for one night only. Compared to years past, it could hardly be called a celebration.

Signe's hands beat into the dough as she worked it, smoke rising steadily from the warm fire. The room was hazy, lit with several torches along the wall as she kneaded the dough to bake into loaves for tonight. Astrid and the two little ones, Bo and Birgitta, had stopped in earlier and played contentedly on the floor with the twins. Baby Erik dozed in Astrid's arms, and she smiled down at the small boy as she sang a sweet tune.

Watching the scene, Signe felt a pang of envy in her chest. Astrid was born for this — to mother. The gentleness in her tone and actions was precisely what Bo and Birgitta needed as they recovered from losing their own parents and adjusted to a new village. Signe was glad the role didn't fall to her, but felt the hint of regret that she didn't carry those same instincts. She glanced at her children, all three smiling and content, and hoped she had it in her to create a better life for them than she'd had at their age.

A hip nudged against Signe's, and she stood straighter, turning to Yrsa at her side. The older woman's expression was full of empathy, reading Signe as she always seemed to.

"How is it that your hair is the exact shade of the flames?" Signe asked as she brushed some of the flour from Yrsa's bright red hair. The motion drew a small laugh from the woman at her side, and Yrsa shook her head as they began working again. "It's rude of you to be so beautiful at your age. I may steal that violet dress when you take it off tonight."

"Green as bright as your eyes suits you better," Yrsa winked, and Signe smiled. The conversation returned to normal, discussing the preparation for the Solstice the next day. Yrsa had shown up early that morning, and despite the easy conversation, her demeanor seemed off while she helped around the hearth. It wasn't uncommon for Yrsa to volunteer to help, but how her eyes continually glanced at the doors *was* strange. Signe could feel the anxiety rippling off Yrsa, even if she said nothing.

Grunting sounded from behind Signe, and her hands stilled as she turned to investigate.

"Don't run over my children," Gunnar mumbled as Magnus walked backward, carrying a large cask of ale between them.

"I like them far more than you," Magnus retorted, bringing a smirk to Signe's lips as her husband rolled his eyes. Together, the brothers headed for the door, and Signe bit her lip as she watched the way Gunnar's muscles rippled under his shirt. As if he could sense it, his eyes found hers and lit from within as he lifted his brows flirtatiously.

It had only been two weeks since the baby was born, and while Signe's body was still fighting to return to its new normal, she was happy that her ability to heal faster than others seemed to be working yet again as it had in her past. Exhaustion wore heavily on her, but hormones surged in her body as she appraised her husband, wanting to show him how much she loved him. Before she could follow that train of thought, shouting from outside drew her attention.

Gunnar and Magnus set the cask down inside the door, leaving quickly to address the commotion. Signe wiped her hands on a rag nearby and glanced at the children. Astrid watched her carefully, but Signe shook her head, motioning for Astrid to stay here with them.

Signe's hand drifted into her pocket, feeling the cool metal of the dagger sheathed there. Gripping it lightly, she stepped into the faint sunlight with Yrsa on her heels, glancing towards her husband.

Thorsten's ginger hair stood out starkly against the snow as he leaned down with his back to Signe. Gunnar and Magnus stood behind him, the trio making an imposing pair. Before she was close enough to see anything, though, Signe's heart raced as a trickle of power dripped down her spine — the same feeling she'd had so many times before, telling her that something significant was about to happen. Her steps hurried as she approached where the men huddled, her heart pounding with each step.

Soft voices drifted through the air as she drew closer, peering around her husband's back. There, curled into themselves on the ground, lay six more children and a young puppy, hackles raised as he stood guard in front of them. Signe gasped, shoving her husband aside as she glanced down at their tiny bodies.

In the middle of the huddle, draped in heavy furs and wearing pants instead of a dress, was a girl Signe knew instantly. That black hair, those emerald green piercing eyes…

"Viveka?" Signe whispered, falling to her knees in front of the children as she fought to pull air into her lungs. At her words, the girl's head shot up, searching. "What are you doing here?"

"You told me to find you," Viveka's voice whispered from exhaustion. "If ever I needed to escape, you told me to find you."

Signe's hand dropped her dagger in the snow at her side as her hands came out, pulling the girl into her arms in a tight embrace. Signe's body buzzed as emotion flooded her, feeling Viveka cling to her. Sparing only a glance at Gunnar, she noticed his creased brow but said nothing; Signe had never shared much about her past and *certainly* never mentioned Viveka. How could she have explained their tangled story to him?

"I thought I'd never see you again," Signe whispered as her eyes dropped back to the girl, pressing a kiss to her temple. A wet nose sniffed along Signe's face, licking across her skin before Signe should shrug the dog off.

"I knew you'd never return." Viveka's words were muffled, but Signe was sure Gunnar heard them just the same.

"Viveka," Gunnar's voice broke the reunion as he crouched to the ground to pet the dog standing at his side, running his hands through the pup's thick black fur. Gunnar's eyes shifted back and forth between Viveka's face and Signe's, noticing the similarities the girl and his wife shared. "Where do you hail from?"

Signe's heart skidded to a halt as it plummeted in her chest, feeling the weight of every lie by omission she'd told over the last eight years. She pulled back from Viveka, searching her face for only a moment before all emotion left Signe's expression, replaced with a cold, hard exterior.

Palming her dagger again, she pushed to her feet, blocking Gunnar's view of the children behind her. "They're Helvigssons. Draugr's clan."

At the mention of his name, Gunnar's face paled, and the quiet conversation between Yrsa and Thorsten stopped, all eyes on her. Signe's pulse roared in her ears as she met their stares, bracing for what came next.

Gunnar stood slowly but said nothing while waiting for Signe to go on. Draugr Helvigsson had earned his name — *The Demon* — in the only way Vikings made names of the sort. Battle. Bloodshed. Victory.

"This is my cousin," Signe tilted her chin up, daring anyone here to challenge her. Her eyes left her husband and drifted back down to the girl who slipped her hand inside Signe's. Muscles lined her lean frame, but at twelve, she was smaller than many of the young girls in Gunnar's village. Signe's eyes burned as she took in how much Viveka had changed… How long it had been…

"Why are you here?" Signe asked again, and Viveka glanced between her and Gunnar, deciding her following words carefully.

"A man," she swallowed, and the other children huddled closer together, a growl tumbling from the pup's mouth as he bared his teeth in a snarl. "A stranger came to our village on the last moon speaking of Ragnarok. A rebirth. Visitors were always welcomed, and he joined the men in the hall. After a night, Draugr dismissed him and his wild stories, turning him out and on his way, but the man was insistent."

Viveka's eyes ducked momentarily, and Signe placed a gentle hand under her chin, tilting it back until the girl met her eyes again. "I was there, in the back of the hall, listening to the meeting."

"Did he beat you?" Signe whispered, her eyes searching Viveka's body for any sign of injury.

"No," Viveka shook her head. "I was careful, like you taught me. But I was there when the man became enraged. What happened next, I couldn't comprehend. The fire lit his silhouette, shining over the black tattoos painted over his skull, right before he sank his hand into the burning coals of the hearth."

Gunnar's eyes glanced over his men in confusion, but Signe ignored his questioning gaze. The man with the black tattoos… "Why would he burn himself?"

"He didn't." Viveka shook her head again, her eyes wide with disbelief. "When he pulled his hand from the fire, he spoke of unimaginable power. Then he raised his hand to the light, turning it for all to see, and there wasn't a mark on his skin."

Signe's heart pounded in her chest, racing as her mind fought to follow the strange story. "What did Draugr do?"

"I don't know." Viveka's eyes drifted to the ground. "Da found me at the back of the hall and shoved me out of the building."

Signe's hand rubbed tenderly across the girl's arm, soothing her however she could. She remembered the consequences of trouble from the men in her village all too well.

"He didn't beat me," Viveka repeated her earlier words. "He told me to pack. Started throwing my belongings into a cloth and bundling me in furs. I listened carefully as he listed my orders, stopping at each house in town, gathering the children who could make the journey with me."

Her eyes drifted over the small bodies huddled together. "He told you to find me?"

"No," Viveka's chin tipped up as her eyes met Signe's, alight with tenacity. "He told me to follow the dragon."

Ushering everyone into the larger longhouse to the left, Frida had insisted everyone leave the new children to rest. The woman so rarely put her foot down that when she did, everyone complied. They settled on the pallets to the right of the room as Yrsa tended to the children, who were miraculously all healthy, but cold and tired, just as the first group of children had been, too.

Astrid and the other children had returned from Gunnar's, following the rest of the party into the house. As she stepped up to Signe's side, Signe took her baby back, sliding him into the wrap on her chest. No matter Signe's movements, her eyes never left Viveka.

"They're from your home, then?" Astrid asked quietly. Signe hummed in agreement, her mind reeling as she thought through their sudden presence.

"You know these children?" Astrid prodded again, and Signe momentarily glanced at her quiet sister-in-law, trying to determine how to answer that.

"Only Viveka," Signe settled on the truth, or at least part of it. "The others are too young."

Viveka's was a face she thought she'd never see again. Her hair, black as coal, was curlier than she'd have guessed, but everything about her was wildly different from the child she'd left behind eight years ago. Even then, Signe had been well past the age to be married off, but unfortunate accidents happened to each of her betrothed, adding to the rumors that followed Signe for years.

When a baby with emerald eyes was left at Vermund's door, Signe was old enough to be the child's mother. Everyone eyed her and whispered words insinuating that Signe had lost her maidenhead before her wedding. No matter their rumors, Signe's lithe frame was as lean as it had always been — it wasn't possible she'd hidden the baby.

It *had to be* Vermund's daughter. No one but Signe and Vermund had eyes like those...

Nine days later, her uncle knelt on the floor of their large hall, claiming the girl as his own. Signe's eyes had never left the tiny black-haired baby, so different from everyone in their village.

As Vermund left the building that night, he'd stopped in front of Signe, handing over the crying child. Signe's eyes shot up to her uncle's face, confusion written in her expression, as she watched her hero shrug.

"I've no business raising a child," he'd said to her that night.

"What am I to do with her?" Signe asked, holding the baby awkwardly at arm's length. She wailed, and Vermund pushed her into Signe's chest. As soon as the baby's face met the skin exposed above the neckline of Signe's dress, her cries stopped.

"Find a wet nurse for her," Vermund shrugged, his frown etching deep lines into his face as he walked off. She'd stared at his back as he faded into the darkness towards the beach, trying to understand his actions, but found no explanation for his strange behavior.

Four years passed while she cared for the girl, learning from the women in the village. Everyone had always kept a wide berth around Signe, Draugr's forbidden daughter, but the baby girl was irresistible. Charm oozed off her even as a toddler, bringing smiles to the faces of everyone in their clan, and smiles were few and far between under Draugr's rule.

Even now, Signe watched the girl — now almost a woman — as the children leaned into her, seeking her comfort and guidance. This girl would be a leader someday, especially now that she'd escaped the grips of the brutal Helvigsson clan.

"Your cousin?" Gunnar asked, drawing Signe's attention away from the girl. The small black pup wove its way between Gunnar's legs, staring up at Signe with dark eyes full of hunger.

She nodded silently, thinking through the many things she'd never told Gunnar. While she'd never outright lied to him, there was so much she'd left out. But everything she'd worked so hard to escape — to leave in her past — had just walked through the front door.

"Yes," she whispered, her eyes finally finding Gunnar's azure gaze as she spilled her deepest secret. "Her father is Vermund."

"Vermund...," Gunnar's shoulders tensed as his eyes searched her. "Vermund Oathbreaker."

If Signe could cry, tears would've welled in her eyes. She watched as the truth settled on Gunnar's shoulders as he pieced together her many omissions. The man had always been so trusting, never one to pry into her past as she so deftly avoided it.

"Vermund Oathbreaker's daughter is your cousin," Gunnar worked to connect the dots, his eyes glancing anywhere but at his petite wife. "So that means—"

"My name is Signe Draugrsdóttir. Draugr the Demon is my father. I'm the one they called the Demon's Spawn."

16

SIGNE

Gunnar avoided Signe for the rest of the afternoon. Or, at least, that was what it felt like to her. With so many new bodies in the village, this was his job. Runners left the house quickly, heading out to the ten families that made up their village, sending word of the newcomers and feeling out the best placement for each of the children.

Signe observed as Gunnar worked, the small pup never leaving his side. Gunnar did everything with the same golden goodness she loved so much about him, yet he never once glanced in her direction.

It stung her heart, seeing him put this distance between them.

Knowing she'd caused it.

For eight years, she'd loved this man in a way that defied everything she knew. He had taught her how to trust, earning her loyalty each day with his kind and true actions. The more she got to know him — the more time she'd spent with his people — the more she wanted to be like him. Worthy of him.

Good.

That's what she wanted to be.

Even so, she'd never told him.

Deep down, if she admitted it to herself, she was afraid hearing who she was and where she came from — *who* she came from — would change how Gunnar viewed her. He'd finally see how unworthy she was of him. In a span of hours, Signe's life crumbled around her. She could feel the pieces of her carefully crafted identity splinter, breaking apart to reveal the ragged pieces of her past.

Erik let out a soft whimper, drawing Signe's attention back to the baby at her chest. His black hair reminded her of Viveka, her first child. Even if she hadn't birthed her, Viveka was just as much hers as Revna, Ulf, and Erik. Not a day had passed that Signe hadn't thought of her, wondering how she was faring and if she blamed Signe for leaving her. After all, that was what Signe had done. In some ways, Signe was no better than her mother, abandoning her newborn daughter. A fire raged in Signe's veins as her mind trailed down that path.

No.

Signe might not be the best for these children in some ways — too harsh, too strict, not soft enough — but they were *hers*. Even when she left Viveka, she'd done it for the girl's safety. Signe's mother had left to protect *herself*, knowing the life she doomed her abandoned infant to.

While Signe adored her husband, she felt a different kind of love for her children. Viveka, Revna, Ulf, and baby

Erik were the center of her universe. Signe would tear down the world to protect them — nothing and no one could stop her. Not even the foreboding dreams and ominous words of a Seer would take them from her again.

The decisions she'd make now at 27 differed vastly from those she'd made at 19, the day the Seer came to her. Verandi, Signe knew now — she'd recognized the Norn the day she came to the village last fall for Shelbie. Verandi's face was one she'd never forget.

"You must go," Verandi had said eight years ago. *"Your fate — and the girl's — depends on it. Leave and never return."*

The rest of the Norn's words still haunted her in the quiet moments.

"When you meet your father again, Ragnarok will be upon us."

The sun was long gone when the children were all settled in homes, sleeping off the traumatic events they'd shared on the journey to the Eriksson village. Two young boys had gone home with Thorsten, Yrsa took the smallest of the six who seemed to need the most care after the cold temperatures, and two more were fast asleep on a pallet in the back of Frida's home, but Viveka still sat near the hearth.

Gunnar stooped, lifted a sleeping Ulf off the ground of his mother's longhouse, and never glanced in Signe's direction on his way out, with the pup trailing behind.

"Come, Revna." Signe shook her daughter's shoulder lightly where she'd dozed off, leaning against her.

"I'm tired, Mama," Revna whined, and Signe dipped

her chin, placing a tender kiss in her hair. The baby shifted in his wrap on her chest as Signe rose, tugging a shuffling Revna along.

"Viveka, you're welcome to join us." Signe stopped in front of the girl. "My home is always yours."

Her emerald eyes glanced up at her, so similar to Signe's gaze, before shifting to where Gunnar had just left the house.

"It's not you he's upset with." Signe attempted to smile reassuringly at the girl, even as her own heart sank at the words. Dread for the coming confrontation with Gunnar filled her for the briefest moments before strength flooded her veins. She wasn't *wrong* for what she'd done, the choices she'd made. She was protecting Gunnar and their family, just as she protected Viveka, and she'd give Gunnar no choice but to understand that. "Gunnar is a good man. He won't turn you down."

"Tomorrow, then," Viveka answered, glancing around at the pile of sleeping bodies around her. "I'll stay here with the children tonight."

Signe nodded, accepting her response. It was the noble thing to do, and she was glad that was Viveka's chosen path.

Selflessness.

Something she certainly hadn't learned from the Helvigssons.

Even as Signe felt an inner turmoil she'd never allowed herself to sink into, she raised her chin. Standing tall, she gripped Revna's tiny hand and followed her husband's footsteps out into the night. The moon highlighted the glittering snow, creating a peaceful reprieve as the clear night allowed the stars and lights to shine brightly. Magenta strands danced across the sky, shifting as quickly as her mood as she neared her home.

Warmth escaped as she opened the door, quickly closing it behind her. Ulf's small shape was already curled into the blankets on the children's bed, the small dog curled in front of the hearth, but Gunnar was nowhere to be seen. Signe's eyes shifted across the interior of the dimly lit room as her heart thumped loudly.

"Time for bed." Signe kissed Revna's head again as her eyes continued searching the space. Revna yawned loudly as her mother helped her onto the platform, tucking her tightly between the soft furs and the thick woolen blankets. The little girl sighed as she curled into her brother, huddling for warmth.

Signe's hand drifted over her low back as she walked to her bed, rubbing across the growing ache there after a day on her feet.

"Let me help you," Gunnar's whispered words startled Signe, jumping to put distance between them. His hands were raised, eyebrows arched as he watched her. "I didn't mean to frighten you."

"No, it was me," Signe answered, shaking off the tension eating at her every nerve. "I'm more tired than I realized. I thought you'd left."

"Where to?" Gunnar's brows dipped. "This is my home. I wouldn't leave you."

At his words, Signe's eyes glistened in the flickering

light, scanning back and forth between her husband's azure gaze. "You aren't mad at me?"

"No, Signe," Gunnar sighed heavily, a hand scrubbing his face. "I'm not mad at you."

Her breath caught on an exhale, relief swimming through her veins at his words. While she knew she was right, still, she feared the worst.

"I'm *hurt*," his voice broke her racing thoughts, and Signe's eyes snapped up again. "I thought," he paused, pinching the bridge of his nose in frustration, "I knew you were hiding things in your past. Whatever had happened before you arrived here, I knew it must have been terrible. You were cold. Hard. Fearsome. Terrifying. And yet… you stayed."

"Because of you…" Signe's words were barely more than a breath. Her hands itched to reach out and touch him, feel his skin beneath hers, and share his warmth. To *show* him how she felt. "I stayed because of you, Gunnar. Because I love you."

"I don't understand, though." Gunnar's hand dropped to his side as his heavy gaze settled on her. "It's been eight years. *Eight years*, Signe. I've told you every dark secret in my past, every terrible moment that led me to you. I've shared my life, my family, with you. And yet," he paused, his chin dipping as he looked to the floor. "Why would you lie to me?"

Signe fought to pull air into her lungs, chest tight as she tried to slow her racing thoughts. *Think first,* Vermund had drilled into her head so many times. One thing she had learned in her eight years was that Gunnar responded to reason — one of the many reasons he was so good. Everything was black and white to him. She just needed him to understand.

Before she could answer, he lifted the baby from Signe's arms and walked around her towards the bed. She watched as he sat carefully on the edge of the bed, holding the baby to his chest as he moved across it. When he gently set Erik down in the center, Gunnar shifted his body closer to the wall, rolling away from her, his back to the room.

Signe's heart raced as her feet were planted on the ground. Her breath left her in heavy falls, despair like she'd never known settling into her bones. She couldn't seem to make herself move. Words were lost to her as only the baby's soft coos mixed with the wood popping in the hearth.

How could she fix this? Explain it to him?

Yes, he'd shared his past with her. Yes, he'd shared his family... but loving, wonderful people surrounded Gunnar. This was his whole life. Everything he knew. While Signe was honored to share this life with him and be accepted by the Erikssons, she couldn't even comprehend the thought of explaining everything she'd seen with the Helvigssons. The things she'd done...

Once he knew...

Once they *all* knew...

Nothing would ever be the same.

Exhaustion finally made the decision she couldn't seem to make on her own as her body drifted down next to the baby on the bed. She lay, hand resting lightly on tiny Erik, staring at Gunnar's large back at an arm's length. Signe could reach across the bed and touch him, yet it seemed a chasm had suddenly opened between them.

Squeezing her eyes shut, Signe forced herself to breathe deeply.

This wasn't the end.

It wasn't even the *beginning* of the end.

Signe. *Victory.* As an infant even smaller than the one next to her, she persisted. She would now, too.

She'd fix this, no matter what it took.

17

SHELBIE

A wet line slid across my skin as a single tear dripped down my temple, pooling on the pillow. Sorrow filled me as Signe's overwhelming grief flowed through my veins, making me feel as if I'd lived it. As if it were me…

Why did every one of my dreams seem so *real* lately? Dreams were a fictional reality drawn from deep within my subconscious, only a story my mind told me. I knew nothing about Signe's past other than how she'd met Gunnar competing in Winter Nights eight years ago, and yet my dream had painted me a vivid picture of her broken past. But this was only my mind fabricating a story to feel closer to the woman I'd befriended.

Not real.

Not my grief.

Not my story.

I swiped my hand across my tears, sniffing quietly to pull myself back into the present and clear the lingering sadness. Eyes still closed, I reached across the bed towards Domari, needing to feel his solid presence.

He *was* real.

This was my life.

I didn't know my story yet, but I felt like it was just beginning.

My fingers moved across the soft cotton sheets, and I cracked my eyes open to see his handsome face as my first sight of the day. But the bed was empty.

I sat up in a rush, panic settling in.

"Domari?" I whispered as fresh tears pooled, emotions from before slamming down around me. Was this all the time we'd be granted? Was that the meaning of my dream? I'd watched as Signe's life crumbled around her, broken-hearted as she feared she was losing Gunnar, and now I'd lost Domari as well? I choked back tears, my heart shattering at the thought, on Christmas morning, no less.

Before I could sink any further into my despair, the sound of clanking pans reached me. Ripping the covers back, I dropped my feet to the floor and held my breath as I padded down the hallway to the kitchen. Relief flooded me as I turned the corner to see a shirtless Domari staring down at the stove, mouth downturned into a scowl as he glared at the knobs.

My pounding heart settled as I stood out of sight, clutching my chest. Wrangling my reckless emotions back into place, I watched as he muttered to himself in frustration, his back flexing as he tensed. I was mesmerized by his bare arms, ten black bands tattooed above his wrists, moving in the morning light streaming through the window.

Jeans hung low across his hips, and I bit my lip as my earlier despair morphing into something else entirely.

Domari was real, and he was *stunning*.

After the third time, he turned the knob and then turned it back off when the stove didn't immediately light, I stepped into the kitchen, chuckling.

"Need some help there?" I asked as I walked up behind him, circling him with my arms and nuzzling into his warm back.

"I was going to cook this meat. How different can it be from over a fire? But there's no fire…"

I grinned as I placed a kiss along his shoulder blade and let go of him. I cranked the knob and set the pan over the burner. "It takes a few minutes to heat. You were doing it right. And bacon sounds delicious." I stepped around him into the kitchen and headed for the fridge. "Coffee?"

"What's coffee?" he asked, still studying the burners below him.

A scoff left me as I grabbed my cold brew jug from the fridge and two glasses, pouring us each a cup. I added some milk and a dash of cinnamon to mine, but Domari drained the glass of cold black coffee before I could doctor his. My eyebrows climbed into my hairline as I waited for his reaction, a chuckle rising in my throat that pushed the lingering sadness down a little further.

His face clouded in confusion as he stared at the now empty cup, tilting it back and forth. "This has an odd taste to it," he said, and I grinned. "I don't dislike it." He glanced up and then down at mine, now creamy brown with my fixings. "What's yours?"

I held it out for him to try, and instead of taking a sip as I expected, he drained it as well. A laugh sputtered out of me; I shouldn't have been surprised by this, as he chugged everything, but it was wildly amusing.

"Different," he said as he handed the cup back. "Yours is sweeter like you. I think I like the dark one better. Cold and bitter, like me." He winked at his comment, and I laughed again, feeling more myself with each passing moment in his presence.

Together, we cooked the bacon, chatting while we stood in the kitchen, and the sorrow that had clung to me from my dream eased. Maybe I didn't know my story yet, but the more time I had with Domari, the more I dared to hope he was part of it.

"Question," I asked as I jumped onto the counter to sit, chewing on a piece of perfectly crisp bacon. Domari raised a brow in my direction, sipping another cup of black iced coffee. "What do you know of Signe's past? She didn't grow up with the Erikssons, right?"

Domari nodded, setting his glass down as he studied me. "No, she didn't. I honestly don't know what clan she's from — Gunnar never said, and I never asked. She arrived in the village to compete in Winter Nights eight years ago, and Gunnar fell for her instantly, but after I'd already left for the Varangian Guard. Why do you ask?"

"Nothing," I shrugged, thinking back over the dream once more. "I had a dream about her last night. Must have been thinking about your family before I went to bed." I took another bite of the bacon, chewing slowly as it dawned on me how much he'd be missing his family right now.

As if sensing the direction of my thoughts, Domari stepped to between my knees, his hands settling on my waist. "I'm glad I'm here with you, Shelbie," he said, his eyes steady on mine, and I felt the honesty in his words. His beard tickled across my skin as he kissed me lightly, patting my legs before he stepped away, heading to change for the day.

The day passed quickly as I short-circuited Domari's mind by showing him the laundry machine, and we sorted out his new clothes. Seeing men's clothes mingled with mine in the closet was strange, feeling much more permanent than I'd allowed myself to think of this arrangement. This home was new to both of us, and we were starting here together.

After we finished laundry, Domari made the rounds, checking on the horses while I showered. My phone rang as I was styling my curls in the bathroom, and I answered it on speakerphone.

"Aunt Shelbie!" a high-pitched voice called out, and instantly, I smiled. "I can't see you!"

"Sorry, Charlotte," I laughed, propping my phone up on the mirror, not realizing she'd FaceTimed me. "Merry Christmas, girlie! What did Santa bring you?"

My eldest niece began her monologue, carrying the phone around as I went on a dizzying tour of my parents' house, trashed with remnants of gift wrap and tissue paper everywhere. Despite the mess, my chest ached, knowing I was missing out on this time with them.

A squabble broke out between my three nieces as they battled for the phone until my mom reached down, plucking it from their fingers. "We wanted to check on you, sweetie," she smiled brightly, the same blue eyes as mine shining back at me. "You're not alone for Christmas, are you? You should have driven back up. And look at those curls! I like your hair that way."

I glanced in the mirror, brow drawn, as I stared at my reflection, noting my bouncy golden curls. That was how I usually wore my hair, which seemed like a strange compliment, but I shrugged it off. "I'm headed over to Charlene's. We've been busy getting me settled and working on the ranch this week. Want to see the house?" I spun in a circle, holding my phone up to show them the small space around me.

"Wow, it's… colorful," my brother Jacob said from over my mom's shoulders, his eyes squinted as he took in the floral wall behind me.

"No comments from the peanut gallery unless you're offering to fix it for me." I held a finger up at the phone, pointing at him. Jacob held up his hands, and my mom swatted his stomach.

"It looks great, honey. Nothing a little paint can't fix. Doesn't look like you've finished unpacking yet?" I shrugged, listening as she continued to tell me all about their morning, but I couldn't stop glancing at the door, worried Domari would walk in while we were on the phone and I'd have to explain his presence.

"You seem busy," my mom said, her lips puckered when I looked back at the phone.

"Sorry." I forced a smile. "Just distracted."

"You sure you're okay, Shelbie?" she asked, her eyes softening, wrinkles creasing the corners of her freckled face so like my own, the perfect picture of a concerned mother. As much as I loved her, I didn't want to get into the nitty-gritty of my life, so I forced myself to take a deep breath to calm myself for her.

"Yes, I'm sure, Mom. I love you guys. Merry Christmas! Miss you!" I waved and blew kisses to my family on the other side of the screen.

The silence of the house after I hung up the phone was deafening, leaving me to my thoughts. I *hated* silence, feeling the heaviness of my thoughts so much more with nothing around to distract me. So I did what I did best and ignored it all, moving to the kitchen to finish the cheesecake I'd baked yesterday, flipping on Christmas music while I worked.

Domari returned to the house an hour later, showered quickly, and dropped a kiss on my head where I sat on the couch scribbling nonsense in my journal. When we were both ready, I grabbed a few small gifts I'd picked up, and we walked over to Charlene's.

Her house was warm and aromatic, the smell of the fresh-cut pine mixing with the potatoes cooking in her oven. Charlene's eyes focused on the cheesecake in my hands, and she snagged it, heading to the fridge.

"This looks perfect, Shelbie," she said as she put it away. Feeling festive, Charlene had upgraded her typical blingy, rhinestoned attire for a tacky Christmas sweater, complete with battery-operated blinking lights on the tree emblazoned across her chest. Red tinsel was wrapped around her high, teased ponytail, and tiny Santas dangled from her earlobes. As always, my forest green sweater looked plain in comparison.

"I'm not a baker, so it might be handy to have you around here." Her eyes crinkled with delight. "And this is the first time I didn't have to go feed all the horses in God knows how long, so I guess Domari is okay in my books, too."

The three of us chatted easily while I translated back and forth between them, and it surprised me how open Domari was with her, answering her many questions about his life and past. I couldn't help but stare at him throughout the meal, and his dark eyes sparkled every time our gazes crossed.

I gathered the plates after dinner and carried them to the sink, but Charlene stopped me with a hand on my back. "Let's do gifts first. I can clean up after."

"Are you sure?" I hated the thought of her having to clean everything alone after she'd also worked so hard on the meal.

Her hand slid down from my shoulder to my elbow as her hazel eyes softened, and she smiled. "It has been so long since I've had anyone here on Christmas. I'd forgotten what this felt like. Yes, I'm sure." She nodded, pulling me from the kitchen into the living room. "Let me spoil you first."

I hugged her tightly, and she swatted me on the butt. "Enough of that, girl," she laughed. "I used up my entire sappy emotional allowance for the year with that one statement."

We walked together to her living room, where Domari had already parked himself in a chair, hard cider in hand. He sipped from the bottle as I slid to the floor at his feet, crossing my legs as I leaned back into his jeans. I grabbed the bag of gifts I'd brought over with me and dug my hand inside.

"You first, Charlene." I grinned up at our hostess. She eyed me carefully as she took the present I held for her and sank onto the couch.

"You didn't have to get me anything," she mumbled.

"Shut it, lady. Open your present." I shot a pretend glare at her, and she chuckled, shaking her head.

Paper ripped as she opened the box and unfolded the tissue. A cackle bubbled out of her as she held up the small turquoise tee and spun it around. *Ass down, Zippers up,* the tee read in rhinestones across the chest.

"Well, I wasn't expecting this," she beamed, wiping a tear from her eye. "This might be my new favorite!"

I clapped, delighted that she was so happy with her gift. This woman had given me so much; it was the least I could do.

"My turn." She rubbed her hands together excitedly, reaching down and surprising us both when she handed a giant gift box to Domari.

"For me?" he asked, glancing between her and me. I shrugged as Charlene nodded.

"Open it." She perched on the edge of her seat, waiting, and I was immediately on guard after spying the maniacal grin that took over her face.

Domari undid the paper as he'd seen Charlene do and

lifted the box top. Inside was a black-felt cattleman's hat. The woman giggled as he picked it up, unable to contain her excitement. I stuttered a laugh at the confused look on Domari's face. "It's a hat. Cowboys wear hats like that here. Try it on."

So he did.

Charlene moaned, clutching her chest as she slowly slid off the couch and onto the floor. Domari rose suddenly, ready to help her, and I couldn't contain myself, giggling uncontrollably.

Glancing between her and me, Domari eyed me carefully. "Why are you laughing? Is she hurt?"

"No," I gasped, trying to catch my breath. "She's dramatic; that's what she is."

He was still visibly confused, though, and I swiped the tears from my eyes, staring up at him. Domari was gorgeous in his tight black tee, dark jeans, and boots. Add that hat... I didn't blame Charlene even one bit for pretending to faint. He was breathtaking.

"Put him on the cover of a Western romance and call it a day," Charlene said from her position on the floor. "The beard. The shirt. The jeans. The boots. THE HAT. I've died and gone to heaven. Hopefully, Nash will forgive me because I'm having impure thoughts about another man."

"He's mine, lady," I swatted her leg, and it set her off cackling again. Meanwhile, Domari stood there, eyes shifting back and forth between Charlene and me in a puddle of laughter on the floor.

"I'm sorry," I finally said to him when I remembered he

couldn't understand what Charlene had said. "You're so beautiful; you killed her."

At that, he grinned widely and tipped his hat forward.

"I can't take it anymore." Charlene fanned herself.

"Don't die on me, Charlene." I grabbed her hand, pulling her up to her feet.

"Wouldn't dream of it," she answered once she settled back on the couch with a heavy sigh.

We passed out several more presents between us after that. I'd bought Charlene a new turquoise halter for her horse, and she gave me black fringe cowboy boots I never would've bought myself. They were fabulous, though. Domari was delighted with the beard-trimming kit I gave him and planted a kiss on my lips in gratitude.

"I didn't get you anything," he said after we finished opening presents. "But I can think of a few ways to repay you for your kindness." His expression turned devious, and I blushed.

"And that's my cue." Charlene slapped her hand down on her legs. "Time for you two to go home and unwrap some more *gifts.*" The eyebrow waggle at the end was so mischievous and meddling that I couldn't help but laugh, even as I shook my head.

"Ready to go home?" I asked Domari as I rose to my feet. He nodded, gathered our presents, and made for the door.

18

DOMARI

The front door clicked as it shut behind Domari, the sound breaking the silence that had accompanied them across the yard. Shelbie had seemed slightly off most of the day, but the gift exchange and dinner with Charlene seemed to help settle her.

Domari slid Shelbie's coat from her shoulders as she shrugged out of it, placing a gentle kiss on her nape as the fabric slid down her arms. She turned to him, the warm, unguarded smile he adored shining brightly on her face, all shadows banished.

How his life had changed so much in a matter of months was still shocking. Right now, he should be at home with his own family, standing in the warm, smoky air of Frida's longhouse for their Solstice celebration. He'd be drunk off ale from a horn, listening to Magnus's terrible poetry or Björn's deep voice. Thinking of them filled his heart with longing, but even as much as he missed his family, he couldn't deny how deeply he felt about the woman in front of him — being here, with her, able to hold her.

Time had conspired to snatch her away, and Domari had almost resigned himself to life with half a heart. She carried the other piece of it, and only with her had he ever felt whole.

Stopping next to the couch, Shelbie flicked on a lamp and stooped to the ground, petting Thor. She spoke to him lovingly, her curly blonde hair hanging loosely over her green sweater, flattering her curves and freckled skin. As she stood and turned back to him, a blush spread across her pale cheeks, noticing Domari's eyes on her.

"Did you have fun tonight?" she asked, one eyebrow raised in question.

"I always have a good time when I'm with you," he nodded, stepping forward, and lacing an arm around her waist as he pulled her chest flush to his. Slowly, he ducked his head, placing a reverent kiss on her lips. Then another.

Shelbie's eyes glittered in the faint lamplight, switching back and forth between his as she studied him, her chest rising and falling rapidly.

"I may not have a gift for you," his voice rumbled through his chest, the emotion he usually hid deep evident in the timbre, "but you. You're a gift to me, Shelbie."

Tears pooled in her eyes as she stared up at him lovingly, and he slid the pad of his thumb across her cheek, wiping them away before they could track down her face.

"I pictured my life full of battles and bloodshed," Domari went on, his fingers still resting on her skin as he tilted her chin towards him. "Never did I ever picture you. Your warmth. Your laughter. Your smile. Your love."

Shelbie's eyes expanded as she hung on every deeply felt word, hearing the honesty there, soaking it all in.

"You have captured my heart so completely, Shelbie." Domari's voice dropped to a whisper, her pulse beating rapidly beneath his fingers on her neck. "Until my dying breath, I'm yours. That's the only gift I can offer you, which is still not enough. Not what you deserve."

Her breath caught as she listened. Domari leaned down again to offer her a tender kiss, and Shelbie's fingers curled into his black t-shirt. As he pulled back once more, her forehead rested on his shoulder, and he wondered if she could hear his own heart thundering under his ribs.

"You should offer to give Magnus lessons, so no one ever has to hear about *billowing bosoms* again."

Domari's laugh shook his body, bouncing her head lightly as he recalled his young cousin's drunken proclamations from Winter Nights.

"He is terrible with words," Domari agreed, smoothing her curls down the back of her head.

"So bad." Shelbie chuckled, glancing up at Domari through heavily lidded lashes. "This wasn't bad, though."

His eyebrow cocked, staring down at the girl he loved with his whole heart. "No?"

"Could have been better." Shelbie shrugged, unlacing her arms from his waist as she drew back. She bit her lip to stop the smile from spreading as she moved further into the living room, her heated gaze sweeping over Domari's body and leaving fire in its wake. "No mention of how much you love not breaking your neck kissing me because I'm so tall. Or how beautiful I look with my bedhead in the morning. Or my ability to not burn a frozen pizza. Most of the time."

"Ah." Domari quickly covered the space between them as she turned her back to him. His hands slid under her sweater, shifting over the heated skin of her soft belly. "Maybe I should have mentioned *your* billowing bosom then, too?"

Her laugh quickly turned to breathy hums of pleasure as Domari's hands continued their path upward, tugging her back into his embrace. Shelbie had held back physically since he'd arrived, not letting it pass heated kisses, and he hadn't dared to push her. But when her hands settled over the top of his, pushing her shirt up and over her chest, he didn't hesitate to pull it over her wild curls.

His teeth scraped across her shoulder, feeling the naked skin beneath him as he wove his fingers under the strap of her bra, pushing it down her arm. "I love how your skin feels," he breathed against her. He kissed up her shoulder to her neck, and her head tipped back onto his chest.

"And the sounds you make when I touch you," he whispered as his hands skated across her torso, leaving a trail of goosebumps in their wake. A moan escaped her as she squirmed beneath him.

"Every day that we were apart, I dreamt of you," Domari said as he stamped open-mouthed kisses down her back, unhooking her bra, then letting the fabric fall to the floor. "Dreamt of your silken skin. The way your mouth moves on mine."

Shelbie spun, sealing her lips to his. Their tongues

tangled, sliding and stroking, as Domari gripped her tightly, banishing every inch of space between them. Moving his hands down to grab her bottom, he lifted her off the ground. Her ankles crossed behind his back as he carried her down the hallway.

Before reaching their bedroom, he stopped, unable to wait another moment, and pinned Shelbie against the wall. He palmed her ass tightly as he held her suspended off the ground, deepening their kiss. Her hips ground into him, seeking his hardness. Minutes ticked by as heat rose between the two, their movements becoming urgent with need. Shelbie's hands slid over his chiseled torso, and Domari groaned at the feel of her nails raking against him. Everywhere she touched left fire in its wake, ratcheting his fervor higher.

"Off," she said, her voice husky with lust as she gripped his shirt. He moved back from her momentarily, and her feet dropped to the ground as he gripped the back of his black t-shirt in one hand and pulled it over his head, tossing it to the floor. Before he could move, Shelbie sank to her knees, her back to the wall as her hands moved across his belt.

A groan rose through Domari's chest as he watched her kneel before him, staring up through her lashes as she undid the buckle and pushed his jeans down his hips. Entwining his fingers through her silken hair, he bent at the waist, slanting his mouth across hers. He ran his tongue across her lips as he deepened the kiss, eagerness a thrum in his chest, propelling him towards *more*.

She pulled back from the kiss, cheeks rosy with passion

and her gaze hot, then shifted her eyes to his hips. Shelbie's fingers roved over his skin, and his muscles jumped beneath her touch. He couldn't look away, riveted to her every move as her mouth moved closer to him. He released an unsteady breath around the tightness in his chest, waiting, watching.

The feel of her tongue sliding across him had him slamming his hand against the wall above her, his head tilting forward. Domari's chest heaved, fighting for breath with every lick and slide of her tongue, loving how she worked him.

"Haski," he whispered, his voice hoarse as he gripped her hair, fighting the need to rip her back to her feet. Shelbie's head bobbed rhythmically, and the sight mesmerized Domari. He didn't deserve her or this, but whatever he'd done in his life to lead to this moment had been worth it. *"Ástin mín."*

His heart beat wildly in his chest, his eyes squeezing shut momentarily as he wrestled for control. His fingers spasmed in her hair, looking back down at her. Shelbie glanced up at him as she slid her mouth across him, and the moment her eyes met his, he needed more.

Slipping his hands under her arms, he hoisted her to her feet. Domari's lips slammed down on hers as he worshipped her mouth. Lips lingering for a moment, he pulled away and stepped out of his jeans, pushing her in front of him into their bedroom. Gripping her hips almost too hard, he spun her to face the bed. He skated a hand worshipfully down her spine, watching as she shivered under his touch. When he reached her waistband, Domari ripped down her pants and underwear in one swift move, throwing them across the room after she stepped out of the fabric. She gasped, her blue eyes glittering over her shoulder, watching as he nipped his mouth across her skin. Domari's hands slid down to her hips, feeling her smooth skin, craving her taste. Silently, he dropped to his knees behind her, placing a kiss on her waist, then moving down.

"Holy shit," Shelbie moaned, falling onto her forearms on the bed. Her fingers dug into the white comforter for purchase.

Domari didn't stop, his tongue leaving a glistening trail across her skin as he kissed and licked the canvas of her body. He savored every move, every sound she made. She squirmed beneath him, her hips moving until he placed a heavy palm across her ass to hold her still. With his other hand, he slid his fingers through her wetness, pushing into her core.

Shelbie's head tipped forward, resting against the bed as she sighed his name. Domari smirked, loving the sound, while his fingers and mouth worked in tandem, wanting to show her exactly what he felt for her. How powerful, how consuming, his love was. How she owned him, body and soul. Shelbie's legs shook against his chest as he laved at her relentlessly, waiting for the moment she finally imploded.

She cried out, mumbling incoherent words as he felt her squeeze around his fingers. Domari clamped her hips in a rush and spun her to face him. Her movements were sluggish as she fought the fog of pleasure, but he couldn't wait another moment, yanking her down to the floor, straddling his lap. Instantly, he lifted his hips, sliding into her heat as Shelbie's lips parted in a silent scream. Her arms laced behind his head, clinging to him as Domari punched up into her, needing to feel every inch of him wrapped in her. He trailed his lips along her jaw, then down to her neck, his hands holding her waist in a crushing grip as he moved beneath her. He wanted it all.

This.

Her.

She was everything to him.

Shelbie's forehead rested against Domari's as his hips slowed, dragging in and out of her at an even, torturous pace. Sweat dripped down his temple, sliding into his thick beard.

His name slid from her swollen lips; her eyes squeezed shut as he moved. Unable to help himself, he sealed his lips over hers yet again, tongue dancing and stroking. The moment lasted an eternity, yet not nearly long enough as passion demanded an increase in his pace.

His eyes snapped open when her hips shifted to plant her feet on the ground. Their gazes locked as she lifted herself, then dropped back down, her eyes incandescent with desire. Domari needed no further encouragement, wrapping his arms around her torso as he moved.

The drum of skin on skin rang in his ears as their kisses became desperate. Need drove him, heat rising from the base of his spine. Shelbie shuddered, her legs quaking around him as she bit into his shoulder, and Domari groaned as he lost himself. Once his hips stilled, their chests still heaving as they clung to each other, he pressed his lips into her damp hair, not ready for the moment to end.

They knelt on the floor for several minutes, still

entwined while their bodies came down from the high. Shelbie lifted her head from where she rested on Domari's shoulders, glancing back towards the living room, and a chuckle escaped her.

Domari's brow creased as he turned to see what had caused this reaction, noticing the trail of clothes they'd left in their wake and Thor lying on her green sweater with his back to them. A smile slid across Domari's face before he turned her face to meet his once more.

"I love you," he said as he gazed into her ice-blue eyes.

She nodded, his emotion mirrored in her stare, and kissed him gently. "I love you, too."

19

SHELBIE

The night was silent around us as Domari and I lay entwined on the bed, unable to separate. His emotional confession when we'd entered the house, followed by the passion that had consumed us, was a lot to take in. He was exceedingly tender and caring as we'd cleaned up after, and I knew what I told him was the truth.

I was madly in love with Domari.

As happy as the thought made me, I was terrified. Loving a man who had traveled through time to get to me was a terrible idea, and I knew it. The gaping wound left in my heart after losing him once still ached, and I was even deeper emotionally now than I had been last fall. It was reckless of me to be so open with my heart and give in to these emotions, knowing the chance of going through that heartache was so high. My hands rested on his warm chest as I fought to stay positive and not think of all the ways I was sure to lose him again. Simultaneously, I wanted to cling to him forever and run from the enormity of the feeling between us.

"Where did you go?" Domari asked, lightly placing a finger under my chin. I lifted my eyes to meet his, memorizing how his warm brown eyes turned down slightly at the corners, how his beard curled slightly under his chin, how his cheeks flushed when he held me.

"I'm scared," I admitted, my lip quivering as I ducked my eyes again, unable to look at him.

Understanding what I meant, Domari pulled me into his chest, wrapping his arms tightly around me as he pressed a kiss into my hair. "I'm here now and will be for as long as fate allows. There's a reason you were brought to me and a reason I found you again. We're two halves of the same whole."

I nodded, hoping and wishing his words were true. Wanting to believe them.

Never in my life had I felt so unsteady. Focusing on the positive and wildly ignoring the *what ifs* had been my go-to for decades. Aside from mild panic attacks caused by the mere sight of an English saddle, this — probably flawed — character trait had served me well. But faced with the idea of losing Domari again, my optimism wavered. I wanted to believe this could be forever, but I didn't see how. A voice in the back of my mind whispered this was too good to be true.

Domari's hands trailed down my sides, and I forced myself to focus on the feel of him instead. To be in the here and now.

Right now, he was here.

Right now, I could be with him.

Right now, I trusted him with my entire heart, and I knew he'd cherish it always.

I leaned forward, brushing my fingers across his neck as I pulled him down to me for a long kiss, taking my time. He was gentle, intrinsically knowing what I needed. My hand lingered on him, drifting down his shoulders and onto his forearms even after I pulled away from the kiss. I just needed to feel him there with me. Ground myself in the sight, sound, and feel of him.

Tracing a finger across the bands on his arms, I glanced down at his black tattoos. Domari's eyes followed my line of sight.

"Do the bands mean something?" I asked, moving from one to the next, tracing the five on his arm that I could see, knowing the tattoos were mirrored on his other arm as well.

"Each year on the Summer Solstice, I tattooed another band on my arm. Ten total," Domari said, his voice rough and filled with emotion. I glanced up at him, focused intently, propping my chin on his chest. "One for each year I spent in the Varangian Guard before I returned home."

"Was it hard?" I swallowed, knowing I needed to ask the next part. "To be away from your family? To choose to leave them?"

His eyes met mine, sensing the question wasn't only about his past. If he was presented with a choice between returning to his family and staying here with me, what would he choose? It scared me to admit to myself what I wanted his answer to be.

"It was the hardest choice I've ever made," he whispered, voice low and suddenly rough. "I love my family and would gladly die for them, but I fled, Shelbie. It wasn't even three days after our plan to steal the stallions had gone so terribly wrong, and I took off with no intention of returning. I left my clan full of grief, guilt, and remorse." Domari rolled away from me, staring at the ceiling as his hand rested on his broad chest.

"I stayed away because I felt unworthy of them. I couldn't look Erik in the eye after I allowed his daughter to die. I couldn't look at Gunnar, knowing I hadn't stopped his foolish plan and his sister had paid the price. And I especially couldn't look at Raud, devastated beyond belief at the loss of his beloved Tove." Domari stopped, clearing his throat before continuing. "The life of a Guard promised adventure, wealth, and glory. I was young and foolish. I thought I could drown my misery with these things. Escape my pain and guilt."

I nodded, hearing his words, my heart breaking for how miserable he must have been. I had seen his clan's grief for Erik's passing last fall, and Erik was old and frail then, not in his prime as Tove had been when she'd passed.

"Did you like serving in the Varangian Guard?" My fingers skimmed across the bands. Faint light caught on the golden rune charm on my red leather bracelet momentarily, and my fingers stilled.

He sighed, taking a moment to think through his answer. "I don't know. I was good at it. We served the Emperor directly, and they revered the Guard in the city. I worked my way through the ranks quickly until I led our unit. Battle comes easier to me than almost anything else. I fight on instinct, almost an out-of-body experience. Maybe that's just the way of Vikings born in our time, but even before the Norns showed up, I knew my fate was that of a warrior. Although I prefer to protect those I love rather than fight aimlessly for a cause I don't believe in. That's all the Guard was — fighting pointless wars for greedy emperors."

"Is the Guard all Vikings?"

A strange look passed over Domari's features I couldn't quite comprehend, but he didn't turn to face me, letting me trace my hands across his skin in a steady rhythm. "Mostly, yes. But we picked up several warriors after a battle in England. Several Saxons joined us after that."

"So you'd never go back to the Guard?"

His face tilted towards mine, brown eyes shining in the dim light. "No. I came back for you, Shelbie," he murmured, sliding his hands along my neck, ensuring I met his stare. "Before I knew that's why the Norns called me home, I chose you. I left the Guard, left Constantinople, and returned home, not knowing what awaited me was beyond my wildest dreams. *Who* waited for me."

Shying away from the naked love in his eyes and needing to distract myself from the emotions swirling in my chest, I focused instead on the shield on Domari's side. Sliding my hands from his arm down to his hip, I laid my palm flat against the ink. He tensed beneath me, his eyes heating with desire once more.

"What about this one?" I asked, gliding the tip of my finger across his skin slowly, following the curved line.

Domari's eyes slid to my hand, watching it move in a circle, tracing the shield's outer edge.

"My father's shield." Domari's answer was clipped, tone suddenly wooden.

My hand stilled, and Domari's large, calloused hand slid down to cover mine on his hip. He wasn't nearly as open as me, and I gave him time. He didn't have to answer, but I hoped he would. The more I learned about this man, the deeper I fell for him. Strength radiated from him in waves, both physically and in spirit. His eyes closed, squeezed shut as if battling away difficult memories of long ago.

"He was a warrior, in the truest sense," he spoke after a while, and I tucked my arm under my head as I listened. "Njal — the Giant — they called him." Domari's eyes opened, and he turned to me with a mischievous look. "Magnus looks a lot like my father, so you can imagine how large of a man he was to be named The Giant." Domari smirked, eyes far away, and I smiled in return.

Hand still resting over the top of mine on his hip, he laced his fingers through mine as he went on. "The clan I was born into wasn't like Erik's. Not like what you saw in our lands. They were brutal raiders, surviving off plunder more than their crops or trade, and consumed by greed."

That was easy to imagine — the Vikings remembered in our history books weren't the gentle, but fierce, people I'd met this fall. I recalled Signe's fearless strength, Magnus's warm friendship, Gunnar's kindness, and Yrsa and Björn's tender care… my heart ached for his people, missing them as I missed my own family.

"We were joined under Styrmir's clan then," Domari

interrupted my train of thought. "He was a fearsome jarl, but our territory was inland, and Styrmir craved the open sea. From there, he could raid distant lands and skip the hassle of the journey home. The winding rivers weren't domain enough for him, and he led our people in battles against our kind, set on seizing more land."

I listened intently as he spoke, the image he was painting of his past seeming so foreign to me here in the present with my warm house surrounding us, the radiator buzzing on the wall reminding me of just how far from home he was.

"Raids were often, and usually successful. Meanwhile, Erik was gathering his own following as he argued for trade routes further inland, away from the sea. My mother had passed that winter during a difficult childbirth that took both her and my sister, and Njal, my father, was seized with grief. Tora, my mother," Domari swallowed, letting my hand go. His fingers combed into the hair at my temples, his eyes soft and so sad, I ached. "Her hair curled like yours. It was wild but darker than mine. I remember that most about her. It danced in the breeze while she worked in her garden, like an angry storm cloud around her face." He chuckled at the memory, running one of my many curls through his fingers. Despite the curve of his mouth, his eyes pinched slightly at the corners, grief swimming through his gaze.

"Njal was never the same after she died," he continued, his thumb sliding across my jaw after his hand touched my neck. "We moved in with Frida and Erik, living in their longhouse when Tove and Gunnar were only small babes.

Njal was angry at the gods for taking Tora from him, and he drowned his misery in a drinking horn. He became reckless, signing on for every raid Styrmir suggested, looking for a reason to run from his past. From his pain."

My chest tightened as I read between the lines, feeling the sense of abandonment and grief Domari still carried from losing his family. He rolled to his back once more, dropping his hand from me as he became lost in his thoughts. I placed a hand over his heart, wishing I could take away his hurt, and he tangled our fingers, his shoulders easing into the bed.

"Anyway," he cleared his throat. "Styrmir was powerful, but our clan wasn't nearly as large as Egill's, to the west. Tired of Styrmir's encroaching, Egill's clan attacked ours in the night, killing almost everyone. Yrsa and Frida took the children into the forest and helped us climb trees. From my perch, I saw our men charge into battle to defend their families and homes, but they decimated us. My father was easy to spot among the men, taller than everyone, and he fought side by side with Erik and Björn, keeping Egill's men from coming closer to the forest and discovering where we hid. A man snuck by their guard, and Erik charged after him, set on stopping him, but exposed his back simultaneously. Njal was locked in battle, swords crossed when it happened. Everything was a blur, but my father dropped his guard to stop the axe that hurtled towards Erik, his only brother. It slammed into Njal's shield, but he took the blade to the side, sacrificing himself instead. Erik's roar, followed by Björn's brutal strength at the moment, was enough to draw the fight away from us. Protecting us in the forest."

A tear slipped free, sliding down my cheek as the air in the room became heavy.

"I'm so sorry," I whispered, running my hand across his arm, offering any comfort I could.

"It was long ago," Domari nodded, but he slid out from underneath my touch, dropping his feet off the side of the bed. He sat with his back to me as he leaned his weight on his hands pressed into the mattress, shoulders bunched with tension, and remembered pain.

I rose to my knees, laying my chest against his taut back, feeling his warmth radiate from his skin as I hugged him from behind. My chin rested on his shoulder, and I laid soft kisses along his neck. I would take his sadness from him if I could. I would ease all of his hurts.

"What about this one?" I asked, my lips touching down on the black ink of the knot tattooed there. "Is this a happier memory?"

His head tilted my way, a faint smile contradicting the sadness that filled his eyes. "It was, once. Yes."

Darkness consumes him, both inside and out, as the man flings himself into the cave and away from the storm outside. With nothing left to live for, he doesn't even bother to check if predators lurk within. Maybe it would be better that way...

In a matter of days, he'd lost his love, his family, his home, all gone in an instant. Gripping his dark hair in anguish, the man falls to his knees in the dirt, a devastating scream shaking the stalactites above.

"Why?" he bellows, tears streaming down his face. "What have I done to deserve this?"

But no one answers.

The gods never listen to his pleas.

Grief threatens to swallow him as he crouches there on the ground, hidden from all to see, holding a knife over his heart. If he can't be with her, he'd rather be in Hel, hunting her down again.

Heaving breaths escape him as he braces for the pain, feeling the prick of the blade. His hands shake as he presses it into his skin, willing himself the strength to go through with it.

Suddenly, the blade flies from his hand, crashing into the wall at the far end of the cave.

His eyes shoot up, wide in surprise, as he peers into the darkness, listening to his blade clatter to the rocks below, far in the distance.

"Who's there?" he calls, his voice echoing back to him through the empty space.

But no one answers.

Pushing to his feet, he moves through the murky darkness, hands outstretched, inching his way forward into the unknown.

20

SIGNE

The wind died down as Signe stared into the rafters, awake as she'd been so often lately in the night. The baby nuzzling at her breast didn't help the situation, but a general sense of foreboding followed her, even into her dreams. With the arrival of the children from her old village yesterday, she couldn't seem to fight off the memories of long ago.

The longhouse was dimly lit with the last of the hearth's blaze as the rest of her family dozed around her. Gunnar's face was relaxed in sleep as he leaned back against the rough-cut wooden walls behind him. Sometime in the night, he'd rolled to face her, and his hand rested easily on her hip. Warmth radiated from the contact, and Signe felt a hitch in her chest.

In the dark of the early morning, the quiet seemed to stretch around her. Signe's eyes roamed her husband's face, taking in the soft lines forming along his forehead. The stress of responsibility for his family and his village had been a difficult yoke for him to carry, but no one was more perfect for this job than Gunnar.

He was loyal.

He was fair.

He was a fierce protector.

He was genuine and true.

Even after eight years, Signe was in awe that such a man would choose her.

She was brutal.

She was harsh.

She was controlling.

She was *broken*.

Yes, she was strong, and she loved so deeply that it ached. But everything Signe had ever known had driven her with such an intense sense of purpose — no matter the task, Signe couldn't fail. She wouldn't allow it of herself.

Yesterday, she'd seen the hurt on Gunnar's face as he realized how little he knew about his wife. It was written clear as day in the way his eyes down-turned, the frown hidden in his golden beard, and the slope of his shoulders. And she'd done that to him.

She'd failed him.

Signe rubbed her hand across her aching chest as she scanned the man in front of her. Her breath came faster, her heart racing as she fought to contain the emotions trying to escape.

"You're weak," her father's words rang in her head as if called forth by her failure. *"I should have left you in that forest."*

All these years later, the memory clung to her still, cementing how worthless she was.

❄

Signe was barely older than her twins the day she'd tumbled from the roof, injuring her arm with the fall. Tears streamed down her face as she cradled the bruised and battered limb to her chest, walking to find her father in the field. Draugr sent her off with a scolding, a shake of the head, and disgust written in his every movement. Vermund's eyes tracked Signe across the thick grass as she made her way to the healer's, but her uncle said nothing.

The healer was kind, offering a poultice for the pain and tightly wrapping her arm to her chest. The wrap hid the black and blue marks just above her wrist, but the bone was straight and would heal. Signe listened to the woman's words, nodding as she heard her warnings about not climbing trees and rooflines, to stay on the ground and safe while she waited for the injury to subside. Signe's lip protruded as she pouted, kicking the dirt up as she made her way home.

Useless.

Injured.

A burden.

She hid for a day, unable to show her father her wounded arm, but Vermund found her sitting outside the longhouse the next morning, watching the villagers head out into the field for another long day of labor. The women sang as they worked in the gardens, and the sound of axes chopping trees beat like a drum in the forest around her.

"Get up," Vermund ordered as he dropped a wooden spear at her side. Her eyes shot up to his, searching her uncle for his intention as the sun glinted off his spear, hanging loosely from his hand. She crawled to her feet, grabbing the stick from the dirt as she straightened.

"Training begins now," he said, swinging the spear hard and slapping the wood against the shoulder of her injured arm. Signe

screamed, fighting with every muscle in her body not to vomit as the pain shot through her. Instinct told her to curl in on herself and wait out the beating, but her large uncle stooped low, his matching green eyes glaring into her own.

"I always thought you were stronger than this," Vermund sighed in disappointment, and Signe growled.

The pain ebbed as adrenaline flooded her system. She pushed the ringing in her ears aside as she brought up the heavy spear in her good hand, adjusting her grip as she aimed for her uncle's heart. He batted the spear to the side quickly, sending her to the ground with the weight of the movement.

"Get up," he ordered again as she snarled at him from the dirt. He kicked a clod up into the air, and Signe coughed, jumping back to her feet. Her hand tightened on the wooden shaft as the skirt of her dress moved around her, feeling the pressure in her hands as she squeezed the wood and lifted the heavy spear once more. Approval shone through Vermund's emerald gaze, light sparkling there momentarily as he watched her. "Again."

Signe's training with Vermund became a daily routine after that day, learning to fight with her whole body. An injury would never hold her back again, not that day or any after. She learned to wield spears, swords, axes, bows, knives… anything she could get her hands on. Even empty-handed, Signe was a weapon in her own right, driven by an inner fire that couldn't be extinguished, even by her father's cruel words.

Signe blinked away the memories. She turned on the bed, resting the same arm she'd injured so many years ago under her head as she stared into the dark home around her, focusing on where she knew the weapons hung on the opposite wall. Firelight danced off Gunnar's long blade hanging there and her own spear hanging to its right.

Two decades later, Signe could still feel the heat of her anger fueling her through that day and so many others since then. She turned, glancing over her shoulder at Gunnar lying peacefully beside her, and couldn't help but catalog their differences. If he knew the real her — how brutal, how ruthless, how angry she was — would he still choose her?

Her eyes burned with unshed tears as she fought against those thoughts, wishing she could slay them as easily as the foes in her bloody past. The only time she'd allowed herself to cry since that day with her injured arm was when she left Viveka. But the thought of losing Gunnar and everything this family meant to her hurt intensely in a way Signe could hardly understand.

Love, to her, was different. It wasn't a soft, tender thing. It was a fire, blazing bright in the dark of the night, ready to burn down any who challenged it.

Right now, Signe realized as her brow dipped in frustration, the biggest threat to Signe's love — to her family — was her own secrets. She knew, deep down, that she needed to be honest with Gunnar. He deserved to know about her past… But was she ready to face it? To examine the choices she'd made? The lives she'd taken? And for no reason other than victory and greed? Even if Gunnar could choose to overlook her mistakes, could Signe even forgive herself?

Unable to continue this line of thought, Signe pushed

against the soft furs beneath her, sitting with her feet dangling down to the packed dirt floors. She shifted the baby away, moving him into Gunnar's warm chest across the bed. Gunnar's eyes opened at the soft touch, heavy with sleep as he watched her.

"Rest." Signe feigned a smile, kissing the baby and then her husband before rising from the bed.

Her feet touched the ground as the fire in the hearth crackled, drawing her attention. A small black head rose from the floor, the puppy's dark eyes watching her as she stepped towards the hearth, like a moth to a flame. Feeling the heat wash over her skin, she glanced at her dozing children covered in blankets along the wall. Seeing their sweet faces pulled up the memory of the children sleeping in Frida's house across the clearing. Each one had an uncertain path before them, and their lives changed forever at the whim of brutal men. With each breath, each inhale, anger rose in her for what was happening to these children, what was happening to her people. Signe's jaw clenched as she stared into the flames, searching for a sign. A direction. Anything.

But no one was there to guide her. And Signe didn't need to be told how to handle a ruthless enemy leaving bodies in his wake.

Signe's spine straightened as she paced to the far side of the longhouse, sliding the dagger into its holster along her thigh. Her eyes glanced to the spear Vermund had given her so many years ago, faintly glowing red in the low light. With one last look behind her, she tiptoed from the house and out into the night.

❄

The moon was long gone, but the lights and stars still danced overhead as Signe's feet crunched through the snow, her eyes scanning for unseen enemies, knowing she wasn't alone. Standing in the clearing in front of Frida's longhouse was another. The pinks and greens above illuminated a slight frame, hair black as night and green eyes that matched her own.

Signe lifted the fur she carried in addition to her cloak, draping it over the girl's shoulders and then her own, before sinking them to the ground against the house.

"How have you been?" Signe asked, and the question sounded idiotic even in her head.

Viveka laughed lightly, her head drifting down to lean on Signe's shoulder. "I survived."

Emotion choked Signe at her words, knowing exactly everything this girl had to *survive* in their village and hating herself even more for leaving her behind. "I never meant to leave you," Signe whispered, the words so quiet they seemed to be snatched by the soft breeze blowing over the snow. "I didn't want to."

Viveka sniffed, wiping a hand across her face, but said nothing.

"Verandi showed up that day," Signe went on, even though she knew the words would be useless. Pain like Viveka had survived, pain that Signe's absence had created, couldn't be explained away. "She told me our only way to survive was apart. But I've missed you every day I've been gone, Viveka."

"Why didn't you come back for me?" the girl muttered after a while, and Signe's heart shattered at her words.

"I wanted to." She swallowed, mouth dry as she thought through her following words. "More than anything, I wanted to." Slipping a hand around the girl's shoulders, she dropped a kiss to her head, hoping Viveka could feel the depth of emotion she held for her. Neither said anything for several minutes, staring up at the night sky above them, clinging to each other after so many years apart.

"Life here is different." Signe heaved a sigh, glancing back to her longhouse across the clearing.

"I noticed," Viveka chuckled, and Signe wished she could bottle the sound to replay in a quiet moment, savoring it beyond anything else. "I have to say; I don't know that I ever pictured you with your own children. You were never the most patient with me."

Signe grunted, and Viveka chuckled once more. "But I kept you alive, didn't I?"

The easy smile dropped from Viveka's face as she stared up at Signe, silently nodding. "That you did."

Signe couldn't bear the sadness she saw in Viveka's eyes, knowing the life she would have had after Signe had abandoned her, so she glanced out at the forest instead. "Is he still looking for me?"

Feeling the weight of Viveka's gaze, Signe turned her eyes, watching as the girl dipped her chin in a silent nod. Instantly, a weight settled on Signe's shoulders, glancing back at the house her family slept within. Rage simmered in her veins at the thought of any harm coming to them or anyone in this village, of the damage done to Viveka in her absence, of the lives taken, but that wasn't a problem for this morning.

Eight years had passed, lulling Signe into a sense of peace, but she should have known better. Draugr had never seen her as an independent person, capable of making her own choices. He *owned* his daughter, and even time wouldn't change that. Pushing the intrusive thoughts away, her focus settled on the girl in front of her, remembering Viveka's words from the night before.

"Explain," Signe ordered, then kicked herself internally for her harsh words as Viveka's eyes widened. "Why are you here? What did Vermund mean by following the dragon?"

"I didn't understand at first," Viveka started. "You know what happened last time I saw a dragon."

"I haven't forgotten," Signe mumbled, flashes of a bruised and beaten young girl rising in her mind.

The day Viveka had come home claiming to have found a white dragon in a cave had been the worst beating Signe had ever witnessed, even on a child so small. After sending his men into the mountains and they returned after a fruitless search, Draugr had lashed out at Viveka, using her as an example for the whole clan as to what happened when lies were spread in front of him. Signe ground her teeth at the memory of Vermund watching, fists balled but never stepping in to defend his daughter against their cruel leader and his punishment. Then Signe had done what no man in their clan had dared to do — she stepped in front of Viveka, blocking Draugr's next blow. Even as his hand slapped across her face, her father hadn't hesitated to continue his beating, leaving Signe black and blue.

"Was it the white dragon again?" Signe asked, unable to even speak the dragon's name. While she hadn't been with Viveka that day in the mountains, some part of Signe had always believed Viveka's story. "Did you see him again?"

Viveka shook her head, shivering slightly in the cold air. "No, not him." Her emerald eyes lifted to meet Signe's, staring intently with honesty, waiting for Signe to catch on to what she implied.

Signe's head reared back as she reeled at this information. "Another?"

"The Dark One." Viveka's voice filled with awe as she whispered the legendary dragon's title, leaning forward as if to emphasize her point. "Hadriel."

Signe wanted to laugh. As with everything, dragon tales loved to tell of good and evil. Hadriel was the dragon that supposedly battled Nidhoggr, the White Dragon, if stories were to be believed. But Nidhoggr, known for his bloodthirstiness, was carved into the front of her father's ships, stained white with blood-red eyes. Viveka's admission seemed far-fetched, but something deep inside Signe believed the girl.

"Hadriel," Signe paused, letting the word drift through the air.

Even then, the distant sound of flapping wings drifted through the valley. Signe's hair suddenly brushed back as Viveka's eyes shifted to the forest.

"Kára said it was the same for them. She never saw anything more than glimpses of Hadriel, but their path was as easy as ours on their way here," she whispered. Signe studied Viveka, remembering the way Kára had reacted the night Magnus told the dragon stories. Before she could ask more, Viveka spoke again. "He's still here."

Signe's eyes darted to the forest. "You can feel him? Can you *hear* him?"

Viveka shook her head, her shoulders drooping. "No," she said sincerely, "I can't. I'm not his Promised."

Signe didn't know whether to be relieved or worried by the defeat in Viveka's voice at those words. Memories returned to her, remembering the many times she'd listened to the story of Lovisa, the battle sorceress Signe had idolized and the first of the Promised. If legends were to be believed, each first-born daughter of Lovisa's descendants was given in servitude to the dragons.

In her worst childhood moments, Signe had dreamt that her mother had been Promised, and that's why she left — to be with her dragon. That, Signe thought, was a good enough reason to leave your only daughter. By the same reasoning, if Hilda had been a Promised, then Signe, as her firstborn daughter, would have been as well. The dream of a dragon scooping her up to fly her away from her terrible life had rocked her to sleep, carrying her through the longest nights, battered, bruised, and alone.

To be chosen as a Promised was something Signe could barely comprehend. As legendary as the dragons were, the Promised fighting at their sides matched before birth. The Dragons' chosen — blessed and cursed with powers that allowed for healing, sight, or communing with the gods.

Signe's green eyes scanned Viveka as they'd done so

many times before, wondering what secrets Viveka's mother had kept when she left her infant on a fearsome warlord's doorstep. What secrets lay in Signe's own mother's past?

Shoulder to shoulder, the two gazed over the trees, listening to the sound of the wind, branches rustling like giants moving within. Together, they watched the darkness swirl around them on the longest day of the year, huddled in their furs. Long pauses of silence passed between them as they watched the stars in the night sky, feeling the world around them turn. The air was bitterly cold, but Signe grew numb to the feel, just as she'd been numb to her own emotions for so long.

Viveka spoke quietly, whispering more about the harrowing trip they'd made across the frozen lands to end up here, at her home. She told of how the dragon never left them, guiding them the entire way as he hovered overhead, clearing the worst of the snow to make it easier on the children. She spoke of the wash of heat they'd felt when the children shook from the cold. She spoke of how the animals in the surrounding forests fled from their presence. She spoke of the fresh kills they happened upon, left as if in offering *to* legendary beings, not *from* one.

A dragon.

The more Signe listened to the girl, the harder her mind worked to believe the tale. It had been years since she'd last seen Viveka, but even still… Signe trusted her. Dread pooled in Signe's stomach as she fought to understand what was happening to her. To all of them. Fate was pulling them towards some unknown destination, and Signe wanted to lash out against it.

But the feel of Viveka slouching, energy draining from the girl as she leaned into Signe's side, was enough to still her racing mind. Without thinking, Signe's hand drifted down to the girl leaning against her, rubbing her palm across her arm.

Signe's chin tilted towards the sky, her long blonde hair falling nearly to her waist as she stared up at the twinkling lights above her, listening to the sounds of the surrounding night. Suddenly, the sound faded, and Signe's spine straightened as her head swiveled, searching out the predator that would silence the other night creatures.

There, to her left, darkness pooled above the forest. The tingling sense of awareness she'd felt so many times in her life drew her focus in as her heart beat rapidly in her chest. Waiting. Watching.

It moved.

Signe's breath caught as she watched the darkness spread, drawing closer, rising higher, weaving in and out of the pink and greens above. Her eyes darted through the sky, seeking the source… *feeling* it. Hand drifting to the dagger strapped to her hip, Signe gripped the hilt, ready to leap into action at a moment's notice. Still, Viveka slept, unaware of whatever moved towards them.

Willing her heart to slow, Signe forced her breaths to even, sinking into a killing calm she hadn't felt in ages as that awareness moved closer. Her head tilted momentarily to the girl at her side. No matter how much time had passed, the sight of the wild black curls dipping down over the pale face resting on her shoulder had Signe's heart seizing.

The darkness receded as quickly as it appeared, and the sounds returned as if Signe had only imagined it. Adrenaline pumped in her veins as she fought to release the pent-up energy, the clouds from her warm breath coming in great puffs as she tried to settle herself. Minutes ticked by as the lights swirled overhead, undisturbed. That same *feeling* that had drawn Signe's attention to the forest was gone, and she took a deep breath, holding it for a moment before releasing it. She gently shook Viveka's shoulder, helping her stand and return to the warm house.

Today was the Solstice celebration, and there was work to be done.

21

SIGNE

Hours after their morning conversation, Viveka's words still filled Signe's mind. She'd returned to her home, gathered baby Erik from the bed, and wrapped him tightly to her chest, feeling his steady heartbeat against her own. Shoving her emotions aside as Signe had done so expertly her entire life, she padded to the hearth to bake for the day's festivities.

Today was a celebration. They'd glimpse the sun sometime later, but the day would remain mostly dark. The longest night. Tomorrow, the sun would return, even for mere moments more than today — a promise of a brighter future, of good fortune to come.

"Good morning." Gunnar's voice was scratchy from sleep as he approached her from their palette. His chest was bare, and no matter her mixed feelings towards her husband at the moment, she couldn't take her eyes off his chiseled chest. Tattoos scattered across his skin; the knot tattooed on his neck matched Domari's — four strands, interwoven together, inseparable, and a band of runes covered his collarbone from shoulder to shoulder. The black ink had faded over the years, but it was still prominent against his clean, pale skin.

Gunnar's lips tipped up as he watched his wife appraise him. His movements seemed unhurried, intentional as he lifted his arms, slowly pulling the shirt over his chest. Signe cleared her throat, dropping her eyes back down to the dough in front of her, but she didn't miss the deep rumble that rolled through Gunnar's chest as he moved closer.

"About Viveka," Signe said, the words rushing out before she lost her nerve. Gunnar said nothing, and her eyes rose again to find him, reading his reaction. Gunnar stood back from the table, expression shuttered as he waited.

"I'd like her to stay here," Signe went on.

"Of course." Gunnar nodded without hesitation, scratching his fingers through his beard along his chin. "Is that all?"

She opened her mouth to go on, but words were lost on her. She didn't know how to mend this rift between them. Would he even believe the tale Viveka told her this morning? Feeling wildly protective of the girl — of *all* the children — Signe's mouth snapped shut.

Gunnar's jaw worked, frustration creasing his brow as he stepped into her space, and anger rose in Signe to match him. He backed her into the table, her backside bumping up against the wood as he loomed over her, pushing in. Signe's eyes shifted back and forth between his, so close she could hardly focus, but she refused to cower. Her hand lifted between them, resting over the baby's back, and

Gunnar's eyes tracked the movement, hurt flashing in his eyes once more.

"I love you, Signe," Gunnar whispered as he deflated visibly before her. "I loved you the moment I met you, even when I knew *nothing* about you."

Her heart jolted in her chest at his words, more true than even he knew.

"And I love you now," he continued, placing a hand on her hip and pulling her gently into his chest. His mouth dropped to her ear. "You can't change that. I will not leave you. I will not judge you. I will not betray you. So get those thoughts out of your mind."

Signe breathed heavily through her nose, the sound echoing through the quiet house.

"But you *will* be honest with me," Gunnar went on, and her head snapped up at his words, eyes expanding at the tone he took with her. It was fierce and demanding — one she'd heard him use countless times on others, but never on her. "I will not allow secrets in this house."

"Or what?" The words left her mouth before she could even think through the stupidity of the statement. She was challenging him, even now.

But Gunnar said nothing. He pulled back suddenly and turned away from her. Nevertheless, she saw the flash of pain on his face as he walked away.

A silent scream filled Signe's head as she raged internally. Why was she like this? Why, even now, when he was extending his terms, showing her what she needed to fix this rift between them, did she push back?

Ripping the door open, Gunnar shrugged into his cloak

and left the house. Signe's hands slammed down hard on the dough in front of her as she watched, feeling the wash of cold air from outside as she punished the bread for her crimes. The baby cried at the sudden noise, and Signe sank to the ground, folding in on herself.

"I'm sorry," she whispered, brushing her shaking hand across the baby's soft tuft of hair. But it wasn't only the baby she spoke to. "I'm so sorry."

The words were choked, filled with emotion Signe didn't know how to let go of.

All day, Signe fought to control her emotions, to return to the same calm, but demanding, nature the Eriksson clan expected from her. It had taken her years to settle into this role, to hang up her anger and weapons side by side, but the sense of foreboding, of imminent danger, wouldn't release her.

Rage fueled her.

A berserker in the form of a woman, ready to be unleashed on the world.

Standing in her doorway, Signe closed her eyes, forcing those feelings down as she'd always done, willing her breath to even, her heart to steady. Slowly, she lifted her lids, green eyes shining bright as she stepped forward, ready to play her role once more. Fur cloak billowing behind her in the wind, Signe stomped through the snow towards Frida's home, listening to the sounds leaking from within.

The door was open, and Signe paused, scanning the

room from outside. The space was crowded as all ten families gathered in the longhouse. Ale flowed freely, passed around in drinking horns. Laughter rang through the room, and Signe breathed in the cold air. Her breath fogged as she exhaled, forcing herself to step through the door.

"How's my nephew?" Magnus boomed, pulling Signe into a crushing hug before she could even adjust to the change in temperatures. She cringed at the contact but had grown used to the big man's affections over the last several years. The more she pushed away from him, the more he seemed to think it was a game, pulling her in for more.

"He'd be better if you weren't crushing him," she shot back, and Magnus chuckled as he released her, running his large hand over Erik's black hair lovingly.

The thought of Magnus being a father soon was jarring for Signe. Some days it was hard to comprehend the hulking, bearded man in front of her was the same boy that had been counting facial hairs, combing the few pale ones he managed to grow when Signe had joined their village eight years ago. Despite Magnus's obnoxious habit of hugging Signe without permission, she couldn't help but adore him. His constant smile was a bright spot in her life, and his attitude was catching.

"Drink with me," Magnus grinned as he passed her a horn, the contents sloshing over the brim. Her chin tipped up, appraising the man in front of her as a loud hiccup escaped him.

"I see you started early," she chuckled with a shake of her head.

"Well, *someone* needs to lighten the mood," Magnus

retorted, bumping her shoulder with his elbow. "We both know it won't be you and Gunnar." He took a long sip of his ale, eyeing her the entire time.

Magnus wasn't wrong, but the words stung just the same. Instead of answering, Signe lifted the drinking horn to her lips and took a deep pull. She was pleasantly surprised that Magnus had filled hers with mead instead of ale. Their casks of mead were low, but the sweet, crisp taste hit her tongue and burned the back of her throat.

"I've missed this," she said, sipping again, although less of a guzzle than before.

Before she could duck out of his reach, Magnus leaned down and planted a loud, wet kiss on the top of her head. "Be nice to him, sister." With that, he walked away.

Her eyes trailed Magnus as he circled the room, laughter following him in every conversation. Magnus was at his best a few ales in — jovial and entertaining, easing the never-ending pressure of Viking life. Tonight, that was desperately needed. He mingled with the other clan members, stopping to pick up children and swing them in wide arcs, passionately kissing Astrid until her cheeks flamed red.

Signe shook her head as she watched from her spot near the door. The only problem with Magnus's drinking was that it didn't take long for him to become obnoxious. How a man so large could get drunk so fast was still a mystery to her. From how he was going, he wasn't too far off from poetry recitations; Asgard help them all. Another time, she would have laughed at his actions, but tonight was different.

Several villagers stopped to chat with her where she

stood at the entrance, asking after her, the baby, and the new children. She smiled, chatting easily as expected, but could hardly break her gaze from Gunnar.

Light from the sconces on the wall flickered over the room, washing the entire scene with a golden hue. Smoke rose from the hearth at the center, where several men stood in a circle, including her husband.

Gunnar seemed stiff. His shoulders were tense, jaw tight, betraying more about his unease than anything else, even though he drank and smiled with the villagers. Signe sipped at her mead, her head swimming with the strength of the alcohol she'd watered down for months during her pregnancy. The buzz was enough to loosen her, drawing her away from the tumultuous thoughts that had swirled inside her head for days.

Without conscious thought, she drifted closer to her husband, floating through the room with every sip. Gunnar always seemed to be aware of her position, but tonight, he was avoiding her gaze. With the mead thrumming in her veins, the hurt transformed into anger — a much more familiar emotion for her.

"Hold the baby for me?" Signe stopped next to Astrid. Her young sister-in-law reclined on one of the palettes in the wall with Viveka and Kára, and several children played at their feet, including Signe's twins.

"Of course." Astrid smiled, taking Erik from Signe as she unwrapped him. Signe undid the fabric wrap she wore around her chest and left it piled on the bed, faking pleasantries with the girls as a plan formed in her mind. Viveka's eyes never left Signe, that green gaze burning into Signe's skin as if sensing where her mind had gone, but the girl said nothing.

Adjusting her crimson dress, snug and low-cut, showing ample cleavage even under her fur-lined cloak, Signe sighed as her back straightened and lifted the drinking horn to her lips once more.

"Thank you." Signe smiled at Astrid. Astrid had already focused on the children again and shooed Signe away from the wall.

With her children cared for, Signe wove her way around the room's periphery, sipping at the sweet alcohol as she mingled, the skirts of her dress and cloak swishing around her. Magnus had worked his magic — everyone was laughing and festive as Björn sang, his voice deep and melodic. The beauty his voice portrayed always was shocking to Signe, so unexpected from the bear of a man, his grey beard hanging down almost to his belt.

But Signe's focus wasn't on him. Her eyes were locked on the golden man in the middle of the room who had yet to glance her way. Light from the torches sparkled off his amber locks, and the room's heat seeped into her bloodstream.

She was done letting Gunnar ignore her. If he wanted the truth... she'd give it to him. The alcohol thrumming in her veins urged her into action, unable to wait even a moment longer to get this over with.

Her hips swung with every pass she made around the room. Eventually, she caught Gunnar's gaze, holding it for only a moment before moving on, chatting with each of the men in the room. Soon, she noticed Gunnar's eyes never left her. Her lip tilted as she smirked, working her way towards the door.

She locked her eyes on his for one beat... two... before turning and walking out.

The chill of the cold air should have been enough to snap Signe out of the drunken haze she found herself in, but heat flowed in her veins, blaming it on a combination of alcohol and hormones. Before she had time to even step to the side of the house, the door swung open and shut again behind her.

Signe stepped into the shadows, hand drifting down into her pocket and through the hole sliced there, as it was in every one of her gowns. The metal along her leg was warm to the touch as her fingers closed around it.

She watched as Gunnar turned, brow creased while he searched the clearing for her. She drew back as he stepped towards her, waiting for the right moment. A split second before his gaze swung towards her, Signe lunged, pinning her large husband to the wall, silver metal glistening in the moonlight as she held the dagger to his throat.

"Signe..." Gunnar uttered as confusion settled over his face. She pressed the blade harder into his throat, watching the muscles move. His eyes drew down, searching hers for the meaning of her actions.

"You want honesty?" Signe's teeth clenched as she fought her instinct to push the blade further and draw blood as she'd done so many times before. "I'll show you honesty. *This* is who I am, Gunnar."

His eyes glanced back and forth between hers as he

breathed shallowly, lifting his hands into the air in surrender to her much smaller frame.

"I'm the *Demon's Spawn*. Draugr the Demon is my father. Do you *know* how I earned my name?" Her eyes were slits in the moonlight, fury coursing through her veins as her cloak rose behind her, lifting in the wind.

Gunnar said nothing, staring down at her as his lips turned down.

"I've killed more men than I care to count. Hel," a bitter laugh escaped her, "Magnus probably can't even count that high. And I did it for *sport*." She spat the words at him, her hair lifting in the wind as the moonlight cast deep shadows across her fearsome expression. She'd never hurt him, but she needed him to *understand*.

"I earned my name by being the first one to rage into battle on every pointless raid my father allowed me to join him. I'm vicious. I'm ruthless. I show no mercy. I will stop at *nothing* to win."

"Signe — " Gunnar tried to interrupt, but Signe leaned in, pressing the blade harder against his neck.

"No, *Gunnar*," Signe snarled, "you don't understand. I'm the last person you should want in your village. At your side. The mother of your children. I never meant to stay this long."

At her words, Gunnar shifted against her, pressing the blade in deeper until a line of red appeared against the metal.

"Enough," Gunnar hurled the word back at Signe. Her eyes fixated on the vermillion streak left across his pristine skin, and her grip loosened, appalled that she'd drawn

blood. Gunnar seized the moment and yanked her hand away from his neck.

Signe's eyes squinted at the challenge, teeth bared, ready for a fight. But when her eyes caught Gunnar's gaze, it wasn't a battle she saw there.

"Yes, you *are* vicious," Gunnar said, and Signe reared away as if he'd slapped her, but he wouldn't allow it. Gunnar's grip on Signe's wrist tightened as he jerked her body into his and flipped their positions. Rage fueled her again as her back slapped against the wood of the house behind her, shoving back against her husband, but his grip didn't loosen. "You're viciously protective of those that are yours."

Signe sucked in a breath as her head swam with his words. Her body stilled under him, the fight leaving her with each word.

"Yes, you are ruthless," he went on, leaning his heaving chest into hers, feeling her pounding heartbeat against his own. "Ruthless in your pursuit of justice, ensuring what's right is done."

Her eyes burned as she cast them to the side, unable to stare at the man in front of her any longer. Gunnar delicately placed a finger under her chin, lifting her face back to his.

"You show no mercy," he continued, "to those who don't deserve it."

A tear slipped from her eye, betraying the well of emotions buried deep inside her.

"You stop at nothing to win," Gunnar finished, "and I could want nothing more for my people. *Especially* my children. What a fierce, determined example you provide for them. You've taught our children that there's *nothing* they can't do, and I'm so proud of you for it."

Signe lifted her damp lashes, glancing up at her husband in front of her.

"And if you *ever* leave me," he growled between clenched teeth, "I will hunt you to the ends of this earth. There's nowhere you can hide from me, as my heart calls to yours, as I know yours does to mine."

Signe hardly had a moment to catch her breath before Gunnar snatched it, slamming his lips down on hers. Her arms circled his neck, pulling her body up into his warmth, emotions making her almost feral.

She had always known her husband was too good for her, but even now, the depth of his love was incomprehensible to her, even after all of these years. But she couldn't let this go on.

"He'll come for me," Signe drew back, pulling away from Gunnar's embrace, receding into the wall behind her. "Gunnar… you don't understand. My father —"

"Has no claim on you anymore," Gunnar interrupted again.

The intensity of his words sent Signe's pulse into a gallop, matched by the heat in her husband's stare. She parted her lips to argue further, but he cut her off again.

"I don't *care* about your past. I don't *care* if you've left a wake of bodies behind you. I don't *care* if your father is still angry with you for leaving him after all these years," Gunnar seethed, pushing a knee between her legs as he pinned her to the wall with his heavy weight. "He can't have you. You're *mine.*"

Signe panted at the viciousness she saw in her husband, the way he was fighting for her. She shook her head in disbelief as she battled internally to accept what was written plain as day on Gunnar's face.

"Raud knows my name," Signe whispered, fingers digging into the woolen fabric of her husband's shirt, begging him to understand. "He's with my father. It's only a matter of time before they connect me to them, and they will come straight here, hunting me."

Gunnar only shook his head. "Fate is pulling us towards something. I feel it, and I know you do as well. The children. The dragon. Raud." His expression faltered momentarily at the name, but his eyes snapped with fierce intensity. "If what fate has in store includes Draugr coming for you, then we will face him as we've done everything these last eight years. Together."

Feeling the weight of his words, Signe's gaze met Gunnar's, and the cool, still water there as Gunnar warred with his rage matched her fire, balancing her as he always did. Warmth spread from Signe's chest to between her legs, and she rubbed her thighs together beneath her skirts. Sensing her need, Gunnar's hands slid from her grip, bunching in the crimson fabric of her dress.

"If your father shows his face here — in our village — we will be ready. And the moments he shares with my children — my *wife* — will be his last."

Gunnar's lip peeled up in a snarl moments before he tipped his head, pressing his mouth over her pulse in her neck. A slow smirk spread across Signe's face as she watched the stars above, running her fingers through her husband's golden hair.

Tomorrow would bring light into their darkest days. Tomorrow, they would prepare for whatever came next. And they'd meet it together.

22

SHELBIE

Sun leaked through the window as I sat at my desk, lost in thought. Five weeks had passed since Christmas, and I wanted to feel *normal*. Each day, Domari and I worked together to help feed and care for the horses, mucking stalls, changing hay, and exercising them. Once those tasks were done, he tended to focus on the manual labor Charlene needed help with around the ranch, and I sat at my desk, scribbling anything that came to mind. Almost always, I ended up penning my dreams, focused intently on the Viking world we'd left behind. Almost always, they were far darker than the world around me, full of pain and anguish that felt so real, I couldn't seem to shake it.

Lately, whenever I shut my eyes, I was transported back in time. Sometimes I watched myself drop my bracelet under the roots of the Tree, witnessing Domari crashing to the ground, curled over my seemingly lifeless form. Others, like the girl's story on the shore with the Norns, I wasn't sure what made me imagine those scenes playing out like a movie in my mind. And Signe — I had two journals filled with stories I hardly remembered writing featuring the woman, let alone brainstorming these backstories for her. Why was I picturing her and these children so clearly? I felt her pain in my heart, crippling as it washed over me, dragging me under like a relentless tide set on drowning me.

To some extent, I understood why my mind drifted back to the Eriksson clan. It wasn't only Domari I'd fallen in love with last fall — it was his whole village I'd connected with. Magnus and his wild story-telling. Gunnar and his easy confidence. Yrsa and her tender care. Signe, though…

I glanced down at the story I'd written last, the dream that had seemed so real. It was as if I'd been there, watching from above as Signe sat in the snow with a younger girl, hair raven black and curls as wild as my own. I didn't recognize the girl, but Signe… it felt like she watched me. Could see me in the distance. This dream I'd had so many times lately since Christmas, replaying over and over in my mind as my eyes connected with hers across the forest and fields covered in snow.

Something about her seemed to call me as if I could sense she needed me, but that was outrageous. First, Signe was stronger than anyone I'd ever met — she *needed* no one. And the thought of being able to sense others' distress, especially someone a thousand years ago, was even more ridiculous than time travel.

Still, the Erikssons tugged at me. While my life seemed to be a waking dream lately with Domari in my life, everything I'd ever wanted in a relationship at my fingertips, I felt *broken*. A crack was forming in my mind, pulling half of me back to a time I didn't even know how to return to. Melancholy followed me throughout the day, seeping into my bones, pulling me down in a way I couldn't comprehend.

I had hoped journaling and writing these stories down would help distance myself from them, banishing the fictional scenes to paper and out of my mind, but that clearly wasn't working. I even debated telling Domari about them, but I'd seen how he shut down after sharing his own story about his tattoos. I couldn't bring myself to remind him even more of everything he had unintentionally left behind and had no way to return to. My chest ached as I thought of having to make that choice myself, to leave my life and family behind for good.

No.

I couldn't show this side of me to anyone. Everything was still so new with Domari, the last thing I needed was to bring us down. More than ever, these poisonous thoughts needed to stay my own.

Last fall, I'd sank to what I thought was rock bottom, leaving everything I knew behind — my home, my job, even to some extent, my friendships. I could still see the way my parents and Sabrina had looked at me when I'd returned, sad eyes full of pity and worry, and I hated it. More than ever, I was avoiding them, drained by the thought of having to plaster on a happy face when I *should* feel happy.

I *wanted* to be happy.

Domari was here, showering me with love and affection like I'd never known before. Charlene made me feel *seen* in a way I could hardly describe. I loved these sweet horses and this simpler way of life. I was recreating myself, a new and improved Shelbie, focused on what *I* wanted. So why did I feel such never-ending dread? Why wasn't I as happy as I wanted everyone to think I was?

Frustrated with myself, I tapped my pen on the paper, chewing my lip as I stared out at Domari working in the yard, needing a distraction. Thor trailed behind him as Domari carried hay towards the largest barn, drool-worthy muscles flexing in his back.

The front door creaked open as I spun on my chair, turning to where Charlene walked towards me, glancing at the bag of home goods I'd purchased yesterday in town — yet another fruitless distraction.

"Let's have a little girl chat, shall we?" she said as she lifted the bag of home goods, inspecting my new curtains I planned on hanging in the office. "A lot of white in here. You suddenly don't believe in color?"

I shook my head as a laugh escaped me and showed her the one Boho-style pillow I couldn't bring myself to pass up.

"That's more like it. I like that one."

I glanced down at the sunshine yellow and turquoise pattern, bright and cheery. The way I wish I felt. *Wanted* to feel.

"You doing okay, sweetie?" Charlene asked, drawing my attention back to her. "I love having Domari here to help and to stare at, sure. The view does *not* hurt." She paused, turning to watch him out the window with a mumbled sound of approval. "Not at all," she whispered before looking back at me. I bit my cheeks to not smile, because I couldn't disagree with her, but then noticed the way her expression changed as she pulled up the extra chair and sat down, elbows on her knees. "Listen. If he's not the one, if this is what's got you so down lately, you let me know, and we can find the nearest wormhole to shove him through. Go back to just us girls."

"What?" I asked as my eyebrows shot up into my hairline. "Why would you think I'm not okay? I love Domari. I'm happy. This is what I wanted."

Charlene hesitated as she squinted her hazel eyes. "You trying to convince me or yourself?"

My mouth hung open as I fought to come up with any response. It wasn't Domari making me feel this way — but how could I explain it? She'd accepted my explanation of time travel easy enough, but dreams and nightmares ruining even my waking moments? I sounded crazy, even to myself.

"You haven't asked for my advice, but I'm giving it anyway," she said, the light catching on her sparkly belt buckle when she shifted her weight, shining a rainbow across the walls. "If you're hooking your happiness to someone else's horse, you'll always be led astray. Grab the reins of your own life and make yourself happy, baby girl. Figure out what *you* want, what makes *you* happy, and fuck the rest."

"It's not that simple, though," I retorted, my mind reeling from this conversation. "What if this isn't forever? What if he's sent back? I don't even know how he ended up here, or how much time we'll have, or —"

Charlene's scoff interrupted me. "Time is a luxury

none of us have. And unless you can suddenly see the future, we'll never know how much time we have. I didn't know I'd only have 20 years with Nash, but I wouldn't trade any of them, even knowing I'd lose him in the end. Live for today, and stop worrying about tomorrow. That's the best advice I can give you. That, and don't join a cult."

I chuckled, and Charlene grinned at my reaction. She pulled me into a quick hug, squeezing tight, then left without another word.

The door clicked shut behind Charlene, but her words clung to me.

"Live for today, and stop worrying about tomorrow," I repeated over and over as I stared down at my journal. "Right. Just... *let it go*." Thor padded by me, glancing back with an intense side eye as he looked between me and the hallway leading back into the house.

My eyes caught on the motion in the yard, watching as Charlene stopped to talk with Domari momentarily. She waved her hands around as she spoke, and I couldn't help but wonder what the two were discussing. They'd figured out some simple ways to communicate despite the language barrier, but each time I saw the tiny, vivacious woman next to tall, serious Domari, I couldn't help but smile.

Domari dropped the hay at the front of the barn, and turned to stride back towards the house. His steps were hurried, but he didn't look angry, and curiosity banished the last of the darkness from my mind momentarily. I slid my pen inside the journal, holding my place for later, and pushed back from the desk to meet him at the door.

The pink door swung open as I approached, and his

bright eyes were enough to snag my attention. I tilted my head in question, crossing my arms against the cool air whipping through the house. "What are you two up to?"

Domari's face turned up in a downright *grin* that reminded me of Magnus. "Charlene is teaching me to drive." His eyebrows waggled in excitement, and I burst into laughter, already feeling lighter in his presence, loving the way he always tugged me into his arms.

"You're joking."

Tilting his head down to look at me, he said, "There's nothing funny about this. I can sail a boat. I can ride a horse bareback as I charge into battle, wielding an axe. I want to drive a car."

"Fine then." I threw my hands into the air, stepping out of his embrace, but reveled in his cheerfulness —exactly what I needed to pull me out of my funk. "Don't crash my Jeep."

"I don't want your tiny Jeep," Domari huffed as he glanced back over his shoulder, eyes glistening with delight. "I want Charlene's truck."

A chuckle escaped me as I shook my head. "Of course you do."

His teeth flashed in another grin, and my insides flip-flopped.

I really did love Domari.

And I really was happy with him.

He studied me for a moment, a crease forming between his brows as he pulled me into his chest, hugging me tightly once more. "Are you okay?"

I nodded, letting his warmth seep into me and banish

the last of the darkness. Here, in his arms, I *was* okay. It wasn't a lie. But the fact that he could see through my facade was frightening. "I am now."

Pulling back, he knocked a finger under my chin and dropped a kiss to my lips. "I love you."

I drifted through the living room and into the kitchen after Domari left, pouring myself another glass of iced coffee. Dishes stacked in the sink, not dirty, but not *clean* either, and the sight of the clutter bothered me, but not enough to do anything about it. The floors could probably use a good mopping, too. In fact, my house had gotten away from me, and I needed to do something about it.

Putting the pitcher back into the fridge, I leaned against the door, looking back over the mostly-unpacked but cluttered kitchen. My breath caught when I noticed a small wooden figure of a dragon on the counter, meticulously painted black and gold. Lifting it, I felt the ridges along the dragon's spine, seeing how the green reflected from his eyes, so like Hadriel. Memories of standing in his presence, feeling the heat wash over me as he breathed into my space, sent a shiver down my spine. The thought of him was still probably the *most* unbelievable part of my story last fall. I fiddled with my rune bracelet at the thought of the dragon, stirring the milk and cinnamon into my coffee.

Promised, that same raspy voice I imagined so often rang through my head but was soon drowned out by the sounds of crunching gravel outside, and I glanced out the front window. Brakes screeched a moment later, and Charlene's massive white truck lurched forward again. I chuckled, put the lid on my stainless steel cup, and drifted to the front window to watch, the dragon still clutched in my palm.

Peeling back the blue floral curtains, I didn't bother to fight the smile spreading across my face as I imagined the conversation that must be happening inside the vehicle. Over and over it went, until the truck moved forward slowly, crawling across the drive. My neck craned, any thoughts of cleaning gone as I watched the wheels roll slowly over the ground.

Honestly, Thor and I could jog faster than that truck was moving, and that was saying something. I wasn't a runner.

Curiosity got the best of me, and I pulled the front door open, Thor on my heels as I plopped down into a rocking chair on the porch, throwing a blanket over my legs. I sipped my iced coffee — snow on the ground, be damned — in the morning light, watching the truck drive laps around the ranch. Charlene's silhouette stood out starkly in the window every time they passed, white-knuckling the handle above her door, speaking rapidly to Domari.

Of course, he'd only be able to understand one in every ten words she said, which made the scene that much more amusing. It was a wonder the two had become friends, and I shook my head with laughter at the thought.

Setting the dragon down on the armrest of the rocking chair, I pulled my legs up onto the seat, crossed them, and sat back to relax. A horn honked in the distance, breaking the usual sounds of the ranch, and I glanced up. Charlene's ranch was far back on a dirt road outside of town, and we didn't have much traffic near here, so the sight of three cars rolling to a stop outside the gate was jarring.

Especially when I realized who was here.

"Oh, fuck."

23

SHELBIE

"Yoo-hoo!" my mom called, hand waving out the window of my dad's old blue truck. "Surprise! Open the gate, sweetie!"

Panic seized me as my eyes shifted between my parents and Charlene's white truck cruising across the ranch property. I still hadn't mentioned Domari to any of my family, and now, they were here.

All of them.

Behind my dad's truck was my brother Jacob's black SUV, and my best friend Sabrina's behind that.

I was frozen to my chair, heart slamming in my chest as I thought about my messy house, my fragile mind, my secret relationship.

All of it.

Thor got up from the porch, stretching, and tail wagging as he listened to my mom's voice, but I sat paralyzed, feeling my eyes bulging in my head.

Breathe in, breathe out, I told myself as my ears began to ring, chest heaving. *It'll be fine. They're your family. You love them.*

Breathe in, breathe out. Sabrina is going to judge my dirty house immediately.

Thor's wet nose slid into my hand, knocking the dragon off the armrest and onto the wood planks of the porch. Vaguely, I felt myself look to the side, but my body felt stiff and not my own.

Dammit, breathe in, Shelbie.

My feet fell to the ground, body taking over as I uncurled from the chair, fighting for air. The gate opened, creaking on its electronic track, and I put my hands on the arm rests.

Breathe out. This is no time for a panic attack in front of everyone.

I pushed off the arm rests, rising on shaky legs as the cars pulled through the gate, driving straight to me on my little porch. Time seemed to slow as they closed the distance, my heart threatening to break free from my body and run into the woods behind us.

On the verge of hyperventilating, I kept chanting to myself to breathe, to calm down, but that was far easier said than done. Trying to remember what it felt like to smile, I hoped my face cooperated, but couldn't be sure.

My stomach churned as the cars parked, and my parents, Jacob and Lauren, Sabrina and André all came into view. I was going to puke. Sucking air in through my nose, I waited as they walked up onto the porch, overwhelming me completely.

"I've missed you, sugar," Mom said as she wrapped her

arms around me, hugging me tight. Thankfully, I remembered to return the embrace, lacing my arms behind her and holding her close. She pulled back, glancing up at me momentarily as her eyes creased. "You're all clammy. Are you not feeling well? Did we choose the wrong time to stop by?"

I shook my head too vigorously, licking my lips as I fought for words. "No, no. It's fine. You surprised me, that's all."

My dad dropped a kiss to my forehead as Thor pushed his nose into his hand. Other than me — and now Domari, I supposed — my dad was Thor's favorite person. "Good to see you, Shelbie Ann."

The freezing air around me seemed to sear my lungs as I pulled in a deep breath, willing the panic away. No matter how I was feeling, I couldn't keep everyone out here in the cold.

"Hey sis," Jacob said as he slapped my back, staring at the pink door behind us. "Man, it's even brighter in person."

An exaggerated laugh left me, and Jacob's eyes swung back to me, but before he could say anything, his wife, Lauren, stepped up and handed me a brown paper bag. "Sorry we're springing this visit on you. I brought food though. Twice baked potatoes! Your favorite, right?"

The bag fell into my hands, and I glanced down at it. Warm, cheesy, potato-y goodness wafted up from the bag, and the scent was enough to finally even my breathing.

"Yes, thank you. Sorry. Everyone come inside." I pushed open the door, staring into the small space behind us as they all passed me, entering. Sabrina's husband André looked uncomfortable as he stopped at the threshold.

"Excited to see the new digs," he said, his smile looking as forced as mine felt. "Haven't seen you in a while, Fireball."

My eyes rolled instantly at the nickname, and the panic from before seemed to fade some more. I wrapped an arm around André's tall, lean form, so different from Domari's broad muscled chest. André's skin was the richest black, and practically wrinkle-free even though he was several years older than both Sabrina and my own 31. "That was *one time*, André. I can't be blamed that you're so *nice* that you were the target of my drunken confessions."

"I believe your words were, *'I need you to know that if I were a different person, and you were a different person, I'd be madly in love with you.'* It's been eight years, and I still don't know if that's even a compliment."

An honest laugh bubbled out of me, and my chest loosened, breaths coming easier at the sight of his bright smile. "Take it. I do love you."

He patted me on the head, awkward since he was only a few inches taller than me, but André's and my relationship had always been playful like that.

"Please don't hate us," Sabrina said as she stepped up, a timid smile on her face. "Your mom called and asked if I'd seen you lately, and then suddenly, she insisted we all come visit you."

"I don't hate you." I nudged her shoulder, trying to remember how to act like a functioning human. "Where are the girls?"

Sabrina itched her nose, her short, black bob hair cut tipping forward as she ducked her head, and I squinted down at my petite friend. Anytime she was about to lie, she itched her nose. "They're with my mom this weekend."

I didn't know why she'd lie about that, but I followed her inside, hoping Domari's driving lesson would continue on a hell of a lot longer so I had time to think through an explanation for his presence. I hadn't mentioned many details about my trip to Sweden to anyone, and had certainly never mentioned him before.

The door clicked shut behind me, and my eyebrows shot up as I noticed my dad already holding a steamer up to the wallpaper. "Is this some sort of strange redecorating party?"

"You told your mom last week you didn't know how to get the wallpaper off, so the boys and I are going to do it."

I glanced to where Jacob and André stood to the side. Jacob rocked back on his heels, looking anywhere but at me, and André intently focused on the paint bucket at his side.

"Honey, let's get your kitchen organized," my mom called from the back of the house, so I left the men in the living room and moved past them. "You still need to unpack the last of those boxes, it seems. But I can do that. Sabrina, why don't you clean up a little to give us room?"

My best friend didn't need to be told twice, snapping yellow rubber gloves over her tan skin, and began scrubbing at the dishes in the sink as if they'd personally insulted her. Hell, maybe the sight of my dirty house *was* a personal insult.

"What do you want me to do, then?" I asked as Lauren

unloaded the food she'd brought, filling my fridge and cabinets.

"Pull up a chair and let us take care of you." My mom waved a hand in my direction as she opened a box of miscellaneous baking items I'd yet to need, so I hadn't bothered to unpack. "Tell us about life on the ranch. Is Charlene here? I'd love to meet her."

Jacob carried over one of my useless barstools, practically knocking my knees out as he dropped it behind me. I sat, because what else was I supposed to do? And yeah, Charlene was here, with Domari…

"She's here." I nodded, looking back to the window where I saw the truck park outside Charlene's house, Domari stepping out of the driver's side, waiting for Charlene to climb out as well. The tiny woman practically fell out of the passenger's side, bent over, hands on her knees as she gasped for air, as dramatic as ever. My heart kicked back up to a breakneck pace as I watched them walk towards my house, throat tight as panic set in once more.

Why could no one in my life ever announce their presence? I was by far the most chaotic of this bunch, proudly holding the Hot Mess Express title, but, yet every single person in my life never gave me an *ounce* of warning before they just showed up, forcing me to think on my feet.

Please, God, don't let me be weird.

"Well, hey, family!" Charlene called out as she pushed open the door, her caramel hair bobbing in its highly teased state. Her smile was wide as she stepped into the house like she was crossing the stage at a country music concert, but I hardly noticed her, staring at Domari standing in the doorframe instead. "What a fun surprise! I'm Charlene."

My dad stepped forward, hand outstretched. "Steve. Great to meet you, Charlene."

Charlene shook it, holding his hand a little longer than necessary. "Strong handshake. I like that in a man, Steve."

I looked their way only long enough to see my dad blush furiously, spinning back around to the steamer and the wallpaper behind him.

"I'm Janet," my mom said as she closed the distance between her and Charlene, arms outstretched for a hug. "Thank you so much for all you've done for Shelbie. We so appreciate you."

"The pleasure is mine," Charlene said, returning the hug. "Shelbie is a sweet girl, and I love having her and Domari here."

Now I was definitely going to puke.

Domari still stood in the doorframe appraising the crowd of people in our little home, and I honestly couldn't blame him. Everyone was talking loud and fast, crammed into the small space. *I* was overwhelmed, and these were my family, speaking my language.

"So this must be Domari then," my mom said, and I snapped my eyes back to her as my heart skipped a beat. "Another ranch hand?"

"YEP!" I called out when Charlene opened her mouth. Charlene turned to me, brows drawn in confusion as she tilted her head. "Another ranch hand. Doesn't speak English though."

So much for not being weird, Shelbie.

"Oh." Mom nodded and bile rose in the back of my throat. "That's okay. Well, come inside!" She waved to Domari, a welcoming smile on her face, and finally, he moved. With every step Domari took towards me I wanted to run, to flee, to huddle in a corner and rock back and forth. Anything other than stand here and feel my heart plummet into my toes.

Why the fuck *am I so weird?*

Domari stepped up to my side, lacing a hand around my back in a gesture that did not portray the coworker vibe.

"Domari," he said, his voice rich and deep, and my mom giggled. She *giggled.* When he held his hand out for hers mimicking what my dad had done, my mom placed her much smaller, wrinkled hand in his, and he stared down at their joined palms in confusion.

Charlene decided to take matters into her own hands — literally — and reached over, squeezing his hand around my mother's, moving it up and down in a shake.

I died of embarrassment.

My soul left my body.

"I'M STEVE," my dad shouted, and I was jerked back to life, wincing at the sound. "SHELBIE'S DAD."

"Dad," I said, a finger in my ear. "He's Swedish, not hard of hearing."

"Swedish, you say?" Sabrina chimed in, her dark eyebrows nearly in her hairline as she pulled her yellow rubber gloves off her hands, dropping them in the sink and moving across the kitchen to where we stood. "How interesting."

Looking up at Domari, I swallowed, throat dry. "I'm so sorry about this, Domari."

He studied me for a moment, then leaned down and kissed me. In front of everyone.

I thought I died before.

Now I was *dead* dead.

André whooped loudly behind us, and I pulled back from the kiss. "Well, can't say I saw that coming," André muttered to my brother, who stood slackjawed by his side.

The strangest snort-giggle-thing erupted from me, and Domari's eyes narrowed, hand still on my side. "What's wrong?"

"Nothing." I shook my head, so thankful in that moment that he and I could speak fluently in another language that no one else here could understand. "I'm sorry. I wasn't expecting any of this today. And I haven't told any of them about the whole time travel bit. Thought we'd have time to prepare a little before I sprung you on my whole family, but I guess that's not happening."

"Well, I'll be," my mother said, her eyes danced between Domari and me. "Shelbie, you said you were learning to speak Swedish before your trip, but I'll be honest with you. I didn't think much of it. Maybe a few phrases, but not this." Her hand waved between Domari and me. "Color me impressed."

My cheeks flamed pink. I could feel it burning across my skin.

"You should hear the two of them goin' at it," Charlene said, and my brother choked, descending into a coughing fit. André slapped his back, his eyes alight with amusement.

Now I was *actually* dead.

> *Shelbie Ann Smith*
> *1991-2022*
> *Accomplished Nothing*
> *Loved by All*

"She really is fluent," Charlene said, laying it on a little too thick as she tried to recover from her hopefully unintentional innuendo. "Proud of our girl. She did the damn thing. Traveling alone is scary shit, but she did it."

"Sure did." Sabrina smiled, her cheeks pinched to refrain from cracking the huge grin I knew she was trying to suppress.

"Mom, what were your ideas on organizing my baking supplies?" I cried, my voice too loud and high as I fought desperately to change the subject. "Show me what your plan is."

With me acting as translator, Domari began helping my dad as they pulled the old floral wallpaper down, revealing an even worse puke-green color beneath. André had started throwing tarps over the wood floors as Jacob mixed the paint, ready to get started on the other walls.

"Sabrina said you'd like grey," André said when I walked by to see it. "Hope that's okay."

Honestly, I hated grey. It was cold and lacking any personality. Sabrina and I had this discussion when we lived together in college and she didn't like my magenta wall I'd painted in our little rental house, but she tended to override a lot of my ideas when it came to design. I didn't have it in me to be annoyed with her over a paint color, so I shrugged. Grey was still better than puke green.

"Go for it."

Paint fumes wafted through the small space as Thor and I moved down the hall towards my bedroom. I threw the sheets up, pulling the white quilt tight as I made the bed. Fortunately, no one had come back here yet, so I kicked what was left of Domari's belongings under the bed, hoping no one would notice the mens jeans and black shirts right alongside mine in the laundry basket on the floor, let alone the woolen shirt and pants he'd worn when he arrived now shoved deep under the bed. Deciding not to chance it, I threw the entire contents of the basket into the washing machine in the hall closet.

If I didn't specifically volunteer that Domari lived here with me, then that was on them for making assumptions. I didn't know why I was being so weird about this whole thing though. At 31, I had to hope my family would trust my judgment when it came to men and relationships, but I couldn't even remember the last time I'd introduced them to anyone I dated, let alone even came close to *living* with someone.

Plus, something about my happiness revolving around a man didn't stick well with me. I didn't want them to think that I was or wasn't happy *because* of Domari. I mean, yes, he was most certainly part of it, but hinging my contentment in life on a person seemed dangerous to me, especially after Charlene's and my chat this morning.

I'd been miserable in my own life far before I ever met Domari. My trip to Sweden had been the catalyst for change, putting it all into perspective for me.

"We should paint your room sometime too," Sabrina said as she leaned in the doorway to my bedroom. I snapped the washing machine door shut, turning back to where she stood. "Guess you might need to talk to Domari before you pick a color though."

"If your eyebrows go up any further, they're going to merge with your hairline." I pointed to her face, and she swatted my hand out of the air with a laugh.

"So is this why you've been avoiding me?" She brushed her short, black bob hair behind a tawny ear. "When did he arrive?"

"It's a long story."

"And there's no time like the present." Her steely gaze locked on mine, and I fought not to flinch. Even though I knew this was coming from her, it was another thing to be in the moment.

"We obviously met in Sweden," I started, glancing over to where Domari stood in the living room, staring down at the paint supplies André was showing him. As if sensing my gaze, he looked up at me, and whether I meant to or not, I smiled.

"Uh huh," Sabrina's voice drew my attention back as she circled her hand for me to go on. *"Cuéntamelo todo."*

"Well," I paused, "we connected quickly, but then I came home."

"Depressed," Sabrina interrupted. "You came home depressed."

"Anyway," I drew out the word, pushing away from the wall. I needed space between her and I to keep up this ruse. "I thought I'd never see him again, and it was a blip on the radar. But we reconnected, and he came here a few weeks ago."

"Well, I think that's great," my mom patted my arm lovingly, her eyes alight with happiness as she joined us in the hallway. "We're happy for you, and glad we can get to know him, too. Come back to the kitchen so we can put some of this stuff away for you."

Sabrina, though, was squinting at me, reading through my unsaid words. My eyes went large, staring her down as I scrunched my nose, silently begging her to drop it for now. A heavy sigh left me as I glanced down the hall towards where my mom was waiting for us, then back to Sabrina.

"You went and found a Viking," she chuckled, shaking her head as she pushed away from the doorframe, following my mom. I laughed *way* too hard along with her, because if she only knew… Her brows pinched together when she turned back to look at me and I snapped my mouth shut. "I mean, that golden brown hair, and the thick beard, and the tattoos. Very stereotypical of him."

"So stereotypical. Unoriginal. Cliche, even. You know how popular those Viking shows are now. Everybody needs an undercut and a beard."

"You're being weird," Sabrina said as she turned back around, blocking our path into the living room and kitchen. "Weirder than your usual weird."

Don't I know it.

I puffed my cheeks out, holding my breath, then letting it go. "Sorry. You all showed up and caught me off-guard. This house is tiny, and you're everywhere."

Sabrina winced. "I know, and I'm sorry about that. Your mom was getting worried about you though. You had a mid-life crisis on us, Shelbie. Scared the shit out of us when you up and quit, well, *everything.*"

Her words felt like a slap even though I knew what she meant, how it looked from the outside. I *had* quit everything, but I'd also been miserable for so long I hadn't known how to tell anyone, and I'd shed the last of the empty life I'd led before. "So, what, this was supposed to be an intervention? Is that why none of the kids are here? You were going to confront me?"

"When you put it that way, it sounds bad," Sabrina shrugged, and I had to fight not to recoil from her as my eyes stung with unshed tears. "We care about you. All of us here love you, and we want our bright, fun, happy Shelbie back."

I nodded, feeling my face tingle as I fought the well of emotions threatening to overflow, but for once, said nothing. Sabrina studied me, waiting for me to respond, but words were lost to me.

I couldn't be *happy Shelbie* all the time, no matter the circumstances. And now, more than ever, I felt as if I was only a joke. Only the chaotic friend. Only the punchline here to make everyone *else* feel good.

So I gave her what she wanted, and smiled.

24

SHELBIE

Charlene left shortly after we emerged from the hall, the door clicking shut behind her as she went to finish chores around the ranch, leaving Domari and me to spend the day with my family. I wished she'd understood my silent, wide-eyed plea to take me with her, but sadly, telepathy wasn't a skill I had.

With the men crowded in the living room working on the walls, and the women squished in the kitchen organizing, cooking, and cleaning, I grabbed some of my cleaning supplies from under the bathroom sink and dropped to my hands and knees. Taking my frustrations out on the tub, I scrubbed the old porcelain with every ounce of strength I had, feeling the muscles in my arm scream in protest. But with each pass of the sponge, I let myself sink into the negative emotions threatening to swallow me whole.

I'd spent years distancing myself from my family and Sabrina, not knowing how I fit in their lives anymore. Everyone else had moved on, fallen in love, gotten married, had kids, and fulfilling careers. Meanwhile, I'd floundered. I was *fine* at my old job, *fine* living alone, *fine* single. But I couldn't even remember the last time I'd been truly *happy*.

What everyone else *thought* was my happy demeanor was a false facade I'd held so carefully in place, shielding my true emotions from everyone, including myself.

Smacking my head on the rocks in Sweden after being shoved down a hill from a horse had been the wakeup call I hadn't known I'd needed. Finding myself trapped back in time had offered me an excuse to slow down, to focus on *me*, and what *I* wanted.

But, had I just latched on to Domari because he was present? Had I thrown my miserable self at him, seeking out a connection that wasn't there? Had I only fallen for him because he was *also* lost like me?

The inky blackness pulls at me, calling my name as I step into the void. Goosebumps raise on my arms, the darkness all-consuming around me, soaking into my skin as I stare out into nothing. Everytime my mind slips, I seem to find myself here.

Drip. Drip. Drip.

I fucking hate the sound of that water. It feels like a poison, slowly working its way into my mind, ripping me in two. Without thinking, I scream, feeling my hands sift through my hair as I pull.

"Easy, *haski*," Domari said as he grabbed my arm, pulling it away from the tub.

I ripped my hand back out of his grip, falling back on my butt as I fought to draw in air. Anger boiled in my veins, the darkness still clinging to me as I threw the sponge across the bathroom, wanting to scream as I'd done in my mind. "Don't touch me."

Immediately, he stepped back, hurt flashing in his brown eyes, and I hated myself.

"Domari, wait."

But he had already turned to go, leaving me alone in the bathroom again. My body folded in on itself, my head dropping down to the cool tiles, eyes burning with tears I couldn't shed, not here, not in front of everyone.

Breathe in, breathe out.

Breathe in, breathe out.

"Shelbie, honey!" my mom called from the other room, and I pushed myself back up to sitting, eyes closed as I fought to breathe evenly. "Lauren has some lunch ready when you come to a stopping point!"

"Be right there," I called back, hands clenched tight, forcing air in and out of my lungs.

"You good in here?" Jacob asked as he stuck his head through the doorway not even two minutes later.

Not trusting my ability to convincingly smile, I focused instead on putting away the cleaning supplies. "Yep. Just picking up first."

"Lauren brought a baked ham. Smells so good. No promises I'll leave you any, so I suggest you hurry."

"I *said* I'm coming," I muttered through gritted teeth,

and Jacob paused where he'd turned to leave. I could feel his eyes on me, feel the way he watched me, and I fucking hated it. So forced a smile onto my face, hoping it wasn't a grimace, and stood to follow him. "Lead the way."

How I managed to make it through a meal with everyone here was beyond me. We sat sprawled around the living room on camp chairs, the couch, the floor, and the barstools. I sat on the floor, Thor in my lap, as I picked at my ham and twice-baked potato. Domari had left, and after how I'd snapped at him, I couldn't blame him.

I wanted to go find him. To apologize. To ease this ache in my chest. As much as I hated myself for how I'd reacted, for how I felt about so many things in my life, I *did* love him, and how I'd treated him was unfair.

Sinking my hands in Thor's fur to ground me, I joked with André and Jacob, complimented Lauren on her cooking, and chatted with my dad on his plans to hang some new bookshelves for me once the walls were finished. Already, the room was transforming, and it did look better. While the grey was lifeless and cold, one uniform color in both the living room and connected kitchen made the room feel larger than it was.

Thor snatched the ham off my fork as it hovered in mid-air, drawing my attention down to him. "Well, that was rude of you. Domari has been spoiling you, feeding you human food."

My dog glanced at me out of the side of his eye, annoyance written in his every feature, and I couldn't help but chuckle. Wrapping my arms around the fluffy dog, I willed myself to soak up the comfort he always brought me. "I love you, big guy," I whispered in his fur, hoping this dog understood how much he meant to me.

"Want to show us around the ranch before we pack up?" Mom asked, and I sat back up.

"Yeah, I can do that," I said. I needed everyone out of my space, and maybe I could go find Domari, too.

With the paint packed up and saved for me to finish later, everyone bundled back into shoes and coats, following me outside. We toured the barns, and I ran my hand along the horse's noses as I introduced each one, but saw no signs of Domari.

My heart sank as I craned my neck, searching for him, until I heard the sounds of a steady thumping coming from the edge of the forest. My steps quickened as the gaggle of adults followed behind me, Thor padding at my side.

"What's back here, honey?" My mom called out, but I didn't even bother turning around to answer her.

Under the edge of the canopy line stood Domari, now shirtless even in the snow, axe in hand. A large pile of firewood stood to his left as he split log after log, intently focused on his task.

"Honey," my mom turned to me. "Wow. He is… quite the man."

"I suddenly understand so much more about this situation," Sabrina laughed, elbowing me in the side.

"Way to go, sis." Lauren put her hand out to me for a high-five. "Whoa."

Absently, I slapped her hand. My dad, brother, and André worked their way through the snow to Domari, stopping as he handed off the axe to Jacob. My brother lifted the axe, adjusted his grip, then brought it over his head, not nearly as smooth as Domari had done moments before.

"How long do we think it'll take our men to think they should also take their shirts off?" Sabrina asked, and I chuckled. It felt good to laugh, even amidst the darkness in my mind.

"So, tell me." Lauren leaned towards me. "Does that shield tattoo go down further, too?" She waggled her eyebrows at me, and Sabrina cackled as I shook my head, refusing to be goaded.

My mom, however, turned back towards the house. "I don't think I should hear this. La-la-la-la…" She walked inside with her fingers in her ears.

I spun, turning my back to the men as I eased into silence with the girls to my left and right. After a moment, Lauren nudged me with her shoulder.

"He seems like he's infatuated with you." She smiled at me, and I nodded.

"But more importantly," Sabrina laid her head on my shoulder, "you seem good out here."

"I am," I sighed, wanting so badly to believe my own words.

25

DOMARI

Domari watched as Shelbie's family packed up, leaving just as quickly as they'd arrived that morning. Leaving his axe propped against the pile of firewood, he pulled on his black t-shirt again before joining Shelbie on the porch. She laced an arm around his waist, leaning her weight into him as she waved goodbye to her family. The touch was simple and casual, but it meant everything to Domari after her words earlier.

"Don't touch me," she'd said, and his heart had snapped in half.

While Domari was many things, he wasn't a fool. He knew he was broken, desperate for love. For connection. For affection. But he also trusted no one enough to let anyone in.

Why Shelbie had wormed her way into his heart so fast, he still didn't understand. Maybe it's because he could see how broken she was, like him — she hid behind her bright smile just as he hid behind his weapons and stoic demeanor.

But Domari saw her, the *real* Shelbie, even when she didn't know he was watching. And, with her, he *felt* seen — he was so much more than a legendary Varangian Guard and Njal's son in Shelbie's eyes, and that was a feeling he never wanted to let go of.

But with every passing day lately, Domari could feel how she held back from him, how emotionally fragile Shelbie seemed, and panic seized his heart. After losing so much in his life, the thought of losing her again was enough to have him at his breaking point.

The language barrier between him and Shelbie's family had made it painfully obvious Domari didn't fit here in her world, and the day had been torturous for him. He hated feeling useless. Without Shelbie to help him understand their words, he'd felt more lost than ever before, and had needed to escape. For the first time in weeks, he was homesick for his his own family.

The feel of the axe in his hand brought him a sense of peace, but still, it was nothing compared to the way her hands felt when they circled his waist, pulling him into a hug.

"I'm so sorry," Shelbie said as soon as the cars were out of sight, her cheek resting on Domari's chest. "I left you alone, and then I snapped at you."

The fact she could read him so easily was both frightening and exhilarating to Domari. He dropped a tender kiss to the top of her head, his hands stroking down her back. "All is forgiven. But, I need you to tell me what happened."

Instantly, she pulled back from him, her face shutting down again, but he wrapped his hand around her forearm, forcing her to stay. "No, Shelbie. Don't push me away. You're hurting, and I want to know why."

Her ice blue eyes turned up to meet his, lip quivering as she scanned his face, her head shaking slightly.

"If you need time, you can have it," Domari said, tucking a stray curl behind her ear. "But I won't lose you like this, and I deserve more than hateful words, even if you regret them."

Shelbie's chin dropped as a sob escaped her, the heels of her palms digging into her eyes. Domari towed her into his chest again as he sank down to one of the rocking chairs on the porch, pulling Shelbie into his lap. Tears shook through her as he continued to rub her back, fighting tears of his own as she battled through her emotions.

"I'm so messed up, Domari," she croaked, clinging to his t-shirt. "I've been miserable in my life for years and never did anything about it. I feel like everyone expects me to be this bright ray of sunshine all the time, and its been so long since I've *actually* felt that way. I was already feeling pretty low today, and then my family showed up, throwing me off even more. I felt like I had to fake it for them, and its…" she sniffed, wiping her nose on the sleeve of her sweater, "it's hard sometimes."

"Why do you think you need to pretend to be happy?" Domari asked, his fingers running through Shelbie's golden curls.

She sighed, her breaths coming easier. "I don't know. This world is full of so much negativity and darkness. No one needs to know or care about my life or stupid problems."

Placing a finger under her chin, Domari tilted her head up so her eyes met his. "I care."

Her lip trembled once more, and he leaned in, placing his lips over hers, feeling the tears that leaked out of her eyes and onto his skin. "What did I do to deserve you?"

"I've asked myself that same question so many times since I found you on the rocks, Shelbie." Domari swallowed, his throat thick with emotions of his own. "Nothing I've ever done in my life has made me worthy of your love, and yet you give it so freely. Not only to me, but to my people, to your family, to Charlene, to Thor."

"I mean, maybe if you weren't so perfect, it'd be easier to not love you," Shelbie smiled, her eyes red and swollen, but, to Domari, she was more beautiful than ever.

His hands came up, bracketing her cheeks as he gazed into her eyes. "My life has been an empty shell of a life for ten years, and even before I left my village. I've been alone for so long, sometimes its hard to believe you're real. That I won't wake up from this dream to find you gone once more. That's easier for me to believe than this love I feel for you."

Shelbie leaned in, lacing her arms around Domari's neck as she pressed a kiss to his lips. "I'm not leaving you ever again."

The sky darkened around them as they sat in the chair, cuddled close together, sharing warmth. Worn out from her emotions, Shelbie's eyes drooped, her breaths even as Domari rested his hand on her waist. He knew he should wake her and take her inside, but he couldn't seem to make himself move, her words echoing in his head.

As much as he wanted to believe her words, doubt filled

Domari's mind. In the depths of his soul, he believed their fates were intertwined, connected far more than he understood, but he'd been a fool before to make promises like that.

Rubbing a hand across his tattooed neck, his mind drifted back to his promise a lifetime ago, vowing to stay together until Valhalla. Even knowing how disastrously that had turned out between the four friends, he couldn't help the words that came next.

"Nor will I."

26

SIGNE

The sun peeked through the clouds, mirroring the warmth in Signe's heart as she followed behind Gunnar on the way to the barn. With each passing day since the Solstice, the sun appeared more, and the ache in her heart she'd carried for so long loosened. The sound of children's laughter carried through the brisk winter air, and it drew her attention to where Viveka and Kára stood, each carrying one of the twins as they jumped through the knee-deep snow around the house pretending to be legendary Valkyries in battle.

"Why do you think Raud and your father spared them?" Gunnar asked as he followed her gaze, holding the door to the barn open for Signe.

She hummed deep in her throat as she thought about the question, one she'd pondered often lately. "When it came to me, Draugr could never make up his mind. Most of the time, he couldn't wait to be rid of me, discussing marrying me off as soon as I first bled." She could feel Gunnar's steely gaze on her as she spoke, but Signe's eyes were still trained on the children outside. "When that didn't happen, something in him changed. He took me on raids — something I'd only ever hoped to do — and delighted in how I held my own in battle."

"He had every right to be proud of you."

Signe shook her head, images of her past coming back so clearly. The thrumming of her heartbeat in sync with the paddles on the water, the ocean breeze in her hair, the war horn followed by cries and howling that broke out as they charged onto the beaches of far-off lands. "It was never pride. You aren't *proud* of a sword you wield in battle; you covet it. That's how Draugr always treated me — a prized possession."

Gunnar's warm hand slipped beneath Signe's chin, turning her face towards his. He stooped, making sure his eyes were level with hers, and Signe swallowed at the seriousness of his countenance. "You belong to *no one* but yourself."

One brow hitched at his words, her lips tipping up into a smirk. "Not even you?"

"I've laid claim to your heart, *elksan min*, but no, you don't belong to me." His hand slid to rest along her neck, thumb brushing across her racing pulse, sending a wash of heat through her body. "But don't mistake my words. If anyone were to attempt to take you from me, the power of Asgard couldn't stop me from getting you back."

A chuckle rose through Signe as she leaned into her

husband's side, hand resting on the baby tucked into his wrap on her front. "You consider your strength equal to the gods now?"

"If I was fighting for you, yes." Gunnar smiled, dropping a kiss to Signe's upturned mouth. With a slap to her bottom, he turned and walked into the barn.

Signe stayed in the doorway, glancing between her cocksure husband and the children she loved so dearly. Viveka's black curls bounced in the wind, and Signe couldn't help but grin at the sight of her carrying around Revna, their emerald green eyes matching in the sunlight, a sight she'd never even allowed herself to dream.

Turning to where Gunnar stood amidst the horses, Signe couldn't help but notice the empty stall on the far end for Domari's horse, Mjölnir. She watched her husband work, noticing the way he didn't dare to even look in the direction of the empty stall.

Each day that ticked by and Domari hadn't returned weighed heavily on Gunnar, but he didn't speak of him often. The sting of Domari's last departure after Tove died mirrored this disappearance too closely, and she knew the grief Gunnar carried over that loss. As her thoughts wandered to Domari, Signe was relieved that the foreboding she felt so often lately didn't come. Maybe she hadn't spent enough time with Domari to have that same level of connection with him, but still, deep down, she believed that wherever Domari was, he was safe. He would come home.

"When Viveka arrived, everything changed," Signe

continued, mostly to distract her husband. "She was left on our doorstep for Vermund, with no sign of the mother." Gunnar looked to where Signe stood leaning against one of the posts in the center of the barn, then back down to the horse he was tending to. "Vermund thrust her on me, and made sure I had everything I needed for the girl, but she quickly became my responsibility."

"How old were you?"

"It was my fourteenth winter. Only slightly older than Viveka is now." Signe shook her head, remembering the way she felt holding the tiny baby in her arms. That day, trying to work through how to care for someone other than herself, had been the most frightening in her life, even though she'd already been through two raiding seasons with her father's men. "For the next five, I took care of her. By the time Viveka was two, another one of my suitors fell through, and I stopped raiding all together because I worried too much about the girl while I was gone."

Gunnar dropped the horse's hoof he'd been cleaning, leaning across the railing as he stared at his wife. "And you think that your history with Viveka has something to do with these new children?"

Her chest tightened as she thought through her words. "Viveka was used against me regularly, Gunnar. Draugr threatened her to make me obey. Hurting her would have been far worse than hurting me, and he knew it," she whispered, eyes burning with remembered pain. "If I had to guess what my father's intentions were, these children are a message. He's flaunting what he sees as my weakness, thrusting them on me, knowing I will not be able to protect them all if it comes to battle."

Silence stretched between Gunnar and Signe as they stared at each other, allowing Gunnar time to soak in her words. She wished they weren't true, but the tingling in her spine told her that her worries were founded. Draugr would come for them, sooner or later, and expect her to sacrifice herself for these children.

He knew his daughter, after all.

Embers popped in the fire as Signe added another log, the longhouse dark around them that night. Viveka and Kára had moved in with them after the Solstice, taking over Domari's empty pallet, and slept soundly with baby Erik between them. Revna and Ulf snuggled into their furs, curled around each other as they were every night, and Signe's heart lifted as she adjusted their blankets.

Between the contentment of having her family whole once more and the way Gunnar made her feel, Signe could never have imagined this life for herself. Each night, wrapped in Gunnar's warm embrace, Signe tore open another invisible wound, exposing every secret and buried pain, recounting the many things she'd never told him. Each broken piece of herself she revealed only seemed to draw him in, and Gunnar rewarded her for each facet of herself she revealed with a passion that Signe had never known.

Children safe in their beds, Signe moved to her own

platform, loosening the ties of her dress as she watched the door, waiting for Gunnar to return from checking on the animals for the night.

While she'd always been in love with Gunnar, now it was different. She *craved* him. Craved how she felt as he held her, hanging on her every word each night. Craved the adoring look in his eyes as she shared her darkest moments. Craved how he kissed away her most painful memories.

The door opened and closed quietly behind Gunnar, and his azure eyes met hers as he crept across the floor. Stopping at each of the children's beds, he laid gentle kisses to their heads before moving to where Signe reclined on their own pallet, pulling the blankets over her legs.

Heat pooled in Signe's core as she watched him move through the dim light. Shifting towards the wall, she made room for her husband as he lifted his shirt up and over his head. Her nostrils flared as she watched, studying his chest, the muscles corded there, knowing Gunnar's strength was far more than skin-deep. His weight dropped onto the bed, and instead of laying to her right as Signe expected, his heavy, muscled body settled over hers. Her heart slammed against her ribs violently as he pinned her, warring between a deep need to protect herself and the desperate desire to let him occupy her body and soul.

Gunnar's lips sealed over her racing pulse at the hollow of her throat as his hands shifted beneath the blankets, pulling the hem of her dress up to her waist. His hands were slow, lazy even, as they traced across her skin, leaving fire in their wake. Thoughts of remaining strong and aloof started to abandon her, consumed in the conflagration of desire he stoked.

Signe tipped her head back, arching her neck to give Gunnar better access, and he licked his way across her sensitive skin to her jaw, then to her mouth. His teeth nipped here and there like striking sparks from flint.

"What story do you have for me tonight? What piece of you do I get to earn and cherish with all the others?" he asked as his hands slid to the apex of her thighs. She felt the stroke of his voice across her skin, felt the rumble of his question in her chest, and her core clenched with anticipation.

A slow smirk spread across her face as she opened her eyes, taking in her much larger husband above her. His gaze met hers momentarily as he waited for her to answer. The silence lingered as his fingers moved against her slick skin, and Signe moaned softly in his ear. Gunnar's shoulders settled fully, wholly absorbed in his seduction, lowering his guard just enough that Signe seized her moment and tangled her leg with his. A loud puff of air left Gunnar's lungs as she flipped him, splaying him flat on his back against the furs. Signe's grin spread as she mounted him, hiked her skirts to her waist, and straddled his hips.

Last night she'd shared the story of shaving her head to enter Winter Nights, and he'd shook with laughter as she recounted how she'd taken down several grown men at only eight years old. Even then, she had been a tiny demon, relentless in her attacks. His laughter ebbed as she detailed the fallout — her punishment had been brutal and one she didn't like to think back on.

Tonight's story, though, was a more somber tale, and the need for control as she recounted the story rode her hard. Signe ground down into her husband beneath her, feeling his hardness even through the thick fabric of his trousers. Gunnar's large hands spanned her waist as she rubbed against him, holding her in place — in the present, here with him. Signe's eyes met his in the dim light, using this feeling to strengthen her own will.

"Draugr sold my hand in marriage before I could even speak," she whispered the words, painful memories surfacing at how she recalled how little she'd ever meant to her father. Yet, still, all these years later, he hunted her. Her head shook with confusion as she tried to reason through his motives.

Sensing her attention ebbing, Gunnar's hands dipped beneath the fabric of her skirts, palming her bare bottom in a tight squeeze. A challenge. He knew her well enough to know what she needed now was a reminder of her strength; nothing gentle and slow would banish the demons of her past. Fire licked in her gaze as she stared down at him, running her fingers along the black ink painted across his chest, runes for wisdom, bravery, loyalty, and protection in a circle around his collarbone.

"The terms stated that after my first bleed, Bahr would be summoned." Signe's lip curled as she thought of her first betrothed. "Bahr was a boarish, unworthy pig. He often fought alongside Draugr on raids, and stories followed him of his viciousness. Bragging of the women he raped and then murdered was his favorite past time. Of course, this was who Draugr had chosen for me — a man as awful as he was." A bitter laugh escaped her, and Gunnar's grip slid to her waist, dragging her down over the hardness beneath her, sucking the air from her lungs as she was yanked back to the present. His bright blue gaze locked on hers, forcing her to stay here with him at this moment. "Every time he came to our village, he insisted I wait on him, fetching him ale and running his hands over me, even as a child. I growled at him more than once, and it only ever made Bahr roar with laughter.

"I burned my blankets the day I bled." Her voice was husky as Gunnar palmed her harder, reminding her where and who she was with. "Tried to hide it from Draugr. But as always, timing was never on my side regarding Draugr. I bore his black and blue handprint over the freckled skin on my arm for a week after he dragged me from the house. He threw me to the ground before the healer's longhouse, insisting I bathe and prepare for my wedding."

Gunnar's chest rumbled beneath her as she dipped, laying her chest against his, pressing a kiss to his lips. He sipped at her lower lip as his hands roamed her skin, waiting for Signe to go on.

"Bahr arrived four days later. I wore a sapphire gown revealing more of my body than ever before, slits cut high on my thigh and exposing my sides. Even covered by my ermine cloak, I felt exposed. The women braided my hair, laying a circlet of gold on my head, murmuring words of reassurance that rang false and weak. There was no happily ever after for me, not with Bahr or anyone my father would ever choose to ally with."

As Signe relived the harsh truth of her young life,

Gunnar ground into her from beneath, still clad in his trousers, teasing her mercilessly with his body. Her head fell forward onto his shoulder as she moved over him, anchoring her here in the present.

"The hall was overflowing that night; two clans gathered together as one, joined by this new union," Signe's words came amidst heavy breaths. "I stood straight as an arrow with my cloak behind me. While the warmth of the fur was welcome, I was glad it disguised the shake of my hands beneath the fabric. My palm rested on the dagger's hilt as I fought to hide the nervous tremor in my veins. I refused to show anyone how much I was dreading this."

"My strong, clever Signe." A warm hand moved up her thigh, resting exactly where she always wore her dagger. Gunnar's grip was tight as he dug his fingers into her skin, pulling her hips down and fitting them closer together. Breath was sucked from her mouth in a soft gasp as his hands slid between them and over her wetness, circling slowly.

"He touched himself," Signe seethed. Gunnar's hands sped up, painting over this terrible memory with a new one, banishing it with each stroke of his fingers, each brush of his lips to her neck. "His hands rested on his cock over his trousers as I walked towards him through the crowds of my father's people. His beady grey eyes roamed my body, and I fought for air as I moved closer. But I refused to cower to him or anyone."

Signe's teeth clenched, both from the memory and from how her husband's hands moved against her core. She tilted her hips, needing more. Needing everything Gunnar had to offer. Pushing her hands into his warm chest, she rose. Her own greedy hands pulled at the ties at Gunnar's waist, freeing his length, sliding her palm along him as the rest of the scene played out in her head. Gunnar's guttural moan was a physical stroke of triumph down her spine.

Just as it had that day, Signe's chin tipped up. Only, this time, rather than walking towards an evil man, she sank down over the best one she'd ever known. Signe and Gunnar groaned in unison as he stroked into her, so deep she could feel him in her soul. They worked each other as they'd done for years, knowing just how the other liked it as words were lost to Signe momentarily. It would have been easy to let the story end there, to be consumed with the passion flowing between them as Gunnar moved within her. But like poison, the story demanded to be purged. To be laid in Gunnar's safe keeping, as had her heart.

"His hands shifted from his cock to his chest, rubbing across it as I walked towards him," she resumed as she slowed her hips, sliding against Gunnar in long strokes. "Towards my awful future. Anger coursed through my veins like a living thing, moving and swirling under my skin, clamoring to smite that sad excuse of a man."

Gunnar's hips moved, and Signe moaned softly, letting her body fall forward onto him as she let him take over. With every stroke, he reminded her that horrible memory wasn't her life — *this* was.

"He gripped his heart," Signe whispered into Gunnar's ear as he pounded into her from below. "I stepped towards him, and his eyes widened in shock, mouth open in a silent cry, then fell to his knees in front of me. Eyes locked on mine as the life faded from them. His last breath at my feet."

Gunnar flipped them once more, rising above Signe as his beard scraped across her sensitive neck, marking her with his mouth. His hand slid over her lips to contain her moan.

"No one touches you but me," Gunnar growled, his movements becoming uneven, losing their steady rhythm. *"No one."* It was both a command and promise, wrapped in passion, strengthened by a core of unwavering love.

Wind whistled outside while his head dropped to her chest, abdomen flexing as his release tumbled through him. Signe clawed at his back, nails digging in and leaving red, angry lines in their wake as her heart thundered in her chest. Tomorrow she would look at them, and feel both heat and pride, seeing her marks on him just as he'd marked her moments before. Signe surrendered to the high of this moment and burned the memories of old with the sound of the crackling fire.

Gunnar's hands still roamed over her exposed skin, branding her with his touch even after he rolled to her side.

"They said I was cursed," Signe said into the night sometime later. "It only added to the stories told of the Demon Spawn. The whispers followed me. Twice after, my father negotiated for my betrothal, and twice, my soon-to-be husbands met untimely deaths." She leaned into Gunnar's warm chest, resting her head against him as she listened to his steady heart beating for her.

Gunnar's fingers tangled in her pale hair, smoothing it down her back. "No other man could lay claim to what fate already knew was mine. They called you to me, and I knew it from the moment I laid eyes on you."

Warmth bloomed in Signe's chest at his words, and her body relaxed against him, soaking in the heat he offered her.

27

SIGNE

With the weather warming each day, everything in the village seemed to be running smoothly. The men were able to hunt and trap more food, and Signe's sense of dread had eased somewhat as life returned to normal. But that morning, she couldn't seem to focus on her task, even as she stared at the clothes she'd washed and laid to dry next to the hearth. The same ominous feeling she'd felt so many times in her life zipped through her spine that morning as she straightened, glancing to the door. Commotion outside alerted her to the hunter's return, and Signe pushed open the door, pulling her cloak tight around her shoulders and over Erik at her chest.

Hand on her dagger, Signe squinted into the sun as she looked to where Magnus stood with Kára, Thorsten, Kare, his twins, Arne and Bodil, and Björn to the right of the clearing, unpacking a sled. Before she could search Gunnar out, a loud whinny drew her attention to the edge of the forest, watching as a dunn horse kicked its feet up in the air, snow scattering in the wind. Gunnar stood before the stallion, arms outstretched as he worked to calm it, and Signe's pulse sped up as she moved. Dropping his weapons, Magnus took off at a sprint through the snow to join his brother, and bile rose in the back of Signe's throat as she approached.

After weeks gone, Domari's beloved Mjölnir had returned without his rider.

"Gather a search party," Gunnar bellowed as he walked beside the horse, his face full of pain.

"We don't know what happened or where he even went," Signe said as she placed a hand over her husband's chest when he moved to pass her. Gunnar glared down, his blue eyes ice cold as his heart thundered under her palm. "Where would you even begin to look, Gunnar? It's been *weeks* since Domari left. We need you and our people here. Together."

Pleading with her eyes, she begged her husband to understand what she knew in the depths of her soul. No matter how *normal* everything felt, their life right now was the calm before the storm. Her father would come for her — it was as sure as the sun rising in the morning. To have any of their men off traipsing through winter storms searching for Domari would leave them under-protected, and they were already wildly outnumbered from what she knew of Draugr's clan, more than triple the size of the Erikssons, and almost all men able and ready to fight.

A heavy sigh escaped Gunnar as he seized the horse's mane and led him to the barn with the rest of the animals.

Forcing her hand to loosen on the hilt of the dagger, Singe flexed her fingers, held out at her side. Gone were the days of tranquil rest this winter as they waited out the storms. It was time to plan. Defense strategies formed in her mind, thinking through supplies and alliances that would need to be forged — everything the Eriksson clan would need when the time came.

With the peace between her and Gunnar so recently restored, Signe chewed on her lip. As painful as it was for her not to rip control back from him and take charge, she knew her husband was also thinking through everything. Vowing to be better, Signe decided to wait and talk to Gunnar before she executed on her plans. Together, they could prepare their people. Together, they were stronger.

Gunnar leaned against the wall of his mother's house later that night, standing with Thorsten, Magnus, and Björn deep in conversation as Frida congregated the children around her in a circle. Each night, she gathered them for a tale, taking over the role of storyteller from her mischievous youngest son. With her beautiful lilting voice, she wove tales that guaranteed the children went to bed with smiles instead of tear-stained cheeks, and Signe couldn't help but listen in.

"What shall I tell you tonight?" Frida asked as she tucked her long, grey braid over her shoulder, settling onto a bench near the hearth in her home. Her blue eyes twinkled in the dim light of the sconces on the wall as she smiled down at the children in front of her on the floor.

"A love story," Birgitta's high voice said as she leaned into Astrid's knees while she braided the small girl's copper hair.

Revna, on the other hand, made retching noises where she sat with the boys. "Not again," she whined, hands tangled in the black fur of the pup at her side. Signe's daughter bounced on her heels where she knelt on the furs covering the floor, and Signe's lips tipped up at the sight. "How about sea monsters?"

"Tell them Erik's story." Björn's deep timbre carried across the room as he paced to Frida's side and placed a steady hand on her shoulder. Their eyes met briefly, and a silent conversation happened there that Signe didn't understand. Frida's eyes shone with tears as she turned back to the eager young children in front of her, scanning each of their faces.

"This is my favorite story," she said, brows high as emotions choked her voice. Ulf slid to her side, holding his grandmother's hand. Seeing her son's empathy did strange things to Signe's heart, and she hoped he never changed, never hardened like her.

"Deep in the mountains of a forgotten land, the wind blew snow in every direction," Frida began, and the room fell silent around her as everyone listened. "White wisps circled a clearing in a cyclone, but the man trudging through the storm couldn't be swayed from his path. Icicles dripped from his beard as he pulled his furs tighter, shielding himself from the whipping chill. Yet, still, his feet continued to move. One step. Another. Over and over. His progress was slow as he waded through the murderous storm, grappling at nearby trees for balance, but he was undeterred, leaning into the wind and pushing forward.

"The moment his foot touched the clearing, the snow stopped." Frida held up her hands, freezing the room with her words and motions. The breath caught in Signe's chest, already sucked into the story.

"Silence," Frida whispered, leaning down towards the children in front of her. "Not the sound of the wind that had pushed him away from his destination. Not the trees moving around him. Not a snapping of a twig. Not even a hare dared to move in the forest behind him.

"His head swiveled," Frida mirrored the motion, glancing around the room at her captive audience, "looking for the source of the sudden calm. He saw nothing, squinting into the bright white around him, until *there.*" Frida paused, widening her eyes as if she was living the tale, pointing to the back wall of her home. "There, ahead of him, stood three cloaked figures staggered in height and posture. A knowing settled deep in his bones as he stepped towards his fate. This was what he'd come in search of. Who he'd come to find."

Revna shifted on her knees, glancing back at her mother momentarily, and Signe smiled down at the little girl, loving the way her emerald eyes sparkled in the firelight.

"'*We've been waiting for you, Erik,*'" Frida said in a haunting voice, not her own. "'*Your journey has been long, and you have much ahead of you.*'

"Erik fell to his knees in the snow, throwing himself forward until his head rested on his fur-covered arms." Frida slid to the ground, covering her head, acting out the story. "*'They're gone,'* he cried, his body heaving with emotions as he lay prostrate against the cold ground. *'So many lost.'*"

Movement along the wall drew Signe's eyes to her husband, watching as Gunnar and Magnus listened carefully to the story of how their clan began. Signe's heart ached for the father they'd lost last fall, so unlike her own.

Rising back to her seat, Frida continued, "*'But you, Erik,'* the shortest figure stepped forward — a woman — closing the distance between them, *'you have the strength to end it. You always have.'*" Frida's voice wavered, and in the dim firelight, Signe could see the tears lining Frida's bright eyes. Björn slid to the bench beside his old friend, holding her hand.

Glancing briefly at Björn for support, Frida's spine straightened, and she went on. "Erik's head rose at the woman's words, revealing his dirt and blood-caked cheeks, now striped with tears. His eyes searched her face, buried deep inside her hood, until he recognized her. *'Urd,'* he said, eyes wide as he took in the Norn standing before him."

Children whispered to each other on the floor, recognizing the name.

"Her sisters stepped forward to join her, linking hands as their hoods fell back to reveal the faces of the Norns — Urd, Verandi, and Skuld." Frida paused, letting the weight of the legendary trio sit in the room. Signe could feel the hair on her arms standing up. Memories of the Norns' presence last fall rushed to Signe's mind, followed shortly by the memory of the day she left Viveka behind. In Signe's opinion, anytime the Norns appeared, trouble followed closely behind.

"Erik sat back on his heels, kneeling in their presence, overcome that the Norns would choose to answer his desperate plea. *'Tell me what I must do,'* he said, bowing his head. *'Tell me how I can protect those that are mine, the lost and broken, the orphans.'* At the word, he hiccupped a sob, swiping at his face again."

A heavy tear slid down Frida's cheek as she looked down at the children around her, realizing this story was playing out all over again. Signe's eyes darted around the room, taking in Viveka and Kára standing tall, little Birgitta and Bo curled into Astrid's lap. Even Ivar had joined them tonight, sitting with Ulf on the floor. So many children here, and this wasn't even all the orphans who had arrived so far; some were still home with the rest of their villagers.

"*'Go,'* Skuld told Erik, placing her glowing hand on his head." Frida did the same on Ulf's head beneath her, and Signe's son stared up at his grandmother with loving affection. "*'Take them with you, and leave these lands. Head east, along the river. There, in the valley between the river and the mountains you're so desperate to flee, you'll make your home.'*

"Erik's head whipped up at her words, confusion written in the lines of his face. *'How will we survive so far from the shore? How will I feed these children?'* he asked, and Verandi sighed in return. *'You'll raid no more,'* she answered. Gently, she placed her hand under his chin and pulled him to his feet. *'Your path lay to the east. There, you'll find a land untouched and full of riches. Hunt those lands, and follow the rivers. It's a treacherous life and a difficult road ahead to start anew, but you'll succeed. These children in your care will bring about the change our world so desperately needs.'"*

With the story second-hand, Signe couldn't be sure if the words of the Norns were true, but she looked to her husband and clan standing on the wall, wondering what the Norns' words meant.

Frida glanced to her side, squeezing Björn's hand before she went on. "Erik couldn't believe the words he was hearing, but who was he, a lowly Viking, to challenge the word of the Norns? The sisters told Erik that another, his most trusted friend, would join him. Would protect him as he changed the lives of these children for good. And his beloved wife would see to their health while she prepared for the fate ahead of her."

Yrsa stood behind Björn, a weary smile crossing her kind face as she looked at those around her.

"Together," Frida said as she turned back towards the captive children, "it was promised that together, our families would forge a new destiny for the children and that others would join our cause.

"*'We leave this burden only to you, Erik, for you are most worthy of this task,'* Urd whispered to Erik, placing her hand on his chest with her final words. *'Return, gather your people, and leave soon before you draw the eyes of the enemies at your heels. Take the children and go.'*

"Without hesitation, Erik nodded; newfound strength settled in his shoulders as he straightened. *'I will do as you say,'* he bowed again to the Norns before him. When he rose, his eyes searched the women in front of him, desperate for any guidance they would give. That they were here — had answered his call — was more than he could have hoped for.

"*'Thank you, Sisters, for this gift,'* Erik said, eyeing the three for the last time. *'I will not waste it.'* Hands outstretched, the sisters found each other and faded into the storm. Gone."

Frida swung her hands out to the side, and not even the embers in the fire dared to break the heavy silence, hanging on her every word. "Erik turned, shoulders back. Head high. With a deep breath, he took a step back in the direction he came, headed into a destiny fit for only the bravest of men. For it wasn't glory he sought, but a legacy. A future for the children left after the bloody battle he'd barely survived, but had succeeded in protecting the children hidden in the trees."

Voice dropping to barely above a whisper, Frida finished the story with the entire house hanging on her every word. "Life. Family. Safety. A world filled with those things didn't exist for his people, but he would build one. For the children," she paused, glancing to the many children on the floor in front of her, then to her own grown children standing along the walls, tears rolling freely down her cheeks, her eyes lingering on Thorsten longer than the others. The large man ducked his head, red hair swinging down in his face in a show of respect for the woman who had cared for him and so many others in their village, including Domari and Raud. "For the orphans."

28

SHELBIE

The fire crackles in the hearth as light dances around the small, one-room hut, but it does nothing to soften the shadows encasing Verandi. The grey streaks surrounding her face glow in the light, dancing lightly in the breeze drifting through the door.

Urd sits at the loom, her white braid cascading down her back and over her elbow, back hunched in age as she examines the threads in her fingers.

"Not enough," Urd whispers as the soft material slips through her hands, her voice cracking at the words.

Verandi turns away from the fire, shoulders hanging in defeat as she walks to her sister's side. She gently lifts the threads from her sister's hands and lays them across the loom to rest.

"We can't change it," Verandi says with a heavy sigh.

The door slams closed behind Skuld, snow scattering as she removes her midnight velvet hood and removes her cloak. Where there should be a pile of soft snow on the floor, there's nothing.

Magic imbues everything in this space. A cauldron sits over the open fire, stirring itself as the loom continues to work without the guidance of the crone's hands. But none of those things draw the eyes of the sisters, who huddle together, arms slung over each other in mourning.

Skuld heaves a groan as she falls to the floor in a slump, white blonde hair billowing out around her. "This is the end," she mutters, her head dropping into her hands.

"It's *not* the end," Verandi scolds her.

"Hadriel has not forgotten her." Urd shakes her head, bending to run a hand along her younger sister's arm. The Future is always the hardest to bear — unknowns at every turn.

"But she doesn't even know," Skuld's words come out in a whine.

"We still have time."

"But how much? Everyone is present this time — we've seen this so many times. You've seen the runes as well as me. As soon as —"

"Stop." Urd raises her hand to her sister, whose mouth snaps shut at the words. "Don't even speak his name. We all know what's coming, but you're mistaken. We don't know the end. Too much can't be seen still. Hadriel is on our side. Hope is not lost."

Skuld nods at her sisters' words, and Urd and Verandi stand, heading back to the loom. A moment passes, then another while Skuld still huddles on the floor. Her nearly white eyes glance to the window, where the lake sits beyond the hut.

"But he isn't enough…" The words pass her lips in a soft whisper, the sound drowned out by the pops of the fire and the creak of the loom. "Not alone."

❄

Tires crunched on the gravel outside the window as I dropped my feet from where they'd been resting on the arm of the chair in the spare bedroom, staring down at the story I'd written in my journal today. The three mysterious sisters — the Norns — were featured in many of my dreams and stories. Rightfully so, considering I still didn't understand why I had time traveled last fall or why Domari could come here to me. But this scene felt different, and I didn't even remember choosing this to write about. My heart sank as I reread the words, feeling the sisters' sorrow — their hopelessness.

The car door slammed, and I glanced through the window to see Domari and Charlene hopping down from the truck. Ever since their first lesson two weeks ago and my epic meltdown, he practiced driving daily with Charlene after his chores were done on the ranch. Driving had easily become the highlight of his days. While he still rarely smiled, joy creased the corners of his eyes as he advanced from driving on the property to down the road and into town. That was as far as we'd let him go; it's not like I could get a driver's license for the man whose birthday was a millennium ago.

Like excited teens with their first taste of freedom, we went on drives frequently. I couldn't deny the sight of him in the driver's seat of my Jeep, black tee stretched across his chest, tattooed forearms stretched out towards the wheel, and aviator sunglasses on the big man wasn't one of the best sights I'd ever seen. I had several versions of this picture saved on my phone.

I watched as the unlikely friends chatted briefly, then

Domari left Charlene and paced across the yard to our house. The door opened and closed, followed by the coat closet, then the sound of heavy boots across the wood floors came towards me. My heart leaped in my chest as I glanced down at my journal again, scanning the words, a sense of panic taking over my body. Quickly, I snapped the book shut, shoved it under another stack of papers on my messy desk, and grabbed another. Throwing my legs back over the arm of the chair the way I sat often, I began scratching words on the page, my heart racing as I tried to act natural.

"Oh, hey," I plastered a sweet smile as I willed my breaths to even out. "Have fun?"

Domari leaned down, kissed my forehead quickly, then glanced at the notebook in my hand. "It was good. Any new stories written?"

"This?" My voice was higher than usual, and I cleared it. "Oh. Nothing today. You know how it is as a creative. Some days, the words find me. Others, not so much."

He nodded, and I placed my pen in the book, dropping it on top of the stack that hid my other journals filled with tales from his time.

"So, I was thinking," I paused, changing the subject as I stood, walking towards him and lacing my arms behind his back, feeling his steady heartbeat beneath my fingers. "You're always so calm. How do you do that?"

"With you," he bent to kiss me, and I reveled in the caress of his lips on mine, "it's easy to feel calm." His words were sweet as honey, and I couldn't help but rest my head on his chest, soaking in his warmth as his hand moved over my back. "But I have an idea to help you."

Domari let go, turning from the room, and I tipped my head to the side as I watched him go. "Wait, where are you going?"

He said nothing as he moved through the house, putting his boots on once more and opening the closet door. I followed his lead, slipping on my own boots as I watched in confusion. Domari reached into the closet to pull his jacket free, then mine, slipping it over my shoulders. When he ducked to the ground to retrieve his weapons belt still laying discarded on the floor, my nose wrinkled.

"Uh," I pursed my lips, "Surely you've noticed by now that my arm muscles are as strong as fettuccine noodles. Please tell me you're not anticipating me learning to sword fight with you. I remember the way you flung that thing through the air against six men and won during the Winter Nights tournament."

"It was ten," Domari said as he straightened, buckling his belt over his jeans, but leaving the sword sheathed in the closet with his axe.

"Right, right," I nodded. "My mistake. God forbid I deflate your ego."

With a shake of his head, Domari tugged on my hand and led me from the house out into the yard. With the warmer weather as we inched towards spring, most of the snow had begun to melt, but winter still clung in the air just above freezing. I zipped my jacket against the chill air, pulling my curls out from the collar and followed as Domari walked with purpose back towards the edge of the forest where his stack of firewood waited.

"Going to tell me what we're doing yet?" I called, trying to match his massive strides through the woods.

I stopped at the firewood pile, crossing my arms as Domari paused in front of a large tree, pulling a knife free from his belt and began to carve.

"Are you going to scratch D+S in a heart there?"

Domari turned back to me momentarily, his face clouded in confusion, and I waved him off. "Nevermind. Carry on."

He whittled for several more minutes until he blew on the bark, brushed a hand across it, and stood back to appraise it.

A target.

His strides ate up the space between us as he circled behind me, then gripped my shoulders in his hands and walked me closer to the tree. At this point, I was smart enough to keep my idiotic questions to myself, waiting for Domari to reveal his plan.

Domari stopped me, his warm hands circling my hips as they slipped beneath my jacket, laid across my bare skin under my shirt. Heat washed through me as I leaned back into him, but he only adjusted my stance, then brushed my curls to the side, his mouth at my ear. "Ready to learn, *haski*?"

His breath on my neck and his hands on my skin sent a shiver up my spine, so I only nodded.

"Close your eyes." He waited until I followed his instructions, then kissed the nape of my neck, his palm over my stomach. "Good. Breathe in." Drawing air through my nose, I focused on the pine and fresh air scent around me, both from Domari and the quiet forest. "Hold it until I tell you to let it go." My heart beat steadily in my chest as his cheek touched the side of my head, holding me close. "Now let it go."

Pursing my lips, I pushed the air back out, opening my eyes as my breath fogged in the cool air.

"Again."

By the third time I worked through this breathing technique, the tension eased from my shoulders for the first time in what felt like forever. Domari's left hand pulled from my body, and instantly, I missed his warmth and comfort. But I kept my eyes closed, breathing deeply and listening to the sound of the trees swaying around us, the horses in the distance. When something cold dropped into my palm, my eyes snapped open, falling to where Domari's fingers laced through my left hand. A small dagger rested in my palm, its weight seeming to balance itself in my loose grip.

"Ready to throw it?"

"Domari," I deadpanned as I turned my face up to his behind me. "I can hardly throw a ball for Thor, let alone a dagger at a target. You don't want to see this. Someone is going to lose an eye, and I happen to like your pretty brown ones. This is a terrible plan."

A chuckle shook through his body as he leaned into my back, pulling me into his chest, and at that moment, wrapped in his warmth and comfort, I realized how much I truly loved this man. Even with my life feeling like it was crumbling around me, he was here, helping me, seeing *me* like no one ever had before.

"I'll teach you."

Adjusting my grip on the hilt, Domari patiently instructed me how to hold it loosely in my hand and bring my elbow back into position. With his hand wrapped around my own, we went through several motions, his calm voice tickling against my neck.

"Breathe in as you pull back, exhale and release. Ready to try?"

A nervous whimper escaped me as Domari released me, stepping out of the way. "Further. I'd hate myself if I accidentally stabbed you."

"If you manage to throw the knife in my direction instead of the target, we have much larger problems than a missing eye. You know Odin only has one, right? Sacrificed the other for knowledge. Maybe the same will happen to me."

"Stop trying to distract me."

"If I was trying to distract you, I'd tell you that my cock is straining against my jeans from how you rubbed your ass on me just now, and I've decided I much prefer my old trousers. This is terrible. I don't know why I ever let you talk me into wearing these."

A laugh exploded out of me, and I doubled over, gripping my side.

"Bending over in those leggings isn't helping, Shelbie." Domari's mouth was in a flat line, but I could see the light dancing in his eyes. I slowly straightened, wiggling my butt as I found my stance once more to the sound of Domari groaning behind me.

"Breathe. Find your calm first."

So I did, drawing air through my nose in a long inhale,

holding it, as I adjusted my fingers on the hilt, elbow in the air. As I exhaled, my arm moved forward, fingers loosening just like he'd showed me. The dagger flipped through the air as it moved towards the target and my heart raced, eyes expanding as I bounced on my toes in excitement. A loud *thwap* cut through the air as the knife bounced off the tree several feet below the target, not even close.

Domari walked to the tree, bending over to retrieve it, and brought the dagger back. "Try again."

By the tenth time I'd thrown the blade, I was only marginally closer to hitting the target, but each time I centered myself, taking my stance and breathing deeply, I felt the calm I so craved sinking deeper into my skin.

"One more?" I asked as Domari walked towards me from the tree, but he said nothing, bending as he neared, and I cried out in surprise when his shoulder connected with my center, my head suddenly hanging upside down. His broad hand landed on my ass in a light slap, and I gasped.

"We're done for today. It's your turn to calm *me* down."

A broad smile spread across my face as heat bloomed in my core, anticipation for what was to come.

29

DOMARI

The rest of the day was spent lounging around the house, but Domari could feel some of the tension gone between himself and Shelbie. His heart soared every time she laughed easily, wrapping her arms around him, soaking in his comfort. Words were lost when she turned her broad smile on him, eyes alight with joy. How he'd ever lived without her, he didn't know, but he would do anything to keep her at his side.

As they lay in bed, his arms wrapped around her back as he did most nights, he kissed her shoulder. "I love you."

Her hands squeezed tighter around his arms, pulling him in closer. "I love you, too."

The feel of her chest steadily rising and falling as she drifted into sleep was one he feared he was starting to take for granted. The season was changing in Colorado, winter releasing its grip as warmer weather melted the snow on the ground, and his thoughts drifted to his own world.

It had been eight weeks now since he'd arrived here in

Shelbie's world, lost and desolate, and each day that passed was a gift. But in the back of his mind, Domari knew this was too good to be true. Nothing good in his life had ever lasted, and as much as he didn't want that to be the case with Shelbie, he couldn't seem to shake off the nagging in his gut.

Something was coming and coming fast.

Time was running out.

Breathing deeply like he'd taught Shelbie earlier, he soaked in the floral smell of Shelbie's soap, his hand splayed out across her skin, and held her close as his mind drifted off to sleep.

"No," a voice cried, pulling Domari from the recesses of his mind as he jerked awake. Darkness filled the bedroom, faint light leaking through the blinds from the moon, barely enough to illuminate the room. Rubbing sleep from his eyes, he glanced across the bed, seeing the way Shelbie had moved across the space, curled in on herself. Forehead deeply creased, she squeezed her eyes shut, tears leaking down onto the pillow beneath her. *"I want out!"* she cried, never opening her eyes.

Reaching across the mattress, Domari wiped a tear from her face, but she pulled away from his touch, eyes still closed, thrashing in the sheets tangled around her. *"LEAVE."*

Hurt flashed across his face momentarily, feeling that same lonely, sinking feeling that always threatened to drag him under, but he knew her words weren't aimed at him. The sob that racked her body was enough to drag him back to his senses, sitting up in the bed. She'd had so many of these nightmares lately, but never had he seen her this upset.

The day spent throwing knives, then reveling in each other, had been one of their best together yet. He could still hear the sound of her joyous laughter ringing in his ears, the sight of her bright smile as she leaned into him all day. He'd hoped it would've eased whatever troubled her mind at night, but as he watched her thrash, he couldn't help but fear whatever plagued her mind was getting worse. Unable to stand the sight of her pain, he placed his hand on her shoulder, tightened his fingers, and pulled her head into his lap.

"Shelbie," he said, placing a gentle kiss on her temple, his heart breaking at the anguished expression Shelbie wore in her sleep. "Wake up. It's a dream." Lightly shaking her, he turned her face up towards his, placing a gentle kiss on the corner of her mouth. "Wake up, Shelbie."

Her eyes flew open, a gasp pulled from her lips as she stared wide-eyed at the room around her, breaths coming heavily, tears still streaming down her cheeks.

"Hey," Domari whispered, swiping away the tears, "Just a dream."

Sitting up, she fought to even her breathing, and he watched with pride as she practiced the slow inhale and exhale he'd taught her earlier. Lacing his hands through her hair, he pushed it from her face, waiting until she'd calmed down.

"What were you dreaming of?"

Shaking her head lightly, Shelbie pulled the sleeve of her shirt down over her hand, then brushed it over her face, palms pressed into her eyes.

"Maybe if you tell me about it, whatever holds you in its grip will let go," he said, not wanting to push, but knowing how haunted his own mind had become over the years. Sometimes when he closed his eyes, all he could see was red, the blood he'd spilled spraying across his subconscious, following him for years. After ten years serving as a personal guard to Emperor Konstantios and the commander of the Guard in the *Hetaireia*, he had plenty of horrid memories to fill his mind. Until Shelbie, he'd never had anyone he'd even considered sharing those nightmares with, but, more than anything, he didn't want that darkness to haunt Shelbie how it did him. "Tell me."

Her hands dropped into her lap right before she shifted her weight to lean her chest across his. Without a thought, he circled her with his arms, holding her close, kissing the top of her head.

"I don't want to upset you."

Domari peeled back away from her slightly, glancing down at her face. "What could you dream that would hurt me?" Then his face fell. "Were you fucking Magnus? That might be worth crying over."

A chuckle shook through her body as he'd intended, and she swatted at his chest. "God, no. Gross. Although I don't think I'd be crying over that, though. His muscles have muscles. Maybe I take the 'gross' part back now that I'm thinking about it."

Loving the way her demeanor had changed at his teasing, he dropped his hand down her side, tickling her waist. A sudden laugh burst out of her as her knee jerked up, grazing his crotch.

"Holy shit, I'm so sorry," she said, eyes wide as she rose to her knees next to Domari, where he clutched his hands over his crotch, curled in on his side. Trying hard to suppress her laughter, she kissed his face, down his neck. "Don't freaking tickle me. When we were kids, Jacob used to tickle me until I'd threaten to puke on him."

"Lesson learned," Domari answered through clenched teeth, his eyes screwed shut.

"Anything I can do?" Shelbie asked, her soft hands rubbing across his bearded cheek. When he shook his head, she fiddled with her sleeves, still kneeling next to him in the bed. The sheets had fallen, exposing her bare legs beneath her t-shirt.

"I dream of your clan a lot," Shelbie said, twisting the fabric in her hands. "Almost every night, actually."

"What about them?" Domari asked, curiosity piqued, as he opened his eyes to look at her.

"I don't know." She shrugged, staring off into the dark room. "Most of the time it's like watching a movie in my head, but I know the actors personally."

"About Magnus?" Domari asked, rolling to his back, one brow raised.

"Stop." Shelbie laughed, pushing at his side. "Honestly, not really. I did write a story in my journal once of him scaring children with a bedtime story. He was terrible at it. Children were crying."

A smile tugged on Domari's lips as he looked to Shelbie, tucking her hair behind her ears in the faint light. Breath sucked out of him as he watched the way the light played off her features, more beautiful than any woman he'd ever seen.

"I dream of Signe a lot," Shelbie went on, not seeming to notice the way Domari's eyes raked over her. "Sometimes I swear it's like she can see me, but I'm a fly on the wall, observing whatever I'm imagining is happening in their world."

"And what *are* you imagining is happening in their world?"

"Well, Mjölnir returned to the Erikssons, which I know is wishful thinking."

The sound of his beloved horse's name sent a pang through Domari's heart, hoping the brilliant beast *had* made his way back to Gunnar. But it had taken them almost two weeks to get to the Tree, so who knew how long it would take Mjölnir to return? More than likely, his horse was gone for good, living out his days in the frozen mountains with the other wild horses. Losing Mjölnir sat like a heavy weight in Domari's stomach, making him homesick.

"I keep dreaming of children arriving in the village," Shelbie whispered, her lips turned down. "I don't know. It's all made up anyway."

Pulling her back down to the bed and into his arms, Domari savored the feel of her against his chest. "Would you like me to tell you more of my home and my people? Is that why you're dreaming about them?"

Her fingers danced along his chest, blue eyes turned up to meet his gaze. "I'd like that."

Thinking for a moment, Domari glanced around the room, searching for a memory not clouded with grief. Seeing the framed picture of a young Shelbie tangled with her brother Jacob hanging on the wall, skis pointed in the air behind them, he smiled.

"Did you know Vikings ski?"

"What?" Shelbie asked, surprise lighting her eyes as she leaned back to look at him. Unable to stop himself, he placed a quick kiss to her nose, then to the freckles under her eyes.

"Yes, when I was young." He nodded. "My first memories are from before we left Stormyr's clan, living in the mountains along the sea. Our skis were wood, with metal bindings to clip them to our boots, so the general concept is the same as the ones you use." He pointed to the wall, and Shelbie followed his line of sight. "In a world covered with snow, they were convenient and fun. Like everything, we made it into sport."

In his mind, he could picture the day he'd raced to the top of the hill, skis in hand, a bright smile on his face. Raud trailing behind, laughter echoing in the empty mountains as the two boys played, hiding from their fathers in the village below. Like Domari, Raud's mother had passed in childbirth, leaving him to be raised by his father Uhtred. Uhtred was far more concerned with earning Stormyr's favor than raising a son, leading raids often while Raud waited in the village for his return.

"The first time I raced my best friend, we crashed into

each other, limbs tangled as we rolled down the mountain, skis nowhere to be found." Domari couldn't help but chuckle at the memory. "It's one of the first memories I have. One of the best from before Erik moved us from the village. From before my father died."

"We call that a *yard sale*." Shelbie's palm laid flat across Domari's chest as she looked up through her lashes at Domari, her lips tugging up into a smile. "When you fall and lose your skis and poles. It's called a yard sale. I hate hiking back up the mountain to find my skis, but have done the same more times than I can count."

Domari smiled, trying to banish the dark thoughts that followed his story. The best friend Domari knew so many years ago — the one he'd rolled down the mountain with — was long gone, replaced with a bitter, broken man. The last time he'd seen Raud, he'd held a knife to Shelbie's throat, and Domari had known a deep-seated terror he'd never felt before.

As if sensing the change in his thoughts, Shelbie's hand slid to Domari's jaw, turning his face towards her. "Thank you for telling me that. I love picturing you as a carefree child."

She placed a gentle kiss on his lips, and the feel of her smooth skin under his fingers drew him back to the present, away from the memories that so often dragged him down. Wanting to banish the thoughts of the past, his hand slid up her bare thigh, loving the way her breath caught at the feel of his touch. Domari flipped her onto her back, rising above her, deepening their kiss as he pushed her shirt up over her stomach.

Shelbie's fingers tangled in his golden brown hair, shoved in every direction as he worked his mouth over her body, sliding lower. With a lick of his tongue over her breast, followed by a kiss, she arched into his touch.

As their gaze locked, he smirked, moving his hands down her stomach and to her slick core. The touch of his fingers sliding over her sensitive skin followed by his mouth over her chest had Shelbie throwing her head back, moaning his name. Working her with eager strokes, he reveled in the way her body reacted to his. When her hooded gaze met his once more, he leaned forward, crawling up the bed towards her.

Their kiss was consuming. The passionate fire that burned between them had given way to something else. Something deeper. Something *more*.

"Shelbie…" he whispered as he rose above her, warm skin settling down on hers as his heart expanded in his chest, overwhelmed with the love he felt for her. Tears gathered in Shelbie's eyes as her arms circled his neck, pulling him back into the kiss. It was gentle, full of unspoken words and promises of forever.

His body rose for a moment until he brushed against her, seeking entrance. Shelbie lifted her hips, and he sank home, filling her. The sound of her contented moan pushed him, seizing her lips with his as he worshiped her body. Tongues tangled as she held on, the weight of his body pushing hers deeper into the mattress with each slow thrust.

"*Domari.*"

The way she groaned his name, fingers digging into the

skin on his back drove him mad. His thrusts came faster, deeper, craving how complete he felt in her arms.

"I love you so much," she said, her voice almost unrecognizable it was so filled with lust.

"*Ástin min.*"

Everything seemed to explode as Shelbie's body pulsed, pulling him under a tide of emotions and sensations he had no choice but to give into. Domari's forehead dropped to her shoulder as he thrust again, hard, seating himself completely, and groaned his release. Sweat dripped off his chest, coating them both as he lowered himself onto her, finding her lips once more, bodies quaking.

"Even better than my dreams," he said at last. Domari shifted to the side and pulled Shelbie's back to him. "Wiggle all you want tonight."

Her breathy laugh paired with his hand on her chest, rapidly rising and falling as she snuggled in close, was all Domari had ever wanted in life. He didn't need glory, or battle, or wealth. Valhalla could hold nothing for him compared to the love he felt in Shelbie's embrace.

He only hoped it wasn't too much to ask for forever.

30

SIGNE

The sun lingered in the sky longer as spring approached, but the winter weather clung to the landscape. Gunnar kept the men of their village busy, hunting as much as possible when the weather allowed it. Even with the village somewhat settled, each day that crept closer to warmer weather had Signe's unease growing, fearing the return of raiding season. Some days, the feeling stuck with her to the point she paced, unable to stand still.

Today was one of those days.

Gunnar and the men left earlier, and Signe stood in the doorway of her house, staring out over the trees in the distance. Something was coming; she could *feel* it in her bones. The sounds of the children happily playing behind her faded from her mind as she was lost in thought. Awareness hummed in her veins as she watched for gods only knew what.

Signe could feel Viveka and Kára's eyes on her back while

she paced near the door, clenching and unclenching her hands as adrenaline pumped into her system. Finally, unable to stand it any longer, Signe removed Erik from the wrap on her chest, handing him over to Viveka as she slid a sword into her sheath and a cloak over her shoulders. With a last pat on the dagger at her hip, she pushed the door open on creaking hinges.

The sun was out, although hidden behind the clouds, as Signe stepped into the biting wind in search of *something*. Her boots crunched across the new snow while she moved away from the house, letting her senses take in the scene around her.

Suddenly, a cry split the air, snow scattering as if afraid of the sound. Signe lifted her arm, covering her eyes as she searched the sky and surroundings for the source of the noise.

Even the talk of dragons lately hadn't prepared her for what she saw there, hovering far above the trees. The enormous predator shifted, blocking out the sun with his dark wings as fire erupted from his mouth. The heatwave rustled the trees, snow scattering to the ground with the force. Heart racing in her chest, Signe was so focused on the dragon above, she almost missed what was below him.

Children.

Dozens of them.

"Frida!" Signe shouted, panic clawing at her as she screamed, drawing anyone nearby. Cloak billowing behind her, Signe raced through the knee-high snow towards the crowd. Huddled together, the children moved as one towards her.

The dragon screeched again, sending another plume of fire far over the children's heads... herding them.

Warming them.

Protecting them.

That's what he was doing.

Hadriel — *The Dark One* — was delivering these children directly to her doorstep.

Chills spread across Signe's cheeks as she raced towards the scene, not even a lick of fear biting her heels as she ran towards the massive predator. Her eyes flicked above, unable to comprehend this scene as she neared the children, watching as the dragon descended to just above them.

Why Hadriel had chosen her — the Erikssons — she didn't understand, but the dragon's gaze was locked on Signe as she fell in the snow in front of the children, hands grazing over their small, dirty frames in search of injuries. His green cat-like eyes blinked twice as he ducked his head, almost in a nod, and turned in the sky, retreating to the mountains.

"Children!" Frida exclaimed as she dropped to Signe's side, breathing heavily. Yrsa was right behind her, always where she needed to be, gathering the smallest of the children to her first. Together, the two older women dried tears, calmed fears, and hugged the children to their chests.

Signe rose to her feet, glancing out over the crowd, heart thumping loudly in her ears. There were twenty-two children here, a wide range of ages, and not a single adult in the group. They'd come alone, as they all had. Signe's breaths fogged the air as she panted, eyes scanning the clearing for any sense of danger. But the feeling in her chest that had been bothering her for days was gone.

This was what she'd been waiting for.

Emotions shuddered in her as a killing calm spread over Signe, one she'd felt so many times before. Spinning in a circle, her gaze caught on the sight of the dragon fading in the distance, pulling something from deep within her. She watched until he was only a speck on the horizon, fading into the morning light. With each beat of his wings, Signe's breathing evened out, and an unnerving stillness took place there instead.

"They're coming." Her words came out barely above a whisper as Signe tipped her chin up. She pulled in a lungful of air, so cold it was painful, and her eyes closed. Voices in the clearing stopped as everyone turned towards her, cloak billowing behind her in the wind, red-blonde hair floating, energy emanating from her skin. Power flowed from her, through her, *in* her, in a way she hadn't felt since the last time she stood on a battlefield.

When Signe opened her eyes, Yrsa's gaze locked on hers for a moment — two — before Yrsa nodded in agreement. Signe's hands drifted to her hips as her chest expanded, searching the forest for danger.

The attack wouldn't be today, but she knew without a doubt these children were a message from her father. Without even asking, Signe was willing to bet her own treasured dagger when they learned where these children were from, they would discover they came from different clans, all inching closer to their own from the shore.

Raud and Draugr were on the move, headed for Signe.

In Draugr's eyes, children were a weakness, and he was sending them *all* to her, sure she would defend them and spread herself too thin. Her father knew her well — there wasn't a single child here she wouldn't die for in an instant. But her father had *consistently* underestimated her.

"Call a village meeting." The words were firm, a command from a leader, and Frida's eyes glanced at her daughter-in-law.

"Gunnar—" Frida started, but Signe's hand rose to the air, cutting her off.

"I will not wait that long. The meeting is tonight. We have wasted enough time," Signe retorted, holding firm control over the conversation. "Yrsa, return home and stop at Thorsten's on your way. Let his family know. Send your sons to the rest of the villagers. When the men arrive back from hunting, prepare them all. We will meet at sundown at Frida's to craft a plan."

"The children —" Frida began again, but Signe's emerald gaze locked on her. Frida's mouth snapped shut, eyes scanning Signe, then Yrsa, once more, before her shoulders slumped, her eyes downcast.

Guilt should have eaten at Signe for the harshness of her words, but she *had to* make them see what was coming. Signe softened her voice, trying to be sympathetic. "Take the children to my home. Get them settled. They have been through enough, and they will be ever grateful for your care and hospitality. You were fated for this role, Frida."

The older woman's gaze was rimmed in red as she rose to her feet, lifting the smallest child — no more than three,

Signe guessed — to her hip and moved across the snow, the children following in her wake.

The men returned from their hunt later that afternoon, towing back two deer and a wild boar — a highly successful hunt for this time of year. The happiness on Gunnar's face faltered as he came into the house and noticed all the new children milling about.

His head whipped around the room, finding Signe in the back, then crossing the room to her in several strides. "What happened?"

Signe quickly informed him of the children's arrival and Hadriel's appearance. Gunnar scrubbed a hand through his short golden hair, shoulders tense as he took in this new challenge.

"They're coming, Gunnar," Signe said as her feet stopped, shoulder-width apart. Ready. Posed. "My father. Maybe Raud, too. He's sending a message to us. Warning us of what's coming." Gunnar's eyes settled on Signe's as his jaw ticked. "We need to prepare for war."

"In winter?" he asked, his eyes closing in frustration. Fingers rubbing his forehead, he continued, "Why would they be doing this?"

"I don't know," Signe whispered with a shake of her head, resuming her pacing. "The timing is terrible, difficult, and dangerous for us, with the storms sweeping in so frequently. But I *feel* it, Gunnar." She clutched at the fabric of her blue skirts, wishing she could rip the feeling from her body and don the armor she still kept beneath their bed. "We can't be unprepared with these children here."

"There are thirty-two new children in the village, Signe." Gunnar's eyes found hers as she turned, defeat already written in the lines of his face. "Thirty-two new mouths to feed. A few deer and a boar can't fix this. Not for long. Hunger and shelter are as much a threat as whatever you sense is coming."

Words dammed in Signe's throat as she took in the implications. Thirty-two children, most likely all orphaned, and hers to protect. Erik chose that moment to let out a soft wail, hands fisted against her chest where he was wrapped once more. Signe's eyes glanced down to his tiny frame as she adjusted him to nurse.

He was so small — so delicate. But the men coming for them were anything but.

No matter what the children had said before, they hadn't been spared from the goodness of these men's heart. Signe knew better — there was no *goodness* in her father's heart. It was a game, and he was moving pieces on the board. Raud was the unknown factor for Signe, the part that didn't fit.

"What are you thinking?" Gunnar asked her as he sidled closer, lifting his large palms to run across her shoulders. "Tell me."

"Their motives don't make sense." Her brow creased in confusion, brows nearly touching. "Raud is bitter, yes. Your father banished him after your sister's death." Her husband's face crumpled at her words, twisted in grief even now, ten years later. "But *why?* Why would he do this?"

Gunnar's chin tilted up to the ceiling, pausing before answering. Several moments passed before his gaze returned to her on an exhale. "He blames me. This is my punishment for the raid that killed Tove. Just like I couldn't protect her, I can't protect these children." His shoulders shrunk with the words, and Signe knew Raud wasn't the only one who blamed Gunnar for Tove's death. Gunnar blamed himself, too.

"Gunnar," Signe started, working to ensure her words were sensitive — something that didn't come easily to her. "Stealing the horses was your idea, yes. The poor planning was yours, yes." Gunnar winced at her words, and she scolded herself for her delivery, placing her hand across Gunnar's heart, beating rapidly under his skin. "But her death... her death isn't on you. It wasn't then, and it isn't now. No matter how desperately you want to protect us all, you can't."

"If something ever happened to you," the words were choked in Gunnar's throat, his fingers tracking across her jawline, "I would stop at nothing for vengeance."

Signe laughed, and his eyes drew up in confusion. "You're wrong." Signe shook her head with a smile. "You *would* stop. Of course, you'd be broken-hearted for ages and never able to look upon another woman again because none could ever live up to *me,*" her words drew a chuckle out of her husband as she'd intended, "but you would stop. You would never punish innocents the way Raud is. The way my father is."

Gunnar's eyes glanced between her own, feeling the depth of the emotion at the moment.

"But I," Signe went on, her fingers trailing over Gunnar's broad chest, "*I* would never stop." He lifted her chin, and the gaze that met Gunnar was forged in fires he would never understand, no matter how much of her past she'd shared with him. "I would do *anything* to protect you," Signe growled as heat spread through her veins, the anger a tangible thing. "To protect our family. To protect this clan."

His fingers danced across her jaw, feeling the tension radiating from her as he brought his forehead down to rest on hers. "Tell me what to do."

Signe's spine snapped straight at Gunnar's words, understanding that he was handing her the reins for this. "Call in every favor you have. Every ally of ours needs to be alert and ready to move." The words tumbled out of Signe's mouth in rapid-fire. "We need able bodies. We need children relocated. We need weapons and defenses. Our men are trained, but this isn't Winter Nights. This isn't a game. This is life or death, and what's coming—"

"It shall be done." Gunnar stopped her words, and her chest swelled with gratitude for this man, able to set aside his pride to do what was best for his people.

"Come." His hand reached down to grasp hers and pulled her towards the door, out into the cold evening, directed towards his mother's longhouse. "Our clan is waiting for your lead."

31

SIGNE

"How are the defenses coming?" Gunnar asked from where he perched on the edge of a table near the hearth in Frida's longhouse as he'd done so often lately. Sconces lined the wall, casting a smokey haze over the crowded room. The black pup — Freki, they'd named him at last — sat alert between Gunnar's legs, eyeing those around his master while he chewed on a bone from their latest hunt. Freki had grown over the last several weeks, his frame filling out with all the meat the greedy puppy could find. His paws were immense, telling just how large this dog would grow to be, and Signe couldn't help but love the way he stood defensively at Gunnar's side.

Unlike Gunnar's calculating calm, Signe's body hummed with anxious energy. She paced along the perimeter of Frida's longhouse, unable to sit still. From the stiffness of Gunnar's body language, Signe knew he'd prefer if she sat to listen like the rest of the men in the room, but unease rippled under Signe's skin.

Two weeks had passed since the last of the children had arrived, and Gunnar had followed Signe's advice, calling in every favor owed to him. Two weeks of relocating children to other villages. Two weeks of training in the makeshift training grounds outside the house. Two weeks of preparing for battle. Two weeks of dread settling deep in Signe's bones.

Fortunately, Gunnar's father had been gracious to other local clans — never grasping for more power, but always looking out for his neighbors just the same. When word spread of the potential threat to the Eriksson clan and the now-homeless children, several clans stepped up to join their cause. In those two weeks, men and women from the Larsson, Ohlsson, and Salversson clans had arrived, promising more to follow.

"We've narrowed the paths coming into the village," Thorsten's deep voice broke through Signe's mind, his familiar bright red hair catching her eye in a sea of unknown faces. While Signe was glad to see so many allies willing to join them, the sight of so many strangers sent unease rippling through her. So she paced. "We left felled trees strategically through the forest to push any incoming parties from the west into a narrow opening."

Gunnar nodded at his words, and Signe breathed a sigh of relief. With no fortress around them, her village would use the land's natural resources, making it difficult for a large force to get to them.

"The river remains frozen," Björn reported next, "and

we've broken through the ice where we can. It will freeze over again in the next storm, but for now, it's impassable."

Kare and Arne conversed with several allies, matching flaxen heads bowed low over the table with men whose names had escaped Signe at the moment, discussing weapons stores. Signe's eyes scanned the room, delighted everyone seemed to take the threat seriously, yet her heart sank as she counted heads.

Never in her wildest dreams would this be enough to take on her father and his forces. No amount of preparation could overcome the number of *bodies* his force contained; the last time she'd fought alongside the Helvigsson clan, they were over two-hundred strong — four times the size of the group gathered here. The most vicious men fought for her father, seeking the lifestyle Draugr provided, and eight years wouldn't have changed that.

Gunnar carried the conversation, doling out orders that showed the extent of his forethought and knowledge. Signe watched him as he bore this burden of worry gracefully, offering wisdom and strength as he encouraged everyone in the room to trust him. This meeting was one of many they'd hosted lately, and the number of allies arriving was increasing by the day. But it still wasn't enough.

"The last of the women and children are set to move tomorrow," a deep voice rang out, and Signe's head snapped to attention. Her heart raced in her chest at the words, even though it had been her idea to move those unable to defend themselves to another village. It would be a long and tedious journey for them as they made their way to the Larsson village on the shore, but she knew it was the right decision. "Those that haven't already left will leave with my men at first light."

Signe watched as the man continued to speak, fighting to recall his name. Asmund, she thought. His dark beard hung down just below his collarbone, neatly trimmed and blending in with the bear pelt he wore across his shoulders. The battle axe sheathed at his side was so broad that she debated if she'd even be able to lift it, but Asmund's arms were corded with muscles, showing he knew how to wield it. His broad chest moved with his motions as he explained the path they'd take away from the village, following the hunting trails to hide their passage as much as possible as they made their way closer to the sea.

Someone else spoke up, reporting on the training grounds now occupying the clearing between Gunnar and Frida's longhouses in the village. The men had been running training exercises for the last two weeks, and Signe joined in where she could, but it wasn't as much of a concern for her. Spears, blades, bows… they *sang* to her in a fearsome lullaby. It was a tune she could never forget, and her aim was always true, no matter how long it had been since she'd last touched a weapon. Lost to her thoughts, she jerked to attention when a large body settled next to her against the wall where she stood.

"I know this will be hard on you," Asmund said in a low tone meant only for her, crossing his muscled arms over his enormous chest. "But we will see your children safely to my village and return to fight at your side."

Signe's head filled with pain, a tingling sensation behind her eyes as she nodded, swallowing hard.

"It will be an honor to stand shoulder to shoulder with you and the Erikssons." Asmund's hand drifted to the blade of his axe, resting lightly. "Stories are told of your bravery, Signe." His words made her laugh as she shook her head — *more like stupidity than bravery* — but he continued, "Even as far as our village, stories of the Demon's Spawn lives on, inspiring our girls to fight."

Her mouth fell open at his words, but nothing came out.

"As their father and leader, I'm more than happy to have everyone in my clan able to defend themselves, so I thank you for that." His smile was genuine and kind, and Signe was speechless. "When I return, don't be surprised if women from my village return with me. My daughter will not believe me when I say I trained alongside you."

Signe's head shook as her eyes dipped, unable to comprehend what Asmund was saying. Self-loathing warred with pride at his words. She never thought that her actions — her own misdeeds — would serve this purpose.

"To fight ruthlessly, defending those who need it most, is a great honor." His heavy hand rested on her shoulder, squeezing momentarily. "The gods will be on our side."

Signe's lips parted as she fought for a response, but Asmund had already receded into the room, standing at Gunnar's side. She watched as the two men spoke momentarily before slapping each other's shoulders in solidarity.

"Don't let that head of yours swell too much," Magnus's voice snagged Signe's attention. He casually munched on seeds as he leaned against a table, but his eyes danced with mirth as her gaze met his. Waggling his eyebrows, Magnus threw another seed high into the air, catching it in his mouth.

Her eyes squinted, taking in Magnus's casual posture, and teased, "Shouldn't you be crying over your wife right about now? She leaves in the morning with my children." Instantly, his face fell, and she regretted her harsh words.

Magnus stood, his height towering over her and chest twice as broad. "I've done that twice already today and plan to several more times tonight."

Signe's serious expression cracked at his innuendo, and a chuckle snuck through her smirk. "You're incorrigible."

"I'm terrified," Magnus whispered against her ear, so softly she wasn't sure that's what he said. "Not of battle," he chewed, "but of leaving her. And my children."

Hearing the depth of his emotions, Signe closed the distance between them, pulling her large, annoying little brother into the first hug she'd ever freely given him. Her arms squeezed over his torso as she rested her cheek on his warm chest. Several beats passed before his arms laced around her as well.

"So am I," Signe whispered into the cloth of his shirt. "But if you tell anyone I said that, I will slit your throat in your sleep."

His laugh burst out of him as his chest rumbled under her cheek, and the sound was so catching, she couldn't help but chuckle with him.

"They'll be fine," Signe said as she stepped back from him. "I can feel it."

"As can I," Yrsa said as she stepped into the house, the

flames from sconces dancing in the wind until the door shut behind her. "Their passage will be safe."

Voices whispered as everyone's eyes tracked Yrsa's movements, her graying red hair swishing as she aimed for where Signe and Magnus stood near the wall. Relief flooded Signe at Yrsa's words. While it was true that Signe *did* feel that their passage would be safe, and she was sure this was the right course of action, to hear Yrsa announce it with such confidence eased the pressure on Signe's heart. She trusted the older woman's intuition even more than her own.

"The dragon will watch over them once more," Yrsa said so confidently that Signe's head cocked to the side. Gunnar rose from the table, pacing to his wife's side, Freki two steps behind.

"How do you know that?" Signe asked, but she knew the answer before it left Yrsa's lips.

"I was born a Promised." Gunnar's head whipped to Yrsa at the words, but Signe only nodded in affirmation of her suspicions. The room went silent around them; all other chatter stopped with the shocking confession. "Hadriel isn't mine," Yrsa pursed her lips, emotions battling on her usually calm face, "but I can feel his intentions."

"Tell me." Gunnar's words were a command but spoken in a tone that was still more caring than harsh, something Signe could never attempt to mimic.

"My dragon, Vyara." Yrsa swallowed, and Björn stepped to her side, lacing his fingers through his wife's. "She was gone before my ceremony, so I never received my full powers. We never spoke, but the faint powers of a Promised run in my blood still."

"Powers." Gunnar repeated the word slowly, and her head rose as pride swelled under her skin.

"Yes. Healing is the strongest of my powers, of course. I also have premonitions, although they are uncontrolled and rare." Confidence filled her words as she continued, "But it's clear to me that our loved ones will be protected on this journey. This is a worry we can release to the gods and know that they are watching over them."

"What else have you Seen?" Gunnar asked, the words seeming to slip out before he could rein them back in.

"Hadriel," she whispered, her eyes alight as she glanced around the room. "Something is coming. He can feel it, and he grows more distraught every day that his Promised isn't here."

Gunnar's brow scrunched in confusion at her words. "Who is his Promised?"

Yrsa's lips parted, but before she could speak, the wind whipped through the house as the door flew open. The flames in the sconces winked out, casting the room in eerie darkness. The bright white of the snow outside was near blinding in contrast, casting a shadow over the cloaked figure in the doorway.

"Shelbie," a craggy voice spoke from the open doors. Gunnar rushed to the woman at the door, pulling her into the warmth of the house. "Thank you, my boy." She patted his arm lightly as her dark hair, greying at the temples, tumbled out from beneath her deep blue cloak. "But immortals aren't bothered by things like *cold.*"

"*Verandi,*" Yrsa exclaimed as she dropped to her knees in reverence. At the sound of her name, the rest of the room's occupants followed suit, bowing their heads to the Norn in their presence.

"Rise, my child," Verandi said, placing a delicate, glowing hand on Yrsa's auburn hair. Yrsa stood as Verandi's hand drifted to her cheek in a loving embrace.

"Why did you send her back then?" Gunnar's voice broke the tender moment, eyes focused on Verandi. "Why did you send Shelbie back?"

Rather than answer him, Verandi's eyes drifted to Signe, searching her expression. "Do you remember my words?"

Signe's ears buzzed, the echo of Verandi's prophecy long ago playing in her memory. "When my father and I meet again...," the words were pulled from her mouth as if of their own volition, "Ragnarok will be upon us."

With a sad smile, Verandi nodded. "The fates are changing," she whispered, and Yrsa sucked in a sharp inhale. "Something is stirring, causing this new path to diverge from the one we have Seen for so long. Ragnarok," she paused, her eyes searching the men in the room, "the time is coming. Our world may come to an end. But Shelbie—"

"Is she coming back?" Magnus interrupted, and Signe was shocked at the audacity of his act.

Verandi only chuckled at the large man's words, unbothered by the interruption. "Yes, I believe your friend will return."

"You *believe*?" Gunnar hesitated far more than his brother as he countered the immortal before him.

"The fates of dragons we can't foresee. And Shelbie's fate is woven so tightly with the dragons that it casts a shadow over the future, blurring it. It was by chance we happened upon her thread the first time and found her, not fully understanding how she was lost to begin with. So, we brought her here, hoping to fix the tear in the tapestry of fate. But rather than fix the tapestry, it began to unravel faster than we could control, changing the entire course of the future. So we sent her back, hoping we could undo whatever had begun, but fate has already altered, morphing into something new and terrible."

"Dragons?" Signe's breath caught on the word, the day Viveka cried of the white dragon surfacing. "More than one?"

"My sisters and I," Verandi paused, her eyes darting around the room. The sight of an immortal *nervous* did nothing to ease the tension rising off everyone here. "We believe Nidhoggr must have had a hand in Shelbie's fate for us to be so blind to it."

"What does that even mean?" Gunnar asked, unease rippling through his features at the turn in this conversation.

"Nidhoggr lives," Verandi whispered the words, but the room was so silent that all heard her proclamation. Hearing the dragon's name sent a wave of chills over Signe's skin, bile rising in the back of her throat. "His fate is hidden from me, but unimaginable power is surfacing that can only mean an ancient dragon has resurfaced. We believe he used what power he had to destroy the last of the Promised before Hadriel hatched, hoping to end the bond between Vikings and dragons. By doing so, none could challenge him as he fought to tear down the Tree, splitting the nine realms open at the seams and watching as Ragnarok swallowed us whole."

"He has that power?" The words trembled as they left Yrsa, floating into the thick air of the room.

Verandi nodded gravely, her eyes downcast as she studied the woman before her. "Even as an Unpromised, he has far more power than you can fathom."

"How do we bring Shelbie back?" Gunnar asked. "Is that what we need to do now? Unite Hadriel and Shelbie?"

"Domari went after her," Magnus mumbled, and Gunnar's furious gaze shifted to his brother, blue eyes flaring with anger.

"All this time you've known where Domari was?" he growled between clenched teeth.

Magnus only shrugged. "He loves her. Isn't that worth taking every risk for? I didn't know if he would be able to travel to her, but I spoke with him the night he left. He was broken, and," Magnus's eyes filled with tears as he glanced at his brother, "I wanted to make sure he was okay." The large man sniffed as his eyes shifted from his brother to Signe, then back. "When Mjölnir returned alone, I assumed that meant he found his way to her. I would jump through time for Astrid and — don't even think to lie to me, brother — I know you would for Signe, too."

"Is that even possible?" Signe asked, bringing the conversation back around to Verandi.

"It is." Verandi nodded. "And he found his way."

Gunnar scrubbed a hand over his mouth as a long sigh escaped him, but Signe saw how his shoulders fell.

"Are they coming back?" Magnus said hesitantly — wishfully.

Verandi's brow creased again in thought, but Yrsa answered.

"She has the pendant." Yrsa nodded, and Verandi's brows shot up in surprise. "I gifted it to her before she left the village. If she puts it on —"

"Hadriel will call her home," Verandi finished the thought.

The two nodded in unison, and the room was silent, absorbing all that had come to light.

"Now, as to the other issue at hand." Verandi's gaze shifted to Signe, and her expression softened. "The road ahead of you is one most vital and requires great sacrifice. Your fate has been leading you here for years, for the only way out of this coming battle is through you, Signe. Our time has run out."

32

SHELBIE

After a day spent throwing daggers and practicing my breathing — something we'd done daily over the last two weeks after we finished our chores on the ranch — I felt lighter. It didn't matter that I'd landed not even one in the target in the two weeks I'd been trying to learn — our time spent in front of the target meant so much more than that. While, yes, the breathing exercises helped, the burn in my arm that reminded me how hard I worked helped even more. And the sight of Domari's pride as he watched me try my hardest to sink the blade? *That* was the best.

For the first time in maybe forever, I felt like I could lean *in* to someone, rather than hide the parts of me that weren't bright and cheerful. Even with Charlene I wasn't completely honest, but Domari… it was different. I *sucked* at throwing knives, but never once was he frustrated or annoyed. Never once did he give up on me. Never once did he say we should skip trying again. And the way he held me when I couldn't sleep, when the dreams that plagued me were too dark? I'd never loved anyone more.

I didn't think Domari understood the significance behind me asking for help, or how much it meant every time he shared more of his story with me. But each morning, I woke up full of gratitude for this growing relationship, despite my dark dreams.

Maybe he was right. Maybe my dreams were trying to connect the dots on everyone's backstory. Even though I felt Signe's worry lingering in my mind, I was determined to banish the negative thoughts. The last two weeks with Domari had been *fun* and light, and I needed more.

Domari left early that morning as he did every morning over the last two and a half months he'd been here on the ranch, headed into the barns to work the horses. I took my time with my curls, pulling on a pale blue sweater that matched my eyes and a pair of dark jeans before tying my floral sneakers. Thor grumbled as I bumped him with my foot, moving him from blocking the door, a pep in my step.

Spinning my car keys on my finger, I jogged across the yard to Charlene's house and pulled open the door. "You in here?"

"You bet," Charlene answered, coffee mug in hand as she walked down the hall in leopard-print pajamas. I grinned at the sight of her, still rumpled from sleep, hardly able to believe this was my same perfectly-put-together friend.

"Did you sleep in?" I asked, my lips tipped up as I tilted my head.

"Well, your beau is doing everything for me lately, so

why the hell not?" Charlene sipped at her coffee, throwing herself down on the couch in the living room and flicking on the TV. "Don't mess this up, Shelbie. I don't know if I can go back to my days starting before 10 a.m."

I laughed, shaking my head. "Trying not to."

"Good." Charlene winked. "You love him, don't you?"

Biting my lip, I sighed. "I do."

Seeming to notice my outfit, Charlene asked, "Where are you off to?"

"I feel like all we do here is work, which is fine. But Domari never stops. I don't think he'd be comfortable going out on a date, so I decided I'd bring one home to him."

Charlene set her coffee cup down on the side table, turning towards me with wide eyes. "So you're headed to buy some new lingerie? Crotchless panties? Oh! Edible ones!" My cheeks flushed, and Charlene cackled. "Making you blush has become one of my favorite pastimes."

"That hasn't escaped my notice," I deadpanned, which only made Charlene laugh harder.

"Shoo. Go. Spoil our man." She waved me off, and I spun, headed to my car.

Sitting in the grocery store parking lot, I scrolled through my phone searching for traditional Swedish meatball recipes. My plan was to bring the Sweden I'd fallen in love with last fall to him, introducing Domari to his country all over again. The more I thought about it, the more I thought he'd love it.

Ingredients list in hand and confidence exceedingly high, I practically skipped through the store, grabbing ground beef and pork, onions, and breadcrumbs for the meatballs, cream for the gravy, and potatoes for the side, ready to try my damnedest to make this meal happen. I grabbed a new bag of coffee beans and raspberry jam, thinking I could also recreate *fika*, my favorite afternoon tradition after my trip to Sweden. Rather than trying two *new* recipes, I decided on making my raspberry press cookies, perfect with coffee, and those I was confident would be delicious.

With a box of Swedish Fish in my hands, a red candy hanging from between my teeth, I dropped everything into my trunk and headed home. Domari was still out when I got back, and Thor stretched, tail in the air, when I opened the door.

"You hanging with me today, big guy?" I asked, bending down to kiss his furry head after I'd put the groceries away. Thor grumbled, dark eyes glancing my direction momentarily before he curled back into a ball with a huff. "Your life is exhausting. I don't blame you for sleeping 20 hours a day."

Apparently, my dog didn't appreciate my sass because he rose to his feet, pawing at the door. I smiled as I opened it for him, watching as he trotted off towards the barns.

The door snicked shut, and a giddy wave of excitement washed through me. Grabbing the vacuum, I cleaned the floors, then plumped the pillows on the couch, and scrolled through my phone, looking for a playlist. *ABBA Gold: Greatest Hits* played from the speaker on the mantle, and I danced my way into the kitchen, ready to show Domari how much I loved and appreciated him.

My lavender KitchenAid mixer whirred as I dropped in the ingredients for the cookies, turning to preheat the oven. With the sweet almond scent filling my nose, I smiled at nothing and no one, feeling truly happy.

"Smells delicious in here," Domari said as he opened the door, hanging his jacket in the coat closet and kicking his boots off. Stepping up behind me, he circled me with his arms, kissing my neck as I leaned away, exposing it for him. "What are you making?"

"Cookies, first." Sticking my spatula down into the bowl, I scraped off a small piece of dough with my finger, offering it to him. Sucking my finger into his mouth, I squirmed as his tongue moved, his warm hands sliding beneath my shirt and over my belly.

"As sweet as you," he said, releasing my finger from his lips, and my heart melted, feeling so lucky to have him at my side. His gaze turned to the counter, noticing the other groceries. "What's all this?"

I spun in his arms, lacing my hands around his neck. "Well, I wanted to show you how much I love you, so I thought I'd make today all about you." A depth of emotion I couldn't decipher passed through Domari's chocolate eyes, his throat working, so I rose on my toes and kissed him lightly. "Want to know more about what your country is like now?"

Domari's dark brows rose on his forehead as he watched me curiously. "Sweden, right?"

"Yes, Sweden," I nodded, releasing him from my grip as

I spun back to the dough in the bowl, scooping it into small balls before placing them on the baking sheet. "I only spent a few days there, so I'm not an expert, but it's still known for its rich Viking history."

He smiled at my words as his hand slid over to the bowl, copying my motions as he rolled the dough with me. We worked together as I told him about the colorful architecture in Stockholm and what I'd seen when I hiked along the Baltic Coast. The scenery was similar, as most of the country was still covered in forest.

Domari was the most excited for *fika*, the idea of cookies and coffee every afternoon needing no other explanation.

"And what about the music?" he pointed at the speaker in the living room playing *Gimme Gimme Gimme (A Man After Midnight)*. "What's Sweden famous for?"

"ABBA," I replied immediately. "There's a whole museum dedicated to ABBA in Stockholm. I thought about stopping in, but ran out of time."

"Can we listen to it?"

My eyes sparkled with humor, and I bit my cheeks as the opening notes of *Mamma Mia* filled the house, xylophone and electric guitar in rapid succession. "We already are."

His brow furrowed, and I fought back a laugh, singing along when the words began. His eyes were on me, and I did my best to remain stoic, knowing precisely what his opinion was about to be. By the time the song made it to the chorus, his hands clenched, eyes wide as he stared down at the floor.

"*This* is what my country is famous for?" His look was dumbfounded, and I burst into laughter, rocking forward on my toes, hands in the back pocket of my jeans. "What happened to the fearsome warriors? There's nothing Viking about this," he gestured angrily at the speaker, "whatever you call it."

"It's pop music," I said with a chuckle, trying to catch my breath.

"It's terrible, is what it is." He reached over to my phone, handing it to me, and insisted I turn it off.

The raspberry cookies turned out perfectly, and I plated them for our afternoon *fika* a little later that the afternoon. Deciding to keep up my momentum, I went straight to work on the meatballs and potatoes. After scrubbing the potatoes in the sink, Domari left to shower, and I turned back to the stove, ready to put them in the water while the meatballs cooked in the oven.

Drip.

Smile faltering, I glanced at the faucet, reaching over to adjust the handle and ensure he'd turned it off before turning back to the stove.

Drip. Drip.

My hands stilled as I looked to the sink again, waiting to see if the water leaked, but nothing. My skin crawled as I recalled the number of times I'd listened to that same sound in my dreams, over and over, taunting me.

Drip. Drip. Drip.

Dropping the potatoes into the boiling water, I moved away from the stove as my breath caught in my chest. The darkness from my dreams that always seemed to cling to me rose, filling me with a panicked feeling that had my heart racing, my ears ringing as I moved towards the hall, away from the sink.

Promised, the word echoed in my head on repeat, meaning nothing. A shiver raced down my spine as I stood in the living room alone, that same sense of dread haunting me relentlessly, like a shadow in the back of my mind. I breathed deeply, waiting for it to pass.

But it didn't.

My chest constricted, squeezing tight as I fought for air, bracing my hand on the wall. "Domari?"

The sound of the pipes clanking in the walls as Domari showered grew quiet, my mind pulling me away from the present. My head fell forward as I breathed deeply, searching for any sense of calm as I felt along the grey walls of my living room.

Answer me, that voice I had grown to hate rang out in my head.

The pungent sulphuric smell of the darkness I'd sensed so often in my dreams rose, drowning out the sweet aroma of the cookies. Breathing shallowly to fight the feeling of panic rising in me, my eyes screwed shut as I raged against what I knew was coming.

Darkness.

Nothingness.

The stale air of a long-forgotten place.

I sank to my knees, my head falling to the floor as despair swept over me, swallowing me whole.

Drip. Drip. Drip.

It echoed in my head, real and imagined at the same time. Lightning struck across the inside of my eyelids as I panted for breath, struggling against this overwhelming panic, riding me hard even while awake.

"It's not real," my voice was unrecognizable as I clenched my jaw against the tidal wave. *"It's not real."*

33

DOMARI

A loud crash drew Domari's attention away from the shower, glancing out into the bathroom. He reached forward to turn off the water, grabbing the towel that hung outside the curtain. Swiping it over his face and hair, he slung it over his hips and stepped out.

"Shelbie?" he called, worry rising in him when she didn't answer, and his heart rate sped up. Something felt wrong.

Thor's bark turned into a deep whine, pawing at the bathroom door until Domari opened it, stepping out into the hall in his jeans. His chest seized at the sight of Shelbie curled on the floor, hands clutched in her hair.

"Shelbie!" he cried, falling at her side on the hardwood floor. Her body was rigid as he pulled her into his warm chest. He tipped her face back, clutching her to him as he'd done tangled in the roots of the Tree, but this time, she didn't fade.

Domari watched as her eyes cracked open, staring up at

him, but the ice-blue gaze he adored was gone. Shock coursed through him as he fought to pull back from her form — still breathing heavily, thank Asgard — but her eyes were entirely white, her mouth hanging open in a silent scream.

"*Shelbie!*" He shook her shoulders, trying to pull her back from wherever her mind had transported her. "Stay with me!"

Her breaths were shallow as her eyes shifted back and forth, seeing something he couldn't. Understanding dawned on him as he clutched her body to his chest, waiting for the moment to pass. Waiting for her to return. Only once had he ever seen anything like this. Only once had he seen the way Skuld's eyes flashed white as she told him his future.

These weren't dreams Shelbie was having.

They were *visions*.

34

SHELBIE

My eyes peel open one at a time, flickering in the dim light at the sound of groaning wood above me. How sound reaches me in my cave deep underwater, nestled in my home, I don't understand.

Glancing around the space, I look for the source of the noise. It's mostly bare around me, with only a few discarded weapons and jewelry to complete my hoard. Disappointing for my kind, but that has never been my priority. I took what I needed — food to survive and gifts given freely, but never more. My job is to be here, protecting the Tree.

Waiting.

I close my eyes again, resting while I wait for her. My heart. My Promised.

Thunk.

The sound starts again, and I lift my head, peering far above.

A human grunts. Growls. Curses. Confusion clouds my mind as I reason through how someone could be here, under the Tree, in the realm of the Norns.

Thunk. Thunk. Thunk.

Curiosity seizes the better of me, and my wings unfurl, propelling me through the water. I break the surface of the Well with a splash, waves rippling around me as I flap hard for the sky above, scanning the ground below me.

No one is here, save the sisters on their porch on the water's edge.

"Above," Verandi whispers, pointing to the sky where the roots of the Tree dangle down from the clouds, mixing with the lights overhead. "In Midgard. He is above."

My wings beat to hold me in place, hovering among the wisps as I nod. Muscles flex in my back while I launch further into the sky, pulling my wings tight as I break through the Realms.

Treetops loom before me, skirting the large lake. There, in the center, is an island. I coast over the pines, listening to the wildlife flee at my sudden presence as I soar closer.

Watching.

Listening.

Roots claw to the water's edge from the Tree, bare branches rising above the island. There, among the roots, is a man I've seen before. Black tattoos cover his head, painting him in darkness. The same darkness coats his heart, buried deep in his chest, and he calls to me in a way I can't understand.

Sensing my presence, the man pauses in his brutal rhythm, hacking away at the Tree's trunk. Rising to his feet, he watches me high overhead.

"Dark One," *his voice rings out, deep and low in a voice that hardly sounds human.* "I will rise again."

His words make little sense to me, though. He drops his axe as I drift closer, leaving it among the roots, and flees back across the frozen lake.

I watch as he joins with dozens of men waiting there in the trees, pointing east. Fire erupts from me as I screech to the sky, gazing upon the army standing there in the snow.

Hurry, I send out, hoping she can hear me. We are out of time.

I gasped as my mind seemed to drop back into my body.

Hurry, the word rang in my head, and I gripped my chest, pulling at my sweater.

Domari clutched my body, holding me against him as I fought for air. Smoke lingered in the air, billowing out of the oven, and I jumped to my feet, pulling the charred meatballs from within.

"Shelbie," Domari's voice cracked as he rose, following me into the kitchen. "Talk to me."

I willed my heart rate to slow, disappointment over the burnt dinner warring with the darkness still clinging to my skin. Tears lined my eyes as I looked down at the blackened meatballs. "Shit, I'm sorry. I ruined this dinner. I should have known cooking was a terrible idea."

Domari's brow creased heavily as he stared at me. "I don't fucking care about dinner, Shelbie. I care I found you collapsed on the ground of our home."

Danger follows you wherever you go, the last of your kind, the words of the Norns snuck back in my head. Before I could say more, Domari's hands slid to cup my jaw, tilting my face to his.

"Are you ready to tell me what you're seeing?"

I inhaled sharply at his words, my heart racing as he held me while I thought through the daydream I'd just experienced. Raud. The Tree. Fire.

"Or are you going to continue to insist on doing this alone? Even when I can see how much it pains you?" Domari closed the last of the inches between us, pressing his chest against mine as his dark eyes took in the misery I buried deep. His voice dropped as I fought for breath, thumb brushing over my jaw. "You know that's what it is, right? These aren't dreams you're having, Shelbie. You're a Seer."

My eyes scanned his face, searching for some joke, but deep down, I couldn't help but wonder if he spoke the truth. Too many things I'd *dreamt* about his world lined up with the stories he'd shared with me.

"But," I shook my head, unable to wrap my mind around this truth, "No. That's ridiculous. I don't believe in that kind of thing." I held up my hand, turning away from him, but he caught it, yanking me into his body.

His hands slid to my face, making me meet his gaze. "Then tell me what it is, *haski*. Tell me what darkness is stealing you from me a little at a time, what's killing you slowly."

My fingers trailed over his broad chest, feeling how wildly his heart thumped beneath his skin. Even if I didn't believe in Seers, the way Domari was reacting told me *he* did.

"I can't S*ee... the future?*" Nervous laughter escaped me as I prattled on. "You're talking about magic, Domari. I don't have magic. I'm just a normal, quirky thirty-one-year-old girl who loves fantasy novels. Half of the time, I can't even S*ee* where I set my phone down, let alone the future."

"Are you Seeing the future?" he asked, cocking his head as he evaluated my response. "Or the past? The present? What have you *Seen*, Shelbie?"

My mouth fell open at his words, thinking through the many dreams I'd had. Erik trudging through the snow. The girl on the shore during her ceremony — the more I thought about that dream, the more I was positive the woman was Yrsa, my friend and healer. The Norns. Raud... And what about the journals I'd filled with stories of his people? Were those true, too?

With the warmth of his hands on my shoulders, I closed my eyes, allowing my chin to dip as my lip quivered. "I feel like I'm losing my mind, Domari."

Any hint of fight left Domari as he sighed again and pulled me into his bare chest, tucking my head under his chin. My arms looped around his waist, seeking the comfort he was offering.

"In my time, some women are blessed by the gods with powers," his voice rumbled under my ear as my body stilled. "Sorceresses. They practice *seid* — healing arts, prophesying, and even communing with the gods."

I chuckled at that. "Well, I don't think I have any healing powers. Remember how banged up I was when you found me? And the only Norse god I commune with is the black furry one on the floor over there. Does Thor count?"

"I don't think it's wise of me to say no."

A growl rolled out of Thor as he lifted his head in our direction, lightening the heavy load weighing on my shoulders. "That's what you think I'm doing? Do you honestly, truly, think I'm having *visions*? But I can't be one of these sorceresses. I'm not from your time, and magic doesn't exist here in mine."

He hesitated for a moment before answering, and my heart sank at the look on his face. "There's a story I heard long ago. Have you ever heard of a Promised?"

My face blanched at the word, my body going cold. *Promised*, the word drifted into my mind in that same smokey voice I'd heard so many times.

"What's a Promised?" I whispered, dreading the answer.

His eyes shifted to me, searching my face before answering. "It's been a long time since I've heard the tale, but I will tell you what I remember."

Pulling me back into the living room, we sat on the couch. Domari scrubbed a hand over his beard, then turned so he was facing me, and my heart stuttered at the seriousness of his expression.

"Long ago, the daughter of a great Viking warrior was blessed with the powers of a Sorceress. Lovisa. They say she was chosen by the gods, carrying Freya's blessing. Her visions were sought after far and wide, and she reveled in the name she made for herself as a battle mage. Men sailed from distant lands seeking her wisdom and her hand in marriage. To have her on your side, to foresee your enemies, meant a swift victory."

Lovisa, the voice rasped inside my head again, and my breaths grew shallow, hands wringing together while I waited to hear this story.

"Lovisa fell in love with a fearsome warrior, Gudbrand," Domari continued, "and together, the two were unstoppable, as if chosen by the gods themselves. With her Sight, he could sail further than any Viking had, conquering lands and riches never seen in our world. Greed drove them further until Lovisa became pregnant. Gudbrand left her ashore for his last raid before the baby would arrive, and he didn't return."

Blood pounded in my ears as he shared the story, and I shut my eyes, seeing the tale he spun clearly.

"Weeks went by as Lovisa waited for her husband's return and her baby's birth. Her visions contained nothing useful, seeing only mist over distant waters every time she attempted to seek him. Soon, her body prepared for childbirth, but Lovisa was driven by panic, blinded by her husband's absence and the loss of her visions. She climbed to the highest peak overlooking the water, searching desperately for any sign of Gudbrand, but saw nothing except the dragons flying in the sky over the open water."

The heavy beating of wings filled my head, the sound as familiar as my own breathing as Domari went on.

"Lovisa leaned into her staff resting against the rocks as her heart broke, for, deep down, she knew her husband was lost, never to return. The heartbroken cry that erupted from her throat drew the eyes of the dragons above, and the great creatures circled closer to the woman on the rocks. They watched as she fell to her knees in desperation, pounding her fists into the ground as sobs racked her body and magic leaked from her skin. Her pleas were so distressed, the dragon closest to her felt pulled — called to her aid."

Yes, the voice whispered, and my ears rang, vision tunneling.

"That day, it's said that Lovisa struck a deal with the dragon above. If she promised her first-born daughter, whose life would begin in mere moments, in service of the dragons, they would search from the skies for Gudbrand and return him home. Every daughter of her line would be Promised for as long as the dragons roamed the skies, one generation after the next."

Promised, the voice rang again, and my vision faded as I fought to pull air into my lungs.

"Legend says that a stone of the darkest onyx set into the end of her staff glowed as her oath was given, pulsing as her power joined with that of the dragon, tied in life and death."

"My dearest. We have waited for you for so long," the Norns' words from this fall echoed in my head. *"Your story is one I cannot foresee. You have so much in front of you, but danger follows you everywhere, the last of your kind."*

"The dragons are all but gone in our world, Shelbie,"

Domari's voice broke through my thoughts, drawing me back to the present. "Hadriel may be the last."

"Hadriel," his name slid off my tongue as my skin began to vibrate.

My Promised, the voice answered, and chills broke out over my skin.

"Domari," I panted his name as my heart raced, bursting from my chest. "The pendant I gave Hadriel — the one Yrsa gifted me. It was onyx."

His eyes snapped to mine, and something I didn't understand passed through his gaze as he stormed from the room. I watched as he entered our room, but my feet wouldn't allow me to follow, planted in place as I fought to comprehend what this meant. Moments later, Domari's large strides seemed to swallow the space between us. My eyes were drawn to his hands, clenched tight over something there.

"Shelbie." He shook his head as he brought his closed fist up to me, lifting his fingers one at a time off the golden chain in his palm. "This shouldn't be possible, but I think *you* may be a Promised."

My breath caught as I stepped towards him, towards the stone. My vision shifted, blurring the room around me as I focused on the pendant. A golden dragon circled the black onyx, just as I remembered from last fall.

"How do you have this?" I asked as my fingers reached forward, drawn to the stone I'd tossed to the massive black dragon months ago. The air rippled around it as my hand drew closer, pulsing with a rhythm that seemed to match my beating heart.

"Hadriel gave it back to me," Domari muttered as my fingers closed the space between us. "I had it in my pocket when I arrived, but then it must have fallen out, shoved under the bed. I didn't think of it until now."

I was magnetized, unable to move as the cool stone brushed against my skin. As I touched it, an electric sting buzzed under my skin, humming with energy.

"Put it on, Shelbie," Domari's voice sounded far away as I closed my fingers over the chain, lifting it from his hand. "Put on the necklace."

It was as if I watched the scene from a distance as the chain lifted over my head, settling onto my skin, resting against my chest.

Everything went black.

35

SHELBIE

My wings, stretched to either side, move in the wind as I coast over the trees far below, weaving in and out of the clouds. The snow is melting, green returning to this world of white as spring blooms again. This is freedom, soaring so far above the rest of the world and its many problems.

My heartbeat is a loud and steady rhythm in my chest, buried deep beneath my black and gold armor. I circle the Tree, eyes scanning the roots of the sacred site, but she still isn't there.

My Promised.

Frustration wars within me with each passing day, but what more can I do? Banking in the wind, I beat my wings, picking up speed as I circle back in the direction I came. Mountains rise in the distance, large and full of many caves I could call home, but I follow the river instead. To the children.

Smoke billows far ahead of me, and my fire stirs deep in my chest.

Like the embers in my soul, the world is burning. Everything we know, everything these people hold dear, is ending. I'm the only one who can stop it, but only if I have my powers. My eyes spin back towards *the Tree, now far in the distance, but watching it won't make her appear. I had to hope* he *would do that.*

Thunder cracks in the distance as my mind drifts to the Warrior. Fate chose well to pair them together; if only he understood that it's here they need to be — with me.

Promised, *I send out, but she can't hear me. She is too far and doesn't know the stone's power.*

Smoke rises in the distance as I near the village, and worry for the children eats at me. I descend, wings just above the treetops. Wildlife far below scatters, hiding from my large shadow. The cries of humans fill the air, but it isn't me they are frightened of.

It's him.

Tall, with a clean-shaven head covered in deep black tattoos, he holds a flaming torch high above his head. The flickering light does nothing to ease the darkness in his soul — a darkness I thought I had banished long ago. His growl is fierce, and the humans around him cower in his presence. I watch as his vision turns towards me.

"You can't stop me this time, Dark One," *his voice rasps into the wind, barely reaching me where I fly high above. At that, he turns, launching the flaming torch high into the air, where it lands on the roof of a longhouse. Wood crackles as flames engulf the home.*

The sound mingles with a woman's cry, filled with anger and sadness. Her pale hair blows in the breeze as she drops the dagger in her hand to the ground in defeat, a black dog at her side as she steps towards the man there.

"It's me you want," *her voice rings out loud and clear as I circle high above. I can sense the legendary strength in her, pulsing from beneath her skin.* "Leave him."

My eyes shift, following her gaze to more men to the side of the building. Blood streams down the face of a large man with golden hair, head hung low as the streaks drip off his chin. Like the others, he shines with an inner light I'm surprised to see. Behind him stands another man with red-blonde hair, holding a blade to his throat. The blood from the blade mingles with that from the golden man's missing eye, leaving hissing drops as it falls to the snow at his feet.

Hurry, I send with everything I can, watching the scene unfold. Seeing that inner light in the man flicker. Panic rises in me at the sight, knowing how vital he is to so many things yet to come.

HURRY, I send again, putting every ounce of my power into it, feeling the flames in my chest push the word into the world, hoping she answers my desperate plea.

I'm coming, *the voice, high and sweet, rings in my head, and I bank hard with a loud cry, circling back over the scene below as power surges in my veins for the first time.*

Don't let them hurt my family, Hadriel. I'm coming.

36

SHELBIE

A scream — high, and full of hysteria — pulled me back to attention, and it took me a second to realize it was coming from my mouth. My body sagged back onto the floor beneath me, but it was an out-of-body experience, my soul settling back under my skin. Domari's face loomed over mine; his skin blanched, eyes wide as concern and panic wrote their tale across his expression.

"Shelbie," his voice croaked, hands tangling in my hair. I attempted to lift my hands to his face to ease the worry written there, but my body was too heavy — my breath fought to escape me in desperation as my chest heaved.

"*Breathe,*" he commanded, gripping my head in both hands sharply, pulling my eyes to his.

And I did.

"Again." His words were an order, and I followed his instructions as I'd done so many times before.

Breathe in. Breathe out; I chanted the words in my head until my body finally gave in and relaxed.

Eventually, Domari gripped my palm, pulled me into his lap on the couch. His arms wrapped around me so tightly it was almost painful, but the pressure grounded me, reminding me I was here.

"Domari." My voice clawed out of my throat, hoarse and foreign, and my heart raced again with the words I needed to share. "He spoke to me."

Gentler than I could have imagined, Domari loosened his hold on me, hands drifting to my jaw, turning my face to his. My eyes were downcast with everything that warred within me until he jerked on my chin, lifting it. "Hadriel."

Hearing the dragon's name leave Domari's lips had me gasping, eyes flying to his. I opened my mouth to answer, but nothing came out. I nodded briefly, and Domari's expression shuddered for only a moment, eyes closing as he absorbed this new information.

"Is this the first time you've heard him?" he asked me gently, and my eyes searched his for any hint of disbelief — wondering how much I should divulge. Because the truth was, I recognized that smoky voice the moment I felt his wings in the air.

Promised, he'd said so many times inside my head.

Home, he'd chanted when I'd arrived in Sweden.

Yes, he'd roared in my veins as strength surged under my skin in the face of certain death at Raud's hands.

Hadriel had been with me far longer than only moments ago, but how was I to know I heard a *dragon*?

"No," I admitted, choosing honesty this time. "It's not

the first time I've heard him. But I didn't understand before, and it's never been like this."

"Like what?" Domari asked, and no judgment shone on his face or tone, for which I was eternally grateful.

"Like... like we were sharing one mind," I admitted, and the words felt right. "Domari, I was in his head. We were flying, and I saw—" Breath was sucked from my body in a desperate gasp as I fought to stand, running to the door.

"What's wrong?" Domari's voice sifted through the air, but I hardly heard him above the ringing in my ears as I shoved my feet into my boots, heart pounding. His heavy hands on my shoulders ripped me back to attention as my heart broke in two and a sob leaked from my body.

"What's wrong?" He punctuated each word as his hands pushed heavily on my shoulders. But I fought to keep moving — I had to go. *Now.*

"TELL ME," he roared, and I flinched at the sound as a tear leaked down my chin, dropping onto the floor, just as the blood had moments ago in my vision. I shook my head, unable to speak, as Domari gripped my chin again. "You don't leave me. And I will not leave you. *Tell me now, Shelbie.* What did you see?"

"Gunnar." His name broke out of my body as my chest split in half. Domari reared back at his cousin's name, the golden man he loved and admired. "Domari..." I whispered, remembering the blood I'd Seen.

So much blood.

❉

Signe falls to her knees, hands outstretched to be shackled as the skirt of her dress puddles in her husband's blood. "LEAVE HIM," she screams, but her father only smirks. "IT'S ME YOU WANT."

Her words are a desperate plea, and the Demon looming in front of her loosens his grip on Gunnar, tossing his sagging body to the right. Raud's hand flies to the side, ripping Gunnar's weakened form to him before he can fall to the ground. Before Gunnar can recover, Raud's hand raises high into the air, firelight glistening off the metal blade, he swings down and sinks into Gunnar's chest.

"NO." The word is ripped from Signe's throat in a feral cry as her body pulses with energy.

"*SHELBIE!*" My name brought me back to attention as Domari shook my shoulders and I slumped into a sob. "*TELL ME WHAT YOU'RE SEEING.*"

His voice was broken, desperate, and I couldn't bear to tell him what I'd witnessed — to lay this grief on his shoulders.

"He's gone." The words left me of their own volition, and I shook with the tears escaping me, streaming down my face. Blindly, I reached for my keys, Thor at my feet.

Domari's hands fell to his side, and his face paled as he reeled in the bomb I had dropped on him. "What do you mean, *gone?*"

"Domari, we have to go." I slid my arms through my jacket sleeves, pulling it on in a panicked state. "We have to go back. Everyone is in danger. They need us." Swiping at the tears on my face, I glanced down at Thor. "You have to stay here," I hiccup another sob, falling to my knees.

A deep growl rolled through his chest as I threw my arms around him, hugging him tightly in goodbye. His loud bark right against my ear pulled me quickly back to attention.

"He's coming with us." Domari shook his head, his vision still fogged and chest heaving, but an intense focus settled over his features as he stormed into my bedroom, retrieving the furs he'd arrived with, then ripped open the closet door to retrieve his weapons. "We're all going."

His heavy hand gripped the front door handle and pulled so savagely that the door creaked in a way that couldn't be good. Domari and Thor strode to the Jeep parked out front, loading into it as I stared out into the sunlight.

"I don't know where to go." Panic surged in me again, but Hadriel's smoky voice rang in my ears before uncertainty could pull me under.

To the trees, Hadriel's rasp drifted into my mind, and I gasped. *Go home, Shelbie. Go to where Domari found you. I've opened portals everywhere over the last millennium, searching for you. I never gave up hope that we'd find each other, Shelbie. My Promised.*

Domari loomed over me again where I stood on the porch, frozen in disbelief of what I'd heard in my head. Without hesitation, Domari snagged the keys from my hand and walked back to the Jeep, getting in the driver's seat.

"You can't drive," I protested, stepping off the porch to follow him.

"*YOU* can't drive," he retorted, slamming the door. "You keep fading in and out of worlds."

Words were lost to me, because he had a point.

"Get in," he ordered, the voice of a trained warrior taking charge of the situation. I did as he said, sliding into the passenger's seat. His hand slammed down on the steering wheel as he cranked the ignition, throwing it into reverse. Veins popped along his forearm as it slid to behind my headrest, and his head swung to the side, glancing behind him. The car rolled backward, and I breathed heavily into the tension filling the vehicle. As his head swiveled back in my direction, his hand stopped, reaching over to my face.

"Maybe your vision was of the future, Shelbie." His voice was laced with a hopeful tone, and I felt my heart splinter into a thousand pieces at the look on his face. "Maybe we can get there in time to stop it."

"Maybe," I whispered, but I had no strength to put behind the word.

37
SHELBIE

Domari steered us out of the ranch and onto the highway while I gripped the handle, stepping on an invisible brake as my father did all those years ago when he taught me to drive.

"Take the next exit," I pointed to the left, directing Domari sometime later, absorbed in my breathing as panic fought to override my senses. He nodded in acknowledgment but was highly focused on the road in front of him, hands at ten and two on the steering wheel.

After I was sure he was on the right path into the mountains, I closed my eyes, breathing deeply through my nose and out through my mouth. Repeating it, I worked to ease my racing heart.

I feel you moving closer, Hadriel's smoky voice broke into my thoughts, and I jumped at the sensation, eyes flying back open.

"What?" Domari briefly shot a glance my way, watching my every reaction as carefully as the road.

"Hadriel spoke to me," I said, as my hand drifted over the onyx stone resting against my chest. "Not in a dream, just... talking."

Yes, Hadriel answered, and my eyes gaped again. *The stone is a piece of Lovisa's original staff and will connect us. As you grow closer, it will get easier. Our connection is strongest when we're together.*

I shook my head at Hadriel's words, unable to comprehend that the disjointed words I'd heard in my mind were real. *His* voice. *A dragon's* voice.

"What's he saying?" Domari asked, brow creased in concentration.

"Hadriel's explaining our mental link. It will get stronger when I'm with him, he says."

"That sounds correct, based on the stories I've heard." Domari nodded again, and I leaned back in my seat, forcing my muscles to relax.

Can you hear me, too? I send out as I rubbed my thumbs across my temples, feeling insane.

Yes, my Promised, Hadriel answered. *I've been waiting to hear your voice for so long.*

My heart broke a little at the longing I heard there. *If I was always to be your Promised — from Lovisa's line — why was I born now and not in Viking times with you?*

A growl vibrated under my skin as I felt a wash of heat, almost like I was standing too close to an open flame. *Nidhoggr.*

"What's Nidhoggr? Or who?" I asked, turning in my seat to stare at Domari's profile.

His arms flexed, the ten black bands stacked on his forearms bulging where he gripped the wheel tightly. If Domari gripped it any harder, I'd be concerned he might rip it off the steering column. His expression flickered from worry to fear so quickly I might have missed it if I hadn't been studying him.

"What's Hadriel saying about him?" he finally answered, and I shrugged, repeating the question to Hadriel in my head.

Nidhoggr must be to blame for why you weren't given to me as your fate was promised, Hadriel answered, his words laced with a growl. *The white dragon is ancient among our kind, and his power is unimaginable, but has faded over time as the dragons died off. Dragons are nothing of what we once were, and like leaders grasping for the last of their dwindling influence, he lashed out. The Norns and I have wondered for years what changed our fates, to separate us against Lovisa's Promise, but lately… I've sensed a power rising once more. A power far greater than my own without you.*

That doesn't sound good, I thought to myself, a chill running down my spine.

The only answer we can think of is that Nidhoggr must have used the last of the magic he had to try to end the fates of all Promised before you were born, changing fate forever. A dragon's magic isn't meant to work that way as we are the protectors of Fate, of the Tree of Life. Not caring that the dark magic would steal his life force, he severed our ties anyway. But he didn't erase your fate, just moved *it. That we found each other is a work of the gods.*

"What?" I said aloud, rather than answering Hadriel mind to mind. "I'm so confused. He says Nidhoggr is to blame for why I wasn't given to Hadriel as my fate had been woven. It sounds like I was supposed to be born in your world, but using his magic, he changed my life?" My head jerked back as my brow dropped, utterly lost in this conversation. "What the *fuck* does that even mean?"

"Nidhoggr," Domari said, then paused, clearing his throat before beginning again. "Nidhoggr is a white dragon, spoken of in Viking legends. He was ruthless, set on destruction above all else, tearing down entire villages, torching them as if for sport, not even to feed. To see the white dragon was a sign of great foreboding. Draugr, the most fearsome and ruthless Viking jarl of our time, paints him on their ships, a warning for all to see of the viciousness to come. But it's been twenty years or more since anyone has spotted the white dragon in the sky. I thought he was long gone."

Is Nidhoggr gone? I asked Hadriel, fearing the answer.

Not gone, Hadriel growled in my head, and it felt as if smoke was rising in my own throat. *But yes, it has been twenty years since he's shown his face. Since I destroyed his wing. Hardly punishment enough for what he has done to our bond.*

What does that mean? I sent back, desperately searching for answers to *any* of this, and then summarized what Hadriel had told me to Domari. With each new revelation I shared, the Jeep picked up speed, and Domari gripped the wheel harder.

Because, Shelbie, he calmly explained, *Nidhoggr wants to destroy us all. He wants Ragnarok to begin. In order for that to happen, you and I can't be together. We're the last hope for our world, and the only power aside from the gods that could even think to stop him.*

Dread pooled in my stomach as I swallowed, afraid to

ask my next question. "Domari," I whispered, and he glanced in my direction as my chest rose and fell in heavy pants. "What's Ragnarok?"

The engine gunned as Domari stomped on the gas, flicking his blinker on while he changed lanes, speeding into the mountains. I gripped the door, thrown back in the seat as the lines on the pavement flew by us rapidly, blurring at our speed. Domari didn't answer me, but my heart was racing so quickly that I fought to pull oxygen into my body, and my vision darkened.

The now-familiar, all-imposing darkness surrounds me as it has so many times, but the scene is different than before. Now, a faint, red light shines up ahead. I move towards it with tentative steps, hands out as I feel my way through the darkness, feet shuffling over the rocks below me.

Drip. Drip. Drip.

The stupid water echoes around me, and I fight the urge to growl into the space, so tired of this incessant dream.

No, *I remember.* Not a dream. A vision.

"What is this place?" my voice echoes off the unseen walls as I inch closer to the red light. "Where am I?"

But no one answers.

A warm breeze blows my curls from my neck, the sulphuric smell coming from the direction of the red light, which seems strange. I've never noticed a light before.

Stepping closer, the hairs on my arms stand up. I gasp as my skin seems to light on fire, a bright pulsing green light shining from my chest, illuminating my hands in front of me for a moment.

The onyx.

"Hadriel, can you still hear me?" I ask, voice quaking as I stare at the glowing stone.

But he doesn't answer.

I'm almost to the red light ahead of me now, and my strides grow longer as I work towards it, answering the pull I feel there. My chest burns suddenly, a hot poker against my skin as my fingers fly to my chest, rubbing across the onyx.

"SHELBIE," Domari's hand slapped down on my arm, shaking me violently as I gulped in air, choking on the darkness that still clung to me. A wet tongue slid over my ear, and it shook the last of the fog from my head.

"Ew, Thor." I pushed my black dog back and into the back seat again.

"You were gone," Domari growled, furious energy pouring off of him into the car. "Your eyes went white as you slumped in the chair, and then you were *glowing*. Your skin was pulsing light, like the Norns do."

I shook my head in disbelief, all of this so wild and beyond my imagination. Remembering my vision, my fingers drifted over the onyx pendant around my neck. I gasped, pulling it away from my skin as pain radiated through my body.

It *burned*. Not just hot to the touch — it had burned me, a bright red raised mark in the shape of a dragon emblazoned on my skin where the metal had singed my skin.

Don't go into that darkness, Hadriel's voice rang in my head, and it sounded almost nervous. *You were lost to me there, our connection severed. I couldn't answer you.*

That can't be good, I thought to myself, and then chuckled maniacally. This was all so outrageous.

We barreled down the highway, but fortunately, traffic was relatively light. Trees and mountains flew past as we twisted and turned on the interstate up into the mountains, closer with every passing minute to our destination.

"You can slow down a little bit," I mumbled, white-knuckling the door handle around a sharp turn as I clenched my teeth. "In fact, do you want me to drive?"

Domari eased off the gas but only shot me an expression that said *no* far more clearly than any words could have.

"Okay." I smiled nervously. "All right, well. Let's slow down now that we're in the mountains. We have another hour on this road, so try not to kill us before we can even get back in time. Sound good?"

Domari didn't answer me, focused on the road ahead as his jaw worked, showing the tension we both felt. I let my gaze drift to the rock wall rising high above the Jeep as we ascended deeper into the mountains, moving closer to the forest where Domari had been waiting for me.

Hurry, Hadriel sent, and I squeezed my eyes shut as I fought for breath.

I'm coming as fast as I can, Hadriel, I sent back, trying my best to remain calm as I sent out my next question. *Are we too late? Is...* I hesitated, unsure I wanted to know the answer to the question pulsing inside my head.

So much blood.

Were my visions true? I asked, unable to send the question I wanted to know.

Hadriel's silence was an answer in its own right, and a tear leaked down my face as I peered out of the corner of my eye towards Domari.

Hurry, Hadriel sent again, and I scrunched my nose, trying to quell the tears threatening to fall.

"Quiet," Frida leans over the children, hushing them as she pushes them deeper into the woods.

Children, far more than I'd ever seen in the village, and most I don't recognize, hurry past her as they follow a tall woman up ahead with long, flowing, almost white hair. She turns, and light shines on her face for a moment, but instantly I know who she is.

Skuld.

She is there for only a moment, then her form disappears. But the children don't react, only following in the footsteps she left in her wake. Astrid passes Frida, heavy belly protruding from beneath her fur cloak. She walks with the children, holding the hand of a small red-headed girl whose curls bounce with each quick step.

Behind them follows another girl, wearing a sword on her belt almost as long as her leg. She carries a small boy on her back in a sling, and he rests his blond head between her shoulders.

The last in the line of children is a dark-haired teenage girl I don't recognize but whose green eyes are familiar to me. Her hair, black as *coal, stands out against the white fur on her shoulders, and the fierce expression reminds me of Signe. A small child sniffs loudly, and the raven-haired teen stops, dropping to a knee in front of a small boy and girl.*

"Mama," the boy sniffles loudly, glancing back over his shoulder.

"No crying, Ulf," the little girl says, and I hold my breath as my vision zooms in on the trio there. "Mama is brave. No man can defeat her."

The teen pauses as emotion wars on her face before she dips her chin in a nod. "Revna is right, little wolf. Have I told you of when she fought ten men at once?" Her eyebrows waggle as the boy glances up into her face when she rises. He wipes his shirt over his nose and places his hand into her outstretched palm.

Frida stands nearby, eyes rimmed with tears as she pats a wrap on her chest.

A baby.

"Come." She holds out her hand to Revna, and the small girl frowns as she walks past, hurrying into the forest and mountains beyond.

"Come back to me," Domari's voice was thick, like syrup, as it drifted into my consciousness, pulling me back to the present.

I shook my head to clear the fog of the vision, peering out the window for any sense of where we were now. A ski resort was to our left, and I gasped as I realized how long I'd been out. Each of these visions seemed to be holding me under their spell longer. "We're getting close, Domari."

He nodded at my words, and relief seemed to shine through as his eyes quickly glanced in my direction. "Do I even want to know what you saw this time?"

I licked my lips, debating my answer. I'd seen Domari with the children in the village and knew how he felt about Ulf and Revna. "Everyone appeared fine." I smiled tentatively, deciding to skip over the fact the children were on the run.

His chest expanded as he breathed deeply, nostrils flaring. But I wasn't fooled for even a moment — Domari was far from calm. Veins bulged in his neck, tension riding him hard as we rocketed towards our final destination.

"Two more exits," I sighed, trying to calm my nerves as I glanced out at the mountains I'd seen so many times before. "We're almost there."

38

SHELBIE

The wheels skidded to a halt, and I was thrown forward, my seatbelt digging into my shoulder. Before I could recover, Domari threw open the door, and it swung, hinges creaking loudly at the abuse.

"Easy, there." I tentatively grinned at Domari as I unbuckled myself, reaching behind me to Thor. Domari only glared back at me, his impatience at my hesitancy written in every line of his body.

As I walked around the car to his side, he tightened his belt around his waist, supporting his sword. He lifted his black shirt, adjusting the knives holstered all along the belt, and I swallowed hard. His grip was tight around his axe, and his jaw worked, making him look every bit the part of a Viking warrior, even with the modern jeans and tee.

How will I be of any use in a battle? I thought, forgetting someone was waiting for my words in my head.

Together, Shelbie, Hadriel answered, and I jumped. *Together, you and I are a force of power this world hasn't seen in decades.*

Hadriel, I hesitated as I sent back. *I don't have any powers other than these visions, and those I have no control over. I don't even know if what I'm seeing has happened or not yet. They could be the past or the future. I have no way to tell.*

Panic shot through me again for the millionth time that day as my mind drifted back to the blood, to Signe's screams, to the knife protruding from Gunnar's chest.

Your powers, Shelbie, he answered, and warmth spread through my chest, a fire burning beneath my skin, *have yet to show themselves, my Promised. You've had only a taste of the power we can wield together.*

I didn't answer him after that — what on earth could I even say? The fact I could even roll with the many punches thrown at me right now was a miracle in itself. Thor paced at Domari's side, hair raised and showing the tips of his teeth below his upper lip.

"Ready?" Domari held a hand in my direction. The gesture was kind, but the look on his face said I didn't have a choice. It was time to go, whether I was ready or not.

I bobbed my head and stepped into his grip. Snow still covered most of the path, but it was tamped down between snowshoers and the warmer temperatures lately. The slushy mixture sucked at my boots, but Domari set a quick pace, and I fought to keep up. Thor jogged at Domari's side, alert as ever, as we rushed to the finish line.

I panted heavily, rubbing a hand across the stitch in my side as we made it to the clearing, feeling even more useless than before. Domari dropped my hand, pacing in a circle, looking for any sign of what would come next.

"I marked the tree closest to me when I arrived,"

Domari shot over at me as I worked not to toss up the contents of my stomach from the uphill run, breathing in deep gulps.

I look exactly *like someone ready for battle,* I shook my head at my inner ramblings but stopped when I remembered what I was supposed to be doing. *Hadriel? What next? How do we get back?*

Domari marked the portal, the dragon answered immediately, his voice already clearer in my head. *As you approach it, your onyx will glow with power. I'm here, at the Tree, waiting for you. When you're near me — close to your side of the portal — it will light with power.*

"He says you marked the portal," I said aloud to Domari. He held a hand up, showing he'd heard my words.

I stepped out of the clearing and towards the aspen grove where I'd found Domari three months ago. The trees were clumped tightly, the many roots growing into hundreds of trees along the slope, all nearly identical. Thor paced at my side, teeth now bared as we circled the trees. Domari paced off to my left, but that felt wrong. I glanced his way before turning right, closing my eyes briefly.

There, further ahead and slightly to the right, something called me. I turned my shoulders square to the direction I felt, then opened my eyes.

"I think it's this way, Domari," I shouted over my shoulder, and he stopped, running back to my side. His hand laced with mine as I stepped closer to the pull, feeling a hum in my veins. Thor's warm body pushed against my leg with every step, offering the only support he could. My fingers drifted down through his soft black fur as we stepped closer. A dull green light began to pulse around us, and I gasped as I dipped my chin to stare down at the black pendant, now alight.

I feel you, Hadriel's voice came through my head, his tone both excited and anxious.

My eyes scanned the trees before me, looking for any sign of a marking, as Hadriel had mentioned. As my gaze drifted slightly to the right, off-center from our current path, I noticed the rune carved in the bark of one aspen, taller than the others.

I dropped Domari's hand as I stepped past him and Thor, drawn in by an invisible rope, pulling me to my destination.

Yes, Hadriel said again as I stepped within arm's reach of the tree. My pendant glowed so brightly it washed the dark forest in green, pulsing light, casting eerie shadows over the still scene around us.

ᚾ

"Here," I whispered, pointing to the rune with a shaking hand. "Domari. It's here."

He said nothing as he stepped into my side, placed a hand around my hip, and turned me towards him. I stared into his eyes, shadows cast across his features in the wash of the green light pulsing at my neck.

"We have no idea what awaits us on the other side of this portal." Domari's voice was rough and filled with emotion. "I love you, Shelbie. Even if," he paused, turning his face away from mine. With a shake of his head, he continued, "Even if I were to lose you... If we don't get through this together, I will follow you through the nine realms, waiting for our eternity together in Hel."

"But we'll make it out of this, okay?" I smiled through the tears that slid down my face freely, lip quivering with each word. "We're going to save them, and everyone will be fine." I nodded, as if my proclamation could reassure me.

His hands slid to my jaw, pulling my face into his in a tender kiss, sealing the raw honesty of his words with each passing moment. As we broke apart, my head fell to his chest for only a second, then I wiped the tears from my cheeks, turning back to the tree.

"Let's do this." I laced my fingers through Domari's, glancing down to see that he had a firm grip on Thor, and stepped towards the tree. The light at my neck grew brighter with each step, and I squinted into the blazing green glow. Bringing my hand up to block it, I glanced to where the tree was only moments before.

With one last look at Domari, I squeezed his hand tightly and stepped into the light.

39

SHELBIE

Colors swirled around me, lights pulsing so vividly I could hardly see. Deep maroons faded into a bright magenta, contrasting with the greens and yellows that overwhelmed me in their neon brightness. White dots speckled my vision — stars — racing by as I fell endlessly. A scream ripped free from my throat, but the sound never reached my ears.

As I drifted towards my destination, my body was weightless, suspended in space and time. It was almost as if my mind and soul had lifted out of my physical body, separated entirely at this moment, but pressure pulled on me, anchoring me in this form. I screwed my eyes shut, unable to take the barrage on my senses any longer.

Let go, Shelbie, the words rang in my head, and my fingers loosened their hold. Something shifted underneath my skin with the words, expanding until I felt like I would burst, split in two.

I was burning, lit from within, fire rolling through my veins in angry pulses as my mind broke.

Let go, the voice said again, and oxygen was sucked from my lungs in a gasp as the flames seared my skin. Pressure crushed against my hand, and I pulled against it, trying to break free of whatever gripped me — trying to ease the sensations overwhelming me, body and soul. Pain flooded my every nerve ending, alight with the fire now, burning alive.

Make it stop, I cried, but the words never left my head.

Come to me, the voice said, growing louder. *I will ease your pain.*

I reached towards where the voice came from, lifting my hand from the crushing pressure, moving towards whoever, or whatever, promised to end this torture.

As my eyes opened, the colors stopped. The stars were gone. The pain ebbed.

Instead, everything was dark.

Drip.

Drip.

Drip.

My breath came in heaving gasps, fighting to fill my lungs as the green light shone from my pendant, illuminating the darkness I'd visited so many times in my dream. Rock walls rose above me on all sides, a slow trickle of water worked its way towards the back of the cave. Stalactites hung suspended from the ceiling, water dripping from them, appearing like long teeth ready to gobble up any who stepped foot into the cave. But there, something in the back of the cave — it called to me. The dull red light.

Hadriel? I sent out, feeling the pendant pulse against my skin as I stepped deeper into the cave. I glanced behind me as my brow scrunched. Something wasn't right — I forgot something. But the pull — it tugged me forward, unrelenting.

Come. Promised, the voice urged again, insistent. I paused, willing my mind to clear, realizing the voice was different.

Something had changed.

Still, I couldn't stop.

My feet shuffled across the rocks beneath me, feeling my way through the eerie scene I'd imagined so many times, now cast in the harsh green light of the pendant glowing bright around my neck. It flickered, the stone changing color for only a moment — flashing red, then back to green. I stopped, staring down at the onyx in confusion, fingers rubbing across the stone.

Hurry, the voice demanded, and this time, the pendant blazed a fiery red. I gasped as the heat of the stone singed my palm. Holding it by the chain away from my skin, I dropped to my knees, placing my hands against the cool stone, trying to ease the burning pain.

COME, the voice shouted, anger laced in the word. My head seemed to split, a pain so intense I fell to the ground, clutching my skull.

Help me, I cried out, desperate for relief from this agony. A cool breeze shifted through the cave, blowing my hair from my neck, where I lay curled on the ground, carrying the masculine smell of pine and fresh air mingled with sweat.

Domari?, I sobbed in my head, unable to find my voice. *I need you. I can't do this alone. Please.*

My hand that wasn't burnt squeezed in pain, fingers bending as they were crushed in an invisible grip, but my mind hardly registered the new sensation, lost to the misery in my head.

40
DOMARI

Domari clutched at Shelbie where she lay, cradled between his body and the Tree roots where they'd landed. They were back in his time, but Shelbie's eyes had gone white, fogged over as her body lay limp in his arms.

"Hadriel! What's happening?" he cried, pulling Shelbie onto his lap in a crushing grip. "Her skin is burning! She's on fire!"

But the dragon didn't answer, only flaring his wings as the ground shook with his fearsome shriek.

The onyx pendant shone brightly against her pale, freckled skin exposed beneath her coat. A green light cast around them, radiating up into the sky. Reds and greens mingled as they danced overhead, but Domari was too frantic to appreciate the beauty above.

"Come back to me, Shelbie." Domari shook her shoulders, teeth clenched as worry ate at him. Each time she'd faded out in the car had seemed to pull her away for longer, lost to the visions in her mind. Still. Unseeing. He watched as her chest rose and fell, still taking in oxygen in heavy gasps, the way she had been for over an hour since they'd arrived through the portal.

Thor whined loudly at her side, placing himself between her and the dragon as his hair stood on end. Domari glanced up, away from Shelbie, for only a moment. At any other time, he would have laughed at seeing a dog staring down a gigantic dragon.

"Hadriel could swallow you whole, Thor," Domari said aloud, and the dog turned in his direction with a furious gaze. He whined again as he stared at Shelbie, and Domari fought the urge to do the same.

"Shelbie." Domari's voice shook as he rubbed his thumb across her cheek, blazing hot under his skin. "I need you. I can't do this alone. Please don't leave me."

Suddenly, the pendant around her neck changed from green to red for only a moment. "Hadriel," Domari whispered, fear turning his blood cold as he glanced up at the dragon. "What does that mean?"

Then, the green turned bright red, and Shelbie's mouth flew open in a soundless scream. Welts rose across her hand, laying on the rocks, and Domari panted heavily as anxiety wove through him.

Hand him a sword. Hand him an axe. Hand him an enemy he could slay for her. Even a dragon... but this... whatever was happening to her... he couldn't fight.

And that broke him.

"*NO,*" he roared into the night, and the dragon prowling the shore above him matched the sound, fire pluming above him in great waves, heat washing over his skin.

"YOU CAN'T HAVE HER," Domari screamed as he pulled Shelbie's unburnt hand up in a crushing grip. *"SHE'S MINE."*

With his free hand, Domari clutched the pendant's chain, sucking in a breath as the heat of the charm seared into his skin, and ripped it free from her neck.

41

SHELBIE

My back heaved off the ground as my eyes flew open, sucking in air as if I'd been drowning. Fractured, craggy lines sliced through my vision, breaking up the glaring colors overhead. I could hear nothing above the ringing in my ears; sight and sound flooded with the sudden change of scenery.

Gone was the darkness of the cave. Instead of stalactites above me, I stared at what I now realized were tree limbs. My head turned slightly, the only movement I could make as I fought to settle my soul beneath my skin again. My hair scratched across something soft underneath me, and I turned more towards the scent of pine.

Domari.

His face was white with anxiety beneath his beard when my eyes finally found him. I watched as his eyes searched me, lips moving as he spoke, but the sound was still muffled as if I were underwater. I closed my eyes as I fought to even my breathing and felt his hands grip my chin roughly. My eyes snapped back open, and the look on Domari's face was now furious.

"Don't leave me," I thought he said, but I couldn't be sure. I fought to lift my hand, laying it over his, where he gripped my face and patted his skin.

"I'm here." I forced the words to pass my lips as my eyes closed again. I felt as his lips grazed mine tenderly, and a splash of water dropped onto my skin.

Sound reached me first — a wet, slurping noise close to my ear. Next, I felt a cool slide across my cheek repeatedly. I pulled away from the feeling, head rearing away from it as the smell of *dog* drifted through the air.

"Thor." I lifted my hand, sinking them into his thick fur and pushing him away from me. "Stop."

Crunching snow sounded around me as I fought to open my eyes. Before me squatted a mountain of a man. He had warm brown hair streaked with gold, longer on top, and shaved closely on the side. Chocolate brown eyes I would never forget drifted over my face, and my heart warmed at the view.

Domari.

The man I loved.

"Hi," I said weakly as he crouched in front of me. He grabbed my hand and pulled me into a sitting position.

"That's it?" his voice was rough as he repeated his words from earlier this winter, and I watched as he fought to force a weak smile. "After all of this, I get one word?"

I chuckled then, dropping my eyes as my hands drifted to my side into the snow on the ground. As my palm touched the cool moisture, I gasped, pulled my hand back against my chest, and glanced down. Red, raised ridges rose across my flesh, where a deep burn was etched into the sensitive skin. The burn was in the shape of a rune — *perthros* — the same one I wore on my bracelet. But, there, through the middle, was a slash. My thumb grazed over the red ridges lightly as I lifted my face back to Domari squatting over me.

"What does this mean?" I showed him the mark, and he tenderly pulled my hand into his lap, inspecting it.

"A fate defied." His eyes rose to meet mine before shifting to something over my shoulder.

Following his gaze, I turned to find a giant black dragon at my back, eyes glowing bright green as smoke rose from his nostrils into the cool air. His teeth were bared in anger, but I wasn't afraid. Hadriel would never hurt me.

Why are you upset? I sent towards him mentally, working to make my words soothing and calm. He needed it.

But there was no answer.

"Why can't he hear me anymore?" I asked Domari as panic rose in me once more. Memories flooded me, realizing all that still waited for us. I pushed to my feet, hurrying to Hadriel's side as the world spun around me. "Domari. We have to go. They need us. Why can't he hear me?"

Domari held out his hand, and in it was my pendant. It was dull, returned to a lifeless black onyx in his palm, and I gasped at the welts on Domari's hand — the marks of the chain.

"You were burning." Domari's throat worked with his words, and I stepped into his grip, wrapping my fingers around the cool stone. "The stone flashed from green to red, and you were on fire."

I lifted the chain from his hand and hesitated, staring down at it.

"I can't lose you, Shelbie." Domari's voice cracked. "Not again."

Something warm and spiky nudged me almost painfully in the back, and I spun at the feeling. Hadriel chuffed, smoke billowing. His enormous face nudged my hand with the pendant, and I understood his message. My hands rose above my head, and the chain dropped over my curls, settling the charm against my chest. Green light blazed brightly as my hair lifted, curls swirling around me as energy pulsed from my skin.

My Promised, Hadriel's smoky voice rasped in my head, and I smiled at the rightness settling deep in my soul. I lifted my singed hand, holding it towards Hadriel, palm down. He lifted his head gently until our skin touched, mine against his.

Power surged from our contact, pulsing light and energy out in a great wave around us, rippling through the air like a stone dropped into a still pond. I shifted my gaze to Domari, standing nearby with Thor at his side, and grinned at the awe written on their faces. Domari's eyes flashed as he stared down at his hand, watching as the burns from my pendant disappeared.

As I lifted my hand, the glowing orb around us shrunk down, absorbed once more into my pendant. I stared down into my palm and saw, like Domari, the brand that was there only moments before was now gone. My skin was fresh, renewed, and healed as if it had never happened.

He tried to take you from me, Hadriel's voice held more emotion than I'd heard so far, and I gazed up into his green eyes, the same color as my onyx pendant shone moments before. *Nidhoggr's power is far greater than I feared. Somehow, when you came through the portal, the moment before we were to connect, he stole you. Someone is healing him, restoring his power. That shouldn't be possible since he is Unpromised.*

"What's he telling you?" Domari asked, and I turned to face him. Hadriel's head drifted to peer over my shoulder, and I lifted my healed palm to cup his enormous, scaled face above me. Domari shook his head before I could answer, raising his hand to rub across his temple and forehead. "This is a sight I will never forget."

Thor's gaze roamed between the dragon, Domari, and me, indecision racking him.

Ready to fly, my Promised? Hadriel asked, and my heart jumped at his words. *His people — your people — need you.*

My pulse rocketed as I remembered what we'd come here to do. "We have to go."

Domari glanced out over the still, mostly frozen lake with a calculating look. "Getting across will be difficult."

A giggle erupted as I slapped my hand across my mouth, glancing back at Hadriel, then over at Domari and Thor. Domari's brow drew down; his eyes now slits boring into me as he cocked his head to the side in an appraising look. Before I could explain, the ground shook as Hadriel lowered himself to his belly, wings slightly outstretched. I spun, walking to his side, and Domari watched wide-eyed as my fingers grazed the dragon's smooth scales. Hadriel's wing dipped down and forward, and I lifted my foot to step up into the joint he offered towards me. My body flew up and over his large torso, settling between his shoulders along his neck.

"No, Domari." I held my hand out to him with a smile that split my face in two, showing every tooth in my mouth as a giddy feeling bubbled inside me. "I don't think it will be difficult at all."

42

SHELBIE

Laughter broke free from me as we soared through the sky, trees flying by underneath us in a carpet of green and white. My eyes shut as my head tilted back, breathing in the fresh mountain air. The wind whipped at my hair and was bitter cold, but the feel of the warm dragon beneath me countered it. Domari's hands laced around my waist tightly, and I felt him shift against my back. My heart raced, adrenaline pumping through my blood with each flap of Hadriel's black and gold wings, like they had in my visions.

Is Thor okay down there? I asked in my head, sending it to the dragon beneath me.

I don't care for his fur in my mouth, Hadriel answered, and I chuckled. *I wish he would have allowed me to carry him in my talons as I'd planned.*

Yes, well, he's always been stubborn, I sent back.

At least he has stopped clawing at my cheeks. That was unpleasant.

My shoulders shook, and Domari pulled me tighter into his body. *Please don't accidentally roast him. I like Thor the way he is.*

I've never accidentally roasted anything, Hadriel shot back defensively, and I suddenly wondered if dragons could roll their eyes. He was as sassy as everyone else I loved.

My fingers loosened their hold on Hadriel's spined shoulder blades, feeling secure in my seating.

I will not let you fall, Hadriel sent out as he felt my shift. My muscles relaxed as I breathed deeply.

"You okay back there?" I said aloud, and the sound quickly carried away from me.

"Don't let go," Domari growled in my ear, and I grinned. This was the lightest I'd felt in months. Rightness settled deep in my bones with every flap of Hadriel's wings.

I was born for this.

Made for this.

Fated for this.

My Promised, Hadriel's voice was full of pride and contentment, and I felt it deep in my soul.

Domari's hands tightly gripped my waist as I let go, letting my arms lift to the side as if I had wings of my own. "This is even better than *Titanic.*" The words whipped out of my mouth as Domari's grip crushed against my torso, anchoring me to the dragon under us in any way he could. "And you're so much hotter than Leo."

Mumbled words answered me from Domari, but nothing I could understand over the sound of the wind whipping around me. Hadriel banked hard to the left, and a part-terrified, part-exhilarated scream left me as my hands flew back down to Hadriel's warm back, gripping tightly onto the horns I'd held. He dipped closer to the trees, and the grin dropped from my face as I stared ahead.

In the distance, smoke rose between the trees, close to the frozen river below. Domari stiffened against my back, and my heart raced to the beat of a drum. Nausea rolled through me as I took in the scene below us. The river was mostly frozen, but trees were lodged on the ice, breaking it in places where water flowed below.

"Good," Domari said near my ear, his beard tickling against my skin. "They prepared. The river isn't safe to pass how they've broken through the ice. An army couldn't easily walk there, and boats can't traverse the waters yet. They'll be forced into the forest."

Sensing the direction of my thoughts, Hadriel said, *The forest is nearly impassable as well. His people have worked hard to slow any incoming enemies, forcing them into a narrow line.* I relayed the message to Domari.

Domari's grip on my waist tightened, and I felt the same tension flowing through my veins. But no matter how hard the Erikssons had worked, something was still burning. Smoke rose in a black cloud above the tree line, like a beacon of death drawing us in. With every beat of Hadriel's wings propelling us closer, my heartbeat picked up speed. Homesteads came into view, and I began counting them, working my way towards the center of the village.

"Domari," I whispered tentatively as my worries were confirmed. "The smoke—"

"It's either at Gunnar's or Frida's, I know."

Acid rose in my throat as we neared the smoke, and I dreaded what I'd see there, knowing what I'd see — I'd already *Seen* it.

"There's something I need to tell you." I forced the words out of me as I glanced to our left, where the trees were denser, leading away from the village and noticed the incoming storm.

Silence met me, but I continued, clearing my throat before I spoke. "The children, Domari. There are many of them here — far more than the inhabitants of this village. I think they're fleeing at this very moment." Domari said nothing, but his hands gripped me tightly. Thunder rumbled in the distance, and I glanced over my shoulder to see the dark clouds headed our way. "Hadriel, is that true?"

Yes, the dragon answered me, and I nodded my head. *They're not far enough from where the battle is just beginning. But you must choose...*

"Choose?" I asked aloud as panic surged. "Choose what?"

Your visions — they are both happening now, the dragon responded.

A manic, nervous giggle left me and my vision began to black out.

"What's he saying?" Domari growled his frustration at being left out of the conversation. I couldn't blame him. Lightning flashed, casting the world in an eerie light, only adding to my nerves as I sat high in the sky.

"He says we have to choose. Both of my visions are happening now, and he can't help both." The words were a whimper as they left me, and I was distraught with this revelation. Hadriel banked to the left towards where he said the children were, and we saw the men working their way through the forest towards the children's path. Painted with black, I counted 40 men holding their weapons at the ready as they stealthily worked through the trees. Several heads glanced our way into the sky as we flew overhead, pausing as they watched the great predator fly above them, but none retreated.

"Where are our men? Where are my people?" Domari asked in an angry growl as he watched the scene below us unfold, and I repeated his question to Hadriel.

They're between the children and this group, but they are far outnumbered, Hadriel answered. *Gunnar and Signe have gathered allies, but not enough arrived yet.*

"They can slow these men but can't stop them," I summarized for Domari as we banked back towards the smoke. "But Domari… Gunnar is going to die."

"HE CAN'T DIE," Domari shouted viciously as emotion overtook his cool calm, thunder rolling ominously as it echoed his words. "Take me to him, Hadriel. I will stop his death on my own. You and Shelbie return and get rid of the men after the children. Feast on their bones. Flay them alive. No man who would willingly hunt a child deserves to live, Hadriel. *End them."*

I will have to leave Thor with Domari to use my fire, Hadriel sent, and I cried out in distress.

As if he, too, could hear my thoughts, Domari squeezed my side. "I won't let anything happen to Thor."

I nodded, understanding this was the only way. Swiveling in my seat, I grabbed Domari's face in a crushing grip and slammed my lips against his for only a second.

"I love you," I said with a nod. "Don't die, please."

He nodded, brushed a thumb across my cheek, and placed one more kiss on my forehead. "Let's go save our people."

My heart threatened to break free from my chest as we circled the scene below us, moving closer to where the smoke rose. Flames licked along the roof of Gunnar's barn. Just as I'd Seen, Signe was on her knees, pleading with the men in front of her.

Twelve men I didn't recognize stood to the right of the building, the largest of them one I remembered from my visions as Signe's father, Draugr. A scar split through his brow, etched deep into his pale skin and up onto his scalp, and his pale red hair had been shaved to follow the same line of the scar — accentuating it rather than hiding it. His black cloak was slung over one shoulder, leaving the other corded arm exposed, strength and power oozing off of the older man.

Draugr held the dagger in his tattooed hand, digging into the skin of Gunnar's throat as blood seeped from where Gunnar's left eye once was. His golden hair leaned against Draugr's shoulder, fighting to put any distance between his neck and the blade, but it was of no use. I assumed the others were Draugr's men, the way they circled him, carefully eyeing the dragon in the sky above.

They whispered to each other, adjusting their shields in one arm and loosely holding axes, spears, and swords at the ready with the other.

Raud stood apart, posed between Signe and the burning house, flames from the torch in his hand casting dancing shadows across his skin. Furs were strapped to his body beneath weapons belts, everything as dark as the images tattooed on his scalp.

"You can't stop me this time, Dark One," Raud taunted the dragon above as déja-vu swept over me, witnessing this scene once again. As I watched, something in his dark gaze flickered, and the onyx at my chest heated. My gaze was glued to him, knowing what would come next. The torch flew through the air as it landed on the roof of the longhouse.

This shouldn't be possible, Hadriel sent to me, but I dismissed his words, focused intently on the scene below.

"Lower Hadriel," Domari said. The dragon did as he was told, tucking his wings in a dive. The beat of Hadriel's wings sent a gust of wind over the scene below, Signe's red-blonde hair blowing around her. The sight of her dagger dropping to the ground in front of her in defeat broke my heart in two.

"*It's me you want,*" Signe's words echo in my head again, full of distress as the strongest woman I knew knelt in front of her enemy. "*Leave him.*"

Domari's grip on me loosened as I felt his heat loss at my back. I glanced behind me to watch where he stood crouched on the dragon's back with one hand on the beast below him, the other loosely holding his sword, axe sheathed at his side. His face instantly transformed from the man I knew and loved. In its place was a fierce, battle-hardened warrior ready to protect what was his.

It's time, Hadriel sent, and I repeated the words aloud to Domari as we lowered onto the scene.

Is there nothing we can do to help? I sent back frantically, panting heavily with adrenaline as Domari's body tensed, ready for the jump he was about to make.

This area is too small. I can't ignite the warriors without also harming Gunnar and Signe.

I nodded as seconds ticked by, and my eyes burned with tears that wanted to fall but couldn't. Heat licked my face as we neared the scene, now only a beat away from us. Everyone in the clearing paused, overseeing our descent. Draugr shouted something to a man behind him, and I watched the scene unfold in slow motion as a spear launched into the air in our direction, headed for Hadriel's belly.

NOW, Hadriel's voice shouted into my head. I gripped tightly to his horns as Hadriel banked to the left. With the shift, Domari flew through the air, emitting a piercing battle cry. I warred between wanting to close my eyes and an inability to blink for fear I'd miss any moment of this. A slightly soggy and very angry Thor dropped from Hadriel's mouth, and I wished I had it in me to laugh at the ridiculousness of it all.

Anxiety rippled off me in waves as I watched both my dog and my man drop a few feet to the ground. My skin ached, too tight on my body while time ticked by impossibly slow. Thunder clapped in the distance as Domari's feet slapped to the ground, dropping to a crouch while he eyed the enemy in front of him.

Every hair on Thor's back stood on end. My dog stalked towards Signe, fangs bared in a furious growl as he flanked her left side, opposite the smaller dog on her right. Together, they faced down the man in front of her. Together, they were protecting her.

Desperately, I wished there was something I could do to help. As if summoned by the thought, fire seemed to coat my skin as a wave of power washed over the scene, nearly knocking everyone below off-balance.

Domari's eyes glanced up quickly to me, alight with pride as he rose to his feet, stepping towards Signe. Before anyone could react to his sudden arrival, Signe's head turned, locking eyes with Domari.

Instantly, she rose, her foot swinging out to the side as Domari tossed his sword to her. Signe caught it effortlessly, continuing her side swipe as she spun, rising to her feet. By the time Domari had closed the distance between them, his axe was drawn, and the dogs both bared their teeth at the warriors' hips.

In a flurry of motion, the four charged towards the men holding Gunnar.

We must hurry, Hadriel said, as he pulled us away from the scene below.

It took every ounce of my willpower to turn my face away from the burning house, trusting Domari and Signe could do this. Could somehow take on twelve men. Could save Gunnar from the death that was approaching fast.

Could spare Signe from the hands of her father. Could defy this fate.

Find the others for me, Hadriel, I said as iron settled in my bones, reinforcing whatever confidence I had. In what abilities, I didn't know. But I thought I'd done that power ripple thing, so maybe I wouldn't be completely useless. *Find the children.*

With that, Hadriel's wings stretched, propelling us with a new speed as smoke rose from his nostrils, oozing from his mouth.

43

DOMARI

An eerie calm settled over Domari as his vision focused, flashing images of men moving, showing their weaknesses to him before anyone had even recovered from the blast of magic Shelbie had caused.

Working with the same goal in mind, Signe did precisely as he hoped, spinning to catch his sword as he tossed it to her. He'd never fought with the woman before, but he trusted Gunnar and Magnus's judgment of her. At the moment, he had to.

The angry growl rolling off Thor drew Domari's attention, watching as the dog bared his teeth at the scene in front of him and was surprised the dog was still functioning after he rode in a dragon's mouth. Unbothered, Thor stepped forward to Signe's side, another smaller black dog on her right. Signe never glanced towards the beast, eyes shifting from Raud to where Gunnar stood, a blade to his throat.

The sight of the crimson streaks down Gunnar's face

and throat, dripping down his chest, flamed the fire of Domari's inner rage, boiling over as Signe and Domari's movements instantly synced, stepping together into the fray.

Lightning flashed, thunder cracking loudly as the storm grew closer, snow drifting down from above as Domari dropped his shoulders, axe held in his grip. Signe bared her teeth in an expression as savage as the animals flanking her, slicing through the first of the men to step between her and her husband.

Together, Domari and Signe moved through the men, eliminating them far faster than he'd expected. Both dogs moved as if made of shadows, ushering enemies within their reach, waiting for the promise of death Domari and Signe issued with their every move. Pride for the woman at his side swelled in his chest as they fought, refusing to give in to the fate handed to them.

A sickening crunch sent blood splattering across Domari's face, painting him in the brutality he swung with each strike of his axe, the same rightness he'd felt so many times in battle before settling deep in his bones.

This.

Domari was made for this. To right the wrongs of others. To collect payments for misdeeds in blood.

Raud moved, catching Domari's attention, and Domari split from Signe's side as she cut down another man. Her focus was intent, working towards her father, who stood back, holding Gunnar with the blade still at his throat.

Fury built in Domari's veins aimed at Raud, ire clouding his vision red as lightning struck the longhouse behind them. Domari's axe fell heavily, severing the arm of the man that stood between him and Raud with a single swing, but the cries of pain were nothing compared to the pulse pounding in Domari's ears.

Fire licked at the wood structure, consuming it, but still, Raud watched the scene with a sneer.

"What do you *want?*" Domari ground the words out through gritted teeth towards his long-lost friend, gripping the wooden handle of his axe tightly as he spun it at his side. "Is this it? Revenge? Punishing us for the fate promised to you? Still throwing tantrums over not getting your way."

Raud shook his head condescendingly as the barn roof collapsed behind him, sending sparks up into the air. Domari studied him as another man charged from the side. With a shift of his hips, he swung the axe up and into the man's torso before he could even move to block the deadly blow.

"Impressive." Raud clapped, his grin flashing in the fire raging behind him. "Still killing with instinct alone. If only your instincts were to protect, then maybe you wouldn't have killed my Tove."

The words stung, even though Domari had thought the same ones thousands of times in his mind over the last decade. "We all made mistakes that night, Raud. Tove, too. She didn't follow the plan, and I couldn't find her. Her death isn't on your hands, or mine, or Gunnar's."

"LIAR." Raud's eyes flashed as his face screwed up into a grimace, veins popping on his neck. But the moment passed quickly, the expression shuttering and returning to a calm facade in an instant. That confused Domari. Never

had his friend been able to control his wild temper like this before.

"All this?" Raud continued, waving his arms out over the longhouse and through the village. "Meaningless. There's no glory here. No victory. No purpose. You *survive* and call that living."

"Compared to what?" Domari scoffed, looking at the dead men scattered around the yard in front of the house. "Murdering innocents for no reason? What does that win you?" Domari's eyes darted momentarily towards Signe, watching as she moved with fluid grace, cutting down men as if they were made of smoke.

Domari didn't know these men, but the red-blonde hair of the one standing behind Gunnar, knife in hand, matched Signe's exactly. Her father, Draugr the Demon, if the fragments of visions Shelbie had shared on their drive were to be believed. Even if Domari didn't know the man, he knew *of* him — most Vikings did. His savage expression lingered on Domari as they eyed each other.

Blood pumped in Domari's veins, thundering under his skin. His skin tingled with electricity as he returned his focus to his old friend. "Do these deaths bring Tove back to you, Raud? Does it fix anything?"

Raud screamed, his face morphing into rage momentarily before the furious, broken expression shuttered, leaving behind a calm exterior once more. Flames reflected in Raud's dark gaze. Domari watched as Raud closed his eyes, twisting his neck to the side in a twitch as if battling some unwanted thought. When he reopened his eyes, red shone there.

With his teeth bared, Raud pointed to the fire blazing behind him. His voice had changed, sounding like he'd inhaled smoke, rasping heavily. "Power is fading from our world, Domari, and I will bring it back. What this world needs is a rebirth. A new beginning. To end those who are filled with weakness. To bring back the warriors of old. Before rejoining Tove in Valhalla, I will destroy you and everything you've ever loved."

As Domari stepped closer to Raud, Draugr *tsk*ed him from where he stood off to the side. "I wouldn't move if you want your precious Gunnar to draw another breath."

"Leave him out of this." Domari shifted his view to the Demon. A smug grin filled the older man's face as he appraised Domari. "I'm twice the warrior Gunnar is." Domari pointed at the seven dead men he'd left in his wake. "Use me."

"I don't care about either one of you." Draugr turned his eyes to stare at Gunnar, blood trickling down over his blade. "But *her* — my *daughter* — I care very much about."

"I don't remember you caring much about me until I decided to leave," Signe shot, eyes squinting as she appraised her father. Her chest heaved as she kicked a foot into the man impaled on Domari's sword, shoving him to the ground to die amongst his peers.

"You *ran*, is what you did," Draugr spat back at her. "A coward move."

"And this isn't?" She tilted her head, challenging her father. "You send children to me, one after the next, expecting *weakness*," she hissed the word at him, "because I loved the child thrust on me. Because I couldn't — *wouldn't*

— follow your orders and mercilessly take the lives of innocents on your raids."

"Love *is* weakness, Signe," Draugr hurled at her as the few remaining in the clearing watched with bated breath. "If I didn't have this man — your husband — by the throat, his life depending on my mercy, what would you do?"

Fire brimmed in Signe's eyes, fury transforming her into a ruthless warrior ready for bloodshed, giving the answer he sought. But Signe didn't move from where she stood, bloody sword hanging at her side.

"You prove my point with every breath," Draugr continued. Raud chuckled, shaking his head as he stepped to join the four remaining men at Draugr's side.

"Look at him." Draugr waved a hand towards Raud. Raud's smug smile fell, a scowl replacing the look of only a moment before. "The things that man has done for love are unimaginable."

Draugr cocked his head to the side, appraising Domari next. "And you. The Varangian captain returned home." His lips turned up in a sinister smile. "I've heard stories about you, and from watching you fight just now, those stories are true. A god among men on the battlefield. I do so wish you would join my fight, but love's poison is written in your every move." His smile fell into a look of disgust. "Weakness should be cut out at the heart."

With his words, he pushed the blade deeper into Gunnar's neck, and Signe screamed, shifting forward on her feet as she dropped Domari's sword to the ground.

"Don't even think about it, my daughter," Draugr

laughed as Gunnar gasped for air. "If you even attempt to stop my heart, as I've seen you do so many times before, your husband will follow me in death."

"*I'll do anything,*" she bellowed, and Gunnar's eye searched Signe's face, remorse battling with a look of pure love. "I'll go with you."

The words were a sob, the most emotion Domari had ever heard from the woman, but precisely the ones her father was waiting to hear. His blade at Gunnar's throat loosened for only a moment, and Gunnar sagged in relief.

Domari shifted forward onto the balls of his feet, waiting for an opening. Before he could move, Raud shouted in frustration, sinking the knife in his hand deep into Gunnar's left shoulder, just above his heart.

"*NO!*" Signe screamed, launching herself forward at the remaining men. Weaponless, she clawed and punched at the men who seized her, watching as Gunnar slumped to the ground, gripping the knife still embedded in his chest. Within moments, the two warriors touching Signe released her, hands clawing at their chests as they backed away from her, eyes wide in surprise. Shock coursed through Domari as he watched the men drop to their knees, the life fading out of their eyes with not a single drop of bloodshed.

"See?" Draugr spun on Raud with a furious glare. "*Weakness.* Take Signe and Gunnar alive — you won't harm them any further. My plans will not be ruined by your impulsive need to satisfy an age-old vendetta that means *nothing.*" Spittle flew through the air as Draugr shook angrily, warring with Raud at every word.

"You." He pointed a shaking finger in the air towards

Domari, whose hand slid to his knife, waiting to launch it as Raud had done. "I would suggest you stay right where you are."

"You've seen me fight, and you still doubt I can take you on?" Domari answered honestly and boastfully, adrenaline pumping as he prepared for battle again. His breathing slowed, sinking into the calm as he slid the knife under his belt and flipped the hilt of his axe in his other hand. "Care for another demonstration?"

Draugr laughed, his eyes crinkling in delight at the challenge, but only shook his head. "While I would love to see you try, know that the rest of my men are waiting for me with strict instructions. If I don't return, they are to continue following your children into the forest, picking them off one by one until none are left. Not even my own grandson, still just a suckling babe."

"I'll go, Domari." Signe's gaze shifted to him, and Domari swallowed. Tears lined her eyes, but not a single one fell.

"Signe, you don't have to do this," Domari answered, fury battling with reason with every breath he took, but he knew his words were useless. If Domari was in her place — if it was Shelbie that lay dying in front of him, if it were his children at risk — there was nothing he wouldn't do.

He watched as Signe rose to her feet, her chin tilting skyward in a proud gesture, even now. "Heal my husband, or I will murder you as you've seen me do so many times, snatching the air you breathe." She glared at Draugr as she passed him, walking away from her burning house, away from her village, away from her life.

Draugr chuckled at her words with a shake of his head. "Do as she says." He flicked his hand to where Gunnar lay on the ground, breathing heavily.

Raud hadn't moved in some time. Domari observed him, noticing the shifting colors of his eyes, the twitch of his neck, the tension curling his fingers. If Raud had sought this relationship with Draugr hoping to remain in charge, he was sorely mistaken.

"This isn't you," Domari said quietly, his body humming with unreleased energy, itching for the last of the fight.

Raud heard him, though, his head snapping to Domari's gaze. "You know *nothing*, Domari."

With his final words, Raud stomped after the retreating men, headed along the river's edge. Signe's red-blonde hair blew in the wind, swishing with her every step as she led the way into the forest and towards the mountains beyond.

Domari stood motionless, indecision warring with his need for battle — needing an outlet for the last of the aggression flooding his system.

Home is more than a place, isn't it? The Norns' words floated through his head as he fought to even his temper and regain control. *To be ready for what is to come, you must remember what you are to protect.*

His eyes drifted over the treetops to where Shelbie and Hadriel had launched into the sky, leaving to protect his clan, people, and children. Thor stepped into his side, leaning against Domari's leg, the other pup circling him. Domari's hand fell, running it through the thick fur along Thor's back as a sigh of defeat escaped him. Grabbing his discarded sword from where Signe had dropped it, he wiped it on the pants of a dead man, leaving the remnants of the battle behind. With one last glance to where Raud's party had disappeared, he turned his back to the fire, swallowing the longhouse whole.

"This isn't the end," Domari promised, sliding his hand across his neck — the knot of four strands. "We swore to always fight for each other, and I will."

44

SHELBIE

The Demon's men are to our left, just below the cover of the trees, Hadriel said. I turned, squinting into the morning light in the direction he showed with a bob of his head. *Your men are between them and the children.*

I glanced to where he indicated, further back into the forest. Snow still capped most of the trees, green peeking out from beneath the white. From above, I could make out a small clearing, and sunlight glistened off a large, blond head I knew immediately.

"Magnus is down there," I croaked, forgetting nobody was here to listen to my spoken words. My eyes scanned the scene as we circled, and Magnus glanced up as if sensing my fear for him. His blue eyes sparkled with a grin, recognition flashing in his countenance. Thorsten, Kare, Arne, Bodil, Björn, and even Yrsa waited just outside the clearing, along with a dozen men I didn't know.

Signe has pulled in Gunnar's allies, but most haven't arrived yet,

Hadriel answered my unspoken thoughts. *Too many of Draugr's men are coming for the force assembled here.*

But now they have us. Hadriel's chest vibrated in an answer as we circled the clearing, moving in behind where Magnus and the others waited.

The traps Signe laid are working. Pride filled Hadriel's voice in my head, and it surged in my body as I looked to where the forest paths were blocked by felled trees and rocks, debris scattered to hinder passage. That woman was equal parts an angel and a nightmare, all rolled into one. *Draugr's men are being herded directly into this clearing.*

Hadriel circled again, swooping down above the tree line, and I leaned to the side to see what he was watching. A dozen children hurried through the woods as fast as their feet could carry them, women hustling them along. Frida glanced into the sky as our shadow passed over them, but never paused in her quick steps through the snow.

A girl with hair as black as coal stopped, staring up into the sky as we passed. Light flickered off her emerald eyes, where they bored into the dragon and me. Her right hand raised in a salute, palm up, as she ducked her chin in a show of respect.

"Clear the path for us, Hadriel." Her words were quiet, but I heard them just the same. Hadriel beat his wings hard as he rose into the air, surging forward in front of the children. Flames erupted from his mouth, melting the snow in their path instantly. In answer, my skin prickled as another wave of power erupted, dousing the fire instantly. The knee-deep mounds of snow from moments before were gone, and ahead of the children now stood a clear path up into the mountains I'd descended with Björn last fall. They broke into a run, and Hadriel flew further ahead. Together, we repeated the process as many times as we could.

Breath was sucked from my lungs as my vision shifted momentarily, images flooding my mind one after the next. Just as quickly as they came on, my mind cleared, nowhere near as consuming as the visions I'd had before Hadriel and I were reunited. I hesitated only a moment, glancing down at the children below. Still, I knew the dread pooling in my stomach wasn't merely from the vision itself, but the insistent pull of magic urging me back to the clearing where we'd left Magnus and the others. I pushed the image of our changing course to Hadriel and slapped my hand down on his warm back. Without a word, he silently turned back in the direction we'd come.

Hold on, he sent, and I didn't hesitate. Leaning my body down into him, my thighs clamped hard against his back while my hands firmly gripped his horns. We rocketed through the sky at a speed I could hardly fathom, the wind whipping my hair violently. Hadriel ascended into the sky, gaining height away from the trees. I began questioning why we were pulling away from the scene until he suddenly tucked his wings. As fast as we'd flown, we now spiraled down into a descent, a bullet flying towards the scene below.

I slammed my eyes shut, the force of our descent feeling like it would suck my eyes from the sockets. The sound of Hadriel's shriek overwhelmed my senses, and my eyes flew back open as his wings snapped out, hovering us above the treeline. Snow shook free of the trees as we passed, raining down on the men below as they watched us approach. Forty men stood just inside the clearing as fire exploded from Hadriel's mouth, licking up the bark of the trees at their backs. Men screamed as they raised their shields against the fire, turning to retreat into the cover of the forest.

But, already, it was useless.

A deep cry rose above the others as Magnus stormed into the clearing, face painted black — ready for battle. Snarling like wolves, a dozen men and women followed in his wake, weapons raised high as they descended on their enemy, and Hadriel unleashed again.

The fire consumed the forest behind the clearing, sealing the two armies in. But there were still far more enemies than our people.

How do I do that pulse magic thingie again, Hadriel? I shouted as my fingers slid to the glowing pendant at my neck. Blood pumped so fast in my veins that my ears rang with the sound of it while Hadriel and I circled the scene below. Metal clanged on metal, blood flying as warriors fell. The scene was such a mess I could hardly tell friend from foe.

It's not enough! I shouted into Hadriel's head, but he was focused on the scene below, not answering me. We swooped lower, now above the field, the heat of the fire all around us parching my skin. His talons scraped across the scene, plucking two men from the battle as he hurled them into the fire of the trees. Screams filled the air, and several men paused, staring at where Hadriel was circling again.

We were now the biggest threat — not the battle.

Hadriel roared again, shaking the ground beneath the raging fighters, and I watched as Magnus called out to his people. They pulled in closer, creating a tight-knit force as shields snapped together in a barrier. His eyes drifted to me, and immediately I understood. He was showing us the enemy.

Vikings I didn't recognize cowered as Hadriel swooped low, flames shooting through the clearing, catching the furs of the men still on the field. His talons scraped down again, seizing the one man brave enough to continue the charge into battle against our forces.

Men bellowed, swords clanging against shields as the enemies below realized we had trapped them within the flames and were picking them off one at a time.

YES HADRIEL! I shouted as he circled again.

Realizing their imminent doom, several battle cries broke through the field, ready to die fighting, aiming for Valhalla. Magnus and his troop broke apart, crying out as swords clashed, axes swung, and spears launched. One by one, the enemies fell by the hands of our people or the dragon beneath me. Arne and Bodil fought back to back as I'd seen them do last fall in Winter Nights, swords held high as they moved in tandem. Björn's thick torso moved faster than I could have imagined, blocking his wife as Yrsa stood, spear in hand at his back. Thorsten and Kare held their shields together as they crashed into a group of five men near the fire, breaking them apart, axes swinging wildly at their sides. Magnus moved with the lumbering gait of a bear, all easy confidence and effortless strength, knocking down any who stood in his path.

My skin tingled with pride, and a wash of power flooded the area as my onyx stone pulsed at my neck.

Everyone in the field — enemies and allies alike — fell to the ground in a lifeless heap as the flames all around the clearing went out.

I gasped, shock and panic riding me hard as I stared down at the bodies below. *DID I KILL THEM?*

A deep, smoky chuckle drifted through my mind at my thoughts. *No, my Promised. You don't have that magic.* His words should have been reassuring, but no one below moved.

We landed hard on the ground, my bones jolting with the impact. I pushed off Hadriel's back, gracelessly sliding to the ground as I tripped my way to where Magnus's body lay prone. My hands slid to his neck, covered in ash, blood, and dirt, but feeling for a pulse.

"Please don't be dead, please don't be dead," I chanted as my eyes screwed shut. His heartbeat was steady beneath my fingers, pulsing quickly from the adrenaline of battle moments before. Relief sagged my shoulders as I slumped into a pile next to him.

His back arched off the ground with a heavy gasp, eyes flying open, snapping to the surrounding scene. When his gaze fell on me at his side, his serious expression faded into the grin I'd missed so much. I threw myself at him, wrapping my arms tightly around his neck, crushing him as if to anchor him here with me at this moment.

"Your dragon is eating the bodies," he whispered into my ear a moment later, and I recoiled back, swiveling my gaze behind me.

"Ew, no, Hadriel. Stop," I gagged at the smell of burning flesh, and the dragon's eyes swung to me in annoyance as what I refused to acknowledge was a severed arm dangling from his teeth. "Can you not? Or at least wait until I don't have to watch?"

His green eyes bore into mine, annoyance clear as the lids flickered over his gaze. A sputtering gasp sounded from below, and I looked down to see Magnus turning blue, clutching his side.

"What's happening?" I leaned back over him, scanning his body again, searching for the injury I must have missed. Beneath his ripped shirt was an extensive bruise covering most of his chest and side. His breathing was labored, his eyes screwed shut, but he panted out a wheezing, "Shit. I can't breathe."

Panic rose in me as my hands shook, unsure of what to do. "Yrsa!" I cried, but the healer still lay unconscious to my left. Magnus's hand squeezed down on mine, his breaths rattling in his chest as his eyes expanded. My head shook violently as the tears fell. "*NO*," I cried. "I can't lose you. I missed you so much, brother."

Sensing my distress, Hadriel moved across the ground towards us, nudging his enormous head into my back. *You can heal him.*

Remembering our moment at the Tree when I'd healed Domari's and my burns, I gasped. My hand reached back to Hadriel's head, placing my palm along his scaled face, tears clouding my vision as I gripped desperately onto Magnus's hand.

Light exploded around us, bright green as it circled Magnus, flowing out over the remaining clan in the clearing. His chest lifted off the ground as he sucked in air, eyes wide as he stared at me. Looking down, my skin glowed green with the magic that flowed from the onyx stone, and where I'd touched him, the blue welts beneath his skin faded, returning to normal.

I let out a breath of relief and stood, reaching my hand out to help pull him gingerly to his feet, though given his size, he had to do most of the work himself. Once he was standing and breathing normally, he nodded to show he could manage independently.

With intention, I shifted my focus back to the bodies still lying around Magnus. I rose to my feet, stooping at each body, laying my hand across their necks, feeling for pulses. With each touch, my stone glowed with power, and I watched in awe as I brought them back from whatever stasis spell I'd accidentally cast over them all.

Once everyone seemed to recover, I glanced at Hadriel. *Can you circle above, and make sure we're safe to move?*

With a nod, Hadriel stretched. His wings sent a gust of wind over the clearing, fanning the flames he lit across the fallen enemies, smoke rising high into the sky. Magnus and I helped those around us to their feet.

45

SHELBIE

Hadriel returned to me after checking the area, reassuring me their path ahead was clear, and that we were safe. He landed hard in the clearing, wing tipped down, and I'd climbed onto his back to fly again, floating over the broken scene below.

Lowering to the pasture outside Björn's longhouse, I watched as the last rafters tumbled to the ground in an ashen heap. I dropped to the ground, waiting for those following me from the forest.

Spinning in a circle, I slid my hand over my mouth, taking in the destruction. Black smoke rose high in the sky from multiple spots around the forest, telling me it wasn't only Björn's and Gunnar's houses in this state.

Draugr's men had burned the entire town.

Tears lined my eyes as I moved around the home I'd first seen in the Viking village, memories of Yrsa's tender care when I arrived last fall surfacing. She and Björn had offered me kindness when I'd needed it most, and I was forever grateful for them. To see their lives uprooted like this, destroyed in mere moments, broke my heart.

A few of the horses had escaped their pens, mingling with two goats, and a few other livestock on the edge of the forest, away from the smoldering fire, but everything within was gone. I sank to my knees in the melting snow as grief for the entire Eriksson clan swallowed me.

This is but the beginning, Hadriel said as his warm body shuffled behind me, casting the ground in shadow. *I can't sense what's coming, but if Draugr and Raud have discovered a way to heal Nidhoggr, to bring him back...*

Hadriel didn't need to finish his sentence. My eyes watered in the smoky haze as I took in the world around me, burned and barren. *Why, Hadriel?,* I asked. *Why would they destroy their own people?*

Steam billowed out of his nostrils when I turned to the immense dragon behind me, watching as his lids flickered over the large green orbs. *Ragnarok is the destruction of everything in our world, even the gods. The Tree will fall, the mountains will crumble, and the seas will overflow the lands. Beasts contained within the nine realms will break free, set to consume everyone, even the gods in Asgard.*

A nervous chuckle escaped me as I wrung my hands together. *Well, don't sugarcoat it for me. Why would they want that, though? Why would they want to destroy themselves?*

Hadriel's wings flared, his four feet shuffling through the dirt and snow. *Pride. Greed. Anger.* A chuff rose deep in his throat, a sound I quickly realized was the equivalent of an annoyed expression for him. *The way of life for the true Viking is ending as the world around us changes quickly, and the fearsome warlord isn't as feared or valued as they once were. Within Ragnarok also lays the promise of a new beginning. With the slate clean, the world will begin anew. Fates can be rewritten, and Vikings can rise again.*

A heavy sigh escaped me as my hands dropped into my lap. The thought of this world and these people destroyed had bile rising in the back of my throat, heart racing in my chest. Before I could ask him more, hoofbeats in the distance drew my attention, and I stood, jeans wet from where I'd knelt. A lone rider moved towards me on a horse with two dogs at his side, and I squinted into the sun to watch their approach.

It's Domari, Hadriel answered my unspoken question, and a sigh of relief left me before my stomach clenched again.

Where are Signe and Gunnar? I asked my dragon, and worry tore at me when he didn't answer.

As Domari rode closer, I saw he was riding Mjölnir bareback, and a tiny bit of the tension I held left me. Domari dropped off Mjölnir's back, face smeared in ash and blood, and I ran into his embrace. He crushed me against his chest, and I breathed deeply as my hands roamed his body. Jeans and a t-shirt weren't the same as armor, but I couldn't feel any injuries on his body, despite the blood that caked his clothes.

"What happened?" I asked. Domari's head tilted to the sky as his eyes closed. "You're not hurt? Where are Signe and Gunnar?"

He shook his head and dropped his face back down. His

eyes were sad, and I knew I wouldn't like whatever was coming next. "He took them."

"But," I sputtered, trying to understand, piecing together the last of my visions of blood leaking from Gunnar's chest, him falling to the ground. "They're not dead, right? Signe and Gunnar are both alive?"

"Gunnar will die if they don't get him to a healer soon." Domari's teeth ground together at the words, and then he sighed. "But yes. They're still alive. Draugr desperately wants Signe, and after watching her fight, I can understand why. She took down five men like it was nothing, and two fell at her feet, the life fading from their eyes when I couldn't even see a blow. He'll keep Gunnar alive to ensure her cooperation."

My eyes searched his face, seeking any explanation for this. Before we could speak more, several others joined us in the field, giving a wide berth to the dragon at my back and the smoldering remains of the house to our left.

"Hadriel is fucking huge," Magnus said as he eyed me, grinning despite the blood drying on his body.

How eloquent, Hadriel's voice rang full of sarcasm in my head, and I smiled for a moment.

Domari and Magnus embraced, clapping each other on the back as several others joined our circle. The rest of the villagers trickled into the clearing behind him. Miraculously, we'd lost no one, and the injuries they'd sustained I healed with my magic.

Yrsa's greying red hair flowed behind her as she ran to me, pulling me into a hug. I gripped her tightly, closing my eyes to savor the warmth and comfort she provided, and a tear escaped me when I felt her tremble in my embrace. Björn's hand rested on my shoulder with a look of pride, and I could have sobbed.

"Just in time," he said, kissing my forehead, his thick beard tickling against my skin. "We owe you a life debt."

Yrsa pulled back, her eyes drawn down to the stone glowing at my chest, and a tear trailed down her cheek. It didn't escape my notice that she never glanced around her, taking in the destruction of her home, but I could hardly blame her — the sight of her demolished home was gut-wrenching.

Focusing on me instead, Yrsa's eyes flashed briefly to Hadriel before she lifted her fingers, touching the warm onyx stone at my chest. The moment her hands grazed the stone, I gasped, feeling the power wash over her, illuminating her skin a pale purple, and blowing her red hair from her neck. Yrsa's eyes closed as she drank in its magic, a contented smile easing the crease from her brow. My jaw hung loose as I studied her, in awe of this woman in front of me.

She let go, and the purple glow faded, her eyes drifting open under heavy lids. "I knew it was you from the moment you arrived," she whispered as her hands cupped my face. I paused, hanging on her every word. "Forty years ago, my dragon passed, and it left me incomplete."

Vyara, Hadriel's voice was only a murmur in my head, but it rang true. I'd Seen what should have been their ceremony in my visions.

"My heart was broken, the future Promised to me stolen before it could ever begin. But fate works in mysterious ways. Even though I may catch glimpses of what's coming, I never thought I'd finally get to meet you, the last of our kind."

Björn glanced at his wife, and I watched the silent exchange between them, wondering what she meant.

"Björn and I," she paused, pulling in a deep breath as her hands drifted to my shoulders. "We lost a child. I birthed a still-born girl. She should have been the next Promised, my first-born daughter, but by that time, the dragons had already begun to fade from our world."

My mind reeled, trying to understand why she was telling me this story.

"The Norns," she swallowed heavily. "They came to me then and told me that my baby's strand of fate may have disappeared, but there would be another. Not to take her place, but to join me. That one day, there would be another girl, another Promised, who would need us as much as we needed her. That even through our pain, one day, there would be hope. That this Promised would find me, and I would be your guide in everything to come." She pursed her lips with a tearful smile, and I sniffed back my emotions. She patted my cheek, leaning in as her nose scrunched. "And you did. I have so much to teach you, Shelbie. Our Promised."

Björn crushed Yrsa and me in a hug, pulling us into his body as my shoulders drew together over my chest.

"I need in on this," Magnus sniffled, throwing his big arms over us. I chuckled, a strange sound in the emotional moment.

Magnus's heavy arm over me lifted as he said, "Domari, you too."

"No," Domari answered, and a genuine laugh bubbled out of me then. The group hug broke up, and Yrsa wiped at the tears on her face. So did Magnus, for that matter.

"I knew you couldn't leave me forever," Magnus said as he bumped my shoulder with a grin. "You'd miss me too much."

I rolled my eyes at him, but he wasn't wrong. I'd missed him terribly, and the moment when I thought he lay dying in my arms was one of the worst in my life.

"We need to make a plan," Domari's somber tone interrupted the rest of the conversations a few minutes later, and everyone in the clearing turned to listen. "Raud and Draugr are working together," he said, and the grumbles from Thorsten, Kare, Björn, and the others I didn't recognize told me no one was surprised by this. "Tell me what you know already."

So they did. They told us of the months we'd missed — the children arriving, the preparations they'd made. With each word, Domari's face grew paler, and a heavy weight dropped on my shoulders as I realized every dream I'd had, every story I'd penned, was true.

"What happened, Domari?" I asked, interrupting Kare's report that the force they'd battled was much smaller than expected.

"Where are the rest of the children?" Domari asked.

Several in the clearing glanced at each other with hesitancy. "Some have left in the last few days, headed to other villages. But our own, and the ones we accepted into our village, are, as of this morning, on their way to Asmund's village."

"Hadriel and I cleared as much of the path as possible for them to make it easier. Everyone appeared healthy and on the move," I answered him, but the tension in Domari's face didn't ease with the reassurance.

"Asmund's men were to meet them tonight, to escort them the rest of the way," Björn answered, and Domari's eyes snapped to him.

"How many men?" he asked, and my heartbeat ratcheted back up, panic setting in. "How many men did Asmund send to escort them?"

"I don't know." Björn shook his head, glancing around at the others. "Domari, what are you not telling us?" His eyes scanned the clearing again, taking in who was missing. "Where are Gunnar and Signe?"

"Raud and Draugr left after the fight, and he took them both," Domari finally told them what he'd been holding back.

"Then we'll go after them." Magnus's voice dropped an octave, his smile long gone.

"We can't," Domari sighed, scratching his beard in frustration. "The force you fought was only a portion of his men. The rest are following the children, waiting on Draugr's signal. If Draugr doesn't return with Signe and Gunnar, they'll leave no one alive."

A strangled cry escaped Yrsa as she curled into her husband, but I couldn't take my eyes off Magnus. His chest rose and fell heavily, muscles bunched as he clenched and unclenched his fists.

I glanced towards Domari, waiting to see if he'd reveal how injured Gunnar was when they'd left. Domari's eyes found mine, and he shook his head ever so slightly. I turned back to the rest of the village and saw the depth of emotion we were all feeling. They needed no other burden placed on them at this moment. Silently, I sent up a prayer. *Please keep them safe.*

I didn't expect an answer, but Hadriel lifted into the sky a moment later, taking off towards the children.

The gods are on our side, Hadriel answered. *This is our fate. The fate of your village. Your family. They entrusted us with the lives of the innocents. I will watch over the children.*

The eyes of everyone in the clearing followed the black dragon, a stark contrast against the white clouds above. As one, their eyes drifted back down to me, and I grinned.

They'd seen Hadriel fight — they knew who he would protect. We weren't clear of the danger yet, but a dragon on our side helped our odds.

I lifted my chin as I stared at Domari. "You may not be a crazed warlord like Draugr or the perfect golden boy like Gunnar, but I can think of no one better to lead us."

Domari's eyes expanded as he studied me, hearing the intentional *us*. Magnus stepped into my side, his heavy arm draped over my shoulder as Yrsa pulled my hand into hers, squeezing it tightly.

"Until Valhalla," Magnus whispered, and Domari's eyes snapped to his, grief and determination warring in his expression as his hand moved over the knot tattooed on his neck. His promise to Gunnar, Tove, and Raud. To his people. To his home.

More than anything, I wanted to banish the pain I saw in Domari's eyes. I wanted to be the rock for him he'd been for me. I couldn't leave these people I loved so much, and to my dying breath, I'd fight alongside them to stop what was coming.

"Until Valhalla."

46

SIGNE

Numbness spread through Signe's body that had nothing to do with the cold air around her. The further they strode from her home, the less she felt. Anger and rash actions would do nothing for her now but put her children in harm's way, so she let the chill sink through her veins, taking root. Seizing her heart.

Smoke rose all around her as she walked, following her father and his men away from the village and its smoking remains. They'd burned everything — not only her home, but those of her clan, too. All of it was gone because of her.

Horses snorted ahead as they walked through the forest, making it back to the two dozen men hidden beneath the trees. Without wasting even a moment, Draugr's men bound Signe's hands and threw her over the back of a horse. Breath whooshed out of her as she settled in the saddle, struggling to hold her balance with her hands tied. Nothing mattered to her anymore, though. As long as these men headed away from her family, she'd do anything to keep it that way. To keep them from her children.

Sparing only a glance towards where Gunnar lay on a sled behind a horse, she closed her eyes, waiting for the darkness to take over as the blindfold slid over her face. The horses moved, the saddle creaking beneath her with each step as they walked. Ice covered Signe's heart, leaving behind a creature far colder and more deadly than Signe had ever been. But like the glaciers moving in the waters of the seas she once called home, it wasn't what you could see that was dangerous. It was what lurked underneath.

She listened as the men talked, absorbing their every word, but never spoke. Soon enough, the air chilled even further around them, nightfall imminent. The wind bit into Signe's skin, but still, she felt nothing. Shortly after, the horses stopped, and someone pulled her from the saddle without a spoken word, dropping her to the ground, back against a tree. When they removed her blindfold, she blinked, trying to adjust to the sudden brightness of the fire blazing before her, but her eyes scanned the clearing, only caring about one thing.

Gunnar.

True to his word, Draugr had delivered a healer for him, and Gunnar lay on a sled, chest bandaged tightly. Signe watched his chest rise and fall in the firelight, and a knot in her heart loosened a fraction. He was still alive.

A dirty body dropped to a squat in front of her, and she glanced up at a face she'd never seen before today but knew immediately. Black tattoos covered Raud's clean-shaven head, monsters painted across his skin, devouring the world in Ragnarok. His scraggly, unkempt beard did nothing to draw away from his eyes, deep brown, almost black, rimmed with red.

"I can't put my finger on what's so special about you," Raud said as he sucked on his teeth, silver rings on his fingers glinting in the firelight. "You caught the attention of Gunnar, had Domari fighting for you, and you were even enough to lure your father to join my side."

Raud's hand drifted to Signe's face, running a knuckle along her skin. She fought to control her movements, not to flinch away from him, that icy calm cracking in her veins.

"Why does everyone care?" he asked, his tone full of annoyance as he squinted at her.

Signe bit her tongue, holding in so many retorts she could spit back at the man. Before she said anything, her eyes glanced to the side, where Gunnar lay healing from a stab wound from this jealous, petty, vicious man. For the first time she could remember, she kept her venomous words to herself.

Raud's eyes roved down her body, his ringed fingers tracing across her chest and down to her hips, making Signe's skin crawl. A surge of power zipped up her spine as her breath caught, but she forced it down, staring at her husband once more. She couldn't lose control.

"I see nothing out of the ordinary." Raud shook his head. "Tove was far more beautiful than you. And yet, *no one* fought for her."

Pain and anger warred on Raud's face, overcoming the cool, albeit unhinged, demeanor he'd worn only moments before. Signe watched as he shut his eyes, inhaling deeply, and the calm settled back over him once more. When he opened his eyes, they were no longer deep brown. Instead, his pupils went to slits like those of a reptile, and the colored iris shone only red.

Bright, blood red.

He stood, cracking his neck to the side, and walked back towards the fire, away from Signe. While she wanted to be relieved he'd left her alone, dread sat heavy in her stomach, knowing this was far from over.

Days ticked by as they rode, and Signe did anything to comply with their wishes. She only cared about the fact that when they removed her blindfold each night, she saw Gunnar was alive. He still lay prone; furs draped over his body where he rode on the sled in a sleep stasis. Each day she watched his chest rise and fall, Signe continued to do as they said.

At some point, her father had left their party, and it had been days since she'd seen Draugr, the man she loathed more than any other. The horses traversed a rocky path up an incline, and Signe could feel the horse's feet slap against the rock below. The same as every day before, her hands were bound in front of her, resting in her lap as they moved, but the ropes around her wrist weren't what stopped her from rebelling. The only thing that kept Signe at bay, kept her anger from lashing out against the men around her, was the knowledge that her husband was still wounded.

While Signe was confident she could fight her way out of this, she had no way to heal Gunnar, and his life mattered far more to her than her freedom.

The horse's movement stopped suddenly, and rough hands wrapped around Signe's arm, pulling her from the horse.

"Move," a gruff voice said behind her as they shoved her hard in the back. Signe tripped forward, catching her balance on a rock wall to her right. They ripped the blindfold from her face, and she blinked into the bright morning light, eyes watering as she took in her surroundings.

She knew these mountains. White snow covered the tops of the rocky crags, the sound of the ocean lapping against the shore in the distance. The salty, cool breeze blew through her hair, red-gold strands floating around her face as she stared at the peaks. If she turned around, far at the bottom of the incline, she'd see her father's home.

The hand shoved against her back again, and her feet moved, following the men proceeding in front of her. A cliff rose above them, and a cave entrance stood farther up.

"Climb," the man behind her said, and Signe turned with an exasperated look. As she was about to spit venom back at him, her breath caught in her chest.

Gunnar stood behind him, draped between two men. He was weak, barely able to hold up his head, but his one-eyed gaze met hers for a moment, a bandage covering the other. Signe's eyes burned, but she blinked away any sign of emotion. Straightening, she nodded to him and turned back to the rock face.

Her steps were sure as she climbed up the steep incline, headed for the mouth of the cave where a man stood with a torch. As she neared, a stench wafted out of the cave — sulfuric and smelling of death. She paused, staring into the dark space, lit only by the few torches of the men inside. Stalactites hung from the ceiling — a jaw waiting to swallow any who entered.

Water fell from somewhere in a steady drip, trickling towards the back of the cave. Signe's intuition fired, blazing hot, telling her to leave. She glanced behind her to where Gunnar was carried a few steps behind, head hung as he fought to stand on his own, and her heart sank.

No matter what lay ahead, she couldn't leave him, and Gunnar was far too weak. With a deep breath, she turned back to the cave, skirts swishing around her feet as she continued to where two men stood at the back of the cave.

"Come, girl," Draugr smiled, the torchlight dancing off the smooth skin of his head. A smirk spread over her face as she looked at the scar cutting across his once handsome face, remembering the day she'd watched the blow he'd taken to the head, hoping it would be his last. But, as always, Draugr seemed to defy death, and Signe's teeth ground together as she stared up at the man, wishing she could be the one to end him. Her eyes flicked to the side, noticing Raud sneering at her, pride simmering off him in a way that made her blood boil.

As she neared them, Raud stepped to the side, and Signe squinted into the darkness. Bones lay stacked everywhere, far more than she could comprehend ever accumulating, varying in size. Her eyes drifted higher over the heaping piles of discarded life, and her heartbeat stilled. She stepped back, but someone pushed her between her shoulder blades. There, amidst the pile of bones —a *nest*, she realized — lay a dragon. As white as the surrounding bones, the dragon slumbered in his almost lifeless form, eyes closed.

"Nidhoggr," her father said with a sinister smile. He glanced back at the dragon behind him and then to his left. Signe's eyes followed his and found her uncle, Vermund, standing nearby, hands clasped in front of him. "Viveka wasn't lying. The dragon *does* rest here, right above our people, waiting for his time to rise again."

Signe shook her head, betrayal stinging her as she turned away from her uncle, her mentor for so long, and back at the dragon.

"Signe, why don't you introduce your husband to your family?" Draugr went on, and Raud twitched, neck jerking to the side. The movement caught Signe's attention, watching as anger washed over the man at seeing her husband standing behind her.

Raud's body convulsed, shaking in anger, rage pouring from his veins as he let out a savage growl. "Why won't you *die?*" he spat, arms flexing as he shouted the words into the cavern, listening as the sound echoed off the walls. "Why won't you *all* die? You *deserve* to die for what you did to Tove. For the vengeance you left *unclaimed*." He bared his teeth in his rage, light dancing across the monsters coating his tattooed head.

Signe watched as Raud's eyes closed, calm washing over him as he inhaled, just as he'd done before at the camp. With his exhale, red shone in the cave, not in Raud's eyes but in that of the dragon. The ground shook, and Signe fought to keep her balance as the white dragon's head lifted from the nest of bones and turned to stare down at her.

Draugr made an exultant sound as the men at Signe's back shuffled, moving away from the monster in front of her, but Signe didn't dare glance away from the dragon in front of her. His red gaze penetrated her, seeing right through to her soul and recognizing the feral beast that also lived within her.

"All this time, I've been searching for the wrong thing." Draugr clapped his hands together, spinning his focus back to his daughter as his face shone gleefully. He stepped in front of her, blocking her view of the dragon at his back. "For *years*, I've hunted your mother. Everywhere I've searched, hoping to prove my theory. While you were vicious," he nodded, a look of pride taking over his face, his hand reaching out to brush along her shoulder, and Signe fought not to flinch at the touch, "you were also *weak*. I didn't think it could be true."

"I'm not a Promised." Signe shook her head at him, a smug smile filling her face as she jumped ahead of his monologue. "I can't hear him. Nidhoggr isn't mine."

The sound of Draugr's deep laughter caught her off guard, and her heart raced in her chest, afraid of whatever could cause the triumphant look on her father's face.

"No, no, Signe," he shook his head, glancing at Vermund for only a moment before his eyes found hers again, alight with excitement. "You're not a Promised."

Signe's brows drew down in confusion as she appraised the situation. Raud still stood with his eyes closed, but something seemed to have shifted in him. Her eyes followed his movement as he turned to the dragon, placed a hand on his face, and inhaled deeply. Red, pulsing light shone from his skin with each breath, matching the eyes of the dragon next to him.

"I don't need *another* Promised," Draugr chuckled, glancing at Raud and the dragon behind him. "Not when Nidhoggr has forced himself into Raud's mind, taking what power he can from the man's life force. What I need is *you.*"

He stepped into her space, and Signe fought to keep her balance. She refused to rear back from him, even though this was the man who'd beaten her so many times before, threatened her children, and held her injured husband hostage.

"You, my darling girl." His hand lifted and cupped Signe's face in the first tender moment they'd shared as father and daughter. "I should have known." He whispered, leaning in. "I should have *seen* it. It wasn't until you left me and my men lost their first battle that I knew."

Her eyes scanned his face as he pulled back, still clutching her face as if she was his most prized possession. The ice cracked beneath her skin, threatening to give way as she waited for the words he was withholding.

"*A Valkyrie,*" he sneered, and the fingers cupping her face turned to a harsh grip. "A Valkyrie. I had a Valkyrie for a daughter, fighting at my side, and I missed it."

Signe fought to free herself from Draugr's crushing grip on her face, but the sound of her husband's grunt of pain behind her stilled her movements.

"Now." Draugr stood tall, dropping her face as he lifted his arms, spinning in a circle. "I'll be unstoppable. No one has ever fought with both a dragon *and* a Valkyrie on their side. Not even the gods can stand against me as I bring this world to its knees, free the monsters within, and tear the Tree from the ground."

Signe barely heard his words, her mind reeling with this new information.

A Valkyrie.

Legendary women chosen by the god Odin to fight alongside the Vikings in battle, guiding those worthy of the halls of Valhalla to their final home while stealing the breath from the lungs of those not worthy. To fight with a Valkyrie on one's side was as close as one could get to ensuring victory in battle.

Invincible warriors.

Brutal and bloodthirsty.

Death incarnate.

"I want it *all*, Signe." Draugr's eyes glittered in the dim light of the torches around them as she met his gaze once more. "I want to begin again, to live a life at the top, untouchable, the greatest warrior Valhalla has ever seen. I want Ragnarok. And you'll give it to me, won't you?"

Her heart beat rapidly against her ribcage, fighting the adrenaline coursing through her body as she fought for breath. She turned, glancing at Gunnar, now crumpled on the ground, hand over his wounded shoulder that was leaking blood again, and her heart broke.

"Forgive me," she whispered only for him, her heart breaking as she watched Gunnar's eye glance up at her, pleading. She spun back to her father, meeting his cruel gaze. "I'll do it. Leave Gunnar unharmed. Heal him. Spare my children, and I'll fight at your side."

Raud's grin was vicious as he watched the way

Gunnar's body caved in, a cry escaping him as the pain and grief of Signe's words overcame him.

Signe would selfishly choose the lives of her family over the lives of so many others. She would destroy this world and everyone in it if it meant she could protect Gunnar and her children from her brutal father. She would bargain with the gods themselves if it meant she could shield them from what was coming. Without hesitation, she'd make the same choice every time, in this life and the next.

And Gunnar would hate her for this choice.

Somehow, she'd find a way out of this — to end her father, the white dragon, Raud… All of them. Signe was unstoppable — one of Odin's own Valkyrie if her father was to be believed — and she would watch the world burn for threatening those she loved. Chin held high, ice settled over her green gaze as she eyed her father, holding her bound hands in front of her.

"I'm yours."

**To Be Continued
In Book Three, Fates Defied**

EPILOGUE

Snow crunched beneath her shoes as she ran, not daring to glance behind her. Clutching her stomach, tears streamed down her face, but power surged in her veins, healing her with each forward movement. She couldn't stop, no matter how her body demanded it.

Time was something she didn't have.

Men shouted in the distance, followed by a deep and drawn-out war horn. The sound drove her forward, desperate as she fled, even though her body was at its weakest.

But this was her fate, decreed by the gods.

A sob wracked her as she stumbled, grabbing onto a tree momentarily as she fought to catch her breath. Never had she known emotional pain like this, not even when she'd followed the words of the Norns, leaving her family with only her brother at her side. Not when she'd sacrificed her body to the Demon as they'd told her to, knowing what would come of it.

But the sight of her baby girl, so tiny and yet so powerful... it broke her.

Dragging a sleeve across her face to dry her tears, she stood straight, drawing in a deep breath as the magic washed over her. Like all the Valkyries before her, Odin himself blessed her, and she was as close to immortal as a human could come.

Glancing down, she watched as her body changed, the skin on the backs of her hands glowing with power as it healed her from within, leaving no signs of the childbirth she'd struggled through only hours before.

The war horn sounded again; this time, she dared to glance behind her. Draugr's men were in pursuit, but even by herself, the vicious Vikings didn't stand a chance. Not against her.

A Valkyrie.

Rather than flee, she turned, warm brown hair flowing behind her as her emerald eyes shone brightly in the fading sun. An arrow whizzed past her, sinking into the tree to her left, and her head tilted down as one side of her lips tipped up, but she didn't move.

"There!" a man called, spotting her amidst the trees, and excitement crept up her spine, tingling in her fingers. At once, all three men launched arrows, and she watched as they arced into the air, closing the distance towards where she stood, waiting.

She couldn't change her fate, nor her daughter's. She

couldn't report back to the gods that her task was unfinished. She couldn't stop the end that was coming.

But no one had said she couldn't defend herself if they attacked...

With a deep inhale, blazing white power lit along her hands as she raised them into the air, the ground vibrating beneath her. Fresh snow from the night before shook from the trees overhead, and she watched as the men stumbled, losing their footing momentarily.

Like the men who had shot them, the arrows wavered in their path. Before they could connect with their target, her hands clenched shut, high above her, and the arrows stopped, hovering in mid-air mere inches from her chest. Waiting until the three men could see her, she held the arrows suspended, ensuring they knew she held no bow of her own.

The man closest to her gasped, stepping back as he noticed first the blinding light casting an aura around her and then the arrow trained back on him.

"RETREAT!" he called to the others, spinning on his heel, and the other two turned at his signal, but it was far too late. All eyes settled on her as she pushed her hands forward, watching as the arrows aimed at her heart shot back towards the men. With a heavy thunk, each one stabbed through their cowardly backs and directly into their hearts, killing them instantly.

Any man who would willingly disengage from battle wasn't fit for the halls of Valhalla.

As the men fell, her eyes swept over the clearing, hearing the war horn sound once more. She sucked in a gasp as she noticed the tall form, pale hair blending in with the surrounding snow, eyes the same emerald green as her own.

"Run, Hilda," Vermund nodded, his voice barely above a whisper, but she heard him clearly, his words ringing in her head and clawing at her heart. "I'll take care of her. Your task is complete, and mine has just begun."

Sharing one last glance with her twin brother — the last they might ever share — Hilda spun and fled into the forest, eyes set on the mountains beyond.

ACKNOWLEDGMENTS

First, thank you, dear reader, for taking a chance on me yet again. I'm beyond grateful for every one of you.

To my husband, Chris: You're my number one supporter, and I'm so lucky to have you at my side. Thank you for your tireless devotion to not only helping me talk through every plot hole but also for your unwavering strength.

To my girls: being your mom is my greatest accomplishment. The pride you radiate when you tell people I'm an author is staggering, and I don't know what I did to deserve you two.

To B: Thank you for always pointing out how I can be better, and then reassuring me of your confidence that I'm talented enough to make it happen. I'm so lucky to be on this journey with you. You're fine, obviously.

To Brit: MORE THAN ANYTHING, this book brought me closer to you, and I'm so grateful. I don't know what I would've done without you there at the end. You were my lifesaver, my confidante, my cheerleader, and my rock. I love you so stinkin' much!

To Lex: I can't thank you enough for putting up with me while we relaunched these new editions. You're the real hero, and I adore you.

To Catherine and Mom: I'm lucky to have you as my first readers for everything, and I love you both!

To the entire Bookstagram Community: Keep lifting each other up. Keep spreading chaos. Keep reading books and letting them become your entire personality. You're beautiful, and I love you.

Zippers Up,
    Aimee

ABOUT THE AUTHOR

 Fueled by peach tea and chaos, Aimee Vance believes that life doesn't end for romantic heroines in their early twenties and that everything would be better if magic was real, both of which are prominent themes in the stories she tells.

Outside of writing happily-ever-after endings for hot-mess heroines, she spends her days with her husband, two young daughters, and a rambunctious labrador retriever in Texas.

Fates Illuminated was her debut novel and the first in the series, The Call of the Norns.

 instagram.com/aimeevancebooks

ALSO BY AIMEE VANCE

Call of the Norns

Fates Illuminated

Fates Promised

Fates Defied - Coming Spring 2024

Deadlights Cove
Cowritten with B. Perkins

Smoke Show

Deja Brew

A Very Merry Christmoose (Novella)

Wing and a Miss

Pier Pressure

Karma is a Witch

Made in the USA
Middletown, DE
12 February 2025